ALSO BY
MARY DORIA RUSSELL

The Sparrow
Children of God

A Thread of Grace

A Thread of Grace

A NOVEL

Mary Doria Russell

RANDOM HOUSE

NEW YORK

This is a work of fiction. Though some characters, incidents, and dialogues
are based on the historical record, the work as a whole is a product
of the author's imagination.

Copyright © 2005 by Mary Doria Russell
Maps copyright © 2005 by David Lindroth

All rights reserved under International and Pan-American Copyright
Conventions. Published in the United States by Random House, an imprint
of The Random House Publishing Group, a division of Random House, Inc.,
New York, and simultaneously in Canada by Random House
of Canada Limited, Toronto.

RANDOM HOUSE and colophon are
registered trademarks of Random House, Inc.

LIBRARY OF CONGRESS CATALOGING-IN-PUBLICATION DATA

Russell, Mary Doria
A thread of grace: a novel / Mary Doria Russell.
p.   cm.
ISBN 0-375-50184-3
1. World War, 1939–1945—Underground movements—Fiction. 2. World War,
1939–1945—Jews—Rescue—Fiction. 3. Holocaust, Jewish (1939–1945)—
Fiction. 4. World War, 1939–1945—Italy—Fiction. 5. Holocaust survivors—
Fiction. 6. Jews—Italy—Fiction. I. Title.
PS3568.U76678T48 2005   813'.54—dc22   2004050942

Printed in the United States of America on acid-free paper
Random House website address: www.atrandom.com

2 4 6 8 9 7 5 3 1

FIRST EDITION

Book design by Carole Lowenstein

Alla mia famiglia

with thanks to Susa and Tomek,
who made me reach for more

Quello che siete, fummo.
What you are, we were.

Quello che siamo, sarete.
What we are, you shall be.

—FROM AN ITALIAN CEMETERY

Characters

ITALIAN JEWS

Renzo Leoni, a.k.a. Ugo Messner, Stefano Savoca, Don Gino
　　Righetti
Lidia Segre Leoni, his widowed mother; *la nonna* (the grandmother)
Tranquillo Loeb, her eldest daughter's husband

Iacopo Soncini, chief rabbi of Sant'Andrea
Mirella Casutto Soncini, his wife
Angelo, their young son
Altira, their first daughter, deceased
Rosina, their second daughter

Giacomo Tura, elderly Hebrew scribe

JEWISH REFUGEES

Claudette Blum, Belgian teenager; Claudia Fiori, *la vedova* (the
　　widow)
Albert Blum, her father

Duno Brössler, Austrian teenager, partisan
Herrmann and Frieda Brössler, his parents
Liesl and Steffi, his younger sisters
Rivka Ivanova Brössler, his paternal grandmother

Jakub Landau, organizer for the Italian CNL (Committee for
　　National Liberation); *il polacco* (the Pole)

ITALIAN CATHOLICS

Suora (Sister) Marta, middle-aged nun
Suora Corniglia, novice, later nun; Suora Fossette (Sister Dimples)
Massimo Malcovato, her father; *il maggiore* (the major)

Don (male honorific) Osvaldo Tomitz, priest, Sant'Andrea
Don Leto Girotti, priest, San Mauro; *il prete rosso* (the red priest)

Santino Cicala, infantryman, Calabrian draftee

Catarina Dolcino, the Leonis' landlady; Rina
Serafino Brizzolari, municipal bureaucrat, Sant'Andrea
Antonia Usodimare, proprietress, Pensione Usodimare

Tercilla Lovera, *contadina* (peasant woman), Santa Chiara
Pierino, Tercilla's son; *il postino* (the postman)
Bettina, his sister

Battista Goletta, Fascist farmer, Valdottavo
Attilio Goletta, his cousin, Communist sharecropper
Tullio Goletta, Attilio's son, partisan

Adele Toselli, elderly housekeeper, San Mauro rectory
Nello Toselli, her nephew, partisan

Maria Avoni, partisan; *la puttana tedesca* (the German whore)
Otello Rollero, partisan, interpreter for Simon Henley

BRITISH

Simon Henley, signalman, Special Operations executive

GERMANS

Werner Schramm, deserter, Oberstabsarzt (medical officer)
    Waffen-SS
Irmgard, his sister, deceased

Erhardt von Thadden, Gruppenführer (division commander) Waf-
    fen-SS; the Schoolmaster
Martina, his wife
Helmut Reinecke, his adjutant, Hauptsturmführer (captain), later
    Standartenführer (colonel, regimental commander)
Ernst Kunkel, Oberscharführer (staff sergeant), aide to von Thadden

Artur Huppenkothen, Oberstpolizei (police colonel), Gestapo
Erna, his sister

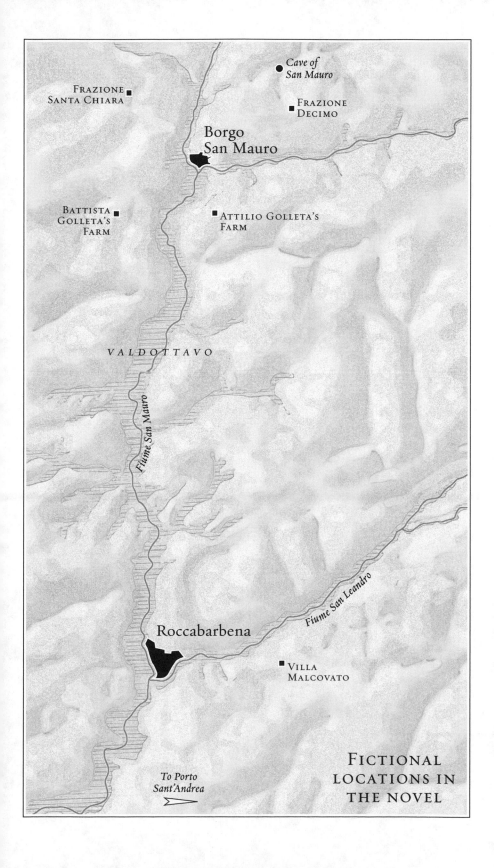

Cave of
San Mauro

FRAZIONE
SANTA CHIARA

FRAZIONE
DECIMO

Borgo
San Mauro

BATTISTA
GOLLETA'S
FARM

ATTILIO GOLLETA'S
FARM

VALDOTTAVO

Fiume San Mauro

Fiume San Leandro

Roccabarbena

VILLA
MALCOVATO

To Porto
Sant'Andrea

FICTIONAL
LOCATIONS IN
THE NOVEL

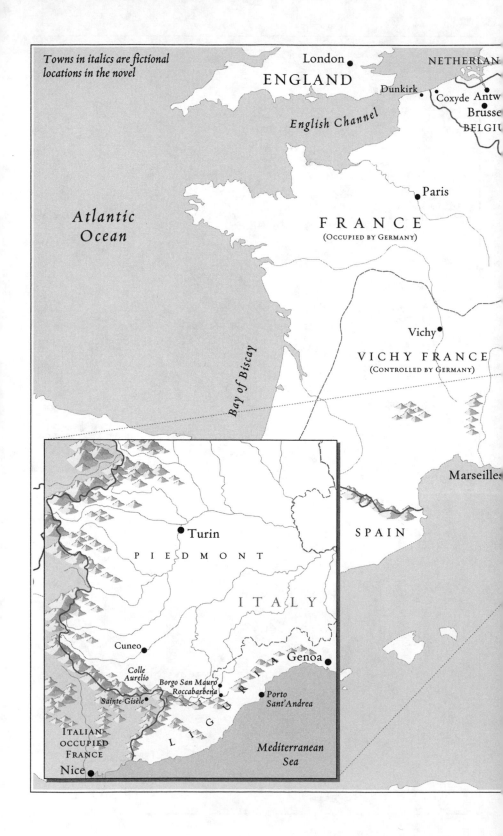

A Thread of Grace

Preludio

This is what everyone would remember about his mother: her home was immaculate. Even in a place where cleanliness was pursued with religious zeal, her household was renowned for its faultless order. In Klara's mind, there was no gradation between purity and filth.

She had sinned as a girl, made pregnant by her married uncle. Adultery stained her soul black, and God punished her as she deserved. Her sin child died.

So did her aunt, and Klara became her uncle's newest wife, dutifully raising her stepchildren, keeping them very clean and very quiet, so her uncle-husband would not become angry and bring out his leather whip. Her husband was no more merciful than her God.

Her second son died, and then her small daughter. Soon after she buried little Ida, Klara became pregnant again. Her fourth child was a sickly boy whose weakness her uncle-husband despised. Klara was ashamed that her children had died. She hovered over the new baby anxiously, told him constantly that she loved and needed him, hoping that her neighbors would notice how well he was cared for. Hoping that her uncle-husband would come to approve of her son. Hoping that God would hear her pleas, and let this child live.

Her prayers, it seemed, were answered, but the neighbors were bemused by Klara's mothering. She nursed her little boy for two years. He'd squirm away, or turn his face from her, but she pushed her nipple into his mouth regardless of what troubled him. She fed and fed and fed that child. Food was medicine. Food could ward off numberless, nameless, lurking diseases. "Eat," she'd plead. "Eat, or you'll get sick and die." It was immoderate, even in a village where mothers expected children to swallow whatever was put before them, and to clean their plates.

In adulthood, Klara's son would have nightmares about suffocation. He would suck on a finger in times of stress, or stuff himself with chocolates. He was obsessed with his body's odors and became a vegetarian, convinced that this diet reduced his propensity to sweat excessively and improved the aroma of his intestinal gas. He discussed nutritional theories at length but had a poor appetite. He could not watch others eat without trying to spoil their enjoyment. He'd call broth "corpse tea," and once pointed out that a roast suckling pig looked "just like a cooked baby."

Whenever he looked in a mirror, he would see his mother's eyes: china blue and frightened. Frightened of dirt, of her husband, of illness, and of God. Klara's son was frightened, too. Frightened of priests and hunters, of cigarette smokers and skiers, of liberals, journalists, germs and dirt, of gypsies, judges, and Americans. He was frightened of being wrong, of being weak, of being effeminate. Frightened of poets and of Poles, of academics and Jehovah's Witnesses. Frightened of moonlight and horses, of snow and water and the dark. Frightened of microbes and spirochetes, of feces, and of old men, and of the French.

The very blood in his veins was dangerous. There were birth defects and feeblemindedness in his incestuous family. His uncle-father was a bastard, and Klara's son worried all his life that unsavory gossip about his ancestry would become public. He was frightened of sexual intercourse and never had children, afraid his tainted blood would be revealed in them. He was terrified of cancer, which took his mother's life, and horrified that he had suckled at diseased breasts.

How could anyone live with so much fear?

His solution was to simplify. He sought and seized one all-encompassing explanation for the existence of sin and disease, for all his failures and disappointments. There was no weakness in his parents, his blood, his mind. He was faultless; others were filth. He could not change his china blue eyes, but he could change the world they saw. He would identify the secret source of every evil and root it out, annihilating at a stroke all that threatened him. He would free Europe of pollution and defilement—only health and confidence and purity and order would remain!

Are such grim and comic facts significant, or merely interesting? Here's another: the doctor who could not cure Klara Hitler's cancer was Jewish.

8 September 1943

PORTO SANT'ANDREA, LIGURIA
NORTHWESTERN COAST OF ITALY

A simple answer to a simple question. That's all Werner Schramm requires.

"Where's the church?" he yells, belligerent and sick—sicker yet when his shout becomes a swampy cough.

A small crowd gathers to appreciate the spectacle: a Waffen-SS officer, thin, fortyish, and liquored up. He props his hands against his knees, coughing harder. "*La basílica!*" he gasps, remembering the Italian. "*San Giovanni—dove è?*"

A young woman points. He catches the word *campanile,* and straightens, careful of his chest. Spotting the bell tower above a tumble of rooftops that stagger toward the sea, he turns to thank her. Everyone is gone.

No matter. Downhill is the path of least resistance for a man who's drunk himself legless. Nearer the harbor, the honeyed light of the Italian Riviera gilds wrecked warehouses and burnt piers, but there's not much bomb damage inland. No damned room for an explosion, Schramm thinks.

Jammed between the Mediterranean and the mountains, the oldest part of Porto Sant'Andrea doesn't even have streets—just *carrugi*: passages barely wide enough for medieval carts. Cool and shadowy even at noon, these masonry ravines wind past the cobblers' and barbers' shops, apothecaries, vegetable stands, and cafés wedged at random between blank-walled town houses with shuttered windows.

Glimpses of the bell tower provide a sense of direction, but Schramm gets lost twice before stumbling into a sunny little piazza. He scowls at the light, sneezes, wipes his watering eyes. "Found you!" he tells the Basilica di San Giovanni Battista. "Tried t'hide, but it didn' work!"

San Giobatta, the locals call this place, as though John the Baptist were a neighborhood boy, poor and charmless but held in great affection. Squatting on a granite platform, the dumpy little church shares its modest courtyard with an equally unimpressive rectory and convent, their builder's architectural ambition visibly tempered by parsimony. Broad stripes of cheap black sandstone alternate with grudgingly thin layers of white Carrara marble. The zebra effect is regrettable.

Ineffective sandbags surround the church, its southeast corner freshly crumpled and blackened by an Allied incendiary bomb. A mob of pigeons waddle through the rubble, crapping and cooing. "The pope speaks lovely German," Schramm informs them. "Nuncio to Berlin before he got his silly hat. Perhaps I ought to go to Rome and confess to Papa Pacelli!"

He laughs at his own impertinence, and pays for it with another coughing fit. Eyes watering, hands trembling, he drops onto the basilica staircase and pulls out the battered flask he keeps topped up and nestled near his heart. He takes small sips until brandy calms the need to cough, and the urge to flee.

Prepared now, he stands. Squares his shoulders. Advances resolutely on massive doors peopled with bronzed patriarchs and tarnished virgins. Curses with surprise when they won't yield to his tug. "I want a pries'!" he yells, rapping on the door, first with his knuckles and then more insistently with the butt of his Luger.

Creaking hinges reveal the existence of a little wooden side door. A middle-aged nun appears, her sleeves shoved into rubber gauntlets, her habit topped by a grimy apron. Frowning at the noise, she is short and shaped like a beer keg. Her starched white wimple presses pudgy cheeks toward a nose that belongs on a propaganda Jew.

Christ, you're homely.

Schramm wipes his mouth on his sleeve, wondering if he has spoken aloud. For years, words have threatened to pour out, like blood from his throat. He fears hemorrhage.

Shivering in the heat, he makes a move toward the door. The

nun bars his way. "*La chiesa è chiusa!*" she says, but Schramm pushes past her.

The baptistry reeks of carbolic, incense, explosives, and charred stone. Three novices scour its limestone floor. The prettiest sits on her heels, her face smudged with soot from the firebomb's damage. Calmly, she studies the Luger dangling in this German's right hand. Behind him, Sister Beer Keg snaps her fingers. Eyes drop. Work resumes.

Schramm shoves the pistol into its holster, pulls off his campaign cap, and rubs a sweaty palm over cropped brown hair. The nave is empty apart from a single man who ambles down the center aisle, neck cranked back like a cormorant's, hands clasped loosely behind his back. This personage studies the swirling seraphim and whey-faced saints above, himself an allegorical portrait come to life: Unconcern in a Silver-Gray Suit.

Distracted by the tourist, Schramm takes a step toward the confessionals and trips over a bucket of water. "*Scheisse,*" he swears, hopping away from the spill.

"*Basta!*" the fat nun declares, pulling him toward the door.

"*Io* need *ein padre!*" he insists, but his Italian is two decades old—the fading souvenir of a year in Florence. The Beer Keg shakes her head. Standing his ground, Schramm points at a confessional. "*Un padre,* understand?"

"*La chiesa è chiusa!*"

"I know the church is closed! But I need—"

"A strong black coffee?" the tourist suggests pleasantly. His German is Tyrolean, but there's no mistaking the graceful confidence of an Italian male who employs a superb tailor. "A medical officer!" he says, noting the insignia on Schramm's collar. "You speak the language of Dante most vigorously, Herr Doktor, but the people of this region generally use a Ligurian dialect, not the classical Italian you are—"

"Butchering," Schramm supplies, with flat accuracy.

"Striving for, one might have said. With your permission, I can explain to Suora Marta that you're seeking a priest who speaks German."

Schramm listens hard, but their dialect is as thick as an Austrian's head, and he gives up until the tourist translates. "Suora tells me Archbishop Tirassa's assistant speaks excellent German. Confessions, however, will not be heard again until Saturday." When Schramm begins to protest, the Italian holds up a conciliatory hand. "I shall point out that in time of war, the angel of death is more capricious than usual. Preparation for his arrival should not be delayed."

The man's voice becomes a soothing melody of persuasion and practicality. Schramm watches Suora Marta's face. She reminds him of his mother's sister, a Vincentian nun equally short and dumpy and ugly. "Like Papa used t'say, 'Christ'll take what nobody else wants.'"

"And so there is hope, even for pigs like you," the nun replies.

Schramm's jaw drops. A stunned laugh escapes his interpreter. Eyes fearlessly on Schramm's own, Suora Marta removes her rubber gloves and apron. Without hurry, she untucks her habit, straightens her gown, folds her outer sleeves back to the proper cuff length. Hands sliding beneath her scapular, she gives Schramm one last dirty look before gliding away with chubby dignity.

Schramm tips a mouthful of brandy down his throat. "*Verdammte Scheisse!* Why didn' you tell me she speaks German?"

"I didn't know! As a general rule, however, courtesy has much to recommend it in any language. This is a small port, but many of us have a working knowledge of German," the man continues, deflecting the conversation ever so slightly. "We've done a fair amount of business with Venezia Giulia since 1918— Pardon! No doubt you would call the region Adriatisches Küstenland."

"Mus' cost a fortune for new stationery every time the border moves," Schramm remarks, offering the brandy.

"Printers always prosper." The Italian raises the flask in salute and takes a healthy swallow. "If you won't be needing me anymore . . . ?"

Schramm nods, and the man strolls off toward an alcove, pausing to admire a fresco of the Last Judgment that Schramm himself finds unnecessarily vivid. Searching for a place to sit, Schramm gets a fix on some pews near the confessionals, takes another sip from the flask. "No retreat!" he declares. Probably aloud.

The tourist's slow circuit of the church is punctuated by murmurs of dismay. A fifteenth-century baptismal font is damaged. A colorful jumble of shattered glass lies beneath a blown-out window. "*Verdamm'* Tommies," Schramm mutters. "British claim're only bombing military sites, but Hamburg is rubble! Dehousing the workers, that's what they call it. *Terrorflieger,* we call it. Leverkusen, München. Köln, Düsseldorf. Rubble, all of them! Did you know that?"

"We hear only rumor these days, even with the change in government," the Italian replies, declining comment on Mussolini's recent fall from power.

Schramm waves his flask at the damage before taking another pull. "RAF pilots're so fugging inaggurate—" Schramm tries again. "They are so . . . fucking . . . inaccurate." Satisfied with his diction, he swivels his head in the direction of his new friend. "They call it a hit if they aim at a dock and smash a church!"

"Very sloppy," the Italian agrees. "A shocking lack of professional pride!"

Slack-jawed, Schramm's skull tips back of its own accord. He stares at the painted angels wheeling above him until his hands lose track of what they're supposed to be doing and the flask slips from his fingers. He aims his eyes at the floor, where the last of the liquor is pooling. "Tha's a pity," he mourns. Laboriously, he lifts first one foot and then the other onto the pew, sliding down until he is prone. "Fat ol' nun," he mutters. Pro'ly never committed a sin in her whole life . . .

A sharp noise awakens him. Coughing and crapulous, Schramm struggles to sit up. His confessor hasn't arrived, but chunks of stone have been neatly stacked by the door. Sweeping shards of colored glass into a pile, the Italian flirts gallantly with the novices. The pretty one flirts back, dimpling when she smiles.

Schramm slumps over the back of the pew in front of him, cushioning his brow on folded arms. "I'm going to be sick," he warns a little too loudly.

The Italian snaps his fingers. "Suora Fossette! The bucket!" The newly christened Sister Dimples scrambles to deliver it, and only just in time. "Allow me," the gentleman says, courteous as a headwaiter while Schramm pukes into the dirty water.

Swiping at his watering eyes with trembling hands, Schramm

accepts the proffered handkerchief. "Touris', translator . . . now you're a nurse!"

"A man of endless possibilities!" the Italian declares, setting the bucket aside.

He has a face off a fresco: bent-nosed and bony, but with a benign expression. Old enough to be tolerantly amused by another's disgrace. Someone who might understand . . . Schramm wants to tell this kindly stranger everything, but all that comes out is "I was tryin' t'make things better."

"Always a mistake," the Italian remarks. "Where are you staying, Oberstabsarzt? Would you like to come back another day?"

Schramm shakes his head stubbornly. "'Dammte Schpageddi-Fresser. Italians're always late! Where is that shit of a priest?"

"Lie down, Herr Doktor." Schramm feels his legs lifted onto the pew. "Rest your eyes. The priest will come, and then we'll get you back where you belong."

"No, thank you," Schramm says firmly. "Hell exists, you know. Any combat soldier can tell you that." The other man stops moving. "I knew you'd un'erstan'! So heaven's real, too! Logic, ja?"

Their moment of communion is over. "I myself am not a devout Catholic," the Samaritan informs him regretfully. "My opinions about heaven and hell needn't trouble you."

"Righ' . . . righ'." Almost asleep, Schramm mumbles, "You're not a bad fellow . . ."

Moments later, he is snoring like a tank engine, and does not hear the hoot of delighted laughter that echoes through the basilica. "Did you hear that, Sisters?" his intepreter asks. "The Nazi says I'm not a bad fellow!"

"For a spaghetti chomper," Suora Fossette amends solemnly.

Musical giggles are quickly stifled when swift footsteps and whispering fabric announce a priest's approach. "Grüss Gott, mein Herr," he says, shooting a stern look at the novices. "I am Osvaldo Tomitz, secretary to His Excellency Archbishop Tirassa."

"Don Osvaldo! Piacere: a pleasure to meet you!" says a well-dressed civilian. "I'm Renzo Leoni."

Tomitz's confusion is plain. Suora Marta undoubtedly told him that the man wishing to confess is an obnoxious German drunk. "How may I be of service to you, signore?"

"Ah, but I am not the one who sought your services, Don Osvaldo." Leading the way toward the confessionals, Leoni presents a Waffen-SS officer passed out cold on a pew.

Nose wrinkling at the sour smell of vomit and brandy, Tomitz snorts. "So that's the Aryan superman we've heard so much about."

"Yes. Disappointing, really," Leoni concurs, but his eyes are on the priest. "Tomitz, Tomitz . . . You're from Trieste, aren't you? Your family's in shipping!"

Don Osvaldo draws himself up, surprised by recognition. In his early forties, of medium height and medium weight, with medium-brown hair framing regular features, not one of which is memorable, Osvaldo Tomitz must introduce himself repeatedly to people who have already met him. "My father was with Lloyds Adriatico. We moved here when the Genoa office opened a branch in Sant'Andrea. How did you know?"

"The name is Austrian. The German is Habsburg. The Italian is Veneto. Ergo: Trieste! As for the rest? I cheated: my father was a commercial photographer. Lloyds was a good customer. I met your father when I was a boy. You must have been in seminary by then. How is Signor Tomitz?"

"He passed away last year. I was teaching at Tortona. I asked for a position here so I could be nearer my mother."

"My sympathies, Don Osvaldo. My mother, too, is a widow."

Satisfied to have established a connection, Leoni returns his attention to the drunk. With an almost professional efficiency, he pats the Nazi down and removes the man's wallet. "Herr Doktor Oberstabsarzt Werner Schramm is with the Waffen-SS Leibstandarte Adolf Hitler, Hausser's Second Armored Corps, late of the Russian front . . . Currently staying at the Bellavista. He's in Sant'Andrea on two weeks' leave." Leoni looks up, puzzled.

"Odd," Osvaldo agrees. "To come from such a hell, and spend his leave in Sant'Andrea?"

"Why not Venice, I wonder? Or Florence, or Rome?" Leoni glances apologetically at the frescoes. "No offense, Padre, but San Giobatta is not exactly a top draw." Leoni replaces the wallet and resumes his frisk. Withdrawing a silver cigarette case, he offers its contents to the priest with exploratory hospitality. "*Prego!* Take half," he urges. "Please—I'm sure the doctor would insist."

"He's not a bad fellow," one of the novices comments, "for a Nazi."

"Suora!" Don Osvaldo cries.

Dimples disappearing, the white-veiled sister scrubs virtuously at the mosaics, but Leoni's laughter fills the basilica. Disarmed, Don Osvaldo scoops his half of the cigarettes out of the case. Leoni offers a light.

"American," Osvaldo notes with some surprise, examining the fine white tissue paper. "I wonder where he—"

"Smoking in a church!" Suora Marta grumbles, trundling down the aisle. Already annoyed, she smells vomit, and her mouth twists. "Swine!" she snaps at the insensible German.

"Judge not, Suora!" Leoni reminds her piously. "I'm inclined to respect a soldier who has to get that drunk before confession. He must have an admirable conscience to be so ashamed."

She holds out a hand. "Give me the rest."

Leoni's brows shoot upward. "*Santo cielo!* Do you smoke, Suora?"

"Don't waste my time, Leoni. Tobacco's better than gold on the black market. We've got orphans to feed."

With a sigh and a shrug, and not so much as a glance at Tomitz, Leoni surrenders the cigarettes. Tucking them into a deep recess hidden in her dark blue gown, Suora Marta lifts the washbucket at arm's length and waddles off to dump its contents. "If I find ashes on that floor," she calls over her shoulder, "you'll eat them!"

"*Sì*, Suora," Don Osvaldo says dutifully. He waits until the nun is out of earshot. "Priest. Monsignor. Bishop. Archbishop. Cardinal. The pope," he chants softly. "And at the pinnacle of the hierarchy? Suora Marta."

There's a muffled schoolboy snicker from his companion. "She hasn't changed a bit. Taught me algebra in 1927. I've got ruler scars to prove it." Leoni taps ashes into a cupped palm crossed with fine lines and gives Osvaldo a sidelong glance. "You looked convincingly innocent for someone concealing stolen goods."

"A sin of omission." Osvaldo takes his half of the loot out of a pocket and divides it with Leoni. "Are you also a soldier? Home on leave, perhaps?" Leoni stiffens, though Osvaldo cannot imagine why. "Forgive me if—"

"I am," Leoni says coolly, "retired from military service."

Schramm's snoring sputters and halts. "I suppose I should call someone about him," Don Osvaldo says, glad to change the subject.

"Don't bother. I'll get him back to his hotel." Affable once more, Leoni makes a quick trip to the side door and brushes the ashes from his hands before returning to Schramm's side. "On your feet, *mein Schatzi*," he murmurs, cigarette bobbing between his lips. "Your *Mutti*'s going to be very unhappy with her *Söhnchen*, little man."

"Sen' 'em t' heaven," Schramm mumbles. "Wha's wrong wi' that?"

"Not a thing," Leoni soothes. Maneuvering the German down the aisle, he retrieves a wide-brimmed Borsalino from a pew, settles the hat at a careless angle, and glances back at Don Osvaldo. "Tell my brother-in-law I couldn't wait for him, would you, Padre?"

"Your brother-in-law?"

"Tranquillo Loeb. The lawyer?" Leoni prompts, glancing in the direction of the basilica offices. "There's a meeting with the archbishop, something about a clothing drive. I don't need to be here for that."

Coming near, Don Osvaldo drops his voice. "But ... Signor Loeb is with the Delegation for the Assistance of Hebrew Emigrants."

"So am I, as of this morning." Leoni hefts Schramm higher and confides, "I just got out of jail, and Tranquillo decided my varied talents would be best applied to the Jewish problem. Something constructive, you understand." Leoni reaches around the German to shake the priest's hand. "A pleasure, Don Osvaldo, and if you would be so kind as to give my regrets to Rabbino Soncini as well—"

"Rabbi—? *Dio santo!*" Darting a look at the SS officer draped half-senseless over Leoni's shoulders, Don Osvaldo mouths, "You're Jewish?"

"A congenital condition," Leoni says, conducting his stuporous ward across the still wet floor.

"*Pazzo!*" Osvaldo blurts. "You're crazy!"

"That runs in the family, as well, I'm afraid. Ladies," Leoni murmurs, managing to tip his hat to the novices on his way out.

Sunlight outlines the two men when the side door opens. Osvaldo throws down his cigarette, crushing it decisively under his shoe. "Leoni, wait! Let me—"

"Don Osvaldo!"

The priest turns to Suora Marta, expecting to be yelled at for the cigarette butt, but the portly nun is running, bucketless, down the center of the nave. "Don Osvaldo! Sisters!" she calls, her dour homeliness transformed by joy. "It's on the loudspeakers—!"

The basilica air first trembles, then quakes with the peal of great bronze bells, drowning everything she says, until at last, substantial bosom heaving, she reaches the baptistry and leans on the arm Don Osvaldo offers and dissolves into sudden tears. "The war," she cries. "The war— Thanks be to God! The war is over!"

SAINTE-GISÈLE ON THE VESUBIE RIVER
SOUTHEASTERN FRANCE

West of the Maritime Alps, beyond what used to be the French border, soldiers of the Italian Fourth Army loiter on a street corner, pausing in their discussion of the armistice to watch a girl dash past. Sharing a match, they bend their heads over army-issue Milites and raise eyes narrowed by smoke. "Another year, and Diobòn!" a Veronese private remarks. "That one's going to be trouble."

The others grunt agreement. The Italian Fourth has occupied this territory only since the end of '42, but that's been time enough to see her flower. "The features are still a bit too large for the face," a Florentine sergeant says appraisingly, "but the eyes are quite good, and she'll grow into those ears."

"Minchia!" a Sicilian swears. "If she was my sister, Papa would marry her off today."

"To keep you from getting your hands on her?" a Roman corporal asks, smoothly ducking the Sicilian's punch.

Flushed with late-summer heat and the importance of her news, Claudette Blum is fourteen, and splendidly unaware of her effect on others. Boys and girls her own age cringe at her infantile exuberance as she pushes and skips and dodges through the crowds that jam the streets of this mountain resort. Old men grumble darkly in German, French, Polish, Yiddish. Their elderly wives shake fingers. Those who could be her parents shake their heads, wondering when that gawky, thoughtless child will settle down. Only the kindest bless her heedless elation. They felt it themselves, briefly, when they heard the news. The Axis has begun to crumble.

They are all Jews—in the cafés and shops, the parks and pissoirs and bus stops of Sainte-Gisèle-Vesubie. The whole of Italian-occupied southern France is awash with Jews: the latest in the flood of refugees who've poured into Mussolini's fragile empire since the early thirties. Word's gone out, in whispers, and in letters passed from hand to Jewish hand. Italians don't hate us. The soldiers are decent men. You can walk openly in the streets, live like a human being! You're safe, if you can get behind Italian lines.

A few months ago, those lines were still expanding. When the Fourth rushed across the border, Police Commissioner Guido Lospinoso arrived from Rome with orders to take care of the Jews in Italy's French territory. Lospinoso did precisely that, commandeering hotels, filling tourist chalets and villas with refugees from across the continent. He encouraged the Hebrews to organize refectories and synagogues, schools for their children, nursing homes for their elderly and disabled. And then? Commissioner Lospinoso left France. He is, to this day, "on holiday," and therefore unavailable to countermand his orders placing all Jews under the protection of Italy's elite military police. Specially selected for imposing size and commanding presence, the carabinieri are, to a man, disinclined to be intimidated by their French or German counterparts.

When Vichy authorities wave Gestapo orders for the removal of undesirables, the carabinieri shrug diplomatically, all ersatz sympathy and counterfeit regret. Artistically inefficient, they shuffle papers and announce that another permit, or a letter from

Rome, or some new stamp is required before they can process such a request, and no one has been deported. But now—

Claudette Blum gathers one last burst of energy and sprints down a hotel hallway, schoolgirl socks bunched under her heels. "Papa!" she cries, flinging open the door. "General Eisenhower was on Radio London! Italy has surrendered!"

She waits, breathless, for a whoop of joy, for her father to embrace her—perhaps even to weep with happiness. "Thank God you're back" is all he says. The room is dotted by small piles of clothing. Two valises lay open on two narrow beds. He lifts a pair of his own shoes. "See if these fit."

Deflated, she takes the worn black oxfords. "Papa, you never listen to me! Italy surrendered!"

"I heard." He picks up a shirt, puts it down again. "One to wear, one to wash. If those shoes are too big, put on extra socks— Wait! Go downstairs first. Borrow trousers from Duno."

"Trousers from Duno? I wouldn't ask him for the time of day! Why are you packing?"

"I blame myself! Your mother wouldn't tolerate this arguing!" her father mutters, reducing socks and underwear to tiny bundles. "Do as you're told, Claudette! We have three, maybe four hours!"

She flounces from the room with a sigh of pained tolerance for a parent's unreasonable whims, but on her way back through the corridor Claudette grows uneasy. Family disputes in half a dozen languages filter through closed doors. Everyone seems angry or scared, and she cannot understand why, today of all days, when the news is so good.

"Believe nothing until it's been officially denied," her mother always said. "The only thing not censored is propaganda, and the British lie as much as the Germans." All right, Claudette concedes, clumping down the stairwell. Maybe the BBC exaggerates Axis losses, but even Radio Berlin admitted that the Wehrmacht gave up ground in Africa and Russia. Mussolini really was deposed in July! The king of Italy replaced *il Duce* with Field Marshal Badoglio, the Fascist regime was abolished, and Badoglio let all political prisoners out of jail. The Italian soldiers said that was true! The Allies conquered Sicily last month and landed on mainland Italy just last week. Could that be propaganda?

Veering between confidence and fear, she settles for adolescent pique, which splits the difference, and knocks on the Brösslers' door. No one answers, but she can hear Duno's father yelling. "Herrmann Brössler's lost everything but his voice," her own father said the first time they listened to an argument in the room below. "He was a big *macher* in Austria. An impresario! Now he's got nobody to boss but his family."

Claudette knocks again, jumping back when Duno suddenly appears. "What do you want?"

Rising onto her toes, she peeks over his shoulder. Frau Brössler's packing, and little Steffi's stamping her feet. "You can't make me!" she weeps, while her nine-year-old sister, Liesl, insists, "Mutti, we can't leave Tzipi!"

Duno grabs Claudette's arm and shoves her back into the hotel hallway. "Ow! Let go of me!" she cries. "Has everyone gone crazy? The war is over! Why is Steffi crying?"

Duno stares with the arid contempt only a fifteen-year-old can produce on such short notice. "Stupid girl. Don't you understand anything?"

She hates Duno, hates his condescension, hates his horrible red pimples and his big ugly nose. "I don't know what you're talking about," she says, rubbing her arm.

"When the Italians pull out of southern France, who do you think is going to march in?"

Her heart stops. She can feel it actually stop. "The Germans?"

"Yes, moron. The Germans."

"We've got to get out of here," she says, dazed. Duno rolls his eyes. "Where can we go now? There's no place left!"

"We're going east. We'll follow the army into Italy."

"Over the *Alps?*"

"It's the mountains, the sea, or the Germans," Duno says, relishing her fear because it makes him feel commanding and superior. "It's Italy or—" He makes a noise and draws a finger over his throat.

"Duno!" His mother pulls the door closed behind her. "What is it, Claudette?"

Claudette has seen a photo of Duno's mother from before the war. Frau Brössler's prosperous plumpness has gone to bone, but if she had any decent clothes now, she'd look like Wallis Simpson: willowy, well groomed. Claudette tucks her wayward blouse back into a skirt she outgrew last spring and decides to cut her bangs. "If you please, Frau Brössler, my father said to ask if I may borrow trousers from Duno."

"Your father is a sensible man, *Liebes.* Come in. We'll see what we can find."

Head high, Claudette flounces through the door, shooting a look of triumph at Duno, who is forced by hard-taught courtesy to stand aside and let her pass, but she stops dead when she catches sight of his father's face. "Liesl, we cannot carry a birdcage over the mountains," Herr Brössler shouts. "No more than we can take your grandmother on such a climb!"

Duno picks up a china-faced doll and hands it to little Steffi. "We have to leave Tzipi behind," he says, kneeling in front of her. "There's plenty of food for canaries here. He'll be very happy. Oma will be all right, too," Duno says, eyes on his father. "The doctors and nurses are staying."

"Thank you, Duno," Frieda Brössler says quietly. "Stop arguing, girls. Bring only what you can carry with one hand!" She holds a pair of Duno's trousers. "Take the woolen ones, Claudette. It will be chilly at high altitude."

Albert Blum pushes tall shutters aside and leans from the window. In the street below, people are hurrying east on foot, but he himself closes his mind to fear and haste. Taking a seat at the little wooden desk, he smooths a single sheet of carefully hoarded stationery. Iron habit demands that his pencil stub be perfectly sharpened. He brushes wood shavings into the wastebasket, wipes the blade of his penknife with a handkerchief, replaces both in his pocket. When he begins at last to write, each letter is precise and regular.

"My beloved Paula, my brave David and darling Jacques," he begins. "Claudette and I are leaving Sainte-Gisèle. I cannot know if this or any of my letters will reach you. I've spent days at bus stops and markets, asking everyone for word of you. I've contacted the Red Cross and the Jewish Council in every town, but nobody's taken notice of a woman traveling with two small boys. In July, I enlisted the aid of a compassionate and resourceful carabiniere," Albert writes, silently blessing Umberto Giovanetti. "He found your names on the manifest of an eastbound train last September, but could learn nothing of your present whereabouts. The Italians have done little to ingratiate themselves with the Vichy government, but this policy makes it difficult to obtain information from French authorities."

Claudette bursts in, trousers slung over one arm, pale but calm. "I'll change," she says. "Give me five minutes."

"Claudette is nearly grown," her father writes, and turns the paper over. "She's like a dolphin, Paula. The woman she will be surfaces now and then, before submerging again into childhood's sea. We are moving on to Italy, where the war is over. Our carabiniere told us of DELASEM, an Italian Jewish organization that operates with government approval. They will find us a place to live, and I'll register again with the Red Cross. There's no more time, my dear ones. May the Lord bless you and keep you. May the Lord shine His countenance upon you. May the Lord give us all peace, and bring us together again! Your devoted husband and loving father, Albert."

He folds the letter, seals it into an envelope, addresses it simply *Paula Bomberghen Blum.* Shrugging into a baggy suit coat, he turns toward his daughter. His jaw drops. "What on earth have you done to your hair?"

She lifts her chin, but tears brim. "My bangs were too long. I cut them." Shamefaced, she picks up her bag. "They didn't come out the way I wanted."

He shakes his head and drapes a topcoat over one arm. "Never mind. Hair grows."

She holds the door open while he takes a final look around the room. They join others in the hallway and descend the stairs in a murmuring flow, but when they reach the hotel lobby, Albert steps aside. Claudette looks back at him uncertainly. "A moment," he says. "Wait at the corner, please."

When she's left the hotel, Albert approaches the front desk, where a bored clerk pares his nails. "My wife may come here, look-ing for us, monsieur," Albert says. "Would you be so very kind as to keep this letter for her?"

The clerk takes the envelope without so much as a word.

"*Merci beaucoup, monsieur,*" Albert says with a small bow. "Please give the owner our thanks for his hospitality all these months—"

"Hospitality!" A sour-faced maid lumbers past, a bundle of linens heaped in her arms. "Who's going to pay the bill, that's what I want to know!"

The clerk is not heartless. He waits until the fidgety little Bel-gian is gone before ripping the letter into tiny pieces. The Ger-mans will be here soon, he thinks. No sense taking a chance for a dirty Jew.

"Pace yourselves," Umberto Giovanetti advises, waving civilians past carabinieri headquarters toward a bridge over the Vesubie. "Long, easy steps."

A reminder, nothing more: they are practiced at this, the Jews of Sainte-Gisèle. For most, this is the second or third or fourth time they've fled the Wehrmacht or Gestapo or local police, mov-ing from Austria or Czechoslovakia or Poland to Belgium or Hol-land or France. Many carry children. Most carry suitcases. Some have fashioned knapsacks from blankets and string. Leaderless, they will attempt to climb the Alps in street clothes, wearing whatever shoes are still intact after years on the run, one step ahead of the Nazis, but not alone this time. Among the bobbing homburgs and swaying kerchiefs are hundreds of gray-green field caps; the Italian Fourth is at their side. The armistice was sup-posed to be kept secret until Italy's armies could withdraw in good order. Instead, the Germans learned of their ally's surrender the same way Italy's armed forces did: on Radio London, when that idiot Eisenhower told the whole world three days early. Now it's every man for himself.

Behind Giovanetti, a squad of carabinieri dig in near the stone bridge that spans the river east of town. "Brigadiere!" one of his men says, nodding toward the crowd. "Your little admirer!"

Claudette Blum waves as she and her father work through the

throng. Umberto blinks, taken aback. Mortified by his reaction, the girl's fingers fly to her forehead. "A new hairstyle!" Umberto exclaims heartily, trying to recover. "How very becoming, Mademoiselle Blum!"

She turns away, blushing, only to confront Duno Brössler's mocking leer. "Mmmmmmberto," he moans, eyes closed in dreamy devotion. Claudette snarls and Duno laughs, crossing the bridge and striding down the road after his family.

Umberto Giovanetti masks amusement with official courtesy. "Here are your passports, Monsieur Blum. You'll need photos, but they're complete, apart from your signatures."

"Passports?" Albert asks worriedly. "Not visas?"

"Naturally, a passport!" Umberto says, brows high. "Any good Fascist can see that you are a member of the Italian Aryan race." He glances toward Claudette. She is preoccupied by a fervent desire to perish from embarrassment, but he drops his voice anyway. "I regret to inform you, monsieur, that your many-times-great-grandmother cuckolded her unknowing husband. You are clearly the descendant of her Italian lover, and therefore eligible for citizenship!" Albert Blum laughs incredulously. Umberto remains straight-faced. "The Romans conquered a great deal of territory, monsieur. As my father used to say, everyone in Europe is a little bit Italian."

"Brigadiere, I don't know how to thank you."

"It was nothing. A telephone call to a cousin. And La Guardia di Finanza—the border police? They're unlikely to check passports under present circumstances. I only wish I had been able—"

"You did all you could, Brigadiere," Albert assures him, "but if you should hear of Paula—"

"Papa! How will Mama find us?" Claudette asks with sudden anxiety. "She won't know where we've gone!"

The carabiniere holds up his hand. "That problem can be addressed when there's a mountain range between you and the Wehrmacht, mademoiselle!"

Umberto Giovanetti has known this little family only a short while, but their fate has become important to him. Small and neat in his late forties, Signor Blum wears a fraying double-breasted suit with a once-fashionable tie and a dented homburg. His worn-out city shoes are buffed to a forlorn gloss. Add an umbrella, and he'd be dressed for a tram ride to an office in Antwerp, but the Hebrew does not look well. His daughter is young, and annoying, and she falls in love with someone new every second day. Even so, Umberto is tempted to tell this gangly girl to take care of her father.

"*Permesso?*" he asks instead. Clicking his heels, he lifts the girl's hand, brings it toward his lips. "Mademoiselle, it has been a great pleasure to know you."

"But . . . aren't you leaving, too?"

Umberto glances at his compatriots busily wiring the bridge for demolition: a rear guard of volunteers who will do what they can to slow the Wehrmacht down. He meets Albert Blum's eyes for a moment before smiling warmly at Claudette. "This is a charming town," he says lightly. "No doubt, some of us will remain here."

The road is level. The breeze is pleasant. The sun is shining. The fretfulness of children and anxiety of parents yield to the novelty of a warm day in the countryside, but soon their pace slackens. Pregnant women and new mothers carrying infants perch on suitcases or lean against trees, resting in the shade. Old people and children quickly feel the strain. Alert to opportunity, French peasants have set up makeshift tables on the roadside, selling pickled eggs, rolls, tomatoes, wine, and water to the passing Jews.

"Papa! You aren't going to pay that for an apple!" Claudette cries. "That's profiteering!" she tells a sharp-eyed woman surrounded by cowed and ragged children. "You're a profiteer!"

"War is hard on everyone," Albert remarks as much to his daughter as to the peasant.

The woman pockets their coins with chilly self-possession. "Good riddance," she mutters at their backs, and Claudette whirls to stick out her tongue.

"Claudette! You've made an enemy," Albert tells her as they walk on. "That woman will always remember that a Jew was rude to her."

"And I'll always remember that a Frenchwoman was mean to us!"

"As long as you don't forget how kind a French doctor was to your mother."

Paula's family is Sephardic-Fleming, wealthy and secure. Claudette inherited confidence from them, as well as height, but Albert himself is the child and grandchild of immigrants who moved from Poland to Germany to Belgium in three generations. His careful clothes, his correctness of manner are protective coloring. He has tailored his soul just as carefully, trying not to give offense. Pride, his grandfather told him, is a Jew's most dangerous luxury. "Your mother and I spent our honeymoon in Italy," Albert says, to change the subject. "Beautiful country. Such warmhearted people! Talk to an innkeeper for five minutes, and you're part of his family."

"What's my name in Italian, Papa?"

"Claudia," he tells her. "Italian is close to French, but easier to learn. Italians talk with their hands, their faces—they make it easy for strangers to understand."

"You should teach me Italian while we walk." She shifts her suitcase from one side to the other. "This'll be my fourth language! German, French, Hebrew, and now Italian!"

How long has the road been her classroom? It seems a lifetime since she practiced penmanship at the kitchen table, while Czechoslovakia and Poland and Finland fell. "Will the Germans come here?" Claudette asked her mother when Holland was attacked.

"Belgium's borders are very strong," Paula said, "and King Leopold has a pact with the French. Finish your homework."

A few days later the bombing began. The Blums packed. "Mama said they wouldn't come here!" Claudette complained while Albert roped suitcases to the roof of their little Citroën. "Why do the Germans keep winning?"

"We expected trenches." He yanked the knots tighter, while David wept and Jacques clambered into the backseat to claim a spot by the window. "Since 1919, we trained for trenches! This time the Germans came in tanks."

Driving along the coast, Albert made Claudette memorize multiplication tables. She squabbled with her younger brothers most of the time, but had reached six fives when the family reached Coxyde. Everyone spilled from the cramped car. Paula and the children pulled off stockings and shoes and splashed into the waves. Albert negotiated an off-season rate for a month's stay in a cottage they'd rented in happier times. War was almost unimaginable in the cheerful resort town, with its fresh paint and bright flowers and sea breeze.

Belgium's defenses held for eighteen days. The Wehrmacht crossed the Meuse, and when they reached the Moselle River, the Blums packed again. "Five sixes are thirty, six sixes are thirty-six, seven sixes are forty-two," Claudette chanted while the Citroën crawled through a stream of refugees headed for Paris. Albert pulled off the main highway onto a country road, only to be trapped at dusk in an immense traffic jam surrounding Dunkirk. They slept in the open that night, and woke to the roar of army vehicles pushing civilian automobiles into weedy ditches, clearing the way for the British retreat, and snapping the Citroën's rear axle in the process.

The Blums trudged south on foot, joining thousands of Parisians now fleeing Hitler's *Blitzkrieg*. "Six sevens are forty-two, seven sevens are forty-nine. Seven eights . . ." For the life of her, Claudette could not remember seven eights. "Fifty-six!" Albert would shout, lugging suitcases, with Jacques stumbling along beside him. Carrying David in her arms, Paula was already limping, but somehow she found the patience to say, "The numbers go in order, Claudette: five, six, seven, eight. You see the pattern? Fifty-six is seven eights."

Claudette was working on nines when the blisters on her mother's feet began to burst and bleed. Albert left Paula with the children in a little wooded valley at the edge of a good-sized village and found a doctor, who bandaged Paula's feet and forbade her to walk another step. Using his influence with the railroad stationmaster, the doctor secured tickets for her and the boys on the next train south. The third-class carriage was horribly crowded, but at least Paula could ride, the two little ones on her lap. The family was to reunite in Nice.

France capitulated. Paula and the boys never arrived. Britain fought on alone. Claudette learned long division in a series of rented rooms, but geography became her passion as they moved

east to smaller towns and cheaper quarters. When Japan joined
the Italo-German Axis, when Yugoslavia and Greece and Russia
and Bulgaria were invaded, when bombs rained on Britain and
the Afrika Korps took Tripoli, she followed every move in an old
atlas Albert had bought in a secondhand shop. Ringed by Italian
garrisons, the Mediterranean Sea was a Roman lake for the second time in history. By the time Albert found their room in
Sainte-Gisèle, the Third Reich occupied most of Europe, its
armies were within sight of the Caucasus oil fields, and Rommel's
tank corps threatened the Suez Canal. From there, Hitler could
disrupt British supply lines and open a sea link to Japan.

Albert was cheered by the Soviet Union's resistance, guiltily
elated when Pearl Harbor was attacked—at last, America would
join the war! But that was when Claudette despaired. The Axis
was invincible; the Americans and Russians could not be beaten.
"If no one can lose, no one can win, and the war will never, ever
end!" she sobbed. "Why won't everyone just stop fighting? Papa,
when can we go home?"

Albert Blum had no answer for her then. And now? Another
year, gone. His wife and sons, still missing. And Claudette is
learning Italian with a suitcase in her hand.

The sun is halfway to the horizon when the first Jews reach the
trailhead. Many are accompanied by soldiers who've traded army
backpacks for Jewish toddlers. Santino Cicala has tried to do the
same, but the first little girl he picked up wailed with fright. Santino set her down, accepting the mother's apology with a shrug
and a grimace. A second attempt went just as badly. At nineteen,
Santino Cicala is built like a dung cart—broad and low to the
ground, and ugly enough to scare children.

Leaning his carbine against a rock, he lies back on fragrant
crushed weeds and waits for someone older to help. Birdsong.
Rustling leaves. Take away the Wehrmacht, he thinks, and a nap
would be irresistible . . . A girl's voice rouses him. "Duno thinks
he's so smart!" he hears without understanding her. "Just because
he learned a few words from the carabinieri! I already know more
than he does."

A gentleman with her says something in French, and the girl replies in Italian, "*Sono, sei, è, siamo, siete, sono. Uno, due, tre, quattro, cinque. Piacere, signore! Mi chiamo* Claudia Blum. Pleased to meet you, sir, I am Claudia Blum. *Io sono di* Belgium."

"*Belgio*," Santino corrects, on his feet and brushing bits of dry grass from his uniform. "*Tu sei di* Belgio—"

Startled, she stops and stares at him. Green eyes, he thinks, thunderstruck. She is tall, with hair like copper wire. He looks down, away, anywhere but at her. "*Piacere, signorina.* Cicala, Santino," he says, introducing himself. She manages to smile politely. Hoping to draw attention from his face, Santino points to his boot. "*Italia?*" he prompts. She nods dumbly. "*Io sono di* Calabria," he says, pointing to the sole just west of the heel.

Her face lights up. "That's where you're from? *Siete di* Calabria?"

"*Sì! Molto bene!*" Slinging his carbine over a thick shoulder, Santino takes the girl's bag in one square hand and turns his attention to the gentleman. "Signor Blum?" The old man nods. Santino gestures for his valise. "*Prego, signore.* My pleasure!"

The gentleman hesitates, but the girl encourages him to hand over the suitcase, burbling, "*Molte grazie! Tante grazie! Beaucoup di grazie,* Signor Cicala. Was that your name? Am I saying it right? We are so tired! You can't imagine! How do you say 'tired,' Papa?"

"*Siamo stanchi.*" Albert hands over his bag. A gap-toothed smile transforms the homely soldier into a gigantic six-year-old. Charmed, Albert touches his chest. "Blum, Alberto," he says. "*La mia figlia:* my daughter, Claudia. *Mille grazie,* Santino."

With nothing to carry, the Blums can manage the pace the soldier sets: climb half an hour, rest five minutes, then climb again. The sun has nearly disappeared when they hear a low rumbling in the distance. "Just what we need!" Claudette says sourly. "A thunderstorm!"

"We're not made of sugar—we won't melt!" her father says with breathless cheer.

Santino sets the suitcases down and flexes his cramped fingers. Artillery, he thinks. Three minutes' rest this time.

Far below, just east of town, Rivka Brössler sits alone, admiring a sunset made glorious by low clouds first gilded, then enameled with Fabergé colors. "The best view in Sainte-Gisèle!" her grand-son Duno told her once. "Do you like it, Oma?" Rivka waved her hand, as though flicking at a fly. It was too much trouble to answer.

Not even the most charitable of her descendants ascribe her present state to age alone. True, she's retreated from the world more decisively since the Brösslers left Vienna, but even as a young mother, Rivka always seemed distracted. Long ago, her family left the Ukraine for the opportunity and relative safety of Austria; they were better off, but something was always reminding Rivka of home.

Her youngest son, Herrmann, grew up in Vienna, embarrassed by his mother's Slavic vowels and awkward syntax. Now, when she speaks at all, it is in Ukrainian, a language Herrmann never learned.

"She's gone back to the Ukraine in her mind," a doctor from Holland told the Brösslers. "Think of it! No one left alive who calls her by her first name. Such loneliness, to be only Mother, or Grandmother, or Frau Brössler, but never Rivka again. You are sad to see her this way, but she's happy in her memories. Sit with her," he advised. "Keep her company. Enjoy her contentment."

Everyone thinks she's senile, but Rivka knows she's not. She's tired, that's all. Tired of Herrmann and Frieda quarreling, of the grandchildren making noise. Tired of new places, new languages. People coming and going, with their names and opinions and rules and demands. Life is one damned thing after another, Rivka decided when they left Austria behind. To hell with it.

Since moving to the Jewish nursing home last spring, Rivka has spent the greater part of every day sitting out on this arcaded wooden balcony waiting for the sunset. Tonight, the air is soft. The scent of roses rises from a nearby garden. Best of all, there's a big storm coming. Rivka settles down happily, listening to booming thunder. She's always enjoyed the drama of a nice storm.

She sneaks a look over her shoulder at the clock. It's past time, but no one's come to bully her into bed. Watching the lightning, she feels like a naughty child, thrilled to stay up late, and like a child, she falls asleep although she'd rather not. Memories blur into dreams, and back again. Who was that girl in the dream? Cousin Natasha! Now, what brought her to mind?

When Rivka wakes again, it's to the sound of footsteps. She doesn't see the soldier enter her room, her attention caught instead by the people running in the streets, just beneath her balcony. "Natasha, look!" she says, before she can stop herself. Now I really am senile! she thinks.

She smiles and shakes her head at her own foolishness, which spoils the soldier's shot. "*Scheisse,*" he swears irritably. Averting his face from the fountaining blood, he presses the gun barrel to the old Jew's skull, and finishes the job.

9 September 1943

PORTO SANT'ANDREA

"Mamma," Renzo Leoni calls, wincing at his own voice. "For God's sake, get the door!"

He doesn't expect a reply. She might be at the market, but it's just as likely that his mother is sitting at the table, content to let him pay the price for last night's binge.

"Signor Leoni!" the rabbi's son yells again. "Are you awake yet? My babbo needs ten men for morning prayers, and I'm only seven, so I can't, so you have to!"

"Your babbo can go to hell, and take the minyan with him," Renzo mutters. He limps as quickly as he can through an apartment crammed with generations of dusty furniture. Piles of knitting and mending slump beside every chair. Books, cinema and fashion magazines, newspapers, and mail obscure every horizontal surface. Before the race laws, peasant girls helped with the endless heavy housework of middle-class families. Now most Jewish housewives struggle to maintain their prewar standards. Not Lidia Leoni. "It's a political protest," she says.

Before Renzo reaches the door, Angelo Soncini has banged on it three more times, kicking it once for good measure. "My mamma says she'll make you breakfast! Signor Leoni, are you—"

"*Belandi*, Angelo! Stop it! You're killing me!" Renzo unlocks the door.

Angelo takes a step backward, staring.

"Inform your esteemed babbo," Renzo tells the boy in a low and careful voice, "I'll be there in twenty minutes, but this is absolutely the last time. Tell your beautiful mammina," he adds with conviction, "that if I come within one hundred meters of food during the next three hours, we'll all regret it." Angelo looks blank. "No breakfast, thank you," Renzo explains. "I'm not feeling entirely well."

Angelo looks a bit stunned, but he nods gravely and takes off for home. Appalled by the amount of noise a small boy can generate during the simple act of descending a carpetless staircase, Renzo closes the door as quietly as he can and shuffles to the nearest chair.

Pretty girls and handsome women gaze at him in the dim, divided light of the shuttered salon. His mother's apartment is his father's Uffizi, its walls a gallery of family portraits, mute testimony to her late husband's professional talent. Beautifully lit, cunningly composed, the largest photo was taken thirty years ago. Round-faced and chubby, the long-awaited son grins toothlessly on his triumphant mother's lap. Around these two, the stair-step Leoni sisters are arrayed, elegant as Romanovs in white organdy, their hand-me-downs kept quietly stylish by their mother's own clever fingers. Rachele, then eighteen and already engaged to Tranquillo Loeb, a successful attorney ten years her senior. At two-year intervals: Bianca, Elena, Debora, and Susanna, each slender and striking, with their mother's aristocratic bearing and Torinese fairness. Then a sad gap: two miscarriages, both girls, and another daughter who died shortly after birth, followed by sturdy little Ester, four in the photo, a proprietary hand resting on her mother's arm. And then? When hope had faded, a son and heir for the proud photographer: Renzo, himself. The little prince.

"Renzo flew before he could walk." That's the family legend, and it's very nearly true. With six sisters to carry him like a doll, his feet rarely touched the ground before he was three, and his earliest memory is of sailing through the air.

It must have been spring, and close to sunset. A small boy awakens from an afternoon nap at his grandparents' home. Downstairs: the high-pitched chatter and squeal of girls, their mother's imperious orders mercifully muffled. Their father, silent, yearns for the peace of his darkroom, no doubt. The boy squirms onto a rush-bottomed chair in front of an open window.

He is alone, and enchanted by a thousand swifts that soar and wheel just out of reach. Dark wings flash against a lavender sky. The birds plunge, disappearing. Sweep upward in tight formation. The rushes prickle his bare feet, so the boy levers himself onto the broad stuccoed windowsill. Squirming forward, he dangles breathlessly, head in the air, rump in the bedroom. The swifts dive again, and in a moment of toddler ecstasy, the boy hurls himself after them, arms wide as wings.

"His maiden flight," Emanuele Leoni called it with perverse paternal pride, telling the story to anyone who'd listen and admire the plaster casts on his son's little wrists.

His sisters watched young Renzo more carefully after that. Escaping their vigilance became part of the game. He did so with a fluid combination of bald-faced lies and physical daring, acquainted at an early age with Sant'Andrea's crowded rooftops and sheer cliffsides. If a few weeks passed without his appearance in the emergency room of the local hospital, the white-clad nursing nuns telephoned to make sure Renzo hadn't been killed. "You should enroll him in flying lessons," one advised when Renzo turned fourteen. "Perhaps he'd learn to control his landings."

In the spring of 1927, over his wife's objections, Emanuele Leoni's son became the youngest member of the Sant'Andrea Aviation Club. And while there was no photograph to record Renzo's initial crash landing, other moments in his son's career as a pilot were immortalized.

"Look at this!" Emanuele would order clients who came to the studio to document an engagement, a wedding, a bar mitzvah. "That's Renzo—he was over the harbor in an old Savoia 17 when the engine shaft broke. See this? That's Italo Balbo himself, visiting my boy in the Benghazi Hospital. Renzo was flying a Macchi 52R with a thousand-horsepower Fiat ASI engine. He set a new speed record just before one of the wings ripped off. Here he is getting his commission in the Royal Italian Air Force. Renzo joined up the day after we declared war on Abyssinia. That snapshot's him in a field hospital in '36. Led a squadron back in a sandstorm. His own engine failed just before he landed, but Renzo didn't lose a single man. See this? The Medaglia d'Argento. My boy's a hero!"

In thirteen years as a pilot, Renzo Leoni crawled out of five bloody wrecks. Blinded by fog, deafened by thunder, he's flown over the Mediterranean and the Alps. He's been lost and low on fuel above the Libyan desert and trackless Ethiopian wastes, and shot at by Abyssinian anti-aircraft guns. But it was Emanuele Leoni who was buried with that Silver Medal; Renzo took it off the day it was awarded, and never spoke of it again.

The familiar sensation rises in his throat. Renzo pushes himself upright and vectors through the maze of tables and chairs and chests, trying not to add bruises to his shins. Centuries of settling have rendered the marble floor uneven, but the uncompromisingly modern bathroom is only ten years old. And surprisingly clean, given his mother's attitude toward housekeeping.

Unwilling to increase the glare off the white ceramic tiles and nickel-plated fixtures, Renzo kneels before the toilet without turning on the light. He brings up bad brandy and outraged stomach acid in two efficient gouts. It takes considerably longer to make his crash-battered knees and ankles straighten, but he gets to his feet and hauls down on the chain, relieved that the plumbing still works after the last English air raid. Mouth sour, he unbuttons his rumpled shirt and pulls off the cotton singlet beneath it. With stately deliberation, he gives the cold-water tap a quarter turn. Splashes his face and chest. Brushes his teeth, and spits. Only then does he confront the man in the mirror.

The asymmetries of his chest are familiar: hard knobs of badly healed ribs on the right, a ragged scar on the left where his collarbone punched through the skin. Dark and anarchic, his hair is a chaos of short brown curls above a broken nose that gives a hawkish look to the lined and haggard face. Two years in Abyssinia, three in Ventotene Prison. A total of twenty-nine months in a variety of hospitals . . . Closer to forty than thirty, his face says, lying.

It's just the hangover, he lies in return, stropping a straight razor.

Friends on leave have carried home lurid tales of drunken parties hosted by German officers. Hitler may be an abstemious health-food fanatic, but schnapps and beer fuel his military, and Renzo can now confirm the stories of prodigious Teutonic boozing. When he got Schramm back to the Bellavista, the German had sobered up enough to drink some more and insisted that Renzo join him. Curious about Schramm, and thirsty himself, Renzo was easy to persuade. They found a tavern near the hotel and sat at a corner table: a comity of two, ignoring the armistice celebration around them.

Night came. The bar emptied. Schramm talked on, and on. He spoke of the eastern front, and the Red Army. He spoke of the Allies, and the Japanese. He speculated about the effect of Italy's surrender on the course of the war. Then, when the yawning waiter deposited yet another bottle on the table, Schramm spoke, at last, of Germany. "Four long years, we fought the whole world to a standstill. Then we wake up one morning in 1918, and the war is lost!" Schramm shook his head in dazed amazement. "One day the empire's there, and the next—pfft! Gone. And who presumes to take the kaiser's place? Friedrich Ebert. A harness maker whose magnificent ambition was to make Germany a nation of bureaucrats! Governments rising and falling like drunks in a gutter. Influenza. That filthy, humiliating treaty! Demonstrations, strikes, riots. Christ! The inflation—!"

"The Jew bankers getting fat while real Germans starved," Renzo supplied, mashing a cigarette into an ashtray. "That was shit, you know. The kaiser financed the war by printing money. Inflation wrecked the banks, not Jews."

Schramm never paused. "Everything we had—gone, overnight. Six million men unemployed, and if you had a job, you were paid in worthless heaps of Weimar paper. Then the stock market crashed, and the whole world went to hell!"

"And of course, it was the Jew speculators who did it."

"Yes, but why?" Schramm asked, surprising Renzo for the first time. "The Jews lost everything, too! The Depression dragged everybody down!"

"Why indeed?" Renzo asked cannily. "This is the subtlety, Schramm. This is the key! For Jews to cause a catastrophe that ruined them along with everyone else makes ... no ... sense. So it must be a conspiracy, right? A diabolical Jew conspiracy! I've had three years to think about this, my friend." He poured them both another drink. "Life was shit. Hitler had the most appealing solution. Just get rid of the Jews."

"Put a stop to all that useless parliamentary crap," Schramm said, remembering. "March together as comrades! Rebuild the German nation—"

"And reclaim your place in the sun!" Renzo declared, chin jutting, mouth turned down, nodding vigorously at his own rhetoric: Mussolini with dark and coiling hair.

"Aha!" Schramm cried, a spongy cough merging with the exhalation. "You Italians did the same thing. Americans, Russians, the Japanese. We all wanted to march behind men who knew what to do! Your family, your teachers, your friends. Newspapers, the radio! All saying the same things—"

"Democracy is degenerate! Greatness lies in struggle! Virtue lies in blood!" Renzo recited grandly. "Say yes to the leader, and you can wear this handsome uniform. Say yes, and you're a patriot!"

"You're part of something big, and new, and powerful! You're better than you were alone."

Renzo offered Schramm one of his own cigarettes. "Say no, and you're a coward and a traitor. Say no, and you're in jail."

"Say no, and you're dead." Schramm lit up, coughed himself blue, and shoved his empty cigarette case across the table. "Keep it! This's my last one, I swear! You should quit, too. Tobacco will give you cancer. We proved it years ago."

Schramm pushed himself up from the table and stood there, slump-shouldered and swaying, far away. "You must learn not to be kind," he told Renzo finally. "Be as blind and as deaf as you have to be. Feel nothing. Only the heartless will survive."

Staring at the hollow-cheeked image in the mirror, Renzo lathers his face. Feel nothing. Believe nothing. Do nothing, he thinks. Lots of practice at that—

The banging on the door begins again. The razor blade knicks his chin. Muttering curses, he hurries down the hall, barefoot and bare-chested, wiping shaving soap and blood from his face. The instant he unlocks the door, it flies open, revealing a short, stout man nearing sixty, who points at him furiously.

"*Pazzo!* Madman! You are going to get yourself killed, and you'll drag the whole family down with you!"

"*Buon giorno* to you, too, Tranquillo," Renzo replies as genially as he can. "Always a pleasure to see my darling sister's husb—"

"Shut that door! What time did you get home last night? Your mother was frantic—"

"Tranquillo, my mother has never been frantic in her life."

"We thought you'd been arrested—"

"For what? Taking a tourist back to his hotel?" Renzo slouches toward the dining room and lowers himself gingerly into a chair.

"Then I find out you're not just drinking yourself senseless again, you're doing it with an SS officer! You were supposed to be helping your own people! Instead you go off with some Nazi and—"

"Schramm's not a Nazi, Tranquillo. He's a combat surgeon."

"You don't think he can be both?" Tranquillo pushes the shutters open, grimly pleased when Renzo swears at the light and twists away. "Let me tell you something. German doctors invented the race policy that put you in prison."

"Tranquillo! Please! Come back and lecture me this afternoon," Renzo suggests, elbows on the table, aching head in his hands.

Tranquillo sits across from him, round arms crossed above a round belly. "Renzo, we have two, perhaps three weeks before the Gestapo starts rounding up Jews—"

"Oh, for Christ's sake, what kind of Jew am I? If my mother didn't live across the street from a synagogue—"

"Renzo, what exactly do you think the word *judenfrei* means? The Nazis don't consult a rabbinical jury to decide if you're pious enough to arrest! In the next twenty-four hours, our existence will become a criminal offense. Renzo, the Gestapo aren't like the Blackshirts! The Nazis won't just force a liter of castor oil down your throat and humiliate the shit out of you, you idiot! They'll—"

"Tranquillo!" Slender and severe at seventy, Lidia Leoni has shut the door to her apartment as quietly as she stepped through it. "War," she declares, "is no excuse for vulgarity."

Startled by her resonant contralto, Tranquillo leaps to his feet, murmuring courtesies. He reaches for his mother-in-law's parcels, but she offers them to Renzo instead, presenting a lightly powdered cheek for a ceremonial kiss. "Take the groceries into the kitchen and put them away for me, will you, please? I couldn't find much—there are roadblocks outside the city." Eyes on Tranquillo, Lidia waits until Renzo has left the room. "You come into my home," she asks softly, "and call my son names?"

Tranquillo Loeb is a decorated hero of the Battle of Caporetto, a respected attorney from whom Catholic clients seek advice, in defiance of the race laws. His modest stature rarely concerns him, but even now, her height reduced by age, Lidia is taller than her son-in-law, and he takes two steps back to compensate. "I apologize, signora, but someone has to explain to him—"

"Explain? Perhaps." Lidia unpins a small stylish hat with a short black veil. "Insult?" She shakes her head and sets the hat aside.

"Signora, he has a criminal record! He's a Communist and a Jew—"

"I wasn't a Communist! I was a defeatist!" Renzo calls from the kitchen. "I said this war would be a disaster, and I was right! We never had the manpower or equipment, and our supply lines were—"

"You're on the police rolls! It doesn't matter why!" Tranquillo's voice drops. "Signora, yesterday we were Germany's ally. Today we are an occupied country. The Wehrmacht has declared martial law. The Gestapo will begin by arresting Rabbino Soncini and me. Renzo's name will be third on the Sant'Andrea list. And don't think a Silver Medal will save you," he yells toward the kitchen. "German Jews with Iron Crosses were deported like everyone else!"

Lidia checks her hair, well cut and iron gray, in a gold-wash mirror hanging above an ebonized walnut credenza, the gleam of its surface obscured by dissident dust. Renzo comes back from the kitchen, rumpled trousers sagging on slim hips. "I gave birth to a perfectly beautiful baby boy," she says to her reflection, "and look what he's done to himself. Put a dressing gown on, Renzo! You know how I hate those scars."

Renzo slouches off to his bedroom. Lidia settles into a straight-backed chair. Tranquillo tries again. "Signora, please! Italy has been invaded—"

"Oh, but Italy is always being invaded!" Lidia replies airily. "Lombards, Carthaginians, Vandals." Propping a pair of reading glasses on a thin-boned nose, she leans over for a sewing basket. "Saracens, Spaniards, Normans. Englishmen. Americans." She peers down through her lenses while threading a needle. "Renzo," she calls, "is this the third or fourth time for the Germans?"

Wrapped in a paisley silk robe, he comes into the salon and flops onto the sofa. "Do Goths and Visigoths count?"

"I suppose they would. The point is, we've seen them all, and we've outlasted them all."

Tranquillo's effort to remain calm is visible. "Signora, Rachele's packing as we speak, and I'm trying to get the Soncinis to leave as well. I have contacts in Switzerland and we can—"

"Switzerland!" Lidia sniffs.

"Terrible food," Renzo agrees. He picks a two-year-old magazine out of a pile on the floor. "Much too tidy."

Lidia refuses to take the bait. "Who knows how the Swiss would treat strangers? I'm sure we're better off among friends."

"Are you willing to stake your life on that?" Tranquillo asks. "In Poland and France, gentiles couldn't line up fast enough to denounce Jewish neighbors! Signora, if you won't leave with us, at least leave the city! Susanna's in-laws are Catholic. They have a tenant farm up in Decimo, don't they? You could—"

"Live in the mountains like a goat? Don't be ridiculous." She stretches a stocking over an ivory darning egg. "I am an old woman and blameless, Tranquillo. I have lived in Sant'Andrea for fifty-one years. My children were born here. My husband and eleven generations of his family are buried here! Four of my daughters lie with them. No one has the right to tell me to leave. Not you, and certainly not the Germans!"

Morning noise drifts in from the street. Most of the bombing has been down near the docks, and this neighborhood hasn't emptied the way others have. "Signor Leoni! The minyan!" young Angelo hollers, two floors down. "Are you coming?"

With an exasperated sigh, Tranquillo pulls out his pocketwatch and steps onto a small balcony overlooking the synagogue courtyard. "Signor Leoni is ill, Angelo. I'll be right down." Returning to the salon, he draws himself up, his bearing still military beneath the weight of his years. "Signora, I have fought and bled for Italy. I yield to no one in my love for my country. I have been married to your daughter almost thirty years. I am a good husband to her, a good father to your grandchildren. I have provided your family with legal advice for three decades. Have you ever had cause to doubt my judgment?"

"You've always had our interests at heart."

"Then believe me when I tell you that every Jew in Italy is in mortal danger, and we have very little time to escape it!"

"I won't be driven from my own home!"

"If you stay here, I won't be able to protect you or Renzo."

Renzo slams the magazine against his thighs. "Who the hell is asking you for protection? *Belandi!* You, of all—"

"Renzo!" Lidia warns.

Tranquillo takes a breath, retrieves his hat, lifts his briefcase. "Rachele and the children and I are leaving tomorrow," he says tightly. "I won't be here for Yom Kippur, Renzo, so if I offended you by offering help, or in any other way this year, I beg pardon." Tipping his hat smartly to Lidia, Tranquillo makes a short bow. "Signora, I will protect your daughter and your grandchildren, as is my duty. Should you reconsider, there will be a place for you with us in Switzerland. *Buon giorno!*"

"Three years locked up in Ventotene for him!" Renzo fumes. "And he has the nerve to offer us his protection! That pompous little—"

"Renzo, *caro,* I've heard it all twice now." Lidia takes a shirt from the basket and begins strengthening a button that's come loose. "You have to admit there's an element of *opera buffa* to be appreciated." Apparently dumbfounded, Renzo mutters something. "I heard that," she says, even though she hasn't. "Stop pacing and sit down."

He stands still, but refuses to sit. "You never told him."

"You asked me not to. I keep my word." She tests the button, clips the thread, tosses the shirt into the ironing basket. "Everything Tranquillo did for those refugees is to your credit."

He starts to say something, but goes instead to the upright piano Lidia bought when Rachele was six and seemed musical. His back to his mother, he plays standing up. Lidia recognizes the piece. "Good Morning, Blues." Count Basie. She tries not to hate this kind of music, primarily because the Nazis do, but for a year after Renzo came home from Abyssinia, he did little more than listen to American jazz. Minor keys, mournful melodies. "I wish you wouldn't play that," she says. "It makes you—"

He bangs the keyboard cover down and disappears into his room.

"It makes you moody," she finishes firmly.

Would things have been different if he'd been born a Catholic? Lidia herself is not so much a Jew as an Italian who celebrates Passover rather than Easter. All her children went to Torah Talmud classes, but they also went to schools taught by nuns. Two of Lidia's sons-in-law are Catholic, a commonplace in modern Italy, where there hasn't been a functioning ghetto anywhere in Italy since 1870. That Lidia lives so near a synagogue is happenstance. Rabbino Soncini is less a spiritual guide than a neighbor, a man who married a girl Renzo once fancied.

Since Mussolini caved in to Hitler's pressure in '38, Lidia has been reminded of her Jewishness constantly by restrictions and regulations that circumscribe her daily life. The race laws are an insulting, but temporary, annoyance. She would certainly never convert, and yet . . . Since he came back from Africa, Renzo's life has been atonement without hope of absolution.

She rummages through the mending basket and slips another stocking over the darning egg. "Tranquillo is a good man," she admits, making her voice carry. "He was a great support to me when your father died, but I have never met anyone so inaccurately named! He believes every story the refugees tell him. I'm sure they've suffered, but honestly? I think they exaggerate. Understandable, of course. Makes them feel more worthy of charity. Saves their pride."

Suspiciously jaunty, Renzo returns, with a silver cigarette case she's never seen before. Casually, he snaps it open and offers the contents to her. "A gift from my new German friend. He's decided to quit smoking. He's got a terrible cough."

Shamefaced, she puts her mending aside and reaches for a cigarette, resting a hand on her son's wrist as he leans over with a match. She smells liquor on his breath, but this is not the time for a lecture on vice. "How long have you known?"

"That you smoke? Since 1926."

Machine-made and elegant, the cigarette is a slim and perfect package of oral gratification, nothing like the harsh Italian tobacco people roll in squares of newspaper these days. "This is wonderful," she murmurs.

"American." Renzo props his hips against the credenza. "The Germans confiscated a smuggler's boat off the coast of Rome. Remember the mafiosi Mussolini jailed down in Sicily? The Allies thought they were political prisoners and let everybody out. They're robbing Patton blind and selling the stuff up here. Cigarettes, oranges, blankets, coffee."

His voice is light, but Lidia is paying attention. "What else did you find out?"

Renzo turns toward the mirror, smoke curling around his face as he tilts his head from side to side to inspect his temples. "Do you think I'm losing my hair? I don't mind going gray, but bald—"

"Renzo, *caro,*" Lidia says wearily, "don't be an ass."

He gets a heavy crystal ashtray from the kitchen and brings it to the table. "Tranquillo's right about the occupation. Schramm thinks Hitler will take the armistice as a personal insult, and he'll make Italy pay."

"Then Jews won't be singled out. We'll all be in it together."

"Mamma, the Germans have something like a hundred thousand troops on the peninsula now. Schramm says Kesselring got his men out of Sicily and onto the mainland last month. No matter what Radio London says, that wasn't a rout." He taps off a coil of ash. "The Germans expected Badoglio to switch sides—they've put eight more divisions into Italy since July. Hitler pulled troops away from the eastern front—that's where Schramm served. Hausser's panzer corps took horrendous casualties at Kursk, but those units are back up to strength now, Mamma, and Schramm says their officers are excellent."

They smoke silently for a few moments, Lidia adjusting her opinions, Renzo watching dust dance on a thin shaft of morning light. "I won't see Schramm again," he says. "He only knows my first name. Even so . . ."

"It was foolhardy, but that kind of information is valuable." Lidia stubs her cigarette out delicately and sets the rest aside for later. "The resistance will need to know what the situation is."

"The resistance!" He snorts. "Eleven boys in Cuneo printing an underground paper? Six Communists in Milan painting 'Death to Fascism' on a wall?" He shakes his head. "Mamma, I just spent three years locked up with hundreds of dissidents representing several thousand political parties. I've seen more organization in an alleyful of cats."

"There were strikes all over the north last spring, Renzo. Huge antiwar demonstrations. I marched in one myself." He gapes at her. "It was the most thrilling thing I've ever done. Twenty-two years of fascism. That squalid little colonial war in Abyssinia— and then an alliance with the Germans, of all people. Five years of being treated like a second-class citizen. My only son in prison! To go out in the sunlight and join with thousands of others and shout, *No more!*" Her needle stabs at the darning egg, and the edges of a hole draw tight. "We shut the factories down, Renzo. We ran Mussolini out of power."

"We've got a Bolshevik in the family, all right, but it's not me."

"There weren't only leftists in those marches, Renzo! There were royalists, Catholic Action people. The Communists will probably run things," she concedes. "They're the only ones orga- nized for an effective opposition. But the whole country's sick to death of fascism, and everyone hates the Germans for dragging us into this war. Everyone hates the Germans, full stop," she mutters, biting off the thread. "They've always been the enemy! And now there'll be soldiers, and we'll fight—"

The ashtray shatters against a wall. Open-mouthed, Lidia stares at the glittering pieces.

"You don't know what you're talking about." He is on his feet, his eyes opaque. Turning his back on her, Renzo crosses to the window. A fragment of breeze finds its way in from the sea. The curtains flutter weakly. His fingers tap the shutter's framework in time to some inner rhythm. "I tried having enemies once, Mamma. It was a mistake."

Abyssinia, she thinks. It always comes back to Abyssinia!

The bronze bells of San Giobatta ring eight. She withstands the chilly silence as long as she can. "All right," she says evenly. "We know what we are not going to do. I won't oblige the Nazis by dis- appearing. You won't fight. We are left with Tolstoy's question: what then shall we do?"

He speaks without facing her. "Go back to bed?"

"That's a plan," Lidia admits drily, "though not quite as ambi- tious as I had envisioned."

His fingers curl into a fist that he touches to the woodwork, once, twice, gently. He backs away from the window and stumbles over a low table covered with books. "This place is a mess!"

"Signor Mussolini is welcome to clean it himself."

When he returns from his bedroom, the remains of the ashtray have disappeared, and she is back to her mending as though nothing has happened. "That shirt came out well," she observes. It was his father's. Renzo lost weight in prison, and she had to cut it down, but the fabric was a pleasure to work with. Checking the collar in the credenza's mirror, Renzo knots his tie. "You're rather overdressed for a nap," she notes.

He shakes out a linen jacket. "I'm going to apply for a job."

"Really?" she remarks, brows lifted. It's illegal for Catholics to employ Jews, and for Jews to own businesses, but getting around the race laws is a popular Italian sport. "What sort of job?"

He jerks his shirt cuffs down to provide a centimeter of reveal. "I met a man in prison whose cousin is a member of the Dairy Association. They need drivers. If you can keep a truck with a gasogene rig running, the foreman won't ask questions."

"Get him to pay you in cheese. I can trade it on the black market." She peers over her spectacles. "You do realize that milkmen are expected to be out of bed before noon?"

He turns from the mirror and smiles at her brightly. "Mamma, you and I have two additional tasks before us this morning, and you may have your choice: clean this apartment, or seduce a priest."

Serenely, she surveys the domestic chaos around her. "How old is the priest?"

Downstairs, the rabbi's wife props her aching back against the open door and bids each member of the minyan a good day as he leaves. "*Buon giorno,*" the first seven say, adding, "*B'sha'ah tova!* May the child be born at a lucky hour!"

Bald and bent, the eighth to leave is Giacomo Tura, but he takes his time about it. With hands twisted by a lifetime of gripping pens and brushes, the widowed scribe waves arthritic fingers over Mirella Soncini's swollen belly. His rheumy eyes rise slowly, lingering on her breasts before arriving at her wry and smiling face. "Mirella! *Chè faccia bella!*" he sings in a raspy tenor. "If you weren't a married woman, *O Dío!* I'd make you mine!"

Mirella waves off his randy gallantry. In her own clear eyes, the war and her third pregnancy have rendered her shopworn and middle-aged at twenty-six, but she knows what others still see when they look at her: an early Renaissance life model, Botticelli blond, demeanor demure, but with a direct and level gaze.

Reaching into the entryway, she grabs a broom and sweeps the night's grime from the low stone steps. "*'N giorno,* Signor Loeb," she says, when the minyan's ninth finally appears. "Is your brother-in-law all right? Angelo said he was ill."

Tranquillo Loeb pushes both hands at the air, miming rejection of Renzo Leoni and all his affairs, and stalks away from the synagogue talking to himself. Mirella decides to go to the source. "Renzo!" she calls loudly. A moment later, he steps onto the Leonis' small balcony. He's dressed, but . . . "Your hair seems to have exploded," she informs him helpfully. "You look like an alarmed cartoon character."

"And you look like a brood mare," he replies. "When you pass small children, it must seem like an eclipse of the sun."

"Diogenes, put down your lantern!" she cries. "I have found an honest man!"

"How are you feeling?" he asks more seriously.

"Huge." She widens her stance and presses her hands against her lower back. "But everything's going well, *grazie a Dío!* Except—" Casting her eyes toward her own door, and then ever so slightly upward, she mouths, "The noise . . ." Every morning, a minyan packs her dining room, waiting for Iacopo to make the tenth. The congregation's secretary and treasurer arrive next. They've had desks in the Soncinis' salon since the synagogue's business offices were converted to a school in 1938. They're followed by refugees queuing for relief money. "Angelo said you had morning sickness!" she tells Renzo.

"An acute but temporary condizion," he tells her with a German doctor's accent. "*Die Prognose ist gut.*"

He's handsome, in a rather world-weary way, but it's increasingly difficult to tell world-weary from hungover. "I still have a headache powder saved up," she offers.

"What he needs is a smack in the head!" Catarina Dolcino mutters, emerging from the apartment lobby. For fifty years, Rina's been the neighborhood portiere; old age and widowhood have merely increased the amount of attention she can devote to stern surveillance. Left fist on a pillowy hip, right wielding a broom like a bishop's crozier, she scowls upward. "You're a disgrace, Renzo Leoni! Everyone in this building heard you come in!"

"*Santo cielo!*" Renzo's mother cries, coming to stand at his side. "Who is that dreary old woman shouting like a fishwife in the street?"

"And who raised such a boy?" A gold crucifix dangles between ample breasts swaying under a cotton housedress as Rina sweeps the sidewalk. "Some other old woman, whose son is a public nuisance! Five in the morning, he came in! He woke the whole neighborhood up!"

"You should have been on your way to Mass by then anyway, you lazy thing! I've already been to the market, and I got the only decent pears in Sant'Andrea!"

Renzo rolls his eyes and backs off the balcony in a strategic retreat. Lidia Leoni and Rina Dolcino have been bickering for decades. One thin, the other round—Stick and Ball, the neighborhood children call them. Once the game's begun, it's impossible to tell who's hitting whom.

Mirella sets her own broom aside, in too good a mood to be drawn into even the most affectionate of arguments. The war is *over,* she thinks for the fiftieth time this morning. The bombing will end. The king will repeal the race laws, and Angelo can go to school with the other children. Soon it will be Rosh Hashana, and life will start fresh. Everything will be as it was before. Except for Altira . . .

Her eyes fill, but she blinks away the tears. Altira is gone, but the new baby will arrive with the new year. It is time, she thinks resolutely, to be happy again. "Have either of you been able to find soap?" she asks the older women. "All this smoke! I'm dying to wash the walls."

"She's getting close," Rina says shrewdly. "I always washed walls the night before I went into labor."

"I have three weeks to go, Signora Dolcino."

"Verdi's had soap two days ago," Lidia says.

"They charge too much," Rina counters. "Try Alesci's instead."

Shops, prices, and the availability of necessities are the topics of the next squabble. It continues long after the rabbi's wife has gone back inside, until Rina runs out of opinions and gazes at the Soncinis' doorway. "Oh, Lidia, I hope the new baby is all right! Mirella went through so much with Altira, poor little thing. You know, I thought at the time it was a mistake to keep that child at home—"

"Don't be morbid, Rina. Mirella has moved on, and so should you!" Lidia leans over the balcony and lowers her voice. "Do you know that new man down at the archbishop's office?"

"Don Osvaldo? Yes, yes. A *Triestino.* Stuffy, but a good heart."

Lidia hesitates. She would trust Rina Dolcino with the lives of her grandchildren, but an unknown priest Renzo barely knows? "I'm coming down," she tells her neighbor. "*Cara mia, we need to talk.*"

MARITIME ALPS
FRANCE

Before the war, climbers from Italy and France hiked in these mountains to escape the heat and noise of urban life. After sunset, they'd hear only the hoot of an owl or the leathery hush of bat wings, and the unnerving nighttime silence could keep them awake in their woolen blankets. Claudette Blum, by contrast, has spent a dreamless night in the deep, unmoving sleep of a growing child, exhausted by the day's exertions, until now.

Her eyelids flutter and snap open in the predawn darkness. All the small noises are near and comforting—her father's soft snore, the soldier's deep-chested breathing—but something woke her up. She rises onto an elbow and listens hard. A moment more, and she slumps with relief, matching sound to sight: the pat-pat-skitter-pat of falling autumn leaves.

They're alone in this small high clearing: Claudette, her father, and Santino Cicala. Most of the refugees spent the night at a mountainside collection point for a logging operation. Their soldiers worked in teams to lift whole tree trunks from a giant's woodpile and heaved the logs onto a huge blaze, sending a column of sparks and smoke toward the stars. Santino shook his head at the fire. "The Luftwaffe will see it." He insisted the Blums move on in a darkness that seemed only slightly less menacing than the Germans.

They'd have been warmer by the bonfire, but Claudette is grateful for the soldier's concern. Her father's optimism annoys and frightens her, but Santino has relieved her of the need to worry, a responsibility her father has obviously relinquished.

A blush of light tints the sky beyond the mountain. Too cold and hungry to go back to sleep, Claudette sits up. Every morning for months, she's awakened to her father's slack face and its gray stubble. He is of no interest, but the soldier is new to her. Santino's face is lined around the eyes, but his hair is thick and shoe-polish black, so tightly waved it looks marcelled. She cannot guess his age, but he is . . . mature, she decides, not old like Papa. Serious, and silent. Not handsome like Brigadiere Giovanetti, but he has a wonderful smile.

Perhaps sensing her inspection, the infantryman rouses, yawning noiselessly. Mouthing, "*Buon giorno,*" and then "*Scusi,*" he rolls to his feet with easy strength and disappears into the woods.

Claudette brushes bits of dried leaf from her hair and rubs her arms to generate some heat. For a few minutes, she sits on one heel, but it does no good. She jostles her father's shoulder. "Papa? Papa!"

"What? What is it?" he cries.

"I have to go!"

He flops back onto the ground, fingers digging into his eye sockets. "*Na, zum Donnerwetter!* For this, you woke me up?" Groaning, he pulls off the pair of socks he wore to keep his hands warm and rummages through his suitcase. He locates the squares he cut from newspaper in preparation for this trek—only yesterday? Handing one sheet to Claudette, he points to a bush.

She's still appalled by the necessity of dropping her pants and squatting, but she's already learned the first lesson of Alpine hygiene: face uphill. This time, the relief is so exquisite, she forgets to be embarrassed. "That's really not so bad," she says, returning to the campsite.

Santino is already back, and he puts a finger to his lips, glancing at her father. Albert chants *Shakharis,* bowing and swaying, eyes closed. Claudette puts herself to work, preparing a meager breakfast for the three of them.

"That's Jewish praying!" Santino exclaims when the chant is complete. "What are those things—those little boxes?"

Claudette meets her father's eyes. This is not a subject she has ever heard discussed. Jews know; goyim never ask.

Unwrapping the long laces of his tefillin, Albert summons his Italian. "The Torah—*la Bìbbia vecchio, sì?* It tells that we should love God with *tutto cuore*—" He taps on the left side of his chest.

"*Tutto il cuore,*" Santino corrects solemnly, accepting the little cube of cheese Claudette offers.

"*Sì.* Love God with all the heart, and *tutta l'anima*—all our spirit *E tutta la forza*—all our strength. The Bible also tells us to bind—*legare, sì?*—bind these words on our hands and in front of our eyes, so we remember them always." Albert shrugs. "Who knows what that means? How do you bind words in front of your eyes? So we write the words about *tutto cuore, tutta anima, tutta forza,* and put them inside the little boxes. Then we tie the boxes to our hands and foreheads when we pray."

Chewing, Santino nods repeatedly, mouth turned down in thoughtful consideration. "*È bello,*" he decides. "That's a good prayer."

"The Torah says we must put those words by the doors of our houses and on our gates," Albert adds, waving toward the forest. "No more house. No more gate. Tefillin are all I have."

"The boxes look like little houses," Santino points out helpfully. "Is that why they're shaped that way? What's wrong?"

Albert is staring at his left hand. "My wedding ring is missing."

Swallowing her second, and last, mouthful of dry bread, Claudette shifts to German, too. "Are you sure you were wearing it?"

"Of course, I was wearing it—I never take it off!" He combs through low vegetation and dry leaves with his fingers. "Don't just stand there, Claudette! Help me find it!"

"*C'è male?*" Santino asks.

"*Mein Ring,*" Albert says, unable to remember the word in Italian. "*Mariage,*" he says in French, and then "*Moglie!*"—wife—in Italian. Albert points to the place where years of constriction have compressed the small muscles of his finger, and makes a circling motion. Santino's face lights up, then darkens with dismay. Dropping onto all fours, he joins the search.

When a few minutes of scrabbling through the stones and twigs produce nothing but scratches and skinned knuckles, Claudette sits back on her haunches. "We'll never find it," she declares, clapping dirt from her palms. "We'll have to leave it behind." Fingers raking, her father ignores her. "Papa, the Germans could be right behind us." She means only to be practical and to justify her impatience, but speaking makes the prospect real. "Papa? Please—let's just go!"

"Claudette, I don't expect you to understand, but I do expect you to—"

A loud, unresonant *crack!* not one hundred meters away startles him into silence. The three of them freeze. Crouched to run, Claudette looks to Santino, who listens, still as a deer. When they hear someone speaking Polish, Santino picks up a branch and mimes breaking it. Smiling reassurance, he gestures for Claudette to resume the search, but she folds her arms across her chest. "That could have been the Germans, Papa!" she insists in a tense whisper. "It's just a ring, Papa!" Terrified now, clutching her father's arm, she tries to pull him to his feet. "Papa, let's go! This is stupid!"

In one motion, Albert Blum straightens and slaps his daughter's face. "It's not just . . . a ring!"

It is the home he and Paula made during sixteen years of marriage, his children's baby photos, mementos of his own youth. It is his orderly office, and meticulously cared-for wardrobe, the reputation he built as an accountant, accurate and scrupulously honest. It is everything that was, and is no more. He's barely slept, freezing and miserable on a rocky mountainside. Every muscle and all his joints ache from yesterday's awful climb, and God knows he's as frightened of capture as Claudette. But months ago, he left his wife and two young sons on a train platform, expecting to see them a few days later. Now they have vanished, like everything else, and Albert Blum cannot—*will not*—accept another loss.

"It's not just a ring," he says again.

Claudette stands. "Fine," she says, refusing to cry. "Let the Nazis catch us. Let them send us to a camp! See if I care!"

Full sunlight bursts over the mountain and finds its way to the ground. Santino lies flat, resting his head on forearms thick with muscle. "There! You see?" she cries, in tones of furious vindication. "Santino thinks the ring is stupid, too!" She wants her father to be humiliated. She wants him to admit he was wrong to care about the ring, wrong to hit her. She wishes the Germans would smash through the trees and arrest them all, this very moment! She'd rather be right than free.

When the slanting light reveals no telltale glimmer in the leaves, Santino starts to rise, then stops, struck by a thought. Reaching for the socks Albert used as mittens during the night, he shakes one, then the other. A small, bright object falls out. "*Ecco, signore!* Here it is!"

Hand trembling, Albert takes the ring from Santino's cupped palm. The soldier smiles at Claudette, who glares resentfully and stomps away. He shrugs, unconcerned. "I have sisters," he tells her father. "Girls are like that sometimes."

Santino hefts the suitcases and trudges up the trail behind Claudette. Albert wipes damp eyes, blows his nose, makes an awkward fist with his thumb over the ring. "My thanks I place before you, O Lord," he whispers, and continues his assault on the unseen summit.

The Alps are not the impregnable fortress walls they seem. Hannibal has passed this way, and Caesar, and Charles VII, and Francis I, and Napoleon. The Romans, the Lombards, the Franks. Russian and Austrian and papal armies have all surged across this mountain range. Ordinary people have fled from one side to the other in times of war, hoping to put high rock and bad weather between themselves and those who'd do them harm.

They've all added to the ancient layered repository of possessions that seemed essential at sea level. Treasured books, silver kiddush cups, and heavy brass candlesticks now come to rest above long-buried cuirasses and pikes. Iron kettles rust atop heavy clay pots. Carved stone deities, who might not be so helpful on the other side of the mountain anyway, overlie flint tools and traces of rush baskets that carried dried fish and red ocher. The trail across these mountains has been in use for seven thousand years.

Time after time, the path crests a rise only to descend sharply before ribboning over an even steeper slope beyond. Chestnut and beech give way to pine and fir, which themselves become dwarfish and gradually disappear. Above the treeline, ancient ice has carved a bowl of rock between two peaks. Barren of all but lichen, its surface is scoured yearly by stones and ice, rain and wind. Stumbling exacts an increasing toll.

The back of Claudette's neck feels charred by the sun. Her muscles are rubbery. Too often, she loses her footing in her father's slick-bottomed city shoes, coming down hard on hands and knees already bloody. Finally she crumples where she stands, waiting for Santino and her father to arrive at her side before bursting into angry tears. "I can't go any farther! I never should have worn these stupid shoes! This is all your fault, Papa!"

"What exactly . . . is my fault?" her father gasps. "The war, Claudette? The Alps? Am I responsible . . . for how hard . . . rocks are?"

Santino says something. Reluctantly, Claudette looks to her father for an explanation. "Save your tears, miss," Albert translates. "You may need them later."

His own dogged momentum broken, Albert, too, sinks onto the bald stone. There's been no water since noon, when the path last snaked past a spring. His toenails feel as though they're being pried off his feet. His swollen fingers look like bratwurst. The ring finger that shrank in last night's cold now throbs like a second heart, and the word "gangrene" flickers through his mind. Oh, Paula! he thinks, worn out with being the object of their daughter's frightened peevishness. I should have taken the boys and left Claudette with you.

To make peace, he holds out his puffy hand so Claudette can see how awful his finger looks. "You were right," he offers. "I should have forgotten about the ring." Her shoulders relax a fraction, and Albert puts an arm around her. "I miss your mother."

"I even miss David and Jacques," she sobs, and laughs at this evidence of extremity. She wipes her nose on her sleeve. "They had it easy, sitting with Mama on that train!"

"After the war, you can brag to them. They'll be sorry they missed this adventure."

They cling to each other until Albert realizes with his body what his mind has resisted for some months now. She's nearly grown, and he has no idea what she does and doesn't know. Shuddering at the idea of such a conversation, he watches a little group tramping down a slope, one gully back. The Brösslers, he realizes. Steffi rides on Duno's shoulders. Liesl has slowed the family down—too big to carry and too small to climb well. Frieda Brössler could speak to Claudette, Albert realizes. I'll ask her when we get to Italy.

A few feet away, Santino has hunkered down on the slanting rock face, glad to rest while the Blums pull themselves together. The sky is vast, Madonna blue, and unmarred by clouds. He can see the French countryside clearly. A swarm of Focke-Wulf 190s would have easy work up here, strafing soldiers and refugees with nothing but moss for cover, but there's been no pursuit. He expects the British or Americans to be waiting on the other side of the mountain, given no more opposition by Italy's armies. His own self-imposed objective is within reach. The Blums are only hours from safety. I'll get them settled, Santino thinks comfortably. Then it'll be south for me. A boat from Genoa or Sant'Andrea. Home.

He looks up, trying not to grimace. An officer told him that the Pass of Aurelius was popular with serious mountain climbers from Italy and France, before the war. The last kilometer is as steep as a ladder against a wall: a challenge for the strong, the experienced, the well-equipped. For the desperate, it's simply necessary.

"How much farther?" Signor Blum asks.

Santino makes two mountains of his fingers and gestures a short distance over the space between them. "Not far," he guesses vaguely, "but a lot of climbing first."

And the mountain begrudges every step. By late afternoon, Claudia has slowed to a crawl, and Signor Blum's lips are blue. Altitude and sun glare off granite have given Santino a fierce headache made worse by hunger, but he hasn't complained aloud. The Blums probably think he's stoic, or naturally quiet. Truth is, Santino's mother tongue is a Calabrian dialect. He learned basic Italian during his four years of compulsory school. His working vocabulary consists of curses and obscenities, picked up in the army. He does not wish to slip and offend a refined gentleman like Signor Blum with bad language, and yet the moment has arrived: his unhappiness demands expression.

Broad back against the mountainside, he takes a deep breath of thin air to power a heartfelt oration concerning the height of mountains, the weight of other people's luggage, the unreasonable ambition of Germans, and the direct involvement of pigs and whores in the parentage of Dwight David Eisenhower, whom Santino holds responsible for this disorganized retreat and who is, without doubt, at this very moment engaged in contracting enviable diseases from shameless women who rouge their lips.

Recognizing the sentiment, if not the words, Signor Blum holds up a bruised and bleeding hand. "Santino, you tried. This's impossible. Leave the valises."

Santino hates to do it, but shrugs philosophically. The only thing worse than dumping the suitcases now, after lugging them so far, is falling off the side of this stinking mountain while trying to carry them over the pass.

Kneeling awkwardly, Albert Blum opens first one bag, then the other. He removes the Giovanetti passports, a photo of Paula with the children. Both toothbrushes and the can of tooth powder. His razor, the remaining squares of newspaper. His tefillin. All these he wraps in his prayer shawl, making a vagrant's gunnysack. The small, silver-bound prayer book he hands to Claudette. "Your mother gave me this siddur on our first anniversary. Keep it in your pocket." He takes out the last of their food—two rolls, a little cheese. Closes the valises, locking them carefully, the better to make them fly. "*Prego,*" he says to Santino, and gestures down the mountain.

Giggling like a schoolkid, Santino flings one suitcase after the other into the sky. They tumble through the air, bounce against the rock face, and sail off into an abyss while the three of them cackle like chickens, witlessly amused. Someone far below yells angrily, but not even Albert can make himself feel ashamed, and Claudette is convulsed by the barrage of echoing Yiddish curses aimed at them like mortar shells.

Squinting into the sun, they sit to share their tiny meal, breaking into helpless laughter whenever one of them remembers the way the suitcase flew, or how the angry man shouted. When they've finished licking crumbs from their hands, they move with new energy, no longer away from capture but toward freedom. Lightweight and more nimble than either man, Claudette takes the lead. Hooking her fingertips into small crevices and pushing upward with her legs, she begins to understand why mountain climbing is a sport, and she scales the wall like a lizard, her nose so close to the hot stone she can smell the rock dust—

The sneeze is completely unexpected. Its spasm loosens her grip. Time slows.

The mountain seems to fall away, lazily tipping eastward while she herself remains suspended in air. I'm going to die, she thinks with a strange detached clarity. I should scream, she decides.

Her shriek shocks time back to its accustomed pace, and before its echo can return, Santino's hand shoots up to support her trousered hip. In a single balletic move, he reaches for a hold and lifts himself, forming a wall behind her with his body.

"*Coraggio,*" he whispers, his mouth so close it brushes the fine down of her cheek. He can feel her heart pound through her back, but keeps his own breath steady. "Courage," he says again. She looks at him out of the corner of an ocean-green eye. When she whispers, "*Grazie,*" her breath is like a kiss.

Four meters below, Albert calls anxiously, "Claudette, what happened? Are you all right?"

"I sneezed and lost my balance," she calls back. "Santino caught me." She still can feel the shape of his square palm, the outline of his short, blunt fingers on her hip. Santino draws back, but before she moves on, their eyes meet once more.

An hour later, the trail levels, widens, hairpins sharply. An abrupt decline reveals a blue infinity of uncountable peaks diminishing eastward toward the darkening horizon. For an endless moment, the three stand silently, between two summits. Santino breaks the spell, stretching into a long, deliberate stride downward. He holds out a hand, steadying Signor Blum as the older man joins him. Then, like a storybook courtier, Santino offers his arm to Claudia.

She is dirty and tired, her hair stringy and her face drawn. Santino's heart catches when she takes his hand and descends as daintily as a fairy-tale princess stepping from a carriage. *"Benvenuti al'Italia!"* he says grandly when both Blums have crossed the border, and he cries a little himself as they weep and cheer, and embrace one another. "Welcome," he whispers, "to my home."

COLLE AURELIO
ITALY

"Boia faus!" Rinaldo Miroglio swears, watching three tattered figures stumble toward him in the dying light.

"What are we going to do with them, Tenente?" asks the corporal at his side.

Not quite twenty-two, Rinaldo Miroglio has been the acting commandant at the Colle Aurelio border post for all of eleven hours. "What about Val di Ponente?"

"The hotels are full, sir. Might be room in Roccabarbena."

"That's too far for them to walk."

Last night, with a solemnity made tinny by the radio, Marshal Badoglio announced the surrender. "Recognizing the impossibility of continuing an unequal struggle against overwhelmingly superior forces, His Majesty Vittorio Emanuele III has requested an armistice to avoid further calamities to the nation." Hostilities between Italian and Allied forces were to cease, but Badoglio ended his broadcast on an ominous note. The armed forces have been ordered to resist attacks from "any other quarter." That can only mean Germany.

Communications to the border station were cut during the night. Early this morning, leaving his lieutenant in charge, the post's captain left for Cuneo to consult with their superiors directly. And while Tenente Rinaldo Miroglio doesn't expect to fight the Wehrmacht, he is dealing with an invasion.

Or, rather, an exodus, and a miracle surely! The Maritimes can be impassable as early as August, but the snows have parted for the Hebrews. All day Miroglio has witnessed emotional reunions. People weep with relief, boast of unexpected prowess in mountaineering, laugh giddily as they tell of terrifying encounters with pursuing Germans, who turned out to be squirrels or chamois.

Rinaldo himself has spent hours coordinating arrangements with local hotels. The innkeepers have been magnificent, refusing to discuss payment with people who have nothing but the clothes they stand in. Waiters assuage hunger with the delicacies and fine meals ordinarily reserved for Fascist officials. Bellhops usher footsore fugitives to thermal pools where they could soak in Roman baths before sleeping—safe at last!—between clean sheets. But hotels have only so many rooms!

Sighing, the lieutenant marches out to greet those he hopes will be the last of the poor wretches. An older man whose arms hang from his shoulders like a scarecrow's shirtsleeves. A pretty girl, all legs and big green eyes. A stocky young infantryman. "Blum, Albert," the gentleman says, fumbling in the pocket of his suitcoat. "We have documents—*abbiamo papiere.*"

"Miroglio, Rinaldo," the lieutenant introduces himself. "Would you prefer Italian or German? Formalities are unnecessary, Herr Blum, but I'm afraid bunks in our barracks are all we can offer. The hotels are full."

"No room at the inn!" the corporal says.

"A recurring theme in Hebrew-Roman history," Rinaldo adds.

The old man manages a smile. "*Grazie,* Tenente. Bunks will be fine—wonderful!"

"I assure you, we'll find better accommodations tomorrow. Tonight, you may take showers in that shed, and Pansa here will bring you something to eat as soon as you're ready."

The stubby soldier watches his Hebrew charges shuffle toward hot water and rest, hardly able to lift their feet. "And you are?" Rinaldo asks.

"Cicala, Santino. Pinerolo Division, First Corps, Fourth Army. We were disbanded, sir. They said it was every man for himself."

"*Sì, sì, sì.* The armistice. I understand."

"Have you heard anything, Tenente?"

"The American Fifth has landed at Salerno. Montgomery's Eighth is also in the south. Our commander expects airborne landings at Rome and Milan anytime now. Maybe amphibious assaults near Genoa, as well. It'll be over by October," Rinaldo predicts. "You're Calabrese?" he asks, recognizing Cicala's accent.

"Yes, sir. And if it's all the same to you, sir, I'm going home."

"I gambled and lost," Miroglio admits. "I was going to study law, but when my university deferment ended, I joined the border police to avoid the draft. Now I'm stuck."

"Borders are borders," Cicala commiserates, "even when a war ends."

"Better here than Russia. Many more behind you?"

"The carabinieri said there were about twelve hundred Hebrews in Sainte-Gisèle. Some stayed behind. Most gave the mountain a try. How many have come over so far, sir?"

"Three hundred at the Fenestre. Twice that at the Pass of the Cherries. We've had a few hundred come through here at Aurelio, so there can't be many more—" A family with three children stagger into view, so tired they're tripping over their own toes. "*Dio santo,* let these be the last!"

"Tenente?" a sergeant shouts from the office door. "Headquarters!"

Miroglio catches the eye of a passing private. "You! Go up and meet that family! Cicala, come with me. The captain may want to talk to you."

They duck through the office door and Miroglio pulls off his cap, tossing it onto a pile of paperwork. Hand over the mouthpiece, the sergeant whispers, "It's not the captain, sir. I didn't recognize the name. Some major—"

Rinaldo brings the handset to his ear. "Tenente Miroglio, at your orders, Maggiore." He gestures for Santino to sit. "I've been told a total of twelve hundred, sir . . . Yes, that's the situation here as well. Most of them are in hotels in Val di Ponente, but some have gone on toward Cuneo . . . I have about thirty in the Aurelio barracks, sir, and more coming—families with children . . . Maggiore, we have a couple of trucks up here, but perhaps you can arrange additional transport? The Hebrews're in poor condition. I'd hate to see them walk any farther . . . Yes, I'll wait, of course, sir."

The office is quiet while Miroglio's line is rerouted. The sergeant reappears, handing Santino a plate of stew and bread with a tin cup of Barbera. The wine is cloudy with sediment and thick enough to chew, but Santino accepts it gratefully, raising the cup in salute as the sergeant leaves. Swallowing a chunk of gristly meat, Santino gestures toward the pass with his fork. "Maybe for Alpini that climb wouldn't have been much, but for regular army and these poor damned *ebrei?* One false step, and we'd have slid all the way to the Riviera—"

Miroglio straightens. "*Jawohl! Ja, mein Herr, das ist korrekt.*"

Santino's fork freezes halfway to his mouth.

Miroglio listens for a long time before saying, "*Jawohl. Ich verstehe.*" When the lieutenant finally replaces the receiver in its cradle, he looks dazed, and very young. "Italy doesn't have a government anymore," he says. "Marshal Badoglio and the royal family left Rome this morning. The city is occupied. The Vatican is surrounded."

Confused, Santino asks, "By Americans or the British?"

"Germans! They've stopped the Allies on the beaches. German command has ordered all Italian troops to disarm. We'll be transported south to reinforce a defensive line close to Naples. Anyone who resists will be shot." Miroglio's Adam's apple works convulsively. "Our post captain was executed this afternoon for refusing to surrender his sidearm."

"*Madonna!* Those miserable, shit-eating sons of bitches!"

Miroglio isn't done. "I've been ordered to keep the Hebrews under guard. The SS will be here noon tomorrow—to take care of our 'problem.' " The lieutenant looks sick. "*Dio santo,*" he whispers. "What have I done?"

"Tenente, you didn't mean any harm—"

Miroglio stands so quickly his chair tips over. "How long will those people last in a labor camp? I've signed their death warrants! What am I going to do?"

They are nearly the same age, both born after Mussolini marched on Rome. All their lives, Rinaldo Miroglio and Santino Cicala have taken orders from fathers, priests, teachers, bosses, officers.

"Tenente? If Germans say noon, they mean noon. Let the Hebrews sleep," Santino advises. "Then get them out of here early."

Miroglio walks to the window. "Where? Where can they go?"

Santino comes to his side. The moon is rising, its light gleaming on stone terraces that descend like a giant's staircase into shadowed ravines. "There must be hundreds of little farms in these valleys. If everybody took a few . . . ?"

"Scatter them around the countryside," Miroglio says slowly. "Spread the risk."

"We should hide, too, sir. If the Germans come here and don't find Jews . . ."

Miroglio looks south. "The Allies promised Badoglio they'd send fifteen divisions into Rome alone—that's what we heard."

"Pardon me, sir, but if promises were pigs, we'd have bacon for breakfast."

"True enough. And if the king's left Rome, we're on our own." Miroglio thinks a moment longer, then rights his fallen chair. Pulling stationery from a desk drawer, he begins to dash off notes. "Rollero, I need you!" The sergeant comes to the door. Miroglio fills him in quickly. "Get a courier in here right away. We'll need to alert Fenestre, the Pass of the Cherries, and every hotel in the valley. I want all the men in the square now, and be quiet about it! We're going to pack up the weapons and ammunition and get out of here by dawn."

Unnoticed, Santino finishes his meal and leaves the office. He shuffles toward the barracks across the square through an anthill of eerily quiet activity as La Guardia di Colle Aurelio begins an orderly if unordered retreat.

Nodding to a sentry, Santino eases the barracks door open, listens to snores and soft sighs, waiting for his eyes to grow accustomed to the dark. Alberto Blum lies prone in the bed nearest the door, loose mouth gaping, eyes sunken into purplish bruises. Claudia sleeps quietly in the bunk above her father.

How old is she? Sixteen? Marriageable, in San Vito—the age Santino's mother was, and prettier, even, than his Mamma in her wedding photograph.

Silently, Santino reaches out and, with one blunt finger, traces the line of her hip in the air above the blanket. His dirt-rimmed nails are ragged from the rocks. Her fine-grained, sunburned skin looks like polished pink marble against the rough army blanket tucked beneath her chin.

She stirs. He snatches back his hand. She does not awaken, but he leaves the barracks quickly, and is halfway across the parade ground before his steps slow.

Hulking mountains blot out half the sky. Santino Cicala grew to squat and solid manhood surrounded by mountains in the rocky highlands of Calabria. A year since he was drafted, and what has he seen in that time but mountains, and more mountains? Up the shank of the peninsula: the Apennines. Here in the north: the Alps, the Dolomites. Everywhere, steep as church spires, Italy's mountains go on forever. Their roads snake and twist and coil—marvels of civil engineering. Bridges and viaducts, culverts and switchbacks and tunnels abound, and every single one will provide German demolition teams with an opportunity to delay or block an Allied advance. Northern Italy is filled with farms and factories. Food for German soldiers and civilians. Fabric for uniforms. Airplanes, trucks, cars. Labor. The Germans won't give all that up without a fight.

"Madonna, I'm *tired*," Santino whispers. Tired of officers and orders. Tired of marching, and of food that tastes of metal. He wants the war to be over. He wants to go home. He wants to build things, not blow them up. He wants a wife. He wants to raise kids. He wants history to leave him alone.

He stares at his own broad feet, sore and blistered in cheap boots—soles gaping, shoelaces frayed and broken. Seven hundred kilometers, vast navies, and great armies lie between him and home. He thinks of Signor Blum, sick and without a wife or sisters to care for him. He thinks of Claudia, and the shape of her against his hand. He looks to heaven, finds the polestar, and empties his lungs of air. "I'm damned if I'll dig ditches for Germans," he tells the night, and enlists in his next war.

10 September 1943

Angelo Soncini's little sister died when he was five. Angelo isn't sorry. Altira was a pest.

Angelo gets yelled at for saying so, but Sara killed his sister. Christian maids weren't supposed to work for Jews, but Teresina and Dafne kept coming anyway. Babbo said they'd get in big trouble, so he made them stop coming, and that's when Sara moved in. "Sara made a mistake," Angelo's mamma told him. "She needs a place to stay until after her baby, and that's why she's our new housekeeper." Sara was from the Rome ghetto, where a lot of Jews were poor.

"She was not bad," Angelo's babbo always said. "She was ignorant."

Except she killed Altira, and that was bad! Even if Angelo isn't sorry. Mamma told Sara, "Don't use that coal oven until we get it fixed." But Sara didn't believe a stove could kill a person. When Angelo and his mamma got back from shopping, Sara was crumped down on the kitchen floor, and Altira's eyes were all rolled up, and the whites showed. Mamma screamed and pushed Angelo out of the kitchen so hard he fell and hurt his knee. He cried, but she didn't pay any attention, and was just yelling and shaking Altira and opening windows, even though it was cold out. Sara woke up, but Altira didn't.

A lot of visitors came while the Soncinis sat shiva. They patted Angelo's hair, and looked sad, and said, "How terrible!" and "Your poor little sister!" and "What a pity!" Angelo went out to play. That's when he heard Signora Dolcino tell Signora Leoni, "It was

a blessing God took that child." So Signora Dolcino thought Altira was a pest, too.

Things got better after Angelo turned six. Nonna Casutto
died, so Angelo's grandpa came to live with them. One time, some
Blackshirts came and shouted slogans in the piazza by the synagogue. Nonno Casutto went out with a pistol. "I'm a Jew and as
good a Fascist as any of you! I fought at the Brenner Pass, you little *finocchini!*" He shot the pistol into the air and laughed when
they ran away. The carabinieri came, but Nonno didn't care.

Nonno Casutto wouldn't go to services either. Angelo's
mamma was always yelling at him. "Your son-in-law is a rabbi!
You're setting a terrible example for Angelo, and you're embar-
rassing me!"

Nonno just sneered, "Religion is a load of crap." Angelo
laughed because Nonno said "crap," so Mamma smacked him in
the back of the head and yelled at him, too. She never, ever said
anything good to Angelo, not once in his whole life. She didn't
care when he cried because he wasn't allowed to go to school with
the other kids. "Your babbo opened a nice new school right here
in the synagogue," she told him. "You'll have the best teachers—
professors from the university! And you'll make new friends.
Everything's going to be fine."

She always lies. Last spring she said she wasn't sick, but she was
throwing up all the time. She's always complaining, too, even
though Angelo's not supposed to. "Iacopo, I can't do it all! The
housework, the cooking—every night you bring people home, and
I'm supposed to feed them and make them welcome. One day
there's no water, the next there's no electricity! My father is a
troublemaker, and Angelo argues with me all day long. The air
raids are driving me crazy. I'm so tired, Iacopo! I'm just so tired!"

She's always crabbing about something.

Nonno Casutto was the only person in the world who really
liked Angelo. "He's a boy! Boys are supposed to be noisy!" Nonno
said. He always stuck up for Angelo, and that's why Babbo sent
Nonno away to live with Zia Etta in Florence.

Now the single only good thing in Angelo Soncini's whole life
is when he gets to go to Signor Brizzolari's office at the Palazzo
Municipale. The secretary has candy, and she gives Angelo some if

he behaves. Behave means you have to sit right next to Babbo, and no talking or fidgeting. That's hard because it's so boring, but today it's even worse than usual, because his mother had to come to Signor Brizzolari, not Babbo, and Mamma always gets all huggy in front of people. Angelo hates that.

"But Signor Brizzolari, what are these families to do?" she asks. "How are they to live without bread? Without milk for their children?"

Sure enough, she rests one hand on her big fat belly and reaches out to place the other on Angelo's hair. He squirms away. "I'm not a baby," he says. "I'm going outside!"

Serafino Brizzolari has children and grandchildren. He cannot help smiling as Angelo, an unwilling prop in his mother's performance, leaves the office to cadge *caramelle* off the department secretary. Even so, when the two adults are alone the bureaucrat shakes his head with ponderous regret. "Signora, I would like nothing better than to help you, but—" He drops his voice. "I'm not certain I can issue ration cards to Italian Jews now, let alone to foreigners!"

"But surely there's something you can do! Signor Brizzolari, a man of your compassion? Your importance! If you can't help us, who can we turn to?"

Like so many Italian women whose menfolk hide from German labor roundups, Mirella Soncini has been thrust into the public sphere despite her advanced pregnancy. She's put together a classic combination of flattery and supplication that would normally bring this little drama to a satisfying conclusion, which Serafino does not fail to appreciate. Nevertheless . . .

Stalling for time, he passes a white linen handkerchief over a heavy round face damp with sweat. Ordinarily he carries his great weight and his responsibilities well, but this breathless September heat is hard on him, and today he feels more burdened than usual by his body and his position. He removes his spectacles, rubbing at the sore spots they make on the bridge of his fleshy nose. "Signora, I am powerless."

"Signor Brizzolari, you can't mean it!" she says, beginning to realize that he does.

"Signora, you must understand my position—"

Angelo steps back into the room, frowning as he chews. "Mammina, isn't he going to give us the ration cards?"

Easing to the edge of the wooden armchair, the rabbi's wife uses both hands to push herself up, and when she speaks, the innocent, flirtatious teasing and operatic pathos have vanished. "Thank you, Signor Brizzolari, for all you've done for us in the past. You have nothing to reproach yourself with." She motions for her purse and the empty shopping bag. For once her son does as he's asked. "Angelo," she says, "look carefully at Signor Brizzolari." Sobered by his mother's tone, the boy turns serious brown eyes toward the bureaucrat. "Shake the hand of an honorable man," his mother tells him. "We are in Signor Brizzolari's debt."

Alone in his office, Serafino Brizzolari shifts his weight to ease the ache where a buried chunk of Austrian shrapnel lies too near the femoral artery to remove. When the rabbi's wife walked into his office, he had braced himself for tears, for outrage, for pleading. Nothing would have been more formidable than the grave and manly gesture of a small Jewish boy, shaking the hand that Serafino studies now.

For twenty-six years, Serafino's own clean hands have had the power to shock him, so certain was he once that he'd never be free of the mud and stink of the Great War's trenches. His white cuffs are immaculate, his suit freshly pressed and spotless. His shoes gleam. His feet, once foul with wet rot, are dry and sweet, even in summer, even if he must bathe twice a day to keep them that way. All these years, and he's still jolted awake at least once a week by shrieks and shell blasts. The dreams are so real that for a few moments after waking, he dares not breathe for fear of mustard gas.

When he left his mother in 1916 and marched away to war, Serafino was a cocky kid, indestructible and convinced of his own courage. Bravado quickly withered under fire, but pride took its place. Determined to drive the Huns from his homeland, he was wounded twice for Italy and the king, but when he limped home from that bloodbath, he was spat on by Bolsheviks, jeered at by trade unionists. The king was a puppet dancing on capital's

strings, they said. Soldiers like Serafino had been duped by speculators who'd grown fat as ticks on labor's blood.

Stunned by the hostility, half-convinced the Reds were right,
Serafino took off his uniform and locked his medals in a drawer,
obscurely ashamed of the deaths and the maimings, the suffering
and sacrifice he had witnessed and inflicted. He forgot courage,
and remembered terror. He forgot the cause, if there ever was
one, and remembered the catastrophe.

Benito Mussolini changed all that. "Better one day as lions
than fifty years as sheep!" *il Duce* cried, and Serafino is still grateful for the pride Mussolini restored in the soldiers who came
home from the Great War and were made to feel ashamed. Even
so, Mussolini has a great deal to answer for. Three hundred thousand Italian casualties in Greece, Yugoslavia, Libya, Russia. The
nation occupied by Germany, invaded by the Allies. The king in
exile, the economy in ruins. And Mussolini himself is the principal marionette in a puppet government Berlin has named the Republic of Salò.

Early this morning, there was a call from Salò: *il Duce's* representatives will be in Sant'Andrea this afternoon, accompanied by
German authorities. Serafino was reminded that he has prospered
in government service, that his family has come through this war
secure, well-housed, well-fed. The only thing required to ensure
the continuation of this good fortune is a simple change of political label, from Fascist to Republican.

My sons are petty tyrants, he thinks. My daughters are vain, my
wife is cold and house-proud. My mistress is a grasping slut. And
I? he asks himself. I am a fat, powerless bureaucrat in a vassal
state, taking orders from an Austrian corporal's lackeys.

Mirella Soncini and her son are already past the mezzanine
when Brizzolari shouts. Standing on the landing outside his office, he waves the rabbi's wife back, then changes his mind. "Stay
there," he calls, and reappears a minute later with a large and
bulging envelope.

He knows he is elephantine and graceless but feels lithe as a
leopard descending the long marble staircase. Beckoning, he directs the rabbi's wife into a recessed doorway in a deserted corridor. "So many have left the city because of the bombing," he

observes airily. "Who knows where they are now? In the mountains? Dead?" He lowers his voice. "If anyone comes back to claim these, I'll think of something. Sell them for cash, signora. Use that on the black market."

Mirella presses the package of ration cards to her breast and beams at her small son. "You see, Angelo? I told you he'd find a way to help! Signor Brizzolari, I don't know how to thank you—"

He raises a clean, dry hand, swallowing nervously. "Just don't tell anyone where you got them!" he pleads. "It's a capital crime to aid enemies of the state."

Enemies of the state? Mirella shakes her head, refusing to believe it. Did Serafino Brizzolari just call us enemies of the state—

"Mamma?" Angelo digs his heels in. "Mamma! You're not listening!"

She stops and looks around, amazed to see how far they've walked. "I'm sorry, Angelo. What did you say?"

"I said I don't see why we have to help the refugees anyway. They talk funny! They touch our stuff! I'm tired of them."

"I know, Angelo. I am, too." Tired of the war, of being pregnant, of sleep broken by air raids and a crowded bladder. And, yes—tired of strangers trooping through her home. For the past three years, Scuola Ner Tamid has made a place for Jewish refugees who've somehow found their way to Sant'Andrea. The Germans are cultured and urbane, but O *Dio!* The Poles . . . Bearded men with bizarre side curls, dowdy women with awful wigs. Thoughtlessly conspicuous, regally unconcerned that Sant'Andrese Jews must bribe officials like Brizzolari to keep them out of the camp for illegal aliens at Ferramonti. They refuse to enroll their children in Talmud Torah because Italian boys and girls study together to become *b'nai mitzvah.* Iacopo says Hasidic theology is the bel canto opera of Judaism: gloriously ornamented, astonishingly elaborate, breathtakingly beautiful. To Mirella, Polish Jews seem obsessed with cutlery and dishes. And they're scandalized that Mirella dresses like any other stylish Italian woman. Are Polish men so oversexed that a glimpse of a woman's hair can plunge them into ungovernable lust? It's absurd.

"I hate them," Angelo told her once. "I wish they'd all go away."
Mirella was distressed, but Iacopo was amused. "Ah, the brutal
honesty of the very young! It takes time to learn hypocrisy. Our
guests steal our time and attention. It's normal to feel outrage at
theft. And you, Mirella? They've stolen me away from you as well."

"I'm proud of your work," she said, "and I'm proud of you."

Mild eyes amused, Iacopo considered this. "Not brutal honesty,
but no hypocrisy either. Instead, discretion!" He kissed her forehead. "Discretion will do nicely."

Two thirds her husband's age, Mirella often feels closer to her
son's resentment than to Iacopo's generosity of spirit. The well-
spring of Ner Tamid, Iacopo provides a reliable flow of reason and
diplomacy during endless meetings with destitute foreigners and
bombed-out congregants. He expresses genuine sympathy for religious instructors whose restless students are delighted when an
air raid interrupts their reluctant study of Hebrew. He soothes the
wounded pride of college professors teaching in Jewish day
schools after the universities were closed to them. And then there
is the ordinary work of a rabbi: making halachic rulings, preparing
divrai Torah, conducting services. Iacopo works and works and
works, and when his public day is over, there is his own need to
study, to be off in his own world—

"Can we?" Angelo pulls his hand out of hers. "You said you'd
think about it, so can we?"

"Can we what, Angelo?"

"Get a puppy! Please, Mamma? I'll take care of it myself."

"O *caro mio!* We've been over this, and over this. No. The answer
is no." Panting, she quickens the pace, even though hurrying
makes her look like a foie gras goose. "They're *treyf,* Angelo: they're
unclean. They have fleas. They carry diseases—"

"But you promised!"

"I promised to think about it, and I did, and it's just impossible. We hardly have enough food for our family and the guests,
and now with the new rationing rules, there's nothing extra for a
great big dog."

"It wouldn't be a great big dog. It would only be a little
puppy—" Angelo moans when he sees the gate of the cemetery.
"Oh, Mamma! Do we have to go here again?"

"You ask the same question every time, and the answer is always the same. Caring for graves is a great mitzvah because it's a good deed we can never be thanked for. Keeping your sister's resting place clean is all we can do for her now."

"But do we have to go every week?"

"We don't have to. I just like to . . ."

Mirella's steps slow, and stop. Angelo, too, takes a breath.

The cemetery is an enclave of peace in a clamorous, dirty city. Stately cypresses guard the gate. Inside, the long strong limbs of six-hundred-year-old chestnuts stretch over neatly swept pathways, sheltering the dead, enclosing their families in hushed dignity. Leaves in unnumbered multitudes are renewed each year. Gnarled roots grip the ground. Generation after generation of Jews have come here to mourn and be mourned. To remember and be remembered.

How long did it take, Mirella wonders numbly, to desecrate a graveyard tended for centuries?

"Mamma," Angelo whispers. "Someone made *caca* on Altira's stone!"

Swastikas are scrawled in dripping black paint. Nearby: a shout of triumph, roars of drunken laughter. They're still here, Mirella thinks. Men capable of shitting on a baby's grave. In Sant'Andrea.

She grabs Angelo's hand, and together they back away. One of the men looks up and points. "Run," she says, and they do: through narrow streets and alleys, past Tranquillo Loeb's shuttered law office, past the cobbler's where Iacopo's dress shoes are being resoled, past the barbershop where Angelo had his first haircut. In the market, she becomes one housewife among many carrying string bags and little parcels, accompanied by a child or two. She works her way through the crowd, around pushcarts with paltry displays of spoiled fruit and withered vegetables—all that's escaped confiscation by the Germans.

Vision blurred by tears, Mirella drags her son along, wrenches away from hands that reach for her, hears nothing of what her neighbors say. Heart hammering, she turns down the narrow passage that leads to the synagogue. Shouting breaks out ahead. Everyone stops, trapped by a checkpoint—

"Thank God! I thought they'd gotten you, too."

The low, startling voice is directly behind her. "Renzo!" Mirella cries softly, finding herself all but in his arms. "They're desecrating the—"

He shakes his head. "Brace yourself," he whispers. "Iacopo's been arrested." Mirella moans. "Don't upset Angelo." Eyes shut, Mirella nods. "Rina Dolcino told my mother. Mamma told me. The whole neighborhood's been watching for you."

The queue shuffles forward toward a pair of pimply soldiers. "*Dokumente!*" one shouts every few moments, brandishing some sort of machine gun. The other boy is younger, less sure of himself, fumbling as he studies each person's identity papers.

Moving forward, Renzo takes Angelo's hand and grips Mirella's arm. There are only two people ahead of them. "Renzo," she whispers. "Our papers say we're—"

"Cry!" he says. Confused, she starts again to protest. "Oh, for God's sake!" he shouts angrily. "You stupid woman!" She backs away, shocked. "How many times do I have to tell you? God in heaven! You have the brains of a chicken!"

By the time they reach the barricade, Mirella is weeping, and Angelo wails as well. "My apologies," Renzo tells the younger soldier in excruciatingly embarrassed German. "My wife is Italian, and therefore an idiot. I never should have married her, but what can you do? It was a lapse in judgment, but it's too late for regrets! Ugo Messner," he says, introducing himself and handing over a fine leather document case. "We're down from Südtirol for a few days, and my wife has forgotten her papers in our hotel. I've told her a hundred times. Carry them always. Women! Might as well talk to a bag of sand. Italians are so lax about this sort of thing. They honor the law when convenient or necessary, and ignore it on precisely the same grounds. We Germans will put things right, though, won't we!"

A few months out of basic training, the soldier probably misses his mother. Faced with a sobbing woman and a squalling child, he hesitates. "All right," he says, relieved to be speaking German. "But she must carry her papers at all times from now on. Next!"

"*Bravissima!*" Renzo whispers delightedly as they walk on. "I really thought you were going to faint! That would have been as good as crying, now that I think of it."

"You pinched me!" Angelo says, sniveling. "And you were yelling at Mamma!"

"We had to fool the Germans, *caro,* and we did it!" Mirella says, as though it were a thrilling episode in a grand adventure. "Renzo, where did you get those papers?"

"From a friend who lives up in Bolzano. Her older brother died last year." Steering them quickly down an alley behind his apartment building, he raps twice, then once more, on the service entrance.

Rina Dolcino flings the door open. "Mirella! I saw the whole thing. Dragged him off like a common criminal. And when I came out to stop them, they—"

"Thank you, Signora Dolcino," Renzo says smoothly, cutting Rina off before she can frighten Angelo.

Upstairs, his mother is waiting for them at her door. "Catch your breath, Mirella," Lidia says, pointing to a chair. "Angelo, come with me. I have a treat for you."

"O *Dio!*" Mirella moans, once Angelo's out of earshot. "Tranquillo Loeb told us this would happen!"

"Fear is what they want, Mirella." Renzo pulls up a stool and sits at her feet. "Don't give it to them."

"But, Renzo, what about Iacopo?"

"Mammina, come and look! Signora Leoni has cheese!"

"Angelo, let your mamma rest." Renzo covers Mirella's hands with his own. "Are you all right? Do you need a doctor?" She swallows and shakes her head. "*Va bene,*" he says. "Stay here while I get things sorted out."

He gets to his feet and leans over, his lips grazing her cheek just as Angelo reappears in the hallway, a generous lump of fontina in his hand. "Mamma!" the child says, scandalized.

Mirella stares at her son, then raises her gaze to meet Lidia's knowing eyes. "Signor Leoni was just being courteous, Angelo," Lidia says firmly. "That's how gentlemen treat ladies in distress."

Hours later, resting on Lidia's bed, Mirella dozes in the brief, heavy sleep of late pregnancy and dreams of Iacopo. "Mirella," he croons softly, "it's time to go home."

She was sixteen and Iacopo almost thirty when they met. Hired away from the *scuola* in Turin, Rabbino Soncini came to Sant'Andrea to serve her congregation as rabbi and cantor. The entire congregation attended his inaugural service, even families like Mirella's that weren't very observant. With a scholar's beard and pallor, Iacopo Soncini had the soft, boneless look of a man who'd never lifted anything heavier than a volume of the Talmud. But that *voice!* Effortless, melodious. Chanting the ancient prayers, commanding attention, drawing her in. The moment Mirella heard him sing, she became the most devout Casutto in three generations.

Cool lips kiss her cheek. Unfamiliar hands grip her arms. She smiles in her sleep, and Renzo sings to her again with Iacopo's velvety baritone. "Mirella?" An aria in three notes. "Wake up, *cara mia.*"

She struggles to sit, startled to find herself surrounded by neighbors. Renzo stands alone in the corner. Iacopo is sitting on the bed, his voice back in his own body. "Everything is fine, *cara.* It was a simple misunderstanding."

"I saw the whole thing!" Rina Dolcino tells everyone again. "Dragged him out like a common criminal! When I tried to stop them, they threatened to shoot me!"

"Oh, Rina!" Lidia says, taking her friend's arm. "Don't make an opera!"

"Babbo," Angelo reports, "Signor Leoni was kissing Mammina."

"And with your permission, Rabbino, I'll do it again." With a sweeping bow, Renzo kisses her hand. "You see, Signora? Your husband is back, safe and sound."

"But how?" Mirella asks, addressing the room rather generally. "Iacopo, what happened? Why were—"

"Renzo was kind enough to alert Don Osvaldo," Iacopo tells her. "The archbishop himself intervened. According to Article Seven of the June 24, 1929, statute, I am a religious leader approved by the Fascist state, required to remain in residence and to fulfill my obligations to the congregation." Iacopo smiles, confident and calm. "The German commandant was satisfied, and I was free to go."

"The archbishop will protest. I'll see to that!" Rina vows as Mirella gathers her things. "And my sister's husband has a cousin in the carabinieri. He'll put guards at the cemetery."

Iacopo thanks Lidia for her hospitality, Rina for her concern. Renzo, more coolly, for swift action. Other neighbors emerge from shadowed doorways as the Soncinis cross the street. *Sì, certo,* Iacopo assures them, everything is fine! He and his family will be perfectly safe in their own home.

And indeed, the mess inside is no worse than normal. Anxiety dissipates in the ordinariness of household clutter and the prolonged process of putting a little boy to bed. On her way back from Angelo's bedroom, Mirella notices the fat envelope that's been tossed onto the table. "I completely forgot," she says, bringing it to Iacopo. "Serafino Brizzolari gave us the ration cards."

"The new ones?" Iacopo opens the envelope and whistles, impressed by the number of cards stuffed into it. Then he reads the list. "Two hundred grams of bread a day, two thousand grams of pasta a month . . . This isn't enough to fatten a finch."

She bustles around the room, putting things right. "Signor Brizzolari said we should sell the ration cards to Catholics and use the cash on the black market."

"What would I do without you?"

"Work too hard and sleep too little." She sweeps crumbs off the table and into her hand, but comes to him for a quick embrace. The child within her kicks, and Iacopo feels it, too. "A boy, I'm sure of it!" she says. "He's rearranging furniture—my liver inconveniences him, so he kicks it out of the way."

"Angelo will be pleased with a brother."

"And you, Iacopo? If it's a girl?"

"A daughter would be delightful. But a *son*, Mirella!" He laughs sheepishly. "Another son would be very fine."

The nights have begun to cool. Fog rises from the harbor. When the bronze bells of San Giobatta strike ten, the sound floats eerily on the mist, then fades, replaced in the Leoni apartment by the steady tick of knitting needles.

"She chose Iacopo." Lidia loosens a length of yarn with a decisive tug. "Mirella has always been a thoroughly conventional young woman." This is not strictly true, but Lidia refuses to undermine her own argument. "It would have been a poor match. Where are you going?"

Renzo shrugs on a gabardine jacket, checks his hair and tie in the mirror over the credenza.

"You are an extremist," Lidia says. "Flying at the sun, or crashing into the sea! You must learn to regulate yourself." Silence. That's how she knows he's truly angry. "Renzo," she says, refusing to be bullied. "The curfew?"

"*Buona notte, Mamma.*"

Rina Dolcino might have pursued such a son down the hall, clutching at his arm in the doorway. Lidia pitches her voice so that it will carry just far enough. "If I were to keep a bottle in the apartment," she asks curiously, "would you drink at home?"

He hesitates. She dares to hope. The door slams shut behind him.

MARITIME ALPS
PIEMONTE

In Alpine resorts and border posts, hotel staff and soldiers move from room to room, and bunk to bunk, regretful but insistent. "The situation has changed," they tell the Jews in low, quick voices. "Italy is occupied. The SS know you're here."

At Colle Aurelio, children are shaken from deepest sleep. Fine, sweaty hair is brushed back from pale, round foreheads. Battered little shoes are tied. A whimpering flock is shepherded from latrine to mess hall, and when everyone is fed, border policemen bundle bewildered boys and girls into military-issue pullovers that hang to the children's knees.

"*Vipere?* Snakes?" a corporal scoffs, when Liesl Brössler asks and Albert Blum translates. "My brothers and I camped all over these mountains when we were kids. You'll be fine!" Nearby, a beardless private fishes Steffi's thin blond braids out of a gray-green collar.

"I've got a sister your age," he says. "Don't worry, *bella.* Everything's going to be fine."

Shifting from foot to blistered foot, Frieda Brössler stares dumbly at a sunrise framed like an oil painting by the rough wooden casement. The corporal offers her a blanket. She smiles spasmodically and wraps it around her shoulders, but her eyes return to the mountains. Aquamarine under a sky streaked with pink and yellow, they break like spent waves from the Maritimes to the horizon. "*Mein Gott,*" Frieda whispers. "*Mein Gott . . .*"

Babies cry. Children whine. Limp toddlers fall asleep again, this time in their mothers' arms. Border guards strap on cartridge belts, sling carbines over shoulders, fasten grenades to D-clips. "It's time!" someone calls. Frieda takes the girls' hands. They follow the others outside, where trucks are being loaded with provisions, light weapons, ammunition.

The young lieutenant is everywhere at once, supervising the abandonment of the post, answering questions in French, German, Italian. Yes, the soldiers will be on the run too. No, they don't expect much trouble. This part of Piemonte is lightly populated, far from any military objective. Don't stop in the nearest valley. Try to get to Valdottavo—it's a big valley southeast of here, very isolated. The roads are gravel tracks, meant for mules and wooden carts, not tanks or armored cars. If you get lost, look for stone terraces. They'll lead you to farmhouses. God—and luck—be with you!

Hefting knapsacks filled with army rations, the strongest Jews start down the mountain alone or in small groups. Others mill about, conferring, almost ready or ready but unsure. Claudette hurries across the parade ground to where the Brösslers stand. "Santino says we can ride partway in the trucks. We'll sit on the boxes in the back. If the driver stops, be ready to get out fast and run."

Overhearing this, a family from Mannheim scrambles into the nearest truck. Duno dashes after them, to reserve space. With a reassuring gap-toothed smile, an ugly young soldier helps Frieda with the girls, then boosts Claudette and her father into the crowded truck.

Somewhere inside, a foot is trod on. Hearing grumbled Yiddish, Frieda reflexively takes command, as though accommodating unexpected guests at her dinner table. "You there, give your seat to Herr Blum. Liesl, sit on your father's lap. Claudette, sit between me and Duno, and take Steffi on your lap." Four more quick commands, and she nods to Claudette's soldier.

He lifts the tailgate into place and bangs on it twice to signal the driver. "Wait!" Claudette cries. "Santino, aren't you coming with us?"

The truck's engine roars to life. Eyes on Claudette, Santino hops away from the exhaust pipe and crashes into Lieutenant Miroglio. "Sorry, sir! I didn't see you!"

"Love is blind," Miroglio says. "Look after them, Cicala. And God be with us all."

Gears grind. The sun rises. Beneath the tented fabric, the air warms. With only a few hours' sleep after the trek over the mountain, smaller children and older adults soon fall asleep. Claudette can't imagine how they manage it, with the truck swaying around switchbacks and jolting over ruts, but as the morning crawls on, her head sinks lower and lower.

An elbow rams her ribs. "Wake up!" Duno whispers fiercely.

She wipes a thin line of drool off her chin and mutters "Sorry" when she sees how wet his shoulder is.

He shakes his head and mouths, "Shut up!"

The truck is motionless. Sunlight flickers on the canvas. Leaves rustle all around. Frieda Brössler lifts Steffi from Claudette's lap. The little girl doesn't rouse, but her sister, Liesl, is stiff with fear. "Wake up, *Liebling,*" Frau Brössler says softly, shaking Steffi. "We have to walk again."

"I don' wanna! Where's Antoinette?"

"Hush!" Her mother hands Steffi the china-faced doll. "Hold her tight!"

Canvas flaps jerk open. Everybody jumps. "The first convoy's gone on, but there're more coming up the road." Santino motions for Claudette to jump down while Albert translates. "We're leaving the truck here."

The driver has nosed the vehicle into a thicket. Duno helps him heap branches against the truck for camouflage while the others assess the terrain. The nearest mountain rises steeply from a stony riverbed. Three days ago, this would have seemed an impossible climb.

Draping rolled-up army blankets over their shoulders and slinging mess kits around their necks, the Mannheimers jump from the truck calling "*Mazel!*" to the Blums and Brösslers. "Claudette," Frau Brössler asks, "may we come with you and your soldier?" Duno starts to protest. Claudette narrows her eyes at him. Frau Brössler stops them both with a look. "Go ask your father, Claudette."

Another quick conference, from German to Italian and back again. The soldier grimaces—a barely perceptible change. It's probably more responsibility than he wants, Frieda thinks. Nevertheless, he takes it with good grace, and lifts Steffi onto his shoulders.

For a long time, the only sound is the crash of vegetation and the huff of their own labored breathing as they climb. "*Mutti!* You're going too fast!" Liesl complains, bringing up the rear. "I can't—"

The flat crack of a single gunshot in the distance silences her. "*Un cacciatore,*" Santino says casually. "A hunter," Albert translates with matching, if breathless, composure.

Everyone above the age of nine stares, first at Albert Blum, then at Santino. A rattling burst of machine pistol fire confirms their silent skepticism, and all discussion ceases. They grip roots, haul on branches, making for higher ground. Knapsacks full of ration cans thump against their backs. Wild berry canes snap at legs and faces. Thorns rip clothes and scratch tender skin. For the next two hours, not even Liesl complains.

"*Mangeremo qui,*" Santino says, unslinging his '91 and leaning the rifle barrel against a fallen log beside a miniature waterfall.

"We'll eat here," Albert translates, dropping onto the log near the carbine.

Clutching Antoinette's china face, Steffi whimpers when the soldier lets her slide off his back to the ground. "What are you crying about?" Liesl snarls. "You got to ride!"

Duno looks around. "We're lost." No one answers. "We're lost!" he says louder.

"Maybe that's good," Albert says. "The Germans will be lost, too!"

"You're always so cheerful," Claudette grouses, flopping onto the ground.

"The truck driver said there was a village over there," Duno claims, pointing. "*Una villa!*" Santino levers open ration tins, playing deaf. "We should have crossed the ridge where that pine tree comes out of those rocks. We're going in circles."

"And you have such a lot of experience in these matters, Mr. Fenimore Cooper?" his father asks. "You know the woods better than a man born here?"

"He wasn't born here," Claudette feels compelled to point out.

"Don't mix in, Claudette!" her father warns, taking a tin from Santino.

"Papa, he's from Calabria!"

Hearing the word, Santino looks up, can opener in hand. He doesn't understand what the Hebrews are saying, but he hears Duno's scorn and accepts it as his due. He's tried to keep them going upward, but when the ground slopes down, is it another ravine or are they going back toward the San Leandro again? I should have gotten a compass from Miroglio, he thinks glumly, but he catches Signor Blum's eye and jerks his head toward the Brösslers. "Tell them not to waste their strength. And quiet down. There could be Germans in the next ravine."

Albert translates. Mouths snap shut. Duno stalks off angrily. The others eat in a silence broken only by Steffi's quiet chatter. "There'll be a handsome nice prince," she tells Antoinette. "He'll have a big pretty castle and soft big beds . . ."

Sharing the fallen tree trunk, Santino and Albert chew companionably, eyes on a valley barely visible through a stand of elms. A low rumble rolls over them. Thunder, not artillery. A moment later, the first drops of rain smack against leaves. Santino pulls out a square of oilcloth and wraps his rifle in it.

Albert asks, "Are you a good shot, Santino?"

"My *nonno* could pit an olive at fifty meters! I'm not that good."

"But not so bad either, eh?" Albert guesses, nudging him with an elbow.

Santino smiles modestly. "We should try to get up to those rocks before dark. Maybe we'll see something."

"Santino, the peasants—the *contadini*—will they help strangers?"

"*Sì, certo, signore.*"

"Even Jews?"

"We're all human beings, signore. Even Turks and Africans." In point of fact, until his unit was deployed in southern France, Santino Cicala didn't know there were still Hebrews alive in the world. If anyone had asked, he'd have said *ebrei* were only in the Bible. Like Egyptians, or those other E-people . . . Ephesians! "Italians don't hate strangers, signore. We hate the uncle who screwed us out of an inheritance. Like Mamma used to say, 'Trust only family, only family can betray you.' She tried to get along with everyone, but . . ." He shakes his head. "Zia Rosa won't talk to her brother, and he won't talk to his wife's nephews, and nobody talks to my cousin Salvatore. My *nonna*—just before she died, she told us, 'Here's who I want you to hate when I'm gone.' Twenty-three names!"

Another crack of thunder shortens Albert's chuckle.

"Must rain a lot here," Santino says. "At home, it's not green like this. Same kind of country, though—mountains, ravines, all cut up. Hard work, sunup, sundown. Every day the same, except for *festas*— saint's days." He scratches at four days' growth of beard. "Strangers mean news, something interesting to talk about. Another thing," he says, warming to the topic. "Farmers always hate the government! All government means to farmers is taxes. Tell people you're running from the government, and you'll always get help."

Albert pulls up his collar and settles his dampening homburg more firmly. "Were you a farmer before the war?"

Santino holds out callused palms scored by short, pale scars. His fingers are nearly twice the thickness of Albert's own. "Dry-stone waller, signore! Harder than farming, but a good wall will last two hundred years, without repairs." His lip curls. "Mussolini built everything with concrete! Concrete is a sin."

"I feel the same way about typewriters," Albert declares, one professional to another. "And calculating machines are an abomination in the sight of the Lord."

The rain's intensity suddenly triples, as though God has drawn a knife through a big cloud's belly. The noise almost drowns out the sound of someone yelling. On his feet, Santino says, "Stay here, and stay quiet."

Crouching slightly, rifle in hand, Santino sprints halfway up the hill, but he stops, furious with relief, when he realizes who's hollering, "*Una via!*" Hair plastered to his skull, the Austrian kid comes sliding down through the brush. "I am correct—I telled you," he crows in bad Italian. "*Una via,* right there! With a *latteria* truck!"

Santino grabs him by the upper arm and squeezes, hard. Duno squawks, and Santino increases the pressure until his own knuckles are white and the boy's eyes widen in pain and confusion. Voice low, Santino says, "If you want to be a man, learn to shut the fuck up."

Wiping tears and rain from his eyes, Duno nods. They return to the others in silence. "He found a road on the other side of this hill," Santino tells Albert. "He saw a milk collector driving by—a man who goes from farmer to farmer and brings the milk back to the central dairy in a city."

Albert translates. Everyone looks at Duno, who is uncharacteristically quiet about this triumph. "There's a reason for a road," Albert points out. "We must be near a dairy farm!"

The girls moan. Herrmann sighs, but Frieda staggers to her feet. "Herr Blum is right," she says, shamed by Alfred's blue-lipped optimism. "The milk van was going somewhere, and the quicker we get there, the better."

Wet day darkens into sodden twilight. The road turns into a gravel track, and then the gravel runs out. The rain becomes a steady downpour that hits the mud so hard, drops leap up like tiny frogs. "Stay on the edges," Santino reminds everyone periodically, gesturing as they splash through the mire. "Walk on the weeds, so you don't sink."

They understand the principle, though they often forget it, tramping down unnamed ravines and over identical ridges. The parents are cheerless, wool blankets draped over their heads. Claudette and Duno pass the time sniping at each other. Santino carries Steffi. When Liesl falls behind, he lets them all rest, balancing exhaustion with exposure.

Night and the temperature fall. Liesl begins to cry, and the others aren't far from it. Even Albert Blum is muttering as he stumbles along behind her. "I tol' you we should've brought th' umbrellas!" he shouts suddenly. "You never lis'en to me, Paula!"

His daughter turns. "We don't have umbrellas, Papa," she says uncertainly. "And Mama isn't here—"

"You shou' be 'n school, young lady."

Duno snickers. "He sounds like he's drunk!"

"*È ammalato?*" Santino asks.

Albert focuses for a moment, bends at the waist, pukes in two thin gouts. It happens so quickly, nobody reacts. "I think I'll just sit here and wait," he announces in a reasonable tone of voice.

"Frau Brössler! Papa's sick!" Claudette calls. "What should we do?"

"What does she want from you?" Herrmann asks. "You're a doctor now?" Frieda starts toward the Blums, but Herrmann grabs her sleeve. "We've got to keep moving!" he says. "We'll all catch our deaths out here."

"Papa's right," Duno says, agreeing with his father for once. "We have to leave them behind."

"I won't hear of it," his mother snaps.

"Mutti, we can't carry him! We left Oma—"

"Yes! Yes, we did! We left my parents in Vienna. We left Oma Brössler in Sainte-Gisèle. Now you two want to leave Herr Blum. Who's next? Liesl? Steffi? Only the strong survive—that's what the Nazis say!"

"Frieda!" her husband gasps, but she pulls her sopping blanket tighter and approaches Herr Blum gingerly. She's never been much good around sick people, but she's seen what nurses do, so she places a palm on his forehead. Her own hands are freezing, but Herr Blum's skin is weirdly clammy and her fingers on his face seem warm by contrast. No fever, so what's wrong? A chill? A bad heart? Too great a strain for too long a time? Duno and Herrmann are probably right, but she can hardly say so now. "Herr Blum needs to get warm. He needs shelter!" she tells the soldier, sketching a roof over her head with her hands.

The lady's gesture is plain, but Santino can only shrug. Of course, we need a house! he thinks. We've been looking for one all day!

The Brösslers start to argue again. Signor Blum is mumbling German, and no one else speaks Italian. Claudia's eyes plead with Santino to do something. He looks up at the ridge that snakes along the track. "Maybe I'll see something from up there," he says, trying not to sound doubtful. Or weary. Or hungry. Or scared. "I'll find something, I promise."

He starts to climb, hands to the ground. The rain is slowing, but midway to the top, he slips on slimy half-rotted leaves and mashes his nose against a rock. "*Gesù!*" he cries, spitting mud. "Santa Madonna, it's probably broke!" Pain, hunger, and helplessness compete to overwhelm him. He slumps onto his knees, letting his bloodied nose drip into the mud. "Madonna," he weeps, over and over, hopeless and alone. "Madonna!"

Without warning, the epithet becomes a prayer. "Santa Madonna! Let there be something on the other side of this hill! *Prego,* Holy Mother! I know I don't go to church much, but I don't ask this for myself. Just help me to help them, Signora. *Prego, prego . . .*"

The bleeding stops. He wipes his eyes, fingers his nose gingerly, looks up. The clouds have begun to part, and a milky moon is reclaiming the sky. Climbing again, and cresting, he stands, eyes straining for the slightest indication of humanity's mark on this dark, soggy landscape: a village, a house, a barn. Anything! he implores. A bridge the Hebrews can sleep under. Haystacks they can burrow into . . .

He sees only more ravines, and more trees. His face twists, but he holds back the tears, determined not to commit the sin of despair. Holy Mother, he prays with an inspired desperation, you ran from Herod. You hid in Egypt. *Prego,* help me find a cave, maybe, or—or—

A charcoal maker's shack.

He stares, open-mouthed. A miracle, he thinks. How else could you explain it? The tiny stone hut slumps behind axed stumps and old hearths, barely visible amid a tangle of weeds taking over an abandoned field. The Madonna must have guided his eyes!

Fatigue vanishing, Santino scrambles down and looks inside. The *carbonaro* is long gone. Drafted, maybe. Dead, or a prisoner now in Russia, God help him. But he left a supply of charcoal on

the stone hearth, and there's a stream nearby. *Bene! Benissimo,*
Blessed Mother! Santino prays, dropping to his knees, sweeping
windblown debris out the door with his hands. I'll leave Claudia
and her father here, but the Brösslers will need a bigger place, he
warns the Virgin. It's a family with three children, so a barn would
be good, if it's not too much trouble.

He clambers back to the Hebrews. The two little girls are
asleep in the mud near Albert Blum, who shakes and mumbles.
Duno and his parents stand, bodies rigid with the effort of holding back hope. Claudia sits wordlessly, and bursts into tears when
Santino nods: Yes, I found something!

"I'm sorry," he says, coming to her side. "I should have prayed
sooner." Looking past her, he tells the Brösslers, "I don't know
how much farther we have to go, but the Madonna will find you a
barn, I promise."

Without Albert Blum to translate, they don't really understand, but Santino's happiness is unmistakable and infectious.
Within the hour, he and Duno have moved the Blums and a supply of tinned rations inside the shack. Duno leaves to rejoin his
family, but Santino lingers, making sure the little fire he built is
going well.

"It's not much, signorina, but it's better than a haystack," he
tells Claudia. "The house is used by charcoal makers. Nobody will
come up here now that the rains have started."

"Santino, *prego!* My father—*il mio papa?*—he said there are people who help Jews. Delegazione Assistenza Emigrati Ebrei.
Capisce?"

"*Sì. Capisco,*" he says, not wanting to leave. "I have to take the
Brösslers to their barn, but I won't forget you. *Capisce, signorina?* I'll
come back!"

"*Capisco,*" she says. Not what he's said, but what he means.

She pulls her sleeve down over her palm and uses it to wipe at
the forgotten blood crusted under his nose. Embarrassed, he tries
to look away, but her cold hands rise to the sides of his face. For a
long moment, her serious green eyes study him, as though learning him by heart, and for the first time in his life, Santino Cicala
does not feel ugly. Emboldened, he takes her head in both his
hands, gently, and kisses her, hard. She does not pull away. "I have

to go now," he says, eyes on hers. He trips over a root but catches his balance. "I'll come back," he says again.

Watching until he disappears into the gloom, Claudette ducks inside the tiny hut and adjusts the army blanket Santino made into a door, to keep the light and heat inside. Rosy in the fire's embers, her father lies curled, inert beneath another blanket, which steams in the warmth. She sits on the packed-dirt floor and listens to the hiss of the fire, watching the rise and fall of her father's chest. His convulsive shivering has stopped, and he snores with comforting familiarity, relaxing into ordinary sleep.

Against her will, her own chest falls into the slow rhythm his provides. Noiselessly, almost calmly, the measured movement deepens. She looks up, to keep the tears from falling. "I miss you, Mama," she whispers in the tiny voice that escapes her thickening throat. "Papa was sick. I was so scared."

Don't be silly, her mother would say. He was very tired and cold. He'll be fine in the morning. Wipe your nose.

Was Papa handsome when you fell in love, Mama?

He was no Maurice Chevalier, I can tell you. But who is?

Santino's short, Mama. He's shorter than I am, I think.

Everyone's tall on my side of the family. Height's not important. Is he of good character? That's important.

He's Catholic, Mama.

Well, Moses married a shiksa. If it's good enough for him . . .

Smiling damply, Claudette cleans her nose on the back of her bloodied sleeve and pulls in a shuddery breath. She adds another chunk of charcoal to the fire, lifts the damp and smoky blanket that covers her father, and crawls in beside him to share her warmth. "We'll be all right, Papa," she whispers. "Santino will come back, and everything will be fine."

11–13 September 1943

Basilica San Giovanni Battista
Porto Sant'Andrea

Boxed inside the confessional, Osvaldo Tomitz slides open the grille to his right, and yearns to hear San Giobatta's bells toll five. Instead he hears a well-known voice whisper, "Bless me, Padre, for I have sinned. My last confession was a week ago, and I missed Mass last Sunday."

In Osvaldo's opinion, Catarina Dolcino has not confessed a single genuine sin since he arrived in Sant'Andrea, but every Saturday old Rina proudly presents a minor misdeed for absolution. "Why did you miss Mass, *figlia mia?*"

"Padre, I was aching so much Saturday evening, I thought it might be typhus!" she whispers. "I decided not to go to Mass and maybe spread the sickness."

"God does not expect you to come to Mass if you're sick. You missed Mass for the good of others—"

"But I felt fine on Sunday morning. So it was a sin."

"No, *figlia mia,* it wasn't."

"Yes, Padre, it was!"

"Look, this is not a debate. I am the priest, and I say you didn't commit a sin when you missed Mass last Sunday."

"Padre, I know it's a sin!" Rina insists more loudly.

"And what seminary did you attend?" Osvaldo demands.

A patrician chuckle issues from another confessional a few meters away. "Surrender, Tomitz," an authoritative male voice advises.

"That was the archbishop, you know," the old lady informs Osvaldo unnecessarily. "You should do as you're told."

"Oh, all right. An *Ave María,*" Osvaldo mutters. "And a *Pater Noster*—for arguing!"

Rina recites a victorious Act of Contrition, and Osvaldo surrenders to a headache. He expected lay confessions to differ from those of seminarians, but old women never cease to astonish him. They are fawningly deferential to priests everywhere but in the confessional.

Before she rises to leave, Rina drops her voice to ask, "Did you think about what my neighbor asked you, Padre? You wouldn't have to do anything. Suora Marta and Signora Leoni and I will take care of everything."

"Signora," Osvaldo says softly, "your friend's son is a criminal—"

"But—no! I mean, yes, he was in prison, but he went for someone else. Remember in '38, when every city had to send ten anti-Fascist Jews to jail? All we had in Sant'Andrea was one Communist and a lunatic, but what does Rome care? Ten is ten! Serafino Brizzolari picked men at random—how else could you do such a thing to your own neighbors? One of them was Tranquillo Loeb, Padre. A war hero! An attorney with a family, with responsibilities! Renzo wasn't married, so he went to the Palazzo Municipale and—"

"Volunteered to go in his brother-in-law's place?"

"He thinks nobody knows, but I hear things," she says smugly. "The Leonis are good people, Padre. Lidia's husband gave money to anyone who needed help. Catholic, Jew. And Emanuele never took the money back. He'd tell them to give it to someone else who needed help." The old lady pauses cagily. "A lot of people put those coins in the poor box, Padre."

"Go in peace, *figlia mía,*" Osvaldo commands firmly, but he adds, "I'll do what I can in conscience."

Sliding open the opposite grille, Osvaldo uses the movement to read his watch in a ray of light coming through a gap in the curtain. It's nearly five, but the ones who wait until the last moment often have the longest list of the most repetitive sins and the most self-serving excuses. It's the war, Padre. Always the war. Death is everywhere. Sordid solace beckons. The mind should focus on the soul's nearness to eternity, but bodies yearn to experience each pleasure life offers—now, before it is too late. Babies are conceived while husbands are at the front; wives do desperate things. Lying and theft become a way of life. Rationing, the draft, a thousand deprivations . . . Osvaldo tries to be compassionate, but he can feel himself slipping into priestly middle age, becoming snappish and judgmental as his capacity for *caritas* erodes. A child next, he prays. Suffer the little children to come unto Thee, Lord. Grant me the blessing of hearing their earnest if unreliable promises to be better next week.

Instead he hears the impact of a heavy man's knees, followed by the stifled groan when a bad leg takes up its half of this body's burden. Serafino Brizzolari. A middle-level bureaucrat at the Palazzo Municipale. The man who sent Renzo Leoni to jail.

"Bless me, Father, for I have sinned. I missed Mass because the air raids kept me awake all night. It's been a savage week, and I was too tired to go to church on Sunday." (Poor thing! Osvaldo thinks, then berates himself for sarcasm.) "I skipped grace before meals ten times, and missed grace after meals about thirty times. I'm a busy man, Padre. I am often called away from my table by matters of state." (Yes, yes! Osvaldo moans mentally. Come to the point.) "—impatient with my grandchildren about twenty times, and with my wife about ten times."

Why, Osvaldo wonders testily, are sins always divisible by five?

"I was short a couple of times with my assistant, but he really is an ass! I had impure thoughts, and I enjoyed them." (Finally! We're getting somewhere . . .) "I forgot my morning prayers about twenty times and my night prayers about thirty times. I touched myself impurely, but didn't enjoy it." (There's a lie, Osvaldo thinks, but he lets it pass.) "I used God's name in vain about fifty times and slept with someone other than my wife three times, and I cheated a man on some black-market meat, but his flour turned out to be wormy anyway, so he was cheating me, too. What can I tell you? There's a war on. For these and all my sins of my past life, I am heartily sorry, especially for being bad-tempered around my grandchildren."

Osvaldo takes a deep breath. "Let's go back to that one about sleeping with someone other than your wife, shall we?"

"Padre, my marriage is empty! My wife is—"

"This is your confession, not your wife's. And in any case, a man who tends someone else's garden can hardly complain when his own has weeds. How long has this been going on? A year? A year and a half?"

"Really, Padre, it's not your place—"

"Don't tell me my place, *figlio mio.* I am your confessor!"

"I shall speak to the archbishop about this, Tomitz!"

"Do that," Osvaldo suggests with acid courtesy. "Better yet, go to the archbishop for your confession and see what he has to say when a man seeks absolution each week with no remorse and every intention of committing the sin again." Leather creaks as Brizzolari shifts uneasily on the kneeler, and suddenly Osvaldo understands. "He already told you to break it off, didn't he! So you came to someone new, and stupid, who would require eighteen months to see through you!" Osvaldo wants to reach through the scrim and shake the man. "Can you possibly believe that God is fooled by such games?" To the silence beyond the grille, he says, "A rosary, my son! And you must break it off with that woman. Now make a good Act of Contrition."

Osvaldo listens to the grudging prayer of repentance. Brizzolari leaves in a huff. Osvaldo gives lurking penitents five more minutes to work up their courage and spends the time trying to convince himself that his own anger was righteous, not just indignation at being played for a fool.

No one else comes. He pulls the curtain aside, stretches cramped muscles as thirty nuns begin to chant their rent-in-perpetuity: a rosary each evening for the soul of Ludovico Usodimare, the pirate-prince who built San Giobatta and Immacolata convent with a modest portion of his stupendous plunder.

Renzo Leoni was right: the basilica is not much to look at. Its plaster swags and plump putti are indifferently molded, though cheerfully painted. Above a boisterous baroque altar, John the Baptist and an unblushing Usodimare anachronistically flank the risen Christ, portrayed as an improbably young man triumphant in the Easter dawn, happy as a soccer forward who's just netted a header. Osvaldo's favorite fresco is an Annunciation: androgynous angel to the left, pubescent girl to the right, a sunburst Dove hovering between them. The composition is sentimental, but it captures the moment when the Virgin's shock gives way to a secret pleasure. Was I too hard on Brizzolari? Osvaldo asks her in his heart. What could I have said that would not have encouraged him to go on sinning?

Quieting his thoughts, he hears an answer. He knows he's doing wrong. Tell him what the right thing is! Go home to your wife. Find a rose, and bring it to her. Treat her with the attention and care you gave your mistress. Love can bloom again. Women are forgiving, and so is God. Earn back your wife's trust, and our Lord's.

He envies the shoptalk of cobblers and waiters. Tailors and barbers can laugh at customers' quirks, exchange trade secrets, discuss technique. Osvaldo Tomitz, who must remain silent about his work, never returns directly to the rectory after hearing confessions. He regrets antagonizing the rectory housekeeper by being late for supper, but he needs fresh air and sunlight on his face before joining his brothers in Christ at the table.

Outside he merges with the crowds that stream away from the port. Women, children, and old men queue for trams and cram funiculars ascending the cliffs to smaller inland towns. The Allies mean to deprive Hitler of anything northern Italy can produce, and their air raids have intensified since the armistice. Porto Sant'Andrea becomes airless and lightless at dusk, its windows sealed with blue paper so the coast won't contrast with the sea, leading bombers toward docks, ironworks, steel mills, and warehouses. When military targets are hard to identify, civilian neighborhoods suffer the consequences. Anyone who can leave, does.

The menace is no longer from the air alone. By order of Field Marshal Albert Kesselring, Italian males between fifteen and fifty are being force-marched south to build German defenses, or stuffed into freight cars and shipped north to German factories. The only men who dare show themselves flaunt black shirts and boots. After a forty-five-day eclipse, the *fascisti* are back, loud and laughing, immune to German labor sweeps.

Radio loudspeakers mounted on the corners of public buildings crackle to life. Republican broadcasts begin with the state hymn, "Giovinezza," and with a travesty of prayer. "I believe in God, Lord of heaven and earth. I believe in justice and truth. I believe in the resurrection of Fascist Italy. I believe in Mussolini and in Italy's victory." Ignoring this ridiculous credo, Osvaldo sprints up long stair-streets, leaving town by way of the Genoa gate. In the distance, a rabble of boys plays soccer on a makeshift pitch, raising dust in the late afternoon's heat. Already sweating, Osvaldo yearns to cast off the black serge cassock, to rid his nose of its smell, his shoulders of its weight, his legs of its tangle. That's out of the question, of course. Even so, he intends to hike up his skirts and scuffle for a football in the heat-burnt grass, taking such pleasure in the sport it seems as confessable as old Rina's missed Mass.

A croupy cough erupts behind him. Osvaldo whirls.

Wearing a civilian suit, and sober, Werner Schramm bends at the waist and coughs until he clears some obstruction. "You're the one . . . who speaks German," he says, breathless. "I want you . . . to hear my confession."

"Herr Doktor Schramm, this isn't the time or place—"

Schramm's spine uncoils. "How do you know my name?"

"We read your papers."

"You read—? How dare you!"

Osvaldo feels his patience snap like a mast in a storm. "You were pig-drunk! Did you expect to sleep it off on a pew, like a swine in mud? You behaved disgracefully toward Suora Marta! You were rude and profane in the house of God!"

"I—my apologies," Schramm stutters. "I have no head for liquor."

Fifty meters away, the soccer players are staring. "Go on with your game," Osvaldo shouts. "All right," he mutters to Schramm. "We can return to the basilica and—"

"No! I mean— Please, I need to see your face." Schramm looks around and gestures toward an olive grove clinging to a nearby terrace, high above the coast. "Over there," he orders, adding stiffly, "if you will."

A tethered goat grazing beneath the silver-gray leaves lifts its horned skull to consider the newcomers. Gulls wheel in air scented by wild thyme and rosemary. Eye level with Osvaldo, the birds cock their heads in passing and inspect the priest with brainless optimism. Food is scarce; scraps for gulls are nonexistent. Don't look at me, Osvaldo thinks irritably. Go find a Franciscan!

"Does heaven exist?" Schramm demands.

Osvaldo blinks. "Yes. Of course."

"One who dies without the stain of sin on his soul goes to heaven?"

"Herr Doktor—"

"Children under the age of reason are not responsible. They cannot sin. If they die, they go to heaven. Yes or no?"

"If they were baptized."

"What of souls trapped in bodies that can never achieve reason?" Schramm asks in the same peremptory tone. "The feeble-minded? The mad? They, too, go directly to heaven. Their stainless souls are freed by death. They are with God."

Osvaldo frowns. "Yes," he says more slowly.

"And if they are not baptized? What about—"

"Herr Schramm, if you wish to engage in doctrinal debate—"

"A priest's office is to instruct the faithful!" Schramm shouts.

The grazing goat shies away, and the German is swamped by another coughing fit. Disgusted by the pulpy noise, Osvaldo looks away to hide his grimace. The paroxysm passes. Schramm leans against the terrace wall, wipes his mouth on a handkerchief, reaches into his suit coat for cigarettes. Osvaldo accepts one, but he puts it in his pocket, unwilling to smoke during a sacrament. "These can't be good for you," he remarks. "Not with a cough like that."

"They're poison," Schramm says flatly, "but useful camouflage." He pulls in the smoke, then makes the little choking sound that comes when one tries to suppress a cough. "Bless me, Father, for I have sinned," he says when he can speak again. "I have murdered 91,867 people."

Osvaldo laughs. You're joking, this laugh says. You can't be serious! "Ninety-one thousand," he repeats. "Eight hundred . . ."

"And sixty-seven. Yes."

The number is absurd, but Schramm does not laugh. He does not smile and exclaim, "Oh-ho! I really had you going there for a minute, didn't I, Father!" He sits, smoking, eyes tracking the flight path of a gull as it veers away, toward the sea.

Confused, Osvaldo attempts to divide 91,867 by 365, but he has no facility with numbers. Make it easier, he tells himself. Ninety thousand divided by 300 would be three hundred a day, for a *year*. If Schramm were a bomber pilot . . . But a doctor? "How?"

"Barbiturates at first. Luminal tablets dissolved in tea. Morphine, scopolamine, if a child didn't die quickly. Then there was a study at Brandenburg, comparing methods. Gas was faster, more humane—"

"Gas?" Osvaldo has no idea what this can mean.

"Carbon monoxide. Twenty, thirty at a time. At Belzec, they decided— It took too long. So we went to prussic acid. I didn't drop the canisters myself, but I decided who— There were trains, and doctors had to decide. You sent them left or right. There were thousands. I was required to decide." Schramm stops, swallows. "I asked for a transfer out of the extermination camp, but—"

Osvaldo shakes his head as though to clear it. "Extermination?"

"I had done research in nutrition, so I was reassigned to Kremer's project at the Monowitz labor camp. There were two medics. They were needlessly—there was no reason to be cruel! So I started doing the intracardiac injections myself. Phenol is quick, and has no effect on the viscera."

"The viscera?"

"To describe the anatomical effects of starvation, it was necessary to preserve organ integrity. Those people were doomed, either way. At least we could derive useful data, but— It was too much, too far! I asked for a transfer again—"

"Herr Schramm, what has this to do with mental defectives—?"

"You're mixing things!" Schramm cries. "That was the euthanasia program."

"Euthanasia?"

"Of the feebleminded, the deformed, the hopelessly ill. You're mixing things! I was a doctor in a state hospital in the late thirties. You have to understand! If their families didn't want such children, why should the nation? If healthy young men died for their nation in war, why shouldn't their hopeless sisters and brothers do the same?"

Head aching, Osvaldo tries to follow, but it's as though he is listening to a conversation taking place on the other side of a plate-glass window, and—

The window! he thinks, recognizing the sudden, impossible

feeling of having experienced this before. His first week in Sant'Andrea: he was sitting in a café, sipping an espresso, reading *La Gazzetta dello Sport*. There was a tremendous *bang!* Flame and smoke erupted from the docks. Wreckage and dust descended. He thought, A steam engine in one of the ships has exploded! But there was a second, a third detonation. Explosions—closer and closer, moving uphill from the port toward the café. All around him, patrons and waiters dove for cover. They shouted that it was an air raid. He knew they were right. He was certain that the concussion from the next bomb would shatter the window, cut him to pieces. He was going to die in a puddle of coffee, but he simply couldn't move. He just stood there like a statue until the planes passed over, and the city burned in relative peace.

The German's words fall like bombs on Osvaldo Tomitz now. Words he has never heard before. Concepts that paralyze him. Numbers that strike him speechless. Places with names so foreign he cannot remember the sounds even moments after he hears them. All over the Reich, there are slave-labor camps—thousands of them, manned by millions who work like beasts on diets of eight hundred calories a day until they die of starvation or disease. Communists, perverts, Slavic prisoners of war, even a few of the healthiest Jews, but not many. The Jews aren't being resettled either. They're being killed in industrial plants, specially built for the extermination of large populations and for efficient disposal of bodies. The death camps specialize in Jews. Gypsies, too, but mostly Jews. Cities and towns—whole countries are scoured for Jews, block by block, house by house. Italy will be next.

"I didn't mean to— I never thought— But you see, I was compromised, because of the T-4 program, and I had to . . ." Schramm passes a hand over his eyes. "I requested transfer to the eastern front. To be a doctor for a combat unit, there was some honor in that."

"Ninety-one thousand, eight hundred. And sixty-seven," Osvaldo whispers. "How can you know the number so exactly?"

"Records were kept. Meticulous records, at the camps. And at the hospital, the death certificates were fraudulent—I lied," Schramm confesses. "I told the families . . . this was part of my medical training! I followed a guide. A written guide. I was to tell parents their child had died of pneumonia, or septicemia. Later, in Russia, it was worse, almost. Thousands and thousands, executed nine at a time by firing squad. There were breakdowns. Soldiers cried and begged to be excused. The officers would scream abuse at them—they were a disgrace to the German race! To the *Vaterland!* So they'd fire at the targets, with tears streaming down their cheeks—"

"Targets?"

"Not all of them cried. Some enjoyed their work—they got extra rations, all the liquor they could hold."

More bombs fall. A noncommissioned officer who held shrieking Jewish toddlers by the hair, shooting them in the head and laughing at the bloody skullcap left dripping in his fist. A Ukrainian volunteer systematically beating people to death with his rifle butt while the SS watched, stunned by his enthusiasm. Living bodies cut apart with bayonets in search of swallowed jewels.

"I am neither a sadist nor a thief," Schramm insists. "I only wanted—I wanted to make things better." He stops, and swallows. "I killed no one at the front," he says firmly, "but there were 632 children in the state hospital, and 220 in the hunger research. I was stationed at Auschwitz for 26 days, and had depot duty for eight days of that time. The average throughput was 9,000 a day. I signed off on 91,015 head. This totals 91,867."

Osvaldo looks at Schramm, at the goat, at the diamond-studded sea sparkling in the distance. Mind racing, he tries to imagine what he can possibly say to this . . . this *demon.* His mouth opens. No words emerge. He lifts his hands, drops them, and begins to walk away.

"Wait!" Schramm calls. "You must— What is my penance?"

Osvaldo turn and stares. "*Mein Gott,* Schramm, what did you expect? *Rosaries?*" Bending suddenly, leaning hard on hands that clutch his knees, Osvaldo chokes back vomit. Trembling, he lifts his eyes. "Shoot yourself."

"What?"

"You wanted a penance."

"You're mad! That's crazy—"

Osvaldo straightens, advances, finger pointed like a gun. "You call yourself a Catholic? You are a disgrace to your faith! Nothing less than executing yourself can possibly atone for what you have done! Commit suicide and condemn yourself to hell. I am your confessor! Obey me, you miserable coward!"

Schramm backs away, looking for someone to whom he can appeal. "You—you're a priest! Suicide is a sin! You have no right—"

"Ah," Osvaldo breathes. "So you are capable of disobeying an order when you know it to be wrong." He shakes his head. "God forgive you. I can't."

"What are you saying? You can't—"

"For absolution, there must be sincere contrition!" Osvaldo cries. "If you'd come to me after three, or even four murders—" Again, the strange laughter of disbelief and shock escapes him. "But to kill, and go on killing? To kill 91,867! Why now, Schramm? Why confess now?"

The German will not meet his eyes, and in the silence Osvaldo Tomitz makes sense at last of the flushed cheeks, the terrible thinness, the horrifying cough. "You're dying," he says. "You have tuberculosis." Schramm flinches. Osvaldo pities him for an instant. "What you feel is not contrition, my son. It's dread. I can't absolve a fear of hell."

"But—what should I do?"

The priest walks away without a backward glance.

"*Please!*" Schramm shouts, his voice cracking. "Someone has to tell me what—"

The hemorrhage is sudden, but not unexpected. The revolting sensation of fluid rising to fill the pharynx comes first. The taste of iron and acid. Schramm sinks to his knees, leans forward, gagging. Salt tears form tiny momentary lakes in the bloody dust. Hot wind rushes past his ears, roaring like a tide, but he does not drown. This time.

RABBINICAL RESIDENCE
PORTO SANT'ANDREA

"You promise?" Angelo Soncini asks as his mother tucks him in. "A brother this time?"

"I can't promise, but—yes, I think it's going to be a boy." Sitting on the edge of his bed, Mirella takes her son's hand, which is reasonably clean for a change, and rests it on her belly. "Wait . . . Did you feel that? This baby is just like you were! All knees and fists and feet, kicking to get out!"

Angelo looks up slyly. "I know a kid who says babies come out the mamma's mouth."

Mirella has prepared herself to be honest, if indirect. "No, my treasure. There's a special opening between a lady's legs that God has made for just such a purpose. When the baby's ready, he comes out down there." Judging from the look she gets, this is a far worse solution to the puzzle than anything Angelo and his young consultants have discussed.

Angelo shakes his head. "That can't be right. Babies are too big for that. Unless—" His eyes bulge. "Do ladies' legs come off?"

"It might be convenient if they did," she admits. "The important thing is, the babies are born, and everyone welcomes them into the family. Especially big brothers! No more questions! Say your prayers!"

Her own prayers are simpler than the Hebrew ones her son rattles through. No raids tonight, please, God! Let my child sleep soundly. Let him dream of baby brothers, and not Altira's death.

So different was her second pregnancy from her first, Mirella Soncini worried almost from the start that something was wrong. If Angelo was like a boxer within her, the new child was like a butterfly, like a breeze on lace curtains. Fluttering, shivering, humming. "The baby almost never kicks," Mirella said, but everyone told her not to fret.

Born at dawn, her daughter quickly flushed as rosy as the light that greeted her, and settled into Mirella's arms like a nestling. That was when everyone else began to worry. Mirella didn't care. In defiance of tradition, she named her daughter Altira, Hebrew for *fear not!*

"All she does is cry and make smells," Angelo complained. "She's almost two and she still can't do anything! Why do you like her better than me?"

"I love you both the same," Mirella insisted. "And you should love your little sister, too! Altira can't do as much as you because she's so little."

But Altira could cuddle. Altira could gaze at her mother with measureless love. She could smile shyly, almost coyly, and throw her face onto Mirella's breast with a surfeit of affection, patting soft flesh with hands like small pink starfish. So sweet . . . But this will be another son, Mirella thinks. A boy, all energy and push.

She makes her ponderous way to Iacopo's office and emits a quiet growl of exasperation at the stacks of paperwork piled on the dining table after a late meeting with the congregation officers. Hoping to reform Iacopo when they first married, Mirella proudly provided her new husband with a nice, big filing cabinet. Iacopo dutifully filled it with correspondence and scribbled notes, but the organization remained more geological than alphabetical. Several arguments later, he declared, "There are two kinds of people, *cara mia:* pilers and filers. Ours is a mixed marriage."

"Angelo's in bed," she says, standing at the threshold of his study. "Shall I wait up?"

Slowly, visibly, Iacopo's mind shifts from the sixteenth century to the twentieth, from Renaissance Hebrew to modern Italian. Mirella waits patiently, breathing in the dust and leathery scent of five thousand volumes. They are her husband's tools and his colleagues, these books. Three millennia of prophets and poets, dramatists and historians, theologians and sages keep him company late into the night. Every surface is laden with texts, laid open or bristling with bookmarks.

When at last Iacopo's eyes focus on his wife, they warm, and in the resonant, melodic baritone that won her, he recites, " 'His heart, aroast upon the spit of longing, turns. He burns! O gaze, gazelle, down from your window, where the tender passion of your gallant yearns—' "

Mirella laughs. "Pardon me, a gazelle with a window?"

"I'm just the translator, not the poet! You can come in, you know. It's only my office, not the holy of holies."

"And take a chance on moving some crucial scrap of paper from one heap to another?" She shakes her head.

"You look tired. Beautiful," he adds, "but tired. Go to bed, *cara mia.* I want to finish this stanza, but you should get some rest."

"In a few minutes. First, I need to clear away a mess someone left in the dining room."

The office door clicks closed. Iacopo Soncini stares a few moments at the rich figuring of its wood. Then it's back to old Pappus, the lovesick innkeeper who yearns for his gazelle. Who now looks into the mirror, and "sees his fallen face and form, his belly—" No. Not belly. "—his *paunch* that pines." Mirella would scoff, A paunch that pines? But that's what the poet wrote, and he liked alliteration. "And eyes that spill uncounted tears. He feels his bald spot's chill; his stray gray locks hang damp with dew . . ."

Iacopo lays down his pen, stretching out the kinks in his own middle-aged back. Poor old Pappus, he thinks. If your gazelle's father permits the marriage, what will become of such a mismatch?

A knock on the front door interrupts his thoughts. Iacopo glances at the clock. It's past curfew. He removes his pince-nez, slipping it into his vest pocket. A German rabbi, beaten in his doorway by SA hoodlums, was blinded by his own shattered spectacles. Seven years since Iacopo heard that story, and still it haunts him.

Unburdened by such fear, Mirella has already opened the door—not to a Fascist thug but to a pale priest. "*Buona sera,*" she says a little blankly. He looks familiar, but there are so many priests in Sant'Andrea. With his forgettable face and anonymous black cassock, this one has failed to make an impression. "Padre . . . ?"

"Tomitz. Osvaldo Tomitz."

Hurrying down the hall, Iacopo leans past Mirella to welcome the priest with a warmth meant to offset Mirella's confusion. "*Buona sera, Don Osvaldo!*"

Mirella presses one hand to her forehead and the other to her belly. "Forgive me, Don Osvaldo. My mind is a sieve these days!"

Making small talk, Mirella ushers their apologetic visitor down the entry hall. No, she tells him, both of us were awake. But, of course! You're welcome here at any time. Fine, *grazie,* and you? Yes, very soon now—at the end of the month, most likely . . .

Iacopo smiles when Don Osvaldo looks around the Soncini's salon. The furniture is lacquer-sleek, the artwork cubist, the chandelier a stark Venini. "You expected something more traditional," he notes when Mirella goes to the kitchen. "All new, when Mirella and I married. Traditional is good, I told her. Nothing looks more dated—"

"—than whatever was breathlessly fashionable eight years ago!" Mirella says, returning from the kitchen with a bottle of wine and three glasses on a tray. "I wish we had more to offer, but this is a very nice sangiovese." She frowns. "Don Osvaldo, is something wrong?"

"Mirella's right," Iacopo agrees. "You're white as snow!"

"Rabbino, you must— Something is—" The unremarkable face twists, and Tomitz looks back toward the door. "I'm sorry. I shouldn't have come. There's nothing I can say!"

"Drink this, Padre," Mirella urges. "Can I get you something stronger?"

"Mirella." There is, in Iacopo's silken voice, a note of soft command. His wife takes one step back. "I have been meaning to invite you to see our synagogue, Don Osvaldo," Iacopo says lightly. "Perhaps now would be convenient."

Tumblers rattle. Well-oiled hinges glide. Footsteps echo on marble, but this is not a lonely sound. For both men, there is comfort in the familiar emptiness of a place of worship at night.

"After the Great War, everyone felt it was time to make some visible statement of our place in Italy. The congregation raised the money for a new synagogue in the twenties. Construction began in the thirties. We were able to employ many men during the Depression." Iacopo opens the etched-glass door to the main sanctuary of Scuola Ner Tamid and switches on the electric chandeliers.

Osvaldo pulls in a little gasp. Carrara walls reflect brilliant light from gleaming silver fixtures. A raised central altar's lectern shelters under a sort of indoor gazebo fashioned of clean-lined chestnut. As modern as the Soncinis' home, the sanctuary's beauty arises from gracious proportions, and fine materials painstakingly polished.

"I am told the style is Italian rationalist," the rabbi says, turning the lights off. "Personally, I prefer the little chapel." He leads Don

Osvaldo down a dark staircase. "When the congregation moved uptown from Porto Vecchio—watch your step, Padre—they saved the *bima* and the ark from a synagogue that was dedicated in 1511. We re-created its chapel down here." He unlocks another door. "Let there be light!"

Illuminated by antique lanterns discreetly electrified, the small square room is as stunningly ornamented as the main sanctuary was serenely unadorned. Heavily carved walnut panels enclose it; their dark riches set off the gleam of precious metals: embossed, chased, engraved. Silver oil lamps on fine gilt chains hang from a vaulted ceiling with a frescoed sky, lapis blue and studded with tiny six-pointed stars leafed in gold.

A stately candelabrum, tall as a man and branched like an es-paliered tree, guards what appears to be an ornate wardrobe inlaid with ivory flowers and jade ivy. "That's the ark," Iacopo explains, "where the Torah scrolls rest." He takes a seat on a mid-Renaissance chair opposite the menorah. "We are commanded to beautify the elements of worship. Our ancestors fulfilled that mitzvah admirably, in my opinion." He motions toward a pew. "*Prego,* Don Osvaldo. What we say here is heard by God alone."

The priest's silence is different now.

"You have been a good friend to our community, Don Os-valdo," Iacopo says, giving the other man time. "I am aware that since you took up your post at San Giobatta, you have encouraged His Excellency and the good sisters at Immacolata to cooperate with the Jewish relief committee. You yourself have helped us find housing for displaced Hebrews. Naturally, when such a friend comes to me with a grave concern, I am distressed. I wish to know if there is some way I can be of help to you."

Osvaldo's lips part, but still no words emerge.

"It must be difficult to hear confessions," Iacopo remarks, one clergyman to another. "Listening, hour after hour, to the shameful and humiliating secrets of others. It must feel like an assault or the onset of an illness. To accept such a burden, to take it onto one's own shoulders—"

"But I am not alone in the confessional!" Don Osvaldo cries, his face twisting. "I am in the presence of One who died in agony to redeem the sins of the world!"

"And yet, you weep," Iacopo observes, offering a handkerchief.

"Rabbino, I have refused a sinner absolution."

Taken aback, Iacopo asks, "Is that possible?"

"I—I don't know. It may be a sort of heresy. But what I heard was so terrible that—that . . ."

"You doubt your savior's ability to forgive it?"

"Or my worthiness to be His priest." Osvaldo moves from place to place in the little room. "What if a penitent is mad? Or deluded. What if he feels such guilt for what he's done in war that he believes himself guilty of other unspeakable acts?"

"Don Osvaldo, why have you not gone to the archbishop with these questions?"

"Because—because what I heard is of great importance to you, and to your congregants. To all of us who—" Tomitz stops. "I'm sorry. Even to say this much—"

"May be breaking the seal of the confessional. Perhaps," Iacopo suggests carefully, "it would be permissible to tell me what you think I might do, were I in possession of the information you cannot convey?"

"You would immediately advise your congregation to—" Don Osvaldo hesitates, but when he speaks again his voice is firm. "To avoid arrest and deportation."

"I am not aware that we are doing anything to invite arrest, Don Osvaldo. The king himself says Italy has no more exemplary citizens than the Jews."

"The king himself has fled the Germans—as you should! Tranquillo Loeb was right, Rabbino. You must all leave as soon as possible."

"And where do you suggest we go, Don Osvaldo?"

"Someplace—anyplace you're not known. Into the hills, the mountains! You could pass for Catholics. I—I'll get you baptismal certificates. You wouldn't have to be baptized, I swear it!"

"A generous offer, Don Osvaldo, and we Italians could conceivably melt into the countryside. But what of the refugees who've come to us for shelter? What would become of them?"

Tomitz sags onto a pew and puts his face in his hands.

"I am working with a German refugee," Iacopo tells him quietly. "He's almost thirteen, studying to become bar mitzvah—a ceremony rather like confirmation. For nearly two years, he and his family have lived in the basement of a bombed-out building near here. They look Jewish, whatever that means. They speak almost no Italian. They have no money. This boy's only possession is a stamp album. Every week, he shows it to me before we begin our study. Three hundred stamps, from all over the world. The Philippines, Bolivia, Tunisia. Algeria, America. Switzerland. Mauritius. Spain, Portugal. Shanghai, Hong Kong, Japan, India. Venezuela, Cuba, the West Indies. I asked him once, 'How did you amass such a collection?' And he answered, 'They're from letters my father received from embassies when we were trying to emigrate from Germany.' " The priest looks up, and Iacopo asks, "Can I abandon that boy, when the whole world has rejected him?"

Don Osvaldo exhales raggedly. "No. Of course not, but surely you have heard the rumors of—"

"Precisely! Rumors! Frightening stories cost the Reich nothing, Padre. They're far more popular than raising taxes. When a Jew leaves German territory, his property is confiscated to finance the Nazi war—"

"Rabbino, what if there were an eyewitness? If I brought someone who will tell you what is happening to Jews who are—"

"Don Osvaldo, what could I do with such testimony?" Iacopo demands, voice rising. "Terrify my congregants? Foment panic? The doors of the world are closed to us! If all you offer is more fear— O Dío! What now?"

"Open up!" someone yells, pounding on the street-level door. "Rabbino, are you in there? Open up!"

The rabbi cringes at the voice, but with anger, not with fear. Muttering apologies, he leaves the chapel, taking the stairs two at a time. Strides across the synagogue lobby. Throws open the door and grabs a man's arm, snarling, "Quiet, you fool! We have enough trouble without you making a public scene."

Flung roughly into the vestibule, Renzo Leoni stumbles into the startled priest's arms. "Don Osvaldo!" he cries. "A pleasure to see you again." He lowers his voice conspiratorially. "If you've decided to convert, you've picked a very poor time for it."

"You're drunk!" Iacopo accuses.

Convicted by his own helpless laughter, Leoni leans against a wall and slides toward the marble floor. "I am not," he allows, "at my best. That, however, is not the topic I wish to discuss! Mirella sent me—"

"You went to my home? You spoke to my wife in this condition?"

"My dear Rabbino Soncini," Leoni says, summoning fluid formality from an unwilling tongue, "as a matter of strict fact, I was looking for *you*. And permit me to observe that if you'd been at home, with your wife, instead of spending your evening with Don Osvaldo here, Mirella would not have been forced to dispatch a reprobate like me to inform you that she is in labor."

The rabbi stares. "She can't be. It's too soon."

"I'm inclined to accept the lady's authority on such matters."

Osvaldo steps outside in time to see Mirella Soncini's belly emerge from her doorway, followed a moment later by the part of her that is pulling on a cardigan. "Iacopo!" she calls loudly. "It's time!"

Her shout galvanizes the neighborhood. Shutters open like windows in an Advent calendar. Heads appear. Words of encouragement sail into the night air. Wearing dressing gowns, Rina Dolcino and Lidia Leoni join Mirella, who motions for her pajama-clad son to come outside. "I'm getting a baby brother," the little boy announces as the ladies usher him into their apartment building.

Osvaldo waves to let them know the news has reached the signora's husband. "Rabbino," he says, "give me the keys. I'll lock up!"

Drawn by the disturbance, a pair of carabinieri appear, flashlights making cones of brightness that sweep through the neighborhood. Apprised of the impending birth, they quickly agree to accompany the signora and her husband to a city hospital a few blocks away.

Renzo appears in time to watch the departure. "It's legal for me to be out after curfew," Osvaldo tells him, "but you should get inside."

Unconcerned, Renzo rearranges himself into a sitting position and leans against the doorpost of the synagogue. "Beautiful evening," he says, eyes on the strip of night sky visible above them.

Shrugging, Osvaldo sits beside him. "The rabbino looked so surprised," he muses, looking at the stars. "I suppose you never get used to it. Every baby is a separate miracle." He lowers his gaze to his companion. "You're not drunk."

"Regrettably: no." Leoni's heavy-lidded attention remains fixed on the heavens. "Iacopo works very hard for the Jewish community. Who am I to deprive such a man of the deeply satisfying pleasures of sanctimony? Besides," he adds, "it was a fair assumption. My intemperance is notorious."

"The rabbi's wife is a beautiful young woman. His distress is, perhaps, understandable."

By degrees, Leoni's regard drops from the stars to the priest at his side. "Signora Soncini is a lady of unimpeachable moral character," he declares with starchy dignity before confiding, "She threw me over to marry Iacopo, but some men can't take yes for an answer."

"There are," Osvaldo notes, "certain practical advantages to an unmarried clergy. How long have you been awake?"

"How long does it take for milk to spoil? Two days? Three? We've got a river of Jews coming over the Maritimes from France, Padre. They thought the war was finished here." He stretches his legs out in front of him and works at his knees with hands that tremble slightly. "I was giving people rides in Valdottavo and then the fucking gasogene rig fouled—" He stops. "Forgive my language, Padre."

"*Ego te absolvo,*" Osvaldo says, wishing bad language were the worst thing he'd been asked to pardon today.

"The peasants up there are taking people in, but they haven't got shit to share. If the Germans offer a bounty . . ." Renzo presses his fingers into bloodshot eyes. "Anyway, by the time I got the conduit cleared, I had a shipment of sour cream. My superiors at the dairy were not pleased. I am officially at liberty to seek employment elsewhere."

"So you wanted to tell the rabbi about the refugees."

Renzo nods, yawning hugely. "I should get home before Mamma decides I'm dead, rather than merely facedown in a gutter."

Osvaldo stands. "I want to help."

"With Mamma? She's used to this."

"With the refugees. The ones already in Sant'Andrea. The ones coming over the mountains. I can get your job back—the man who owns the *latteria* is a parishioner. When Tranquillo Loeb took his family to Switzerland, he entrusted nearly thirty thousand lire to the archbishop's office for refugees. A milk route will be a good excuse to go from farm to farm. We can distribute the money as we go."

"We?"

Osvaldo tugs the synagogue door closed, locks it, pockets the key. "There's a priest up in Valdottavo—an old friend. Leto's a Catholic Actionist. He'll help, and there'll be others. Suora Marta, for one. The sisters can hide people in the convent."

"Mamma thinks the Communists are the only ones organized enough to oppose the Nazis." Renzo considers the priest thoughtfully. "Perhaps she's overlooked a possibility."

Osvaldo offers Leoni a hand. Even with assistance, Renzo's rise is an exercise in mechanical engineering, the separate elements of his skeleton carefully arranged on a plumb line between his head and heels, knees unfolding last. Their eyes meet. A pact is made.

"You can live in the basilica," Osvaldo says. "There's a storage room we can—"

"Wait. Live in the basilica?"

"Your mother asked me for a room where a man could hide."

"Ah, but the room is not for me, Padre." Renzo pulls out an identity card, a pay stub, a half-used ration card. "A friend of mine works for an undertaker. Last week, a Sicilian sailor died of typhus, and Giorgio saved these for me. Had to change the photograph and the occupation, but the rest works. Stefano Savoca's family lives behind Allied lines down in Sicily, so nobody can check the identity. And I've got another set for an ethnic German named Ugo Messner. He died last year. I used to date his sister."

"Then who . . . ?"

"Giacomo Tura. He's a *sofer*—a ritual scribe. Friend of Mamma's. I suppose I should warn you, Padre. In the absence of male supervision, my mother has become a revolutionary. The Communists say they'll give women the vote."

By late Monday afternoon, the cleaning supplies have been removed, leaving a faint chemical smell in the basilica storeroom.

Painted shutters have been pried loose, and the single window fitted with a good, heavy blackout curtain. Along one wall, an iron bedstead waits, its mattress covered by pressed white linens, overlain by a blue woolen blanket—patched, but with fine stitches. In a corner: a chipped enamel chamber pot draped with a square bleached rag. A washbasin and pitcher, a worn clean towel folded neatly beside. A table fashioned from two bookcases topped by a broad plank. Dominating the center of the small room, at an angle to the window: a slanted drawing board and a high stool.

"It's spartan, Giacomo," Lidia Leoni says, "but no one will think to look for you here."

"The sisters will watch for trouble," Suora Marta assures him.

"Is there anything else you need, Signor Tura?" Rina Dolcino asks.

The *sofer* inspects a miniature forest of brushes, quills, and pens rising from glass jars. His gnarled fingers walk in the air above the tools of his trade. Kneaded erasers, cleaning pads, sponges, tapes. Little piles of parchment trimmings that can be turned into glue to restore other documents. Rows of small bottles filled with colored inks. The ladies have smuggled in the entire contents of his studio, including two chunks of Jerusalem limestone that serve as paperweights. He perches on the stool, adjusts the drawing table to a better angle. "I could use more light. My eyes aren't so good anymore."

The ladies think. "Mirrors?" Lidia suggests. "To reflect the light from the window."

"Of course!" says Suora Marta. "We have no mirrors in Immacolata, *grazie a Dio,* but—"

"I'll bring one," Rina Dolcino promises quickly. She's seen Signor Tura coming and going from the synagogue for years, but they have never spoken, beyond wishing one another *'n giorno.* The scribe is a small man, bent from his work, but he has a fine head of white hair and intelligent eyes. The age Rina's husband would have been, if the sugar disease hadn't taken him . . . She blinks and pulls a set of documents from her handbag. "These are the newest, Signor Tura. My brother just got them from the office in Genoa. He'll stay off the street until you're done."

Surprisingly nimble, Giacomo hops off the stool and steps to the window. Holding the identity card to the light, he studies the paper, the printing, the signatures. "I'll have a set of blanks for the engraver by the end of the week. How will you get photos, Lidia?"

"The Catholics who took over Emanuele's studio—they're helping."

"You'll need the stamps," Giacomo reminds her.

"We're working on that."

The three women bid him good-bye. Lidia exits briskly, but Ferdinando Dolcino's widow allows her hand to linger in the scribe's a moment longer than absolutely necessary. She is, Giacomo notices, still quite a striking woman, but before the thought can go further, Suora Marta takes her by the elbow and turns her toward the hallway. Rina flashes a smile over her shoulder. The door clicks shut.

Giacomo sits on the bed. The mattress is thin, but he can't fault the nuns' hospitality. He hasn't eaten this well since before his wife died.

Outside, a cloud drifts eastward, and a shaft of sunlight makes the ink bottles sparkle. Crimson, grass green, cobalt blue. Gold and silver. Sepia and coal black. With such colors, Giacomo Tura has spent a lifetime documenting the happy events of the Jewish community: illuminating marriage contracts, birth announcements, creating invitations to *b'nai mitzvah* and weddings. But he is also a skilled conservator. With bits of paper and parchment collected for decades, he can repair a medieval manuscript's torn corner, mend a gaping hole in a seventeenth-century *ketuba*. Once he even restored a family photograph spoiled in a flood.

Lifting the German document again, the *sofer* studies the color and density of the paper, the ink, the script. Yes, he thinks, laying it aside. I can reproduce this.

He washes his hands. Struggles into the midnight blue scribal tunic. Settles a *kippah* onto his head to remind himself that his work is sacred. "We write the Torah for life, for continuity," his master told him when Giacomo was an apprentice. "Before beginning our task, we blot out the name of Amalek, the biblical enemy of Israel. Thus, we remember the prophesy: our enemies shall pass, and we live." Humming absently, Giacomo selects a tiny piece of parchment from among the remnants. Inscribes on it, in the vowelless Hebrew, the consonants of Amalek's name.

Crosses them out with two lines, crushes the parchment in his palm.

This much is tradition, but he takes up a second snippet of parchment. Smiling grimly at his innovation, Giacomo Tura writes four more letters: *HTLR*. These he crosses out three times, and then he burns the scrap.

$\mathcal{L}$ate $\mathcal{S}$eptember 1943

VALDOTTAVO
NEAR FRAZIONE SANTA CHIARA

"Papa, we should go back down," Claudette says at first light.

She is, her father thinks, almost incapable of silence. Just as she had to crawl and walk and climb when she was little, she has to hear her own voice now, to argue, to test her strength.

"We won't be giving ourselves away, Papa. Someone already knows we're here."

Sitting up, Albert digs crust from the corners of his eyes with numb fingers, and rubs his palms together briskly.

She pulls his topcoat more tightly around his shoulders, defying him to yell at her for being nice. "Look at those rocks." She points at pebbles he was too worn out to brush aside last night. "How could you sleep on those?"

"I didn't," he grumps.

"We're almost out of newspaper," she warns, and leaves to relieve herself.

In Sainte-Gisèle, Albert had a library to visit, and other adults for companionship. Here, there's nothing to read but their diminishing supply of toilet paper, nothing to do but fret and argue. They haven't seen another soul since Santino Cicala left them in the charcoal maker's shack a week ago.

Then, yesterday, two apples materialized. Russet red, mottled with lemony yellow, they'd been placed in the center of a flat rock just outside the hut. Albert insisted that they leave the shack and move farther up the mountain, where they've spent a wretched night.

"You look like one of those scraggly Poles who never shave!" Claudette says when she returns.

You're no vision of loveliness yourself, he thinks.

"Papa, what if it was Santino?" she asks.

He rolls creakily to his knees, and pulls out the velvet tefillin bag. "What if it was Germans?"

"Germans wouldn't leave apples." She watches him wind the tefillin strap. "Papa, what if the Allies—"

"Claudette, please! Five minutes of peace!" He tugs the dirty tallis over his eyes, grateful for this small symbolic tent to hide within. Blessed be our desert fathers, he thinks, and loses himself in prayer.

"I would kill for a newspaper!" Claudette says the moment he's finished. Oblivious to his mood, she glowers at the town that straddles a river far below, visible through half-bare branches. "I'm not joking. I would actually, truly kill somebody for a newspaper," she says. "And I'd torture somebody for a radio!"

"Where would you plug it in?"

It's a good point, but she won't admit it, any more than he'd admit he's as starved for news as she is. This is what I've been reduced to, he thinks. Childish games with my own daughter.

Her tone changes. "Papa? Do you remember what Mama looks like? Without looking at a picture, I mean."

"Of course," he says a bit too quickly.

"I wish I had a photograph of Santino. I think I remember, but he's sort of mixed up with John Garfield."

More like Edward G. Robinson, Albert thinks.

"I'm sure Santino left the apples! He's looking for us, and we're up here freezing and starving for nothing!"

"Why would he leave us apples without so much as a *buon giorno?*"

Albert slips the tefillin into their bag and folds the prayer shawl neatly, remembering the day, years ago, when he was shocked by a newspaper account of a woman who killed her four children and then herself. "How could a mother murder her own children?" he asked Paula. "The mystery," his wife informed him, after a long day with their three, "is how many of us don't."

Claudette stomps around, rubbing her arms. "I can see my breath! Papa, you never listen! We can't stay up here! It'll be winter soon—"

"Oh, for the love of God, Claudette! Will you please shut up!"

Claudette whirls, ready to shout, "Mama told us never to say 'shut up'!"

The words die in her mouth. For an instant she sees a dimly remembered grandfather: Zeide Blum, pallid and pasty under a gray stubble, his lips as blue as his eyes. Something's wrong, she realizes. Not like before. Something else.

"This is stupid," she mutters. "It's not the Germans."

Ignoring her father's strangled shout, she sets off through beeches that glow like gold, their yellow leaves filtering the autumn sunlight. Dirty hair slapping at her neck, she stumbles and slides through glacial gravel and thin crumbly dirt, suffused with a reckless confidence that does not waver until she nears the shadowy edge of the woods.

The ground drops away abruptly. She cannot see the shack from here, but while there's nothing she can interpret as an ambush or trap, caution seems less absurd now that she's alone.

She reties her father's oxfords, crouches slightly, sucks in a nervy breath. Giving herself no more time to think, she explodes from the forest, sprints through the meadow, vaults a fallen tree trunk, dashes through clumps of high, stiff autumn grass. "It's not the Germans! It's not the Germans!" she huffs, but she veers and ducks like a cinema cowboy dodging arrows, knees lifting high. Suddenly the shack comes into view. She alters course, sprints straight toward it. Mouth open, lungs bursting, she skids to a pebbly halt.

The apples are gone.

She groans, crumpling with disappointment. Hands on her knees, she bends to ease the cramp under her ribs, and sees two pears and a good-sized chunk of pale cheese wrapped in white muslin, on a makeshift plate of leaves. "Santino!" she shouts. "Hello? Anybody?"

Nothing. Not even birdcalls.

Working quickly, she gathers a loose bouquet of hardy wildflowers still blooming near the hut and swaps this token of thanks for the fruit and cheese. "*Molte grazie!*" she says loudly, just in case, and scampers up the wooded mountainside, laughing with excitement.

"Whoever it is, they decided we don't like apples!" she yells when her father comes into view. "And they know there are two of us," she says more quietly when she sees his face.

Hand trembling, he points with a combination of fury and relief. "Don't you *ever* do that again!"

"But Papa, they left us food."

"The people in these mountains are illiterate peasants! They're ignorant, Claudette. Priests have been filling their heads with Christ-killer lies all of their lives!"

She bites into one of the pears and moans. "Oh, Papa! Oh, this is beautiful! This is the best pear I ever tasted!"

"They think we poison wells! They think we murder babies and use their blood to make matzoh! They hate us—"

"Name two."

Albert blinks.

"Whenever we said 'they,' Mama told us to name two." Claudette divides the lump of cheese, handing half to Albert. "Mama said if you can't name two actual real people, then you're just being prejudiced. So name two peasants who hate us." She takes another bite of pear, holding his eyes with her own: ocean green and guileless in a dirt-smeared face. "Mama said."

Albert sighs. "All right," he says, capitulating to hunger, and to a heart-deep weariness, and to the ethical precepts of a wife whose face is more difficult to conjure as each day passes. "All right, but just this once."

There are pears again the second day, and more of the glorious creamy cheese; tomatoes and crumbly yellow bread the following morning; a jar of milk and a pile of wild mushrooms next. Claudette pays for each small meal with a fistful of wildflowers, and on the fifth day, there is more than food.

"Papa, look what they left last night," she calls, lugging a thick woolen cape of military green up the mountainside. "Pity it rained last night, but it didn't get too wet." Without waiting for a response, she flaps the blanketlike cloak and snugs it around her father with a practical dispatch that has begun to feel natural. "I saw footprints in the mud this morning," she reports, using the handle of her toothbrush to spread the soft cheese over the cornbread's rough surface. "It's a child, I think, bringing us things."

Their anonymous benefactor has been miraculously faithful, and Claudette has found windfall apples and even raspberries to supplement their diet. They have water from a little creek, but there's never enough food. They've both had awful diarrhea. Her father is thinner and more silent with each passing night. Sunken into craters of bruised-looking skin, his eyes flick toward her, then away. He's still wearing his tie, the knot drawn close to keep a little of the chill out.

Claudette tucks blue-nailed fingers into her armpits in a useless effort to warm her hands. "Papa, look at me!" she pleads softly. "Papa, are you sick again?"

"I—I saw Germans in that town down there," he whispers through cracked lips, stiff with cold. "Soldiers, taking people away. The war's not over . . . I—we won't survive the winter up here. I don't know what to do."

She is, for once, speechless. He raises the army cape with a trembling arm so she can snuggle in beside him. For a long time they stare in silence at the river: a man of forty-nine, a girl not quite fifteen, weighing bad choices.

"We have to trust someone," Claudette says quietly. "Whoever's bringing the food—even if he's only a child, he wants to help us. Let's go down, Papa. Not all the way to the town. Just to the shack."

"All right," he says finally. "All right. If you think so."

They gather their few belongings, and Claudette leads the way along the path she's worn through vegetation crisp with frost. Often, as they descend on numbed and clumsy feet, Albert puts out a hand to steady himself on his daughter's shoulder.

After days in the open, the ramshackle hut seems palatial— warm and windless and dry. Carefully Claudette lays a fire with plenty of tinder to catch the flame of their last match. "The war can't last forever," Albert whispers as she pulls the cloak around him. He is asleep before she can reply, his chest rising and falling in great heaves, laboring for breath even at rest.

All her short and willful life, Claudette Blum has tried to make her father listen to her, and now he has. Whatever happens next, she thinks, it's on my head. She swallows hard and settles down to wait. Save your tears, she tells herself. You may need them later.

NEAR FRAZIONE GORE

Herrmann Brössler is on his knees, pointing through the hayloft window. "Duno, use your eyes!" he shouts. "Look at the woodpiles! Stacked to the roof on three sides. Why is that house attached to this barn by a second-story passageway? Because the farmer has to get to his animals, even when the snow is chest-deep! The winters here are terrible!"

"The partisans can survive in the mountains," Duno shouts back. "And I'm going to join them!"

"You're still frightened of *bees!* You're going to be a soldier now?"

Hugging herself with thin arms, Frieda Brössler takes no part in the argument. She does not notice the mule that snorts and shifts uneasily in the stall below. She does not listen to her husband or her son. The voice she hears is her mother-in-law's. "De optimists, dey died in a vork camp . . ."

When Rivka was widowed a second time, Frieda and Herrmann were pleased and proud to make a home for her. The Brösslers were respected members of the community. Herrmann gave liberally to civic charities and raised funds for the restoration of a lovely old theater in the center of Vienna. Duno and Liesl went to a wonderful school, and Steffi would, too, when she was old enough. Their large, airy apartment was filled with sunlight, art, books. Frieda held lovely receptions for Europe's finest musicians and most famous singers. Important Christians attended her parties. And yet, whenever things went especially well for Herrmann—when he had just booked a popular opera company or presented an exceptionally good *Liedersänger* in a concert the critics loved, Rivka's stories would begin again.

"We had nice house, nice furn'ture. Just like you and my Herrmann," she'd say, her voice tired and thready. "My fader, he alla time helped oders. Good man! Everybody like my fader! But when

I got t'ree year old, dey come und took everyt'ing. Even fork! Even spoon! Dey put us ina keller. My mudder, my fader, my bruders. Dey put us ina keller, and set fire! Set fire, with us ina keller. Gott safe us wit' a rainstorm, 'n we got out, but dey want us to burn."

"We have no Cossacks in Austria, Mama Brössler—"

"Den dey come again anodder time, but we got not'in' for steal. Not even fork! Not even spoon! So dey kill my oncle. Jus' spite. Spite absolutely! 'Cause we got not'in for steal."

"It's not like that here," Frieda would soothe.

"Den dey come again. By dat time, my fader, my bruders, my first husban', dey got nice li'l business, moving furn'ture. Wit' horse, wit' cart. Nice li'l business. Dey come again. Take everyt'ing. My mudder had li'l box of jewel'ry. Li'l box," Rivka would say, palms a few centimeters apart. "Dey take dat. Take furn'ture—we sleepin' on da floor. Take horse, take cart! How we 'sposed to live?"

"That was the Communists, Mama Brössler. The Communists will never take power in Austria."

"Dey'll come again," Rivka would say. "A Jew got somet'ing, goyim gonna take it. Dey don't care 'bout dat Jesus. Dey just t'ieves and murderers."

"Mama Brössler, Vienna isn't like the Ukraine—"

"You an optimist," Rivka would tell her sadly, "jus' like my husban'. We start over. We be all right. But dey arrest him. For not'in! For not'in, absolutely! Dey take my husban' 'n my bruders to Siberia. De optimists—dey all died in a vork camp."

Herrmann's voice cuts through Frieda's memories. "Duno, if we don't turn ourselves in before the deadline, we're *Vogelfrei*— birds free for the shooting! Anybody can denounce us for a reward. We have no papers. We don't speak Italian."

"I do!"

"*Buon giorno? Arrivederci?* How far is that going to—"

"I know a lot of Italian. I learned from the carabinieri, and from the farmer. Papa, we don't have to give up. We can go back to the mountains."

"I don't wanna go up the mountain again," Steffi wails.

"*Mutti,* make them stop!" Liesl pleads.

The Brösslers have been fortunate. The Calabrian soldier found them a farmer who was willing to give them food and shelter. The mule and two cows warm the barn at night. Not even the girls complain about the smell anymore. A week, maybe two, and the Germans would leave the valley, that's what everyone expected.

This afternoon, the farmer brought them a newspaper from Borgo San Mauro. Maps and numbers and arrows told the story: the Allies were bottled up at Salerno, far to the south. In the center of the front page was an article headlined UN PROCLAMA DEL COMANDO GERMANICO. Duno made a great show of reading it, probably guessing at most of the words. The same phrase appeared after a variety of offenses: *sará fucilato secondo la legge marziale.*

Then the farmer showed Herrmann a flyer printed in German and in Italian. "By 1800 hours, 28th September 1943, all Jews present in the district of Valdottavo must report to the German SS commanders at reception areas in Roccabarbena or in Borgo San Mauro. Those surrendering in accordance with this order will be resettled in the East, where work for adults and schools for children will be provided. After this deadline, Jews who fail to report will be shot on sight, as will be anyone upon whose premises they are found."

The farmer murmured something soothing as he laid a callused hand on Steffi's fine fair hair, looking across the valley, talking at length about Attilio. "He's talking about the Huns," Duno said confidently. "Attilio means Atilla."

When Herrmann looked up from the notice, the farmer sighed, "*Mondo cane, ne?*" Kneeling, he scratched the boot of Italy into the dirt with a stick. In the northwestern corner of the map, he drew a triangle pointing south. "Valdottavo," he said, looking toward the valley. A twisting line down the center of the triangle was declared Fiume San Leandro: Valdottavo's main river. A dot poked into the broad end of the triangle was Borgo San Mauro, the railhead town they could see. A bigger dot at the narrow end: the city of Roccabarbena.

"*I Tedeschi,*" the farmer said, drawing SS runes in the dirt, over and over. "Genova. Sant'Andrea. Savona. Roccabarbena. Cuneo. Milano. Torino." The farmer looked at Herrmann before making one last mark in the dirt: Borgo San Mauro.

Herrmann and Duno have been arguing ever since.

"If he wanted to denounce us, he would have already!" Duno yells.

"What if one of his grandchildren says something? What if he's got a neighbor with a grudge? Duno, if that farmer's shot because of us, it would be as though we pulled the trigger ourselves!"

"So we should put the gun to our own heads?"

"If we go now, nobody will be shot."

"You have a touching faith in the Nazis, Papa!"

Frieda looks up in time to see the flat of Herrmann's hand hit Duno's face. The boy's hair swings from his temples and falls around his ears. For a moment, her son is five years old again. Frieda closes her eyes to his stunned shock.

Chickens scratch and chuckle. Cows comment, their voices breaking comically: basso profundo into soprano. The rhythmic thunk of the farmer's ax does not falter. Firewood piled to the rafters, and still a need to lay in more. Clouds have settled like a woolen blanket over the valley. Mountain peaks gleam with snow.

"We're leaving tomorrow morning," Herrmann says raggedly. "Go now, and we live. Delay, and we'll be killed, and we'll take innocent people with us."

"Fine," Duno says at last, his voice lower than Frieda has ever heard it. "Go with the women and children, Papa. I'll take my chances in the mountains."

"Duno! Don't you dare walk away from me! *Duno!*"

Frieda does not realize that she is crying until Herrmann puts his arms around her. "He'll be back," her husband says. "I used to fight with my father all the time! He'll be back, Frieda." Herrmann gathers their youngest into his lap. "It won't be so bad," he tells the girls. "There'll be a kindergarten for you, Steffi—they won't make little children work. Liesl might have to, but you're a big, strong girl, aren't you, Liesl? We can get through this as long as we're together."

He smiles at Frieda, but she cannot rally. De optimists, she thinks. Dey died in a vork camp.

Tears hot on his stinging cheek, Duno clambers higher, determined to leave all evidence of human existence behind. He'll find a cave. He'll hunt and fish. He hates everyone he can think of, but most of all he hates his father. "Fuck you, Papa! Eat shit!" he yells, cursing aloud for the first time in his life. "Fight! Why won't you fight?"

Hands clawing, toes digging, he drives distance between himself and humiliation. We should have fought, right from the start, he thinks. Friends—people you really believed were your *friends*—stopped looking at you. Eyes skimmed past the star on your armband. They were embarrassed for you—*by* you.

Stop seeing real Jews, and it's easy for people to believe lies. Jews are lazy. Jews are ugly. Jews are evil. Day after day. Year after year. Jews are capable only of crime. Jews are only clever enough to cheat good Aryans. The mere presence of fat, hairy, bowlegged Jews fouled public swimming pools. Their hideous, misshapen faces were depraved and disgusting. The only right Jews had was to disappear from the face of the earth!

Legs aching, lungs bursting, he stops to catch his breath, and hears a faint roar that sounds like a river. Mouth gaping, he looks up. A small, hard avalanche peppers his face with stinging dust and pebbles. "Ow! Shit!" he cries, spitting and coughing as the dirt dances past. "Bastards! Shit-eating bastards!" he sobs. "Goddamned, shit-eating, goddamned Nazi bastards!"

When the crisis passes, he sucks in snot and wipes his eyes with grimy hands. Papa's right about one thing, he thinks bitterly. We're *Vogelfrei,* just like Steffi's stupid canary when it got loose. And how do you catch a cage bird, Papa? You close the door to keep it in one room. You draw the curtains over all but one window. Cage birds aren't strong. You chase them from one place to another until they're tired. They move toward the only light in the room, and sit on that windowsill. Then you just scoop them up. Somewhere there's a happy Nazi shit eater thinking, Stupid Jews. Chase them till they can't run anymore, then offer them a school! They'll trample one another trying to turn themselves in!

He can see Colle Aurelio across the main valley. The pass seems impossibly high, nestled between two great mountains. Shadowed gullies and crevasses look small from here, but Duno knows their immensity with the muscles of his legs and the air of his lungs. How, without wings, had anyone crossed such monstrous terrain?

Put one foot in front of the other, he tells himself fiercely. That's how!

The mountains turn gold, then pink, then blue. Bone-rattling cold sweeps downward, sinking off the snowfields. Sweat chills on his skin, raising chicken flesh. "I'll never go back," he says aloud, to harden his resolve. The life he knew is over. He will never take over his father's business or have a bourgeois apartment or buy season tickets at the ballet or have money in the bank. He won't give parties for people who eat his food and mock him behind his back, then spit in his face and laugh when he's kicked into the gutter.

He won't miss his family either. He is done with them. Forever. But he wishes he'd brought some food.

CASA DI GOLETTA
VALDOTTAVO, PIEMONTE

Battista Goletta sets another chunk of beechwood on the stump. "They left a few days ago. I said I'd bring 'em across the valley to my cousin Attilio. He'd've taken 'em. They didn't understand what I was saying, I guess." Battista brings the ax down. "Their boy, Duno, ran off to join the Communists. More balls than brains."

The soldier shifts despondently from foot to foot. "Have you heard anything about an old gentleman with a girl about sixteen, signore? I left them in a *carbonaro* shack up here somewhere. I've been trying to find them, but all the ravines look the same."

Battista leans over to toss a few more splits onto the pile of firewood. "There's *ebrei* over with the Cesanos. No girls, though."

"Madonna. I hope they didn't turn themselves in."

"A lot did," Battista says. The valley was filled with families living in barns, under bridges, in the open. Worn-out women, trying to hold families together. Men, pauperized and impotent. Kids sick, scared of bugs and snakes. Those were the ones who gave up.

"I found a priest," the soldier says. "He said he'll help if I can find them."

"Don Leto?" The boy nods. Battista grunts, unsurprised. "The padre's a Red, just like my idiot cousin Attilio. Landlords. Communists. Priests." He brings the ax onto another piece of wood. "None of 'em work, and they all want something for nothing! Me? I work for everything I got, and I don't owe nobody nothing. Damned Communists . . . They came through here a couple of days ago. Stole two wheels of cheese. Left me a receipt! Thieves." His tone changes. "She pretty?" The soldier frowns. "*La ebrea!* Your sweetheart! Is she pretty?"

"She's not my sweetheart," the boy mumbles, "but she's pretty."

Sweating even in the chill of autumn, Battista swabs his tanned bald head with a thin rag. His sister spun its wool the spring before he married Rosa. His mother wove the fabric, and made a shirt for his wedding after the grape harvest was in. He wore that shirt for the baptisms of his children, and on every Sunday for fifteen years. It served for work ten years more, and then Rosa made squares of it. Carefully hemmed, the handkerchief will do another decade of duty in Battista's pocket. "Looks don't last," he warns the boy. "Can she work?"

"She knows a lot of languages. She could be a teacher."

Battista snorts. "Most of what's wrong in the world is because of educated goddamned fools." Far below, a train whistle wails. They can see the window of its locomotive flash as it pulls domed wooden cattle cars along the riverbank. Battista sends his ax thunking into the stump. "What's your name, kid?"

"Cicala, signore. Santino."

"You hungry, Cicala? You could work it off."

Santino walks over to the toolshed, stretching and bending to study its construction. Battista kneads his aching back, and sees the farm with a stranger's eyes: house, barn, outbuildings, fences, all built with flat stacked stone. Walls buckle where the ground has settled away from them. The door to the toolshed hangs on one hinge. The barn roof has been patched and patched and patched.

"Whoever built this skipped the hearting," Santino calls. "It's cheaper not to, but you have to pack the wall's core, or it's got no strength. That's why you're getting water damage."

In the thirties, this place produced ten times what the Golettas could eat, and Battista's name was listed among the Cavalieri del Lavoro: the Knights of Labor. Mussolini himself honored the virtue of men whose patriotism was measured in productivity and sweat. Now Battista does all he can to keep the place up, but it's a losing battle. "Me and Rosa, we're alone," he explains. "Boys're in the army. Girls're married, troubles of their own. I'm getting old." He claws thoughtfully under a whiskered chin. "I could use some help. Can't pay you anything, but you'd have food and a roof against the snow."

The ugly young face contorts uncertainly. "I told Claudia I'd come back."

"Keep wandering around the countryside looking for her, Germans'll pick you up . . . Course, if you were here working, I could ask around."

Battista's hair is gray, what's left of it. His skin is rutted as a road, but those shoulders are heavy with fifty-odd years of ax-muscle. Santino shakes his head. "They'd grab you, too, signore."

Slyly, Battista stoops and twists, manufacturing a hump worthy of Rigoletto. "A crippled old shit like me, Your Grace?" he whines. "No good to anyone, Your Honor. Just a poor old *cafone* trying to sell a few vegetables." With a pirate's grin, Battista straightens, claps Santino on the shoulder, and jerks his head toward the house. "Rosa!" he yells. "You've got men to feed! C'mon, kid. Let's go eat."

October 1943

Even before his father left, Werner Schramm had a plan to escape his mother and her moods. "Black moods in the Black Forest!" his father called them, after four or five beers. "What've you got to moon about, woman?" He never waited for an answer. "Millions dead in the war! Millions dead of influenza. Who gives a shit about one worthless girl? And fix yourself up, for Chris'sake! Startin' to look like that nun-sister of yours! Ugly old hag."

Everything was fine before Irmgard was born. Well, Papa drank and Mama had her moods, but Irmgard made everything worse. Putting her away didn't help. One morning, Papa boarded the train to Freiburg and never came home. Everyone said, "Werner, you're the man of the family now," but he wasn't. He was the son who was left behind, and in his opinion, the blame lay squarely on Irmgard's huge and freakish head. "Water on the brain," a city doctor said. It would kill her someday, but not soon enough to save her family.

Werner was damned if he'd end up a debt-ridden farmer with a loony mother in the back bedroom and a freak sister in an institution. He had bigger plans than that. He was good at drawing— he'd won a prize at school. His aunt the nun encouraged him to study art. For months, he daydreamed of a Parisian garret where he would paint, unburdened by secondhand sadness. Gradually, Florence replaced Paris in the geography of his imagination. He got top marks in Latin; Italian would be easier than French.

At seventeen, he got a job at the ski lodge and distinguished himself by working harder than any of the aging veterans drifting through the countryside hoping for a handout. Werner washed dishes. Shoveled snow. Cleaned privies. Anything was preferable to his mother's frantic loneliness. For a year he saved in secret, and when he had enough he left, like his father before him: at dawn, without saying good-bye. "One way, third-class, to Florence," he told the Freiburg ticketmaster.

Two days later, he stepped down onto a platform at the Stazione Centrale di Firenze: reborn, sui generis, in Florence, Mother of genius, where painting and sculpture and architecture flourished with jungle luxuriance in the warm Italian sun. A friendly carabiniere told him of a pensione whose owner spoke some German. Schramm paid for two nights, and crossed an inner courtyard where Della Robbia's terra-cotta putti presided over an arcaded square designed by Brunelleschi.

Too excited to rest, he dropped his rucksack on the bed and made a dash for the Uffizi, where art books and holy cards came to life. He gaped at *David,* stunned first by the sculpture's size, then by its power. Altarpieces by Cimabue, Duccio, and Giotto competed for attention with paintings by Raphael, Caravaggio, and Botticelli, which themselves battled bronzes by Cellini and Donatello.

That summer, Schramm did chores at the pensione in return for meals and an attic bed. His thoroughness and energy earned the owner's praise and a few extra lire, which he spent on drawing lessons from an old woman who claimed she was a *principessa* fallen on hard times. She tutored him in Italian, too, and whenever he could, Schramm practiced conversation with the hotel maid, whose angular face, soft breasts, and complete indifference stoked a sexual heat he was too awkward to reveal.

The days grew shorter. Rooms were closed, one by one. The chambermaid was let go for the off-season. With the kitchen ashes hauled out and the coal fire banked, Schramm was free most afternoons and wandered the city munching roasted chestnuts purchased in paper cones. He hiked the hills of Fiesole and Settignano. The Ponte Vecchio, Boboli Gardens, and Lungarno Corsini became his private domain.

The Florentine winter proved cold and misty. Narrow streets and small piazze turned dark and dirty gray. With the tourists gone, there was no one to look down on. Loneliness set in.

Florence taught Werner Schramm many things, the most significant of which was that he had no real talent. Embarrassed to go home, he waited until his nineteenth birthday to send his mother a postcard, giving his address. The response was a telegram from his aunt's convent. "Regret to inform you of your mother's death. Come home. Irmgard needs you."

His aunt and another nun were waiting for him at the Freiburg station. They boarded the local back to Hinterzarten, where he laid wildflowers on his mother's grave and learned that shame was worse than grief. That spring, he sold the farm for little more than an apple and an egg, but he cleared his family's debts. Finally, no excuses left, he went to visit Irmgard.

"The Church will tell you that your mother's suicide was sin," Irmgard's doctor said. "I say the sin is on the heads of those who permit hopeless cripples to drive strong, healthy Germans to despair! It is a perversion of medicine and nature when civilization allows the health of the race to be undermined by these useless wretches." Silver-haired and kindly, with the high forehead and lucid eyes of a scholar, the physician placed his hand on Schramm's shoulder, but looked past him toward a better future. "Someday institutions like this will disappear. Money and effort will cease to be lavished on the weakest and the worst. When you return to Freiburg, you must look up Professor Hoche! Ask about the paper he wrote with Karl Binding. It is persuasive, my boy. Persuasive!"

That summer, his aunt arranged for a scholarship, and Werner matriculated at the University of Freiburg. "If you can't be an artist, you can be art's apostle," she said, urging her nephew to study art history. For want of a better idea, he began his courses, working with diligence if not passion. He inquired about a garret on Goethestrasse. The rent was criminally high, but he was still capable of romantic delusions about artistic poverty, and the *Jugendstil* house was breathtaking: all twining vines and whiplash curves, and slender stained-glass girls with damselfly wings. He did yard work in exchange for Sunday dinners with the family.

At one such dinner he met Elsa Rombach—round and cheerful, with a wholesome prettiness that helped him forget the Florentine chambermaid's more complicated beauty. Elsa's father was an industrialist who disapproved of artists, poets, and other lives unworthy of life. Herr Rombach forbade Elsa to see Schramm, but she lied and made excuses, thrilled by her own cool daring. Werner waited for her at Zur Trotte, where a half liter of Viertele Silvaner could last all afternoon. Around them, students talked earnestly of blood, leadership, strength, soul, heritage, health, and race. Elsa read Rilke aloud, and Werner filled sketchbooks with sentimental portraits of a good Catholic girl who wouldn't put out until he married her.

That year he began to see the future more clearly. Or, rather, he heard the future's voice every night on the radio. Full of faith, full of emotion. Ringing like a bell, calling the masses to worship. Promising a whole generation—a whole nation!—what it yearned for. A task, a meaning. A greatness that would redeem misery and defeat.

Moved, inspired, Werner Schramm resolved to follow the Führer's example. He would give up dreams of artistry and serve the German people. With an introduction from Irmgard's doctor and an energy he hadn't felt since he first left home, Werner made an appointment with Professor Hoche, who even helped him with the paperwork required to change his field of study from art history to medicine.

"I am so proud of you!" Elsa squealed when Werner told her the news. "Papa will make sure you have the right connections when you go into private practice!"

"Professor Hoche thinks I should do research," Werner said cautiously. He'd never mentioned Irmgard to the Rombachs. "There were so many defectives born after the *Diktat* of Versailles. People believe such defects result from bad breeding, but if they were a result of starvation after the Great War, good nutrition could prevent them in the future."

Elsa pouted prettily. "You sound like a scientist already!" Then the idea sank in, and her guiltless, guileless face lit up. "Oh, *Lieber,* yes! Why, you'd be contributing to the health of the whole nation! Papa could never object to a son-in-law who did that!"

Years have passed, and Werner Schramm is in a garret once again, but artistic dreams play no part in his choice of quarters now. He needs a place to hide, and this attic is the cheapest he could find. "View of the sea," the advertisement promised, without mentioning, "only if you sit in the musty upholstered chair near the southern window, lean onto your left elbow, and squint."

From there, he can just barely see an island in Sant'Andrea's harbor. "What is that big building on the island?" he asked his landlady after his first night under her roof.

"*Il lazzaretto di incurabili,*" Signora Usodimare said, crossing herself. "A hospital for incurables. Mostly tuberculars, poor things. You shouldn't smoke so much, signore! It weakens the lungs. You could get consumption, you know."

"Yes," he said, making his face bland. "I'm trying to quit."

To change the subject, he asked her for something to read. Proudly, she offered a history of Sant'Andrea, which he studies daily, a thick dictionary at his side. The lazzaretto, he's learned, was built to isolate victims of the Levantine plagues that Renaissance merchants imported to Europe, along with spices, silks, and ivory. During a single fifteenth-century epidemic, over 150,000 Sant'Andresi died. In hope of a cure, Ludovico Usodimare sailed off to raid Montpellier, determined to capture the mummified body of Saint Roch—a holy relic, sovereign against plague. Alas, the Venetians arrived first and stole the Frenchman's corpse before Usodimare could. A practical man, the prince did some pillaging on his way home and acquired, among other things, a golden salver. This plate, he declared, had once carried the severed head of John the Baptist, and he built the Basilica di San Giovanni Battista to house his souvenir.

"At a stroke," the breathless author informs Schramm, "Ludovico Usodimare surpassed Andrea Doria of Genoa, who only had a church, and miraculously reduced Sant'Andrea's mortality from plague ever after." Natural selection, Schramm replies, setting the book aside. The most susceptible had died off. The surviving population was resistant.

"My late husband was an Usodimare," his landlady reminds Schramm whenever there is the smallest conversational opening to this topic. Dependent on her discretion, Schramm refrains from commenting on the extent to which ancestral splendor has diminished. Like everything else in this charmless city, his room is cramped and innocent of taste. Time and a leaky roof have been unkind to the walls. A threadbare rug adds little warmth to the uneven plank floor. The mattress is lumpy and thin, the linens frayed. The bulb in his reading lamp is of such low wattage as to be useless.

When the sun sinks behind the roofline of the apartment

house next door, Schramm reaches for a bottle and settles back to watch the sky darken mercifully over the scene below. Even before the bombing, Sant'Andrea was a Frankenstein monster sutured together from the decaying ruins of its millennia. Bits of sarcophagi, looted from Egypt, protrude from massive medieval walls. Fluted Roman columns support Gothic arcades fitted with Renaissance portals. Allied bombs have added debris to the architectural mess.

On Saturday, Schramm starts drinking a little earlier than usual. When he's dosed himself sufficiently to control his cough, he dresses in the ill-fitting suit Signora Usodimare purchased at his request. The cinema is half a block away, with no checkpoints to pass, no document inspection at the box office.

By the time Schramm has slipped into the last row of seats, the house lights have dimmed and the *avanspettaculo* has begun. Dancers, comedians, and singers perform before the film in a sort of cabaret act. The jokes are in dialect, but Schramm enjoys the laughter and can follow some of the song lyrics. The show ends with a tenor dressed as an Alpino. Longing for home, and love for Mamma, ensure a standing ovation for the troupe.

The stage darkens. Pulleys sweep dusty velvet curtains aside, exposing the shimmering screen. The latest Film Luce newsreel flickers and solidifies. Audience reaction provides Schramm with an informal referendum on current events. Scenes of Italian humiliation are met with sullen silence. German tanks and armored cars roll into Rome through Saint Paul's Gate. Opposition by adolescent Socialists and middle-aged civilians armed with cobblestones is crushed. The Wehrmacht occupies four-fifths of Italy. Italian territories in France, Yugoslavia, Greece, and Salonika are part of Greater Germany now.

Mussolini's appearance is met with hisses. Snatched from internal exile by SS commandos, *il Duce* wears a dark topcoat and a jaunty hat, looking dapper if a bit dazed when he climbs out of a small plane to shake the Führer's hand.

The scene changes. Schramm straightens. Even the Sant'Andresi, no strangers to Allied bombing, gasp at the result of an American raid on Frankfurt. Burning buildings seem to melt, their bricks pouring through the air, dust rising like a waterfall's

mist. It's enough to make a mason weep, centuries of work reduced to smoking heaps of wreckage. In low tones of outrage, the
narrator vilifies heartless Allied bombardiers for causing thousands of civilian deaths.

The screen brightens. "A sea battle rages in the Aegean sunshine!" the narrator announces. "Defeatist-Traitor Badoglio met
Eisenhower aboard the HMS *Nelson,* but an expected Allied landing in the Gulf of Genoa has not materialized." In the south, Italian Republican units have inflicted five thousand British
casualties at Salerno, but the Axis has lost Pompeii and Naples
after weeks of vicious infantry combat and nonstop dogfights over
southern airspace. "*Coraggio,* countrymen! The German Reich has
come to embattled Italy's aid! The American Fifth Army and the
British 56th Division are stalled at the Volturno! There will be an
all-out defense of Rome! The Gustav Line will hold!" Almost as
an afterthought, the narrator concludes, "The Red Army has retaken Smolensk."

No news of Freiburg, but even Schramm can name the targets.
The Kronenbrücke bridge. The *Hauptbahnhof* and the railroad maintenance yards. Fauler's foundry, Grether's heavy-equipment factory. Herr Rombach's ironworks. Fabric and thread manufacturers
like Mez and Krummeich will be hit, to deprive the Reich of uniforms. "Stay away from anything that might attract raids," Schramm
writes to Elsa in his mind. "Don't believe what you're told about the
war, or about me. Someday I will send for you, and Klaus and
Erwin." But no—there must be nothing incriminating, nothing that
could be held against one's family. "*Mein Mädel,* my darling girl, take
our boys to the countryside, where life is healthier. Never believe
me fallen. One day, we will be reunited." Better, he thinks. Something any patriotic soldier might send his wife. He wonders if it will
be enough to disappear, or if he should try to fake his death. He
wonders if he'll live long enough to bother with fakery.

The cinema crowd stirs, murmurs, and settles in to watch the
featured film. *La cena delle beffe* is a popular costume drama in which
Good (Amedeo Nazzari) defeats Evil (Osvaldo Valenti) for the
sake of Beauty (Clara Calamai). Even Schramm has seen the
movie twice. Celluloid is scarce. Not even directors like Blasetti
make new movies anymore.

Schramm waits until the much-anticipated moment when

Beauty bares the first bosom ever to grace Italian screens. While Signorina Calamai absorbs the cheering crowd's attention, Schramm gets up to leave, but the change in posture upsets the precarious balance in his chest, and the coughing starts again. Three rows up, someone twists in his seat. Schramm freezes. It's the man from the church that first day. What was his name? Lorenzo? Something like that . . . Renzo!

Touching his temple with one finger in a small salute, Renzo turns back to the film. Hurrying outside, Schramm finds the nearest alley, and doubles over to retch up phlegm. Wet-eyed with exertion, he is too preoccupied to be surprised when the Italian appears at his side and exclaims quietly, "Herr Doktor, what a terrible suit! Care for a drink?"

Schramm nods gratefully, and Renzo leads the way through a bewildering rats' nest of dark and twisting *carrugi*, circumventing checkpoints and roadblocks with casual changes of direction. All evidence of occupation disappears as they near the docks. The Gestapo has conceded this neighborhood to the wiry men in cotton singlets who loiter, silent and suspicious, at every turn. Fishmongers and butchers stand in doorways, canvas aprons splashed with rusting crimson. Motionless knives drip blood onto cobblestones. Renzo receives and returns nods and gestures of greeting. Not even the whores smile at strangers like Schramm.

The tavern is small, dismally lit. Longshoremen hunch over low mounds of cheap food. Sailors' thumbs hook the edges of plates in memory of meals tossed by waves. The earthy smells of tripe, dried cod, and chickpeas mingle with the tang of sweat. Renzo takes a small table in the back. The barman delivers a bottle of grappa and two small glasses. Schramm chokes on the first harsh sip, then sighs as its comforting warmth relaxes his chest.

Renzo's drinking is steady and silent. When the bottle's contents are visibly diminished, Schramm sets his own glass down. "Keep that up," he warns, "and you won't see forty."

"Promise?" Renzo wipes his mouth with the back of his hand. "And who are you to talk?"

"Point taken," Schramm says. "What day is it?" he asks.

Renzo gives the matter thought. "Saturday?"

"No! The date! What's the date?"

This takes longer. "October eighth. I think."

"*Verdammte Scheisse.* I got a telegram last month," Schramm whispers, leaning close. "All leaves canceled. Report to your unit immediately! Jesus. October eighth . . . That's a whole month of not reporting immediately."

Closing his eyes, he concentrates on how much better his chest feels, and how glad he is to be here and not in Russia. "Once," he says, "when I was at the front, we set up a field hospital in a town just taken by a panzer division. There were five or ten Reds around every house. Guts spilling out of bellies. Brains drizzling out of skulls. In the middle of the street, there was a forearm. Completely unharmed, except it was all by itself. No body."

Renzo nods and pours.

"On the other side of the street, there was a naked leg, sticking straight up out of the snow. Rigid, like an obelisk!" Schramm takes as deep a breath as he can. "Most of the Russians were dead, but there were wounded. One was firing so wildly, no one could get near."

Renzo's vague eyes come up. "You shot him?"

"No, but I didn't treat him."

"Would've been suicide."

"I knew you'd understand!" Schramm makes a strangled gagging sound, and for once the cough loses a skirmish. "Another man's clothes were on fire," he says, clearing his throat. "When the flames got to his ammunition pouch, it exploded. I was five meters away. It was a miracle I wasn't killed."

"No miracle for the poor bastard with the ammo pouch." Renzo scrubs rhythmically at his face. "God only works for the survivors."

"There was another man—shot through the eyes, from one side to the other. He moaned and moaned, and his face . . . Wounds steam in the cold. Like soup. Did you know that?"

"You told me before."

"I expect I did. I talk too much when I'm drunk." Schramm slumps in the warped wooden chair, fingers curled around his emptied glass. "Nothing I say shocks you," he realizes. "You're a veteran, aren't you."

"Abyssinia," Renzo says, enunciating carefully. "Combat pilot."

Schramm snickers. "Combat! Four hundred crack Italian pilots in the world's best planes, sent to fight the Abyssinian air force—

which consisted of eleven planes, as I recall, only eight of which were actually capable of flight."

Renzo's glassy eyes turn cold. "They had a million men under arms. Mountains favor the defenders. We had superiority in the air, and we used it. That war wasn't the mismatch the British said it was. Fucking League of Nations," he mutters. "If they hadn't slapped sanctions on us, Italy never would've joined the Axis."

"What was it like?" Schramm asks. "To fly, I mean. I've never been in an airplane."

"You ski?"

"Notschrei's about three kilometers from where I grew up."

"Ever jump?"

Schramm nods.

"With a small plane, it's like that, except you don't come down. Single-engine trainers, they leap into the air. And then . . . you're in a different world. On a cloudy day, you get up around two thousand meters, break through into sunshine—" He rubs his forehead with one hand. "Bombers are different. Like flying freight trains."

Schramm tries to imagine it, but all that comes to mind are newsreel memories of Mussolini's inglorious African adventure. Black bodies smeared with ocher, running barefoot into battle against machine guns. Chieftains dressed in leopard skins, with lion cubs on leashes. Men waving curved swords and wooden pitchforks at airplanes strafing them with—

Struck by a thought, Schramm stares at the man across the table. "You're a *Jew!*" he whispers, astonished.

After a long moment, Renzo asks, "What makes you think so?"

"You're healthy. You're a combat pilot. Your country is—was— at war. You're not in uniform. Ergo: you are a Jew."

"And *you,*" Renzo says with a grin of warning, "are a deserter."

Schramm's laugh is quickly lost to a sharp, shallow cough. "It's beginning to look that way," he admits soggily, pulling out another handkerchief.

"Jesus, Schramm! Why didn't you take medical leave?"

Schramm tries again, and this time he manages the long, vigorous gasp required to shift a heavy clot of phlegm. "I'm not sick. I'm dying."

Working it out, Renzo moves back in his chair. "Tuberculosis."

"I fooled myself at first, and then . . . Well, the Reich was desperate for doctors in Russia. Now even amateurs can diagnose the condition!"

"I've seen it before. My father. A friend's uncle." Renzo's brow wrinkles in a muzzy effort to understand. "Why don't you just go home?"

"I'd be executed."

"For deserting, sure, but you must have known for months."

"Time, my friend, is rationed quite severely for the Reich's consumptives. The final solution to the tuberculosis problem. Saves several Reichsmarks a day on hospital care." Seeing no comprehension, Schramm waves the topic off. "Why the hell did *you* go to war? Italy is a beautiful country, filled with beautiful women, beautiful art, beautiful food. Why travel thousands of kilometers to the arse-end of Africa, just to bomb naked savages armed with spears?"

Renzo looks away. "It was . . . complicated. There was a girl my family wanted me to marry." He shudders briefly. "And also the girl I was—" He clears his throat, and Schramm nods with avuncular understanding. "And there was another girl. She wouldn't have me."

"Your true love!" Schramm brightens. "She was a Catholic!"

"There were religious differences." Renzo shrugs. "Anyway, joining the air force was patriotic. And convenient."

"Shall I tell you why young men love war?" Schramm offers dreamily. "In peace, there are a hundred questions with a thousand answers! In war, there is only one big question with one right answer." He pours them each another shot, emptying the bottle. "War smashes all our petty problems and sweeps the shards into one huge, patriotic pile. Going to war makes you a man. It is emotionally exciting and morally restful."

"I believed the lies," Renzo says, leaning back in his chair. "Like every other fool from the Alps to Sicily, I thought I had a share in the glory that was Rome. Mussolini screwed Italy with history, but it wasn't always rape." He reaches out to tap Schramm's glass with his own. "Some of us bent over."

"Would you like to know what the German lie is?" Schramm whispers. "We are the nation of Beethoven and Schiller and

Goethe! We are a great people. But—" Schramm leans close. "Did I compose the *Eroica*? What poetry have I written? Race isn't talent! Greatness isn't just... being German. Who could believe nonsense like that? I'll tell you who! Chicken farmers. Shoemakers. Grocery clerks. Academic drudges. Bureaucratic hacks."

"Put ordinary shitheads in impressive uniforms, give them guns and permission to use them, they'll shoot anyone who threatens their illusions," Renzo agrees. "So what made you put the uniform on?"

Schramm digs out his wallet, extracts a photo. "That's my Elsa with Klaus and Erwin. You should've seen her before she thickened up." He passes the picture across the table. "Lovely girl. And we made strong, handsome children. Sturdy, my two boys! Perfect little Aryans. I joined the party because I wanted what the Führer wanted. I wanted German children to have a better childhood than my generation had after the Great War. They'd have good, nourishing, unadulterated food—wholemeal bread, fresh vegetables! The state would make industries clean up the poisons they were spewing into the air and the water."

"An idealist," Renzo groans. "The most dangerous kind of criminal!"

"Doctors would transcend the selfishness of treating single patients. We'd be physicians to the *Volk!* There'd be no disease, no deformity. No madness, no perversion or divorce. No unemployment—"

"And no Jews?"

"No drunks either!" Schramm sobers a bit. "I knew a Jew in Freiburg. He had a bookstore on Holbeinstrasse... You always hear that Jews are money mad, but—"

"—generally from people who borrow money."

"He always gave me the whole year to pay for my textbooks. He was very decent about it."

"Jews are simply members of the human race." After a thoughtful pause, Renzo adds, "I can think of no worse insult."

"There are plenty of people who can," Schramm warns. "They never saw you. They don't know your name. They don't know anything about you, but they *hate* you. They hate your mother, they hate your sister, they hate your cousin's little baby boy."

Schramm shakes his head. "I never understood the logic. You're Communists to a man, but you own all the banks. You're subhuman, but you're running the world."

Renzo leans over the table. "Never underestimate how soothing it is to have someone else to blame. If Jews didn't exist, someone would have to invent us."

"Oh, I don't know," Schramm says judiciously. "There're always the Jesuits. Or Freemasons."

Renzo drinks off his grappa in a single searing swallow and sets the glass gently on the table. "Secret Jews," he declares, belching. "Every last one of them."

Schramm crosses his arms on the table and leans against them to ease the pressure building in his lungs. "I barely made it through the *Physicum,*" he confesses. "The other students had no fears about their abilities. They made the same mistakes as I did," he says, "but if a procedure went wrong? The patient was weak—a poor specimen. I was afraid all the time, but I had a wife, children, so I kept on. When half the doctors in Germany were fired for being Jewish, a lot of doors opened to mediocrities like me."

Renzo looks at him for a long moment. "At least you're honest."

"Well, my ambitions have diminished. I retain not the slightest desire to improve the world! I just want to live until this fucking war is over," Schramm says, voice fraying. "I want to see my family before I die."

Balancing his chair on its back legs, Renzo retreats into his thoughts, while Schramm's own mind empties of longing and regret. He closes his eyes, drifting in the lovely twilight liquor bestows. Breathing is easy, he thinks. In. Out. In. Out . . .

Renzo's chair levels with a thump. "What would it take?"

Schramm rouses. "What?"

"What would you need? To live until you can see your family again."

Shocked into near sobriety, Schramm studies the unmoving face, trying to read the bones, the eyes, the mouth. "You're serious?" Renzo nods, and Schramm tries to think. "A place to stay, someplace quiet. Up in the mountains—cold, dry air. Plain food, but a lot of it. Nursing—if I get too sick to care for myself."

"What about contagion? If people've already been exposed—?"

"I can't do them much more harm. And there was a study last

year in Denmark—the bacillus is airborne. Sunlight kills it." I might not die, he thinks. I might see my boys again . . . "If there are windows, open air, that would be best for all of us."

Renzo's glass rises. "To pretty wives and healthy children," he declares with drunken decisiveness. "I'll see what I can do."

VALDOTTAVO
NEAR FRAZIONE SANTA CHIARA

Bearded and filthy, Albert Blum peers through the gap between Santino's blanket and the shack's doorpost. Claudette stirs. "Papa?" she asks drowsily. "Was that a hawk?"

"Quiet!" he whispers. "Don't move!"

Her dream hawk's high cry resolves into the piercing voice of a young girl. Claudette scrambles to her feet. "Someone's coming!"

Outside, the meadow is silvery with frost, autumn wildflowers dead or dying. Thick with bulky skirts and lumpy layered sweaters, the girl is only a few steps ahead of a stocky, scowling woman. "Mamma says you shouldn't stay here anymore!" the girl calls, waving frantically. "I knew it was wrong, but—"

"I should cut you in pieces!" the woman shouts. "I should kill you right now!"

Claudette clutches Albert's arm. "Papa, that lady's got a gun!"

"Claudette! Please! I'm trying to understand!"

The language is some peasant dialect. He catches words and phrases, but not enough to be sure, and then—

The woman yanks the blanket aside and lifts the gun stock to her shoulder. Claudette screams. Stubby thumb still tensed on the shotgun's hammer, the woman's shrewd brown eyes travel from the outline of Claudette's small bosom to her tattered trousers and disintegrating shoes. A slow smile appears.

"That's not a *boy!*" Shifting the shotgun to the crook of her arm, the woman reaches out to smack her own daughter in the back of the head. The blow is glancing, but enough to register the mother's dismay before she offers the same callused hand to Albert. "Lovera, Tercilla. An honor to meet you, signore."

Her Italian is slurry but understandable. It's her disposition that confuses him. "*Piacere, signora,*" he says uncertainly. "Blum, Alberto. And my daughter, Claudia."

"That's Bettina, signore. My youngest—she's thirteen." She nods at her daughter, who is gawping at Claudette with a mixture of awe and disappointment. Tercilla leans toward Albert. "I thought she was sneaking out to meet a boy. At her age, you can't be too sure, *ne?* Aren't you ashamed!" she shouts suddenly, rounding on Bettina. "Leaving these poor people out on the mountainside like animals!"

Dumbfounded, Albert accepts the shotgun Tercilla thrusts into his hands. Short even for a peasant, she stretches to pull the army blanket down from the door of the shack and glances around the tiny stone shelter. "Bettina, get that mess kit! And put that fire out. *Prego,* signore, there'll be hot food waiting." Draping the blanket over a short-boned arm, Tercilla asks, "Is this all you have?" Albert nods numbly. "*Poveretti,*" she says, shaking her head.

Claudette demands translation, and when Albert tells her that they're invited to dinner, triumph replaces terror. "I told you they wanted to help us! We're Jews," she tells the mother. "*Siamo ebrei, signora.*"

"*Sì, certo,*" Tercilla says, unconcerned. "The priest said, 'Help the Hebrews coming over the mountains, and don't tell anyone.'" Without warning, she spins around and yells, "He meant the Germans, not your mother!" Bettina giggles and ducks, evidently accustomed to maternal *Blitzkrieg.*

With a last quick inspection of the shack, Tercilla takes the shotgun back and waves the Blums outside. "If we meet anybody, pretend you're stupid. You were bombed out, *ne?*" She taps the side of her forehead: Not right in the mind. "Don't worry," she says over her shoulder when Albert hesitates. "The Germans're looking for Jews, but nobody up here will help those *bastardi.* To hell with them, and the chancred whores who bore 'em."

"What is she saying, Papa?" Claudette asks.

"They don't like the Germans," Albert reports drily.

Taking Claudette's hand, Bettina skips ahead chattering while Tercilla guides Albert to a gravelly trail a few hundred meters down the slope.

"That's my husband's cloak you're wearing," Tercilla says, helping Albert over a tree trunk that's fallen over the path. "Domenico was an Alpino during the last war."

Winded already, Albert sits on the log to catch his breath. "Signor Lovera fought the Austrians?"

"Two and a half years on the line," Tercilla says grimly, watching the girls round the next switchback. "And now? Gone again. My brother Primo, too. They were at the Wednesday market down in San Mauro. Germans came and took all the men! How're we supposed to farm with no men?"

Albert is willing to go on, but Tercilla doesn't notice.

"All I have now is Pierino," she says. "Four girls married off, just Bettina left to settle. But only one son." Cradling the shotgun against her thick little body, Tercilla looks east. "Valdottavo sent thirty-five boys to Russia last year. Two came back. My boy was one of them, *grazie a Dio,* but . . . The priest—Don Leto—he thought Pierino could be a teacher. No more," Tercilla says with quiet finality. She turns to meet another parent's eyes. "This war, signore? It ate my boy alive."

A dozen twisting switchbacks down the mountain, Santa Chiara hides snug in a deep ravine. Not big enough to be called a town, it consists of a haphazard collection of gray stone buildings pressed hard against a mule path. At the high end of the path, an artesian fountain burbles from a plain pipe, water caught in an unadorned stone basin. Along the ridges, narrow terraces crammed with kitchen gardens, grapevines, fruit trees slice into thin, stony soil.

Staircases ax-chipped from tree trunks angle up the outside walls to plank galleries that lead to haylofts or living quarters. Below, there are shelters for a cow or a few goats, a thick-wheeled wooden wagon, and a mule or ox to pull it. Stone oven-shacks squat near chicken coops, where their warmth can keep the birds laying if the winter's mild. Flimsy windbreaks surround stand-up latrines: two logs bridging a cesspit.

Inside each house, polenta bubbles in iron pots that hang on chains from tripods over open fires. Colorful pictures of Madonnas and martyrs brighten walls. Packed dirt floors are freshly swept. Twig brooms lean in corners, ready to whisk away footprints at the last moment. Every now and then, someone steps outside to yell, "Pierino! Any sign?"

Putting aside the book he's reading in the hayloft, Pierino stretches to see as far as possible up the mountain. He shakes his head.

So does his neighbor. The boy speaks so little, you'd think every word cost ten lire, although God knows his mother makes up for Pierino's silence. This morning, Tercilla caught her daughter sneaking out before dawn, and woke up everyone in Santa Chiara. There were accusations and denials, shouting and weeping. Bettina refused to talk at first, but no one stands up to Tercilla for long. "I was looking for mushrooms last month, and I saw an old gentleman and a boy with—"

"You snuck out in the dark to see a boy?" Tercilla yelled. "Did he touch you? I'll kill him!"

"I never even talked to him, Mamma! He never saw me! Don Leto said to help the *ebrei*—"

"*Ebrei?*" Tercilla wailed. "*Dio mio!* Those poor people! *O la Madonna!* How long have you known they were up there? Shame on you! Why didn't you tell me?"

Her neighbors have been cooking and cleaning ever since.

No one among them has ever met a Hebrew, but they've heard that Jews are educated, and dignified, and live in cities. It's a good thing the *ebrei* will stay with Tercilla. She has an oil lamp made of glass, and there are books because of Pierino, who can't do anything but read. Her windows are not just shuttered but glazed, with overlapping pieces of salvaged glass that Domenico carried up the mountain from a city after a bombing raid. Tercilla's brother Primo was a loafer, but Domenico was a match for her drive. He could fix anything, and had more ideas than most people.

Then again, he couldn't fix Pierino. And big ideas didn't save him or Primo from the Germans.

Suddenly one dog after another goes into a frenzy. Barefoot children race to meet the visitors. Hanging faded aprons on pegs, the women of Santa Chiara follow, jamming fists into the pockets of hand-knit cardigans. Old men—ropy with muscle and rank with sweat—arrive last, but in time to see the visitors make the last turn.

Surprise ripples through the assembly. Tercilla's guests are not the august, bearded sage and worrisome boy they've all expected, but a sickly gentleman—"*Poveretto!*"—leaning on Tercilla's arm, and—"Madonna! A girl in trousers!"

"Alberto Blum, Claudia Blum," Tercilla says gravely, when they draw even with Santa Chiara's burbling fountain, "I present to you my neighbors."

The Hebrews shake hands, murmuring, "*Piacere*" over and over as Tercilla introduces fifty-some members of the Brondello, Borgogno, Bruno, Cesano, Chiocchia, and Romano families. Then Pierino steps from the shadow of the barn.

"Your mother tells me you are a veteran and a scholar, Signor Lovera!" the Hebrew gentleman says.

Everyone murmurs admiration for the *ebreo*'s very nice Italian, a language they themselves speak only when dealing with officials. Pierino smiles shyly, and everyone notices with approval that Signor Blum does not offer his hand. Unfortunately, the signorina does, and when she realizes Pierino's right arm ends in a stump just below the elbow, she stammers an apology, which only makes things worse.

Covering embarrassment, mothers briskly dispatch girls for the food and wine. Little boys crinkle up and laugh when Tercilla urges the Hebrews to use the cesspit. Slaps are aimed at small heads, and the boys dance out of range.

When the Hebrews have washed up at the fountain, Tercilla leads the way to her home, stepping aside to allow the guests to pass first under the heavy wooden lintel. Unfamiliar with the smoky, shadowy little house, the Blums stand inside the doorway, letting their eyes adjust to the gloom. Tercilla eases past them and drags chairs toward a long plank table.

Cloaked from neck to ankle like ancient emperors, peasant patriarchs enter next. They settle on mismatched stools and chairs pulled close around the table. Drab in brown and tan, kerchiefed women follow, perching on the earthen platform that rings the room. Excited children run in and out, adding chicken-cackle giggles to the murmuring of adults.

Like a hen-shaped ballerina, Tercilla rocks onto the toes of her wooden clogs and reaches for a jug on the top shelf of a painted cupboard. "This will warm you," she says, pouring a generous measure of violet liquid into the only two glasses in the village.

"Hand this to Claudia, Bettina. It's *genzianella,* signore. We make it from a flower."

The gentleman's eyes widen above a smile when he tastes the liqueur. Hands folded over her broad middle, Tercilla nods with satisfaction and turns to the signorina, who takes a sip and gasps, and chokes, and coughs.

"*È bello!*" Claudia says hoarsely. "It's beautiful."

"*Bel-la!*" Bettina corrects. "*Genzianella è bella!*"

La ebrea repeats the lilting phrase, "*Genzianella è bella,*" as though it were a poem. Everyone applauds delightedly except Tercilla, who is looking at Bettina when she says, "Thank you for the flowers, Claudia."

"*Niente,* signora. It was nothing," Claudia replies before taking a more cautious sip of the powerful, sweet brandy. "We are *molte gra-zie* for the food."

"Another lie!" Tercilla hisses at her shamefaced daughter, but her eyes warm when she looks at Claudia.

The Chiocchia girls are the first to reappear, shyly placing two bowls of polenta before the *ebrei.* Everyone smiles when the signo-rina picks up a wooden spoon eagerly. Thin as a communion wafer, poor little thing. Her father places a hand on hers. "*Prego,*" he says, looking around the room. "You must be hungry as well."

A discussion in dialect, and the eldest among them speaks. "*Prego,*" Cesare Brondello replies firmly. "We ate enough, before. This is for you."

The gentleman surely feels awkward eating with an audience, but hunger takes over, and everyone is pleased by the small moans of appreciation he makes over each new offering. Roasted pota-toes and peppers appear, and bowls of tiny white beans called *denti del bambino,* baby's teeth. "No, no!" he cries. "This is too much!," which spurs the women to greater competition. Chestnut bread, eggs fried with mushrooms and onions, followed by a platter of misty-black grapes and petal-thin curls of hard, salty cheese that melt on the tongue.

At last, satisfied with a job well done, the bustling women move once more to the benches around the room, but they never stop working. Drop spindles are taken from deep pockets. Arms rise and fall rhythmically as locks of wool play out. Tercilla says some-thing to a sparrow-sized woman with wispy white hair, who leans over to nudge Cesare Brondello. The old man draws a folded woolen blanket from beneath his cloak and presents it to Albert. "My grandson is a prisoner in La 'Merica," he says.

A tired young woman wearing a man's padded jacket is next. "My husband served with Pierino. Tomasso's still in Russia." She puts a clean, worn shirt in Albert's hands and pulls a fussy three-year-old onto her hip.

One by one, representatives of each household come forward with a pair of knitted socks, a skirt for the signorina and a kerchief for her head, neatly mended trousers for her father.

Over and over, Albert Blum murmurs gratitude. "You are too kind," he says, stunned by their generosity.

"We all have boys in the army," Cesare's tiny wife explains. "Do unto others, *ne?* Maybe someone in Russia will be good to my grandson."

"*Grazie. Grazie tante,*" Albert says. "May God bring your soldiers safely home to you."

The oil lamps flicker, and Tercilla yanks a homespun blanket across a sapling mounted above the doorway to block the draft. Sitting at last on muscles thick from climbing, she looks taller somehow, though her feet don't touch the floor. "Signor Blum," she prompts, "Don Leto said the *ebrei* might be from Poland, but you speak such pretty Italian, like a Roman!"

"You are too kind, signora—my accent is terrible! We are Belgian. Before the war, I worked for a metal-ore company based in Antwerp. Every year, I traveled to Genoa and Istanbul and Nice to inspect the books of our partners. I was an accountant—"

"Istanbul!" someone cries.

"An accountant?" someone else asks.

The conversation becomes lively and general with questions about the price of firewood and eggs in France, the habits of Saracens, the likelihood that their landlord *il maggiore* Malcovato is cheating them on a shared chestnut crop. Albert answers as best he can, his voice flat and unmusical as he concentrates on finding words and remembering grammar. Often, his Italian fails him, and brief good-natured charades ensue, but he warms in the attention and dignity he is accorded, and feels as though he has awakened from a long bad dream. This is what I was like before the war, he realizes. A man of the world. Competent, respected.

Across the room, Tercilla's eyes meet Albert's and she lifts her chin toward his daughter. He glances back, and smiles. Huddled together on the fireplace platform, Claudette and the other children look like a litter of sleeping puppies, and the adults' voices drop.

When the talk turns to rumors of Mussolini's return, Albert's knowledge falters. He knows less than the peasants do, but that doesn't matter. The story of the mountain crossing is better than politics anyway, and his telling of it takes on the epic cadences of the *Odyssey*.

For all the adventure of the trek from Sainte-Gisèle, what concerns Tercilla and her neighbors most is the awful news that Albert's wife and sons are missing. There are murmurs of approval when he tells them about the carabiniere's kindness, but when they hear how Paula and the boys were put on an eastbound train, Pierino stands.

"What is it?" Albert asks him. "Why do you look at me like that?"

"He has seen terrible things," Tercilla tells everyone. "He cries in his sleep."

"Shut your face, woman!" Cesare snaps.

"What?" Albert asks again. "Pierino, what have you seen?"

The soldier's eyelids flutter. His mouth works. His throat spasms. The word, when it emerges, is like a sigh. "Hhh-hands" is all he says.

Day and night, the Italian troop transports chugged eastward, toward the Russian front. Whenever the train stopped for water and coal, Pierino and the other draftees would get out to stretch their legs.

At nearly every station, on the next track over, there were cattle cars filled with Hebrews. "*Voda! Voda!*" they'd call. Or "*Un peu d'eau!*" Or, "*Wasser, bitte!*"

"*Acqua!* They want water!" someone shouted.

After that, the Italians made sure their canteens were full so they could fill the palms thrust out through gaps in the wooden slats. The Germans' guard dogs snarled, but you could buy the handlers off or distract them while someone else slipped bread or cigarettes into waiting hands. The ladies asked for combs sometimes, ashamed to be so dirty. Children whimpered. Infants wailed, a high peculiar hopeless sound.

An officer who spoke French found a Jew who did as well. "They're taking us to Palestine," that lady told him. "We're going to be resettled."

Back on the troop train, the officer said, "Somebody's lying. They can't be going to Palestine."

"Why not, Tenente? Didn't *il Duce* send a bunch of Hebrews there back in the thirties?" a sergeant asked. "Those refugees from Austria and Germany, remember, sir?"

"*Sì, certo,*" the officer said. Mussolini was crafty. Jewish immigrants would stir up the Arabs—that would make things hot for the Tommies in their protectorate. "But the British haven't let Jews into Palestine for years."

"So where are the trains going?" Pierino asked. No one answered.

The rails ran out, leaving days and days of marching before they reached the front. The Italian Eighth Army was dug in along a line of low hills about a kilometer from the River Don. They had log-and-earth bunkers for each platoon, with interlocking fields of fire to cover the gaps, but even with reinforcements there weren't enough men for a line of continuous trenches, and they had no cement for pillboxes or dragon's-teeth obstacles to stop enemy tanks. Already the Eighth had withstood a Soviet offensive north of Stalingrad, saving the Germans to the south a lot of trouble, but that was stalemate, not victory.

In 1941, the Führer thought Russia would fall as fast as France, and neither Axis army had winter gear for the first Battle of the Don. With a second winter coming on, the Italian reinforcements expected cold. As the days shortened and the weather worsened, they added to their gray-green uniforms a second woolen shirt, a thick sweater, and finally a greatcoat, but no wool in the world could stand up to Russian cold, and their boots were already falling apart.

Warm in fur-lined hats and fur-lined parkas, with felted *valenki* like a second skin over fur-lined boots, the Soviet army waited on the other bank, patient as a glacier. On sentry duty Pierino would smoke, and stamp his freezing feet, and stare across the river. Most of the time, the only sound was the whisper of high, dry grasses, but if the wind was right he might hear a Russian sing, or cough, or sneeze across the Don.

In November, snowy slush coalesced into a veneer of ice. The Reds fired mortars at the river in the morning to see how fast the holes froze over. Soon Field Marshal Winter would build an ice bridge across the river. And then? There wasn't a schoolchild in Europe who hadn't read about Napoleon's Russian campaign. Everyone but Hitler knew what was coming.

The battle began on Pierino's watch. There was no bugle call to arms, just the sudden stunning concussion of eight hundred shells exploding simultaneously. In an instant, all along the Italian lines, ripped and broken men screamed and bled, or flew upward in cones of flame and landed in pieces, or vanished into a faint pink mist that settled on the snow.

The Soviet artillerymen loaded and fired, over and over and over, like clockwork executioners. The bombardment went on so long, Pierino could no longer remember a time before it began, or imagine a time when it would end. The entire 2nd Corps was destroyed before the ground attack began.

When the shelling stopped, ten Soviet motorized divisions and two tank regiments roared across the frozen river. Outnumbered and outgunned from the start, the Italians fell back, clawed their way eastward, and retook ground only to be strafed from the air and attacked again by the inexhaustible Red infantry. Day after day, night after night, the battle went on and on. And through it all: the deafening howl of Katiuscia rockets, the whining roar of diving planes, the grinding metal shriek of tanks. The mind-murdering noise of battle.

"G-G-Gesù! They—they just k-keep c-c-coming!" Pierino wept to a major he'd never seen before. "Wh-why d-don't w-w-we ret-treat?"

"The Germans—" The winded officer gasped, choking on the stench of cordite and blood and shit. "They said . . . hold the line . . . to the last man."

And where could you pull back to? Leave the trenches, you'd be in open country. In Russia. In winter.

Pierino saw the man who threw the grenade that crippled him.

Wiping spattered blood and flesh from his face, he stared witlessly at what was left of his right hand, and looked up to meet the
Russian's eyes for an instant before the grenadier's own head exploded, poppy red.

Cradling his arm as though it were a baby, Pierino bid good-bye
to the battle and four of his fingers, and walked, hunched like a hag,
to a field hospital eight kilometers west of the front. There were no
narcotics, no anesthetics by that time. Appalled by others' screams,
Pierino kept silent while a hollow-eyed, grim-faced medic snipped
away the last shreds of his thumb. "Brace yourself," the medic
warned. Pinning Pierino's arm down, the medic scrubbed mud and
grit out of his lacerated flesh with a surgeon's nailbrush. Blinking
away tears, Pierino watched the chopped meat at the end of his
blunted arm being wrapped with dressings torn from the dead.

The medic cut Pierino's shirt off. "You're lucky these didn't
punch through to the lungs," he yelled, tweezing grenade fragments out of chest wounds Pierino hadn't even noticed. "Get
some sleep," the medic said, and went on to someone else.

Pierino eased a dead man's greatcoat around his own bare
shoulders and shuffled to a tent nearby. There he lay among
moaning, sobbing men, who filled the air with cries of "*Mamma!
Acqua! Prego, acqua!*" He had hardly closed his eyes when a colonel
stuck his head into the hospital tent and shouted, "They've broken through! Run, boys! Run!"

Later, Pierino heard the Soviets took one hundred thousand
prisoners, many of them wounded. He himself flagged down a
truck loaded with salvaged materiél, and begged the driver for a
ride. "We're not supposed to carry infantry," the Neapolitan corporal told him, darting a look around. "Fuck it. Hop in the back."

Pierino hid behind ammunition crates and slipped into merciful
unconsciousness, oblivious to the jarring, springless ride. Sometime
during the retreat, his arm turned septic. He was half dead when the
truck driver dropped him off at an Italian military hospital near
Warsaw. "I can't save the arm, but I can save you," he heard the surgeon say just before the amputation. "You're going home, son."

A bargain, Pierino thought as the anesthestic took hold. Half
an arm was not too much to pay.

By May of '43, he was strong enough to travel. The Italian
trains were crammed with wounded, each man accompanied by as

many orderlies and escorts as possible. Hitler ordered his own shattered regiments to die in Russia, and called his allies cowards. Italy's generals didn't care; their pride now lay in saving their nation's sons and brothers and husbands from pointless slaughter.

This time the troop trains rolled west, with fewer men and fewer legs to stretch while the locomotive took on water and coal. But one thing hadn't changed: the freight cars packed with Jews. "They're going to labor camps," someone in the waiting room said. "That's what I heard."

Two SS officers were waiting in the station for a different train. The smaller glanced up from his newspaper. "*All'inferno,*" he said in clear, supercilious Italian. "They are going to hell."

Stump throbbing, Pierino muttered, "Wh-wh-what's that sss-supposed to mmm-mean?"

The German said a word the Italians had never heard before. It sounded like a curse or a cough, like a man clearing his throat.

A Sicilian draftee assigned to Pierino had an accent so thick even other Italians had to listen hard to understand him. Carmello stood and pointed violently first at the Germans in their fine black uniforms and then toward his own eyes. "I saw! I saw in dat city! Dey pulla d' wife froma d' husban'! Dey dragga d' screamin' chil'ren froma d' papa's arms!" His voice cracked, but not from youth. "Dey break uppa da families!"

A hundred stony faces turned toward the Germans, whose hauteur did not alter under scrutiny. "You Italians," the small one said with soft amusement. "So sentimental! Vermin don't have families. They merely breed. It's a public health matter, really."

He folded his newspaper and stood. His boots were polished to such a reflective shine, it seemed impossible that they were leather. Black glass rather, or obsidian. "I believe I'll have a bite to eat," he said. There was no café in that station, but the other German left as well.

"I saw wit'a my own eyes," the Sicilian whispered again and again. "I saw! I *saw—*"

"What did you see?" Albert Blum asks.

Pierino whirls, startled by this near, real voice, when he had been listening so intently to the remembered one. He takes a breath before he answers, giving himself time. "Fffreight t-t-t-trains, fffull of *eb-brei.*"

And hands. So many hands. You have not seen them, signore? Pierino asks in thoughts that are still fluent. A hundred in each boxcar. A thousand on each train. Train after train, headed toward Poland, from the east and from the west. How many? Pierino wonders. How many in eight months?

Albert frowns. "The Germans said they'd be resettled . . ."

Think, Pierino's face urges. Are the Germans so charitable, signore? Did they conquer the East so that *Juden* would have *Lebensraum?*

"There was a Pole in Sainte-Gisèle," the older man recalls uncertainly. "Jakub Landau. *Ebreo,* but—" He waves his hand around his head. "Very blond, like an Aryan. He said . . . crazy things. He told us, 'They have factories for killing Jews in Poland.' He was such a strange man! Maybe they shoot people for some infraction? For working too slowly, perhaps, or damaging a machine."

Pierino Lovera rubs the stump of his aching arm, and says no more. History will break your heart, he thinks, but I won't wield the hammer.

LEONI APARTMENT
PORTO SANT'ANDREA

"Mamma promised me a brother," Angelo Soncini grumps. "She always lies."

Loosening a crinkly length of used wool, Lidia Leoni peers over her glasses at the misbuttoned shirt, short pants, and unmatched socks of a child who's dressed himself. "Your mother didn't lie, Angelo. Sometimes ladies are quite sure they'll have a boy, and then it turns out to be a girl. Until a baby is born, only God knows what it will be. Don't pick those. You'll get an infection."

He turns attention from his scabby knees to the handbag slumping near him on the floor. Soon, the rhythmic tick of knitting needles is joined by the metallic click of the two gold beads that hold Lidia's purse closed. "My other sister died," Angelo says conversationally. "I didn't care. She was a pest." He glances up. "She was!"

In Lidia's considerable experience, seven-year-olds are frequently morose and sour little people. The best policy for dealing with them is to wait until they're eight, when they get silly.

Click, click, click goes the purse clasp. "Maybe Rosina will die, too!" Angelo says, brightening a bit.

"Your new sister arrived a little early, but I'm afraid Rosina is just fine."

"Accidents happen," Angelo reminds her darkly. "Mamma told Sara, 'Don't use that coal oven till we get it fixed,' but Sara didn't believe a stove could kill a person."

Lidia nods. The boy tells this story nearly every day.

"When me and Mamma got back, Sara was all crumped down, and Altira's eyes were all white, like this." He demonstrates gruesomely.

"My daughter Ester was the baby of the family for four years," Lidia tells him, purling. "When her brother Renzo was born, Ester was very annoyed. She didn't hate Renzo. She hated not being so special as before."

The child watches her hands, momentarily fascinated by the way old moth-eaten sweaters can become a new blanket. "Can I look in your purse? Please?"

She nods. Angelo begins to dig. "I know a lot of dead people," he brags. "Both my *nonne* are dead."

"How sad! My grandmothers are dead, too," Lidia confides, turning the needles.

"And one of my *nonni* is dead, plus Altira." He holds out an ancient candy he's found at the bottom of her purse. "May I have this? Please?" Lidia nods. "Catholic funerals are better than sitting shiva," Angelo decides, unwrapping cellophane so old it disintegrates in his fingers. "You go, and it's over. Shiva lasts forever! After Altira died, there was a scary man. He kept looking in the windows."

Lidia has never been sure whether the scary man was real or just a bad dream.

"One time, a lot of Blackshirts came, and they were yelling, and Nonno Casutto shot at them!"

"Yes, I remember," Lidia says aridly. A stray bullet lodged in her kitchen ceiling that evening.

"The police came. Nonno Casutto didn't care. He wouldn't go to services either. Mamma was always yelling at him."

"Angelo, I live right across the street, and I've never once heard your mother raise her voice in anger." In complete and utter exasperation, perhaps . . .

"She yells soft! May I draw with this?" he asks, squirming around to show her the fountain pen from her purse. "Please?"

Lidia finds him a pencil instead, and chooses a copy of *Cinema* from a pile of magazines. "I suspect there are ladies in this who would look very nice with beards."

"Do you have any little boys like me?" he asks, turning pages.

Lidia had forgotten how much children talk. "My little boy is all grown up. You know Signor Leoni—he's my son, Renzo."

Angelo thinks this information over; at seven, the notion that grown men were once boys is still hearsay. "I know a kid who says Signor Leoni is a *galeotto*," he says slyly. "What does that mean?"

"It means jailbird, Angelo, and something else very vulgar. Don't use that word in my home."

"Now you're yelling at me." Lower lip protruding, he looks for an old woman in the magazine and scribbles furiously through the face of a character actress in her forties. Lidia is flattered. "Everybody's always yelling at me," he mutters. "Angelo, be quiet!" he whines in what he believes to be his mother's voice. "Angelo, you'll wake Rosina up! Angelo, play outside!" This reminds him of his earlier grievance. "Mamma does too lie! She said the war was over, but they bombed us last night again."

"Being wrong is not the same as lying. The war we fought against the Allies is over, but now the Germans are using our factories to make things for their army, so the English are still bombing—"

He's stopped listening. World politics are difficult enough for adults these days. She reaches down to lift his chin. "Angelo, listen carefully. If we can save a life by lying—our own or someone else's—it is our duty to lie. That's why I'm pretending to be Catholic."

"Babbo says that's wrong. Babbo says if he carries the Torah to

God's people, he's safe. 'Cause God protects him. 'Cause he's doing a mitzvah."

"Your father is a very brave man." Foolhardy, but brave. "Just remember: you don't have to tell Germans the truth. If a German asks where a road goes, tell him you don't know, even if you do. Or tell him it goes to Milan, even if it really goes to Genoa. If he asks, 'Do Jews live here?' You must say, 'They all left!' Or you could say, 'We kicked them all out!' Germans will like that. Those lies can save lives, Angelo—"

"Do you know any other dead people?"

This is what's so tiring about children. Endless changes in direction, the constant need to adjust. "Ye-es," she says slowly, summoning patience like a moderately obedient dog. "I know a lot of dead people." She goes back to her knitting. "I had an uncle who died before I was born."

"Then you didn't know him!"

"Don't be pedantic. My uncle fought with the House of Savoia against the ninth Pius. The popes owned the whole middle of Italy back then, and Pius the Ninth was a terrible man. My uncle was killed in battle, but he was so brave, the king gave my grandmother a medal."

"The king? Himself?"

"Vittorio Emanuele the Second! The very king who unified Italy and made us equal citizens, because Jews fought so well." Lidia decides not to confuse the child with her current opinion of the monarchy.

"Who else do you know that's dead?" Angelo asks eagerly. "'Specially soldiers! I'm going to be a soldier, and I'm going to drop bombs and shoot bad people."

After six daughters, Lidia was always shocked when Renzo came home bloody and grinning; she is retroactively comforted that even a rabbi's son starts out as barbaric as her own once was. "Two of my nephews died in the last war, fighting the Austrians. So did my daughter Susanna's first love. Davide was a nice boy, but he was killed before they married. It was very sad. And then there was a terrible sickness called influenza—"

Footsteps in the hallway slow. An envelope slides under the door. Angelo runs over to get it. "Is it a secret message?"

"Just some papers." Lidia flips through the documents. "Very serviceable," she remarks, and goes to the kitchen to sign several of them. "Put these in my purse, please, Angelo."

He does as he's told, then returns to the magazine, looking for more ladies to deface. Belly on the floor, feet waving, he says, "I like it when I stay with you."

"Thank you, Angelo. It's kind of you to say so. I have a grandson your age. He lives in Rome, with his two little sisters. All my grandchildren live far away. Rome, Turin, Florence." Even before the war made petrol scarce and travel dangerous, Lidia didn't get to see her grandchildren often enough. Her daughters rarely visit.

"You're like my Nonno Casutto," Angelo decides, drawing an airplane in the sky over Amedeo Nazzari's fedora. "You let me do stuff other grown-ups won't. One time," he says, sitting up, "there was this air raid, and me and Nonno Casutto sneaked up to the roof to see the fires! I like air raids. My sister Altira—she got scared, but I like 'em. 'Cause after, you can find stuff, and look in people's apartments, and see their wallpaper and toilets and everything."

"Very interesting," she admits.

"I found an unexploded bomb once. I ran for a carabiniere. He gave me *caramelle* for telling."

"That was very brave and sensible, Angelo."

"A kid I know? He said Jews are cowards."

"Nazi propaganda," she snaps. "He's just parroting what he hears on the radio. In the Great War, the oldest man and the youngest to be decorated were both Jews! Remember Signor Loeb? He was decorated after the Battle of Caporetto! And my son, Renzo, earned the silver medal for valor during the Abyssinian—"

"Look! What a stupid hat!" Angelo holds the magazine up briefly. "One time, I saw Signor Ravera walking around with a bucket. His apartment building was all wrecked, and he was crying and yelling." The pencil stills, and Angelo aims a sidelong glance at Lidia. "I looked in the bucket. Signora Ravera's *head* was in there."

Lidia stares, her hands going motionless.

Gratified by the reaction, Angelo adds a pointy beard to the

lady with the stupid hat. The hat has a little bird on it, so he draws
a soldier shooting the bird. "If Mammina and Babbo got killed, I
wouldn't care. I'm not a baby," he boasts. "I know how to do stuff."

Lidia lays her knitting aside, horrified by the bravado, awed by
the courage. Violent death, casual horror—just part of childhood
now. "You are exceedingly competent for a seven-year-old," she
tells him firmly, "but your parents are going to be fine." The mantel clock begins to chime. "*Santo cielo!* Noon already." Eyes narrow-
ing, she considers Renzo's bedroom door. "Angelo, I believe it's
time to play something nice and loud on the piano!"

Lingering in the hallway while his pounding heartbeat slows, Iacopo Soncini listens to the racket inside and smiles in spite of
everything. The signora is playing Chopin's Nocturne in E-flat
while Angelo bangs on the low keys, more or less in time.

Removing his hat, Iacopo knocks, and his hand automatically
brushes the doorpost where a mezuzah used to hang. It's gone, the
nail holes neatly patched. The doors of all eight tenants are freshly
painted; no household's entry attracts attention. "Routine maintenance," Rina Dolcino can claim if things go badly. "I had no idea
anyone in my building was Jewish. Why would anyone pay attention to things like that?"

Small feet pound down the hall to gleeful shouts of "Babbo!
Babbo! Babbo!" Signora Leoni has barely unlocked the door when
Angelo hurtles through it, then stops, mouth open. "Babbo, why
are you so dirty?"

"Rabbino, what happened?" Lidia cries, pulling him inside.

"A little unpleasantness in the street. I was wondering if I might
clean here before I take Angelo home." He glances meaningfully at
his son. "We don't want to worry your mammina, do we!"

"Angelo," Lidia says, equally cool, "show your babbo to the lava-
tory."

Angelo leads him past a crucifix hung prominently in the entry.
A framed picture of Piux XII has joined the family photos in the
salon; the silver menorah is nowhere to be seen. Renzo hunches
over the table, unshaven and comprehensively hung over. Hands
around a cup of ersatz coffee, he looks worse off than the cre-

denza's display of grisly plaster martyrs. Colorful saints merely cast lugubrious eyes toward heaven in attitudes of mild vexation at their torture; Renzo can barely raise an index finger in greeting.

Iacopo bids him a hearty, if ironic, "*Buon giorno*" and retreats behind the bathroom door, closing it more loudly than strictly necessary. He takes his time, wiping gray dust from his black suit with a dampened cloth, washing his face and hands, borrowing a comb to neaten his hair and beard. There's nothing to be done about his spectacles, and the eye will blacken, but it could have been worse. When he cannot put the moment off any longer, he switches off the light.

Angelo leaps up the instant the door reopens. "Babbo, look what I found this morning!" he says, digging something out of his satchel.

"Later, Angelo. Signora, I'm afraid . . ." Iacopo holds out a slip of paper. "A stranger gave this to me on the street."

Unfolding the small note, Lidia reads aloud. " 'Five parcels sent to Switzerland have been confiscated at the border. Do not try to export any more of these goods.' There's no signature." She sniffs in a short breath. "Rachele. Tranquillo," she says numbly. "Their three youngest. That makes five—"

"Babbo, look!" Angelo says, holding what looks like a cigar stub.

"Angelo!" Renzo says sharply. "Sit down and be quiet!" Bloodshot eyes on his mother, Renzo pulls out a chair for her.

Iacopo settles himself across the table from Lidia. "Signora," he says calmly, "I've already seen the archbishop. His secretary, Don Osvaldo, has made inquiries. The Loebs were turned back by the Swiss because they didn't have the proper transit visas. They're in German custody. Archbishop Tirassa himself spoke to the man in charge. The Loebs were not arrested for their race, but because they were attempting to leave Italy illegally. His Excellency has been assured that all law-abiding Jewish citizens of Italy will be treated properly. I think that's true. I've been stopped twice by German soldiers today, and allowed to pass with no trouble."

"And the unpleasantness in the street?" Renzo asks.

"Rabble," Iacopo says. "A carabiniere chased them off."

"Babbo, look—"

"Angelo," Lidia says a little raggedly, "the grown-ups are talking!

Rabbino, I understand that Tranquillo is in trouble, but surely Rachele and the children—?"

"Technically they all committed a crime when they tried to cross the border with false documents, Signora. His Excellency will try to get them released."

"Iacopo," Renzo says, "you have to close the synagogue."

"During the High Holy Days? Never!"

"Take a million, maybe two million lire out of the bank," Renzo continues, voice low and even. "Give all the synagogue employees three months' salary, and tell everyone to get the hell out of the city!"

Lidia shakes her head stubbornly. "Evacuation is collaboration!"

"And I don't have the authority to close the synagogue," Iacopo says. "That's the community president's decision, and he's in Florence."

"Then hide the synagogue records, at least!" Renzo urges. "Take anything with names and addresses to Osvaldo Tomitz. He'll bury them in the basilica's papers. Otherwise, we'll be no better off than the Jews in Rome—"

"Wait!" Lidia says sharply. "What's happened in Rome?"

"Babbo! Look!" Angelo insists, waving the cigar.

"A shakedown. Angelo, *please!*" Renzo pleads. "I got a telephone call through to Ester last night, Mamma. She and the children are fine, but she had to give her wedding ring and Nonna Segre's necklace to the Nazis."

"The Gestapo gave the Roman Jews thirty-six hours to deliver fifty kilos of gold," Iacopo explains.

"If they don't pay up," Renzo says, "Kappler will deport two hundred people to Germany—"

"A great many Catholics are coming to our aid, signora! The gold will be delivered on time."

"Demonstrating that we can be intimidated and robbed," Renzo points out. "Let's not make it easy for them—"

"Babbo! Look!" Angelo yells. Three adults wheel, ready to shout. Angelo holds out his treasure and finally achieves the silent awe he hoped for. "I found it in the street after last night's raid," he says proudly. "The nail polish is still on it!"

It's not a cigar stub. It's a woman's thumb.

RABBINICAL RESIDENCE
PORTO SANT'ANDREA

Underslept and overburdened, Iacopo Soncini closes his eyes behind the cracked lens of his glasses. Listening to the silence of his book-crammed study, he thanks God that Rosina's colicky crying has finally quieted and that Mirella will get a few hours of rest before the baby needs to nurse again.

He eases the desk drawer open and chooses a pen with care, selecting one his grandfather gave him on the day Iacopo became bar mitzvah. "These are the Days of Awe," he writes, wondering if even a minyan will be left for Sabbath services. "When Abraham bound Isaac upon the altar, he was ready to sacrifice his only son at the Holy One's command. God did not require that awful deed: an angel stayed Abraham's hand, and told him to substitute a ram for the boy. On Rosh Hashana, when the year begins anew, the children of Abraham and of Isaac are reminded by the call of a ram's horn that during the following eight days, God considers all His children and decides who will be inscribed in the Book of Life for another year."

Since Italy's surrender, Allied air raids have become more frequent. Targets seem more random. Renzo Leoni has offered to take Lidia, Mirella, and the children to the mountains, where they'll all be safer. Should I have said yes? Iacopo asks himself. Have I waited too long? Dio santo, my son believes that finding a woman's thumb is interesting—like finding a bird's feather or a pretty shell on the beach!

"Wake up from your slumber," he writes. "Examine your deeds! Maimonides tells us that is what the ram's horn proclaims. Turn in repentance, remembering your Creator. On Yom Kippur, we'll rise together to ask forgiveness, so that we might be inscribed in the Book of Life, and together we will be comforted by Jonah's assurance of the Lord's compassion for all creatures. And yet, next year at this time, some of us will be gone."

You've got to close the synagogue . . .

Easy enough to ignore the advice of a dislikable drunk, but Osvaldo Tomitz came this evening to give the same advice, and the priest was even more insistent. "What better target than a synagogue full of fasting Jews on Yom Kippur? Just surround the building with troops and scoop the *Juden* up! Rabbino, the Loebs were not the only ones to be stopped at the Swiss border," Don Osvaldo told him. "Forty-nine Jews were arrested at that crossing. This afternoon we got word that their bodies were found in Lake Maggiore!"

"Never has a year passed in which no one died," Iacopo writes resolutely. "Death waits for all who live—the birds of the air, the fish of the sea, and the beasts of dry land. We who have eaten from the Tree of Knowledge, we alone know that death is coming for us. Adonai, in His compassion and wisdom, has given us the Days of Awe, so that we might turn back toward Him. Some do. Some don't. Some need not return because they've never left. It seems to make no difference. Each year, the Holy One takes life from those whose deaths leave us stunned and bereft. Each year, He leaves among us those whose lives are a curse. Of all His creatures, we alone ask, 'Why?' "

Why my mother, my son, my cousin, my wife? his congregants will ask themselves. Why these innocents, when Hitler and Himmler, Goebbels and Kappler live on.

"I have studied Torah for many years," he writes. "Had I studied alone, I might have come to believe that Torah does not teach us to understand God but simply to belong to Him. Fortunately, we Jews have as our study partners the wise of all ages, sages who lived in the times of the Canaanites, the Assyrians, the Babylonians, the Hellenists, and the Romans."

Iacopo's gaze drifts along the shelves of his library. Bibles in Hebrew and German, French and Italian. The many-volumed Talmud with its centuries-long conversation among past rabbis. Commentaries by Maimonides and Nachmonides, by Rashi and Rabbi Luzzatto share a plank with Aristotle, Plato, Socrates, and Plutarch. Flavius Josephus and Nathan ben Yehiel rest cozily between Machiavelli and Tacitus. Schiller and Shakespeare rub shoulders with Solomon Conegliano. Cantarini, Cardoso, Lampronti. Deborah Ascarelli, Sara Coppio Sullam. So many dear friends . . .

"The sages offer us a way to understand the terrible times when we are driven into exile, when we are beaten and enslaved, when we are killed with less thought than a *shochet* gives a chicken. The

Holy One has made us His partners, the sages teach. He gives us wheat, we make bread. He gives us grapes, we make wine. He gives us the world. We make of it what we will—all of us together. When the preponderance of human beings choose to act with justice and generosity and kindness, then learning and love and decency prevail. When the preponderance of human beings choose power, greed, and indifference to suffering, the world is filled with war, poverty, and cruelty. Bombs do not drop from God's hand. Triggers are not pulled by God's finger. Each of us chooses, one by one, and God's eye does not turn from those who suffer or from those who inflict suffering. Our choices are weighed. And, thus, the nations are judged."

Carefully, Iacopo removes his cracked spectacles. Elbows on his desk, he presses his fingers into his eyes and weighs his own obligations. He cannot abandon the foreign Jews hiding in Sant'Andrea, but he will risk only his own life, not the lives of his family or his congregants.

He can close the synagogue school on his own authority. Suora Marta has offered to enroll Jewish children in a boarding school run by her order in Roccabarbena. The *repubblicani* have closed the state schools, but Mother of Mercy is also an orphanage, and classes are in session. Inland, away from industrial targets, the children can continue their education in relative safety.

On Monday, Iacopo will bring Angelo to Suora Marta himself, and urge other parents to follow his example. And then he will ask—no, he will beg Lidia Leoni to take Mirella and the baby to Decimo, where they can hide on a tenant farm owned by her Catholic son-in-law's parents until the war is over.

Iacopo is aware of the irony. All these years, he has refused to bless mixed marriages, alarmed that so many of his congregation's young people were marrying Catholics—the inevitable result of shared lives, shared neighborhoods, shared values. He considered those marriages heartening proof of Italy's religious tolerance but a threat to Jewish survival. Such unions may be the salvation of the Italkim now.

Replacing his glasses, he picks up his grandfather's pen. "The Jews of Italy have always striven to be a source of generosity in the world, for God has often granted us *koach latet*: the power to give.

For centuries, we Italkim have supported the victims of persecution and expulsion. In the days to come, remember this: when we accept the generosity of others, we are the occasion of the Holy One's blessing on our benefactors for their kindness. May God guide us all," he concludes, "from war to justice, from justice to mercy, and from mercy to peace."

He caps his pen and taps the paper into a neat stack. His muscles are cramped, and his mind seems packed in cotton wool. Even so, before he goes to bed, he reaches for the small Bible he keeps on his desk for easy reference. Holding it in one palm, he opens his hand and lets the book fall open where it pleases. "I cannot go where God is not," he whispers, and draws a finger down the text, stopping midway down a column in Psalms.

"I hear the whispering of many, terror on every side," he reads. "But I trust in you, O Lord."

EN ROUTE TO ROCCABARBENA
VALDOTTAVO, PIEMONTE

Mussolini's trains contrive to leave stations on time, only to slow and stop repeatedly. Damaged rails must be repaired. Military transports sidetrack civilian trains. Locomotives break down, or run out of coal.

"Bring food," everyone advised. "It'll take all night to get there."

Third class was crammed with passengers who would doze and cough and curse, but when Suora Marta boarded, a conductor recognized her from a geometry class in 1931. Crooking his finger, he led her and her companions to a safer and more private compartment shared by three well-dressed gentlemen who treated the nuns with courtesy and smiled at the little boy. On Marta's left, nearest the sliding door, Suora Ilaria drew out her rosary; within minutes, she was snoring peacefully, black beads clutched in fingers clawed by arthritis. Squashed next to the window, the rabbi's silent son stared at the countryside until he, too, fell asleep.

Bookended by her companions in the motionless train, Marta shifts carefully, trying to restore feeling to her thick little legs, without notable success. Unable to sleep, she offers up the pin-cushion sensation and starts another drowsy rosary.

Outside, welders work: demonic in iron masks, lit blue and brilliant white by acetylene torches. Sparks scatter from a section of twisted rail. At last, and slowly, the train makes its way past the workers, onto a different track. The gentleman sitting opposite lifts his chin toward the window. "That's why we were delayed, Suora."

First she sees only her own unappealing reflection. Her breath catches. A young man's body hangs from a rope tied to the cross-bar of a telegraph pole. A placard slung around his neck reads "Saboteur" in Italian and German.

"Troublemakers," the man grumbles as the train's movement smooths out and gains speed. "They only make it harder for the rest of us."

"We must pray for his soul," Suora Marta counters, pugna-ciously pious.

The man snorts, crossing his arms over his chest. No one in the compartment speaks again.

They arrive in Roccabarbena just after dawn. The station isn't large compared to those at Sant'Andrea or Genoa, but this is an important, if small, city. On five tracks flanked by crowds and crates, Roccabarbena gathers in Valdottavo's olive oil and wine, cornmeal and chestnut flour, pork and fruit, and sends this bounty to the coast in exchange for manufactured goods, dried cod, sardines, and anchovies.

Small valise in her right hand, Suora Marta has only her left to deploy, and debates which of her charges to hold on to: the little boy or an old nun in her second childhood. Either might wander off.

Suora Ilaria's veiled head tosses and swivels; she reminds Suora Marta of a horse trying to see around blinkers. "This didn't use to be here," Ilaria says, glaring at the railway station. "I'm sure this didn't use to be here!"

Marta grips Suora Ilaria's elbow. "Stay close," she tells the boy. "We have to show our papers."

They shuffle forward. A carabiniere gives the nuns' documents a cursory inspection and smiles at the child, who is not required to carry any. "This didn't use to be here!" Suora Ilaria informs the policeman. "Are you sure this is Roccabarbena? I'm sure this wasn't here!"

"Suora Ilaria grew up here," Marta explains, "but this is her first visit in a long time."

"The station wasn't built until 1927, Suora." The carabiniere hands the documents back to Suora Marta. "*Poveretta*," he mouths, with a sympathetic glance at the old nun.

The view beyond the station is pretty: low mountains in pale sunlight, a cool mist rising over the two rivers that converge just south of the city. Leading the way, Marta keeps her charges moving through telescoping arcades that increased in height and grandiosity as Roccabarbena grew from minor Roman town to busy Fascist railhead.

Already the workday has begun. Merchants roll up iron *saracinesce* to reveal storefronts. Housewives sweep stoops or shake out string bags and greet neighbors on the way to the market. People look startlingly clean and healthy, without the grimy gray pallor of those who live with air raids on ever-diminishing rations. Roccabarbena has escaped Allied bombing. Food is close at hand.

"You're a lucky boy," Marta tells the rabbi's son. "This is a good place to live."

His silence borders on rudeness. She lets it go for now, distracted by Suora Ilaria's increasing agitation at the changes in her hometown. All evidence of the past forty years annoys and frightens the old girl. And I'm beginning to feel the same way about this century, Suora Marta thinks.

They cross the Piazza Centrale and board a crosstown trolley that deposits them at the base of a hill. "Watch!" Suora Marta tells the child. The trolley rotates on its huge wooden turntable so it can return to the piazza. "That's Mother of Mercy up there," she tells him then. "See the walls?"

There's no reply from the boy, but Suora Ilaria's mood improves with every step. "This is how it used to be," she declares happily, bending beyond her ordinary stoop into the long uphill hike. "We always walked!"

There's no fuss when they arrive. The portress takes Ilaria to a room. Suora Marta shows the boy to a visitor's W.C., drops her own valise, and heads for the sisters'. When she returns, the child is waiting by the front door. "Are you hungry?" He shakes his head. "Come with me," she says.

He follows her down a long, cool hallway to a door giving onto a stone pathway bisecting the convent's high-fenced garden. They pass through a gate into the schoolyard. The weather is clement, the windows open. Singsong classroom chants drift out on the breeze: multiplication tables, irregular verbs, prayers being learned for First Communion.

"That will be your room," Suora Marta says, pointing. "Your teacher's name is Suora Corniglia." She expects a question: is she nice? The rabbi's son keeps his own counsel. "She's young, and new to teaching," Suora Marta tells him anyway, "but she has a good heart. You'll like her."

They enter through a side door, but instead of bringing Angelo directly to Suora Corniglia's classroom, Suora Marta escorts him to an empty office. Pulling the door closed, she takes a seat at a desk, studies the silent child standing in front of her. "*Figlio mio,*" she asks quietly, "do you know why you are here with us?"

He does not nod so much as hang his head more dejectedly.

"When you answer me, you must say *Sì,* Suora or *No,* Suora." It is a correction, but not a severe one. She is merely teaching him the rules. "Let's try again. Do you know why your father brought you to us?"

"*Sì,* Suora," the boy whispers.

"That's better, but you must look at me when you answer. From now on, when someone asks your name, you must say—" It will be easier for him to remember if the false name is similar to his own. "You must say Angelo Santoro."

The boy scowls at his feet. "I don't want to lie."

Suora Marta blinks. Yesterday the terrible rumors were confirmed. Eleven hundred Roman *ebrei* were deported on Yom Kippur, the Jews' holiest day. The Vatican immediately ordered that all Catholic institutions be opened to refugees, but this must remain a secret, or the Church's status of diplomatic neutrality will be nullified. "Don't think of it as lying," she suggests, cagey as a Jesuit. "Think of it as pretending. Again: what is your name?"

He looks up briefly. "My name is Angelo Santoro," he says, and adds, "Suora."

She smiles. "You're a quick learner, Angelo Santoro. Come here to me, child." He moves around the corner of her desk, feet scuffling reluctantly. "Angelo," she whispers, lifting his little chin with one finger, "this is very important. You must never, ever tell anyone why you are here. You must pretend to be a Catholic, and do everything the other children do."

"Sì, Suora."

"I'm going to bring you to your new teacher now. Suora Corniglia also knows why you are here. She'll help you learn our ways, and tonight she'll show you where you'll sleep."

The child's hangdog silhouette is outlined vaguely by misty light from the window. For an instant, Suora Marta sees the dead partisan's head canted at a horrible angle.

"Angelo, if anyone finds out why you are with us, we could all be punished. So you must be brave, like a soldier! Promise me," she whispers. "Promise on your word of honor that you won't tell anyone why you're here."

"Never," he swears, eyes stinging with tears he refuses to let fall. "Never, Suora!"

Sunlight breaks through fog and low clouds, its sudden dazzle mocking Angelo Soncini's dark and wounded pride. He sucks his lips between his teeth and bites hard.

Never will he tell a living soul that his father sent him away because he was too noisy, and made his baby sister cry.

DIVISIONAL HEADQUARTERS
12TH WAFFEN-SS WALTHER REINHARDT
PALAZZO USODIMARE, PORTO SANT'ANDREA

These are the times when one is simply happy to be alive. All is right with the world. Suffused with a sense of unassailable well-being, you know you are where you should be, doing what you were meant to do.

This is war's importance and its essential function, Erhardt von Thadden thinks. War provides an arena in which the best demonstrate their strength by cleansing the world of its worst. A perfect system, really . . . I should write a paper.

The Schoolmaster. That's what von Thadden's officers call him. Tall, spare, and born to instruct, he would still be a university professor but for a fortuitous guest lecture to some military cadets. When he walked into their classroom on the last day of June in 1934, he was merely an honorary major in the Security Department's Cultural Activities section. He joined the organization primarily to further his study of Aryan philology, but national service came naturally to a von Thadden. And the smart black uniform with its silver runes was handsome.

He'd just begun his lecture when the first of the SA queers were brought to the Gross-Lichtenfeld wall. The cadets rushed to the windows when they heard the first volleys. Appalled by the distressingly unprofessional executions, the boys turned to von Thadden in confusion. Without hesitation, he left the classroom and took charge of the proceedings at the wall. By the end of the day, the Party's Blood Purge had entered German history, and Erhardt von Thadden had *earned* his commission.

Nine and a half years later, he has risen to the rank of lieutenant-general in the Waffen-SS. Command sits easily upon him, despite his academic past. Erhardt von Thadden cannot deny it: he is a man of many talents.

Shaved and dressed by 0600 hours he returns briefly to the bedroom to kiss his sleeping wife's forehead. He leaves the palazzo's private rooms, crosses an inner piazza, and strolls down a polished marble hallway to his office. Oberscharführer Kunkel stands at the door ready to hand the Gruppenführer an espresso. Before accepting it, Erhardt holds his arms away from his body and pirouettes for his staff sergeant's inspection.

"Your collar, Gruppenführer," Kunkel murmurs indulgently. The Schoolmaster's inattention to dress is famous.

Von Thadden checks his reflection in a gilt-framed mirror. "*Ach!*" he cries, smoothing the offending fabric. "This morning," he promises Kunkel, "I shall make a special effort to keep the coffee off my uniform."

For the next half hour, von Thadden reviews the night's events, scanning dispatches and reports laid out on a superb neoclassical table. When the Gruppenführer sets those papers aside, Kunkel materializes with another stack: notes prepared for the morning's briefing. At 0700 sharp, von Thadden heads for the library, pausing just outside a grand ballroom filled with rows of gunmetal gray desks. Typewriter keys smack sharply against paper, voices murmur, telephones ring. When the C.O. appears, men stand and salute. Von Thadden raises his own hand more casually as he passes. Behind him, chair legs squeal, and his staff goes back to work.

"*Heil* Hitler," he murmurs, entering a small room walled with four hundred years of finely bound books. Officers come to their feet, salute. A man in civilian clothing raises his right arm straight, forty-five degrees off horizontal. The soldiers' attention is on their commander, but the civilian's eyes rest with conspicuous devotion on the photo of the Führer that has replaced a portrait of the Sant'Andrese pirate who built this palace.

"How nice to see you again, Artur," von Thadden says, forcing the civilian to acknowledge him. "Gentlemen, we have a guest this morning: an old acquaintance of mine from our days in München. Herr Artur Huppenkothen—formerly of the Vienna Office for Jewish Emigration, currently Oberst der Polizei in Sant'Andrea. He will be addressing us later in a discussion of joint operations."

Kunkel pulls down a large map mounted on the wall. Von Thadden reaches for a wooden pointer and strikes a pose behind the lectern. "I know what you're thinking," the Schoolmaster says, looking over his shoulder slyly. He does not join the burst of surprised laughter, but his eyes sparkle.

With the pointer, he quickly outlines a triangle of territory angling north-northwest. "Gentlemen, our area of responsibility runs from the Port of Sant'Andrea here, inland to central Piemonte." *(Tap, scrape.)* "The arc of land along the Gulf of Genoa is Liguria, which takes its name from a pre-Roman tribe. Piemonte means 'foot of the mountain,' the mountains in question being the Maritime Alps. Eastern Piemonte is a large, fertile plain. Highly developed agriculture. Rice, corn, wheat. Western Piemonte is composed of long river valleys bordered by high saddles of low but steep wooded mountains, all of which are ribbed by numberless ravines."

Von Thadden clears his throat and looks around. "Kunkel? Where is the water?" he asks mildly.

"Sorry, Gruppenführer. Right away, sir."

"Valleys," von Thadden continues, "often take their names from their rivers. Valle Stura. Valle Gesso, Valle San Leandro." *(Tap. Tap. Tap.)* "The pattern is broken in our area of authority. The Romans called this Vallis Octavii—Eighth Valley. Italian is, of course, merely Vandalized Latin . . ."

He pauses to take note of who chuckles first: Helmut Reinecke. No surprise there. Always in the front row, like a diligent young graduate student, but an excellent combat record. Artur Huppenkothen, on Reinecke's right, makes a show of boredom.

"Like everything else in this once great empire," von Thadden resumes, " 'Vallis Octavii' has been corrupted—the present inhabitants call it Valdottavo. The valley forms a great funnel pointing south-southeast, with the San Mauro River running down the center. Saint Mauro is the patron of the region. Some sort of bishop in the reign of Pope Sixtus the Fifth." He pauses for effect. "Or was it Fiftus the Sixth? Difficult to keep all these popes straight . . ."

From the staff: smiles all round. Huppenkothen looks out the window.

"Despite the terrain, Vallis Octavii was famous for peasant farmers whose capacity for hardship and toil earned the poet Virgil's praise. The land is all but untillable, its soil imported by sailors in sacks, so the story goes, and hauled up the mountains on muleback. The peasants are tough, secretive, hostile to outsiders and—"

"Communists," Huppenkothen says in a loud, flat voice. "The place is rotten with them."

Von Thadden goes on as if Artur had not spoken. "Transport is fairly primitive. The San Mauro River is broad, shallow, rocky, and unnavigable. Torrential in spring and autumn, frozen in winter. In summer, the river may dry up altogether. Mule paths connect high hamlets with villages. Gravel tracks connect some of the larger towns. Paved roads and a railway parallel the riverbed."

Kunkel delivers mineral water in a Murano goblet on a silver tray. Von Thadden takes a sip and continues: "Note that at the narrow ends of these two valleys, the San Leandro and San Mauro rivers converge." *(Scrape. Scrape.)* "Together they have carved out a wedge of land. The city of Roccabarbena"—*tap*—"sits on that wedge, at the funnel's narrow end. The Roccabarbena railway switching station collects freight and passengers from both Valle San Leandro and Valdottavo. Four bridges cross the rivers at Roccabarbena." *(Tap. Tap.)* "Two are Roman, built for foot and wheeled traffic. The others are railway trestles, built in the 1920s by Herr Mussolini."

He lays the pointer down. "By December, German engineers will finish blasting a tunnel from Valdottavo into the plains northeast of the region. This connection will allow food, goods, and laborers to be delivered to the *Vaterland.* Armaments will flow southward to the Gustav Line, below Rome. Your thoughts?"

The discussion of tactics for controlling supply lines is routine, methods for securing them standard. Roccabarbena's bridges and Valdottavo's railway line are of clear strategic importance. "And the Communists in the region, Gruppenführer?" Helmut Reinecke asks, with attention to detail. "Indigenous or imported?"

"Both," Huppenkothen says.

"Yes—and perhaps now is the time to turn things over to our Gestapo colleague," von Thadden says mildly, backing away.

The men shift in their chairs. Artur Huppenkothen takes the podium, realizes it is too high for him, and sidesteps it. Behind him, the Gruppenführer leans against a wall lined with books, arms crossed just below his medals. Von Thadden catches Reinecke's eye, and glances toward Huppenkothen's heels, which are undoubtedly raised by lifts. Reinecke's lips twitch. Suspicious, Huppenkothen glances over his shoulder. Von Thadden smiles encouragingly, like a teacher urging a shy student to get on with his book report.

Artur is a remarkably colorless man: pale skin, pale eyes, a pale scalp showing through thinning blond hair. His cuff links are fashioned of unadorned gold, the better to draw attention to the red monogram *AH* embroidered on his shirt cuffs. These are Artur's own initials but, one is invited to note, also the Führer's. Artur always dresses with strict attention to grooming, his shoes polished to a high gloss, his trousers pressed to a fine edge. He thinks all this will win respect, but others see it as a confirmation of a widespread speculation. If he hadn't informed on his own lovers to Himmler, Artur Huppenkothen would have been executed in 1934 like the rest of Röhm's SA fairies.

"Our department has completed an assessment of the Jewish problem in northern Italy," he begins, pulling a sheaf of crackly onionskin from a leather document case. "The infestation is pervasive," he says, rattling the report to prove it. "As soon as our Führer began to drive them from the *Vaterland,* Jews ran like rats for Italy. But the Jew also has deep roots here—"

Von Thadden interrupts. "If I may add a bit of background for the men, Artur? The earliest Roman synagogues predate the Vatican by centuries. Historians estimate a tenth of the population of the Empire was Jewish at the beginning of the Christian era. Many Romans converted to Hebrew monotheism," von Thadden says with a wry smile. "Women generally, adult males being reluctant to undertake circumcision."

Huppenkothen clears his throat as the uncomfortable chuckles fade. "Your commander is, of course, correct. The oldest Jew community in Europe is that of Rome. Soon, however, we shall say that it *was* in Rome. Deportations have begun," he says, regaining his momentum, "but our task is daunting. The Jew has infiltrated Italian society at all levels, and in every sphere. Not only trade unions, but also the military and the government—"

"In Italy," von Thadden interjects helpfully, "the Jew is not closely associated with commerce. Until recently, he was prominent in the Italian armed forces."

"Accounting, no doubt, for the poor showing Italy has made militarily," Huppenkothen snaps. "Even the Catholic Church has been subverted here—not at the highest levels, but among so-called worker-priests who stir up discontent among factory workers and the peasantry. The Fascist Party itself was filled with Jews from the beginning, even on Mussolini's Grand Council. *Il Duce*'s daughter nearly married one! Race mixture has been extensive here, even in the face of the 1938 laws. Native-born Jews have been provided endless exemptions to the laws. A Jew could be Aryanized if he had served in the armed forces, or—"

"Knew whom to bribe in the registry," von Thadden murmurs.

Huppenkothen soldiers on. "The race laws were not enforced

at all in Italian-occupied territories. The Italian foreign minister Count Luca Pietromarchi has Jewish blood. He is married to a Jewess—"

"Really?" von Thadden asks. Needling Artur is almost too easy, but someone has to keep the little queer in his place. "I thought that was only a rumor."

"The Italian Foreign Ministry never surrendered a single Jew from any of their territories," Huppenkothen says, his bearing rigidly erect, to make the most of his inadequate stature. "Not from Greece, Salonika, Russia, or Yugoslavia, not from southern France—"

"My dear Artur, handing over undesirables to another government would have meant a loss of sovereignty." Von Thadden addresses his men. "That, of course, is no longer an issue for the Republic of Salò."

Huppenkothen gathers his papers and replaces them in the document case. "Our survival as a *Volk* demands that we free ourselves and Europe of this ancient racial cancer." He looks at each of the officers in the room. "The malign influence of the Jew festers in every city and every valley of this country. We must be hard. We must be ruthless. Be assured," he says directly to von Thadden, "the Gestapo takes note of those who fail in this regard."

The room remains silent until the small man's footsteps are heard no more. The Schoolmaster strolls back to his place behind the lectern. "Herr Oberstpolizei Huppenkothen's devotion to the Aryan race is admirable. It is a devotion I endorse, a devotion I share, but the Waffen-SS is a military organization, gentlemen. Our priorities must be well ordered. Reinecke, do you have the figures I requested?"

"*Jawohl,* Gruppenführer. On 8th September, there were approximately thirty-five thousand native-born Italian Jews, or less than half a percent of the national population. To this, add several thousand foreign Jews smuggled into the country from France and Yugoslavia by Italian troops last month."

"For a total of . . . ?"

"Best estimate seems to be forty-five thousand, Gruppenführer. Although with the deportation from Rome, that number has already dropped."

"So, forty-four thousand Jews, two-thirds women and children. Leaving—?"

"Fifteen thousand men, of whom a third would be too old to fight," Reinecke says, having anticipated the calculation. "Say, ten thousand potential combatants."

"Make that *ten* potential combatants!" a Standartenführer in the last row retorts. "These are Jews we speak of!"

"Worse," someone else calls out. "Most are Italian Jews!"

"How many gears does an Italian tank have?" another asks.

"Only one: reverse!" comes the answer.

Suddenly the room erupts with jokes. How do you stop an Italian tank? Shoot the soldier pushing it! Did you hear about the Italian rifle for sale? Never been fired, only dropped once! What do Italians call half a million men with their hands in the air? The army! Did you hear about the new Italian flag? It has a white stripe—on a white background! Did you hear? Did you hear? Did you hear?

Reinecke looks increasingly troubled, but von Thadden lets the men enjoy themselves. All their lives, they've been taught to sneer at the *Untermenschen* of the world, but when the laughter wanes, he warns them, "In war, as in chess, underestimating the enemy is a mistake. We who have served in Russia know that Italian soldiers can be formidable and ferocious fighters."

"Particularly the Alpini," Reinecke says earnestly.

"Obersturmführer Reinecke was seconded to an Alpine unit during the first battle of the Don," von Thadden informs the others. "Bear in mind as well: the Badoglio government surrendered, but *il Duce*'s Black Brigades are united with us in opposition to the Allied invasion of Italy, and to the Bolshevik threat to Europe. Other demobilized soldiers," he grants, "consider us an occupying force. They could pose a substantial threat. Furthermore, Italians are a notably tenderhearted and generous people, and such altruistic softness inevitably leads to collectivism. If Bolshevik Jews join and subvert Italian resistance forces, they must be considered the vanguard of the Soviet army."

He waits in the chastened silence for his words to sink in. "Garrison all population centers with over one thousand inhabitants. Conscript laborers and clear fifty meters on either side of all railroads and paved highways. Burn everything that can give cover to saboteurs. Shoot anyone who resists. I want anti-aircraft guns around all bridges and at two-kilometer intervals along the whole of the railway from Sant'Andrea to Borgo San Mauro. Establish supply-line patrols—every four hours, round the clock, starting at seventeen hundred hours this afternoon. Dismissed."

Chairs rumble. Low voices murmur. The staff meeting breaks up, but von Thadden motions for Reinecke to remain. "Your given name is Helmut, is it not, Obersturmführer?"

"Yes, it is, Gruppenführer."

"And your wife is Anneliese? Expecting, I believe." Reinecke nods, a little startled. Von Thadden smiles warmly. "Shall I arrange leave for the event?"

"The Reich comes first, sir."

"Of course! But I'll see if we can't find a few days for you to go home. Or," von Thadden offers craftily, "your little family could join you here. The presence of a man's wife and children does so much for morale, and I want my adjutant to operate at peak efficiency. The rise in pay grade will not be unappreciated by a new father, eh, Hauptsturmführer?"

"I— Thank you, Gruppenführer. This is most unexpected."

"I've had my eye on you, Reinecke. I pride myself on recognizing merit. You've earned this promotion." Von Thadden extracts a slip of paper from his breast pocket. "Contact this man about the arrangements."

Reinecke reads the name. "Ugo Messner. German, sir?"

"Of German blood—a *Volksdeutscher* from Bozen. Charming, and very helpful with finding accommodations, furniture, and so on. Get cracking, Reinecke! My Martina is lonely, and she loves babies. Your Anneliese will be good company for her."

FORMER RABBINICAL RESIDENCE
PORTO SANT'ANDREA

Erna Huppenkothen rubs at a smudge on the credenza with the corner of her apron and adjusts the lace tablecloth on the dining table. Fine porcelain and lovely silver are already laid at Artur's place. She has prepared his supper herself. Plain, sensible German cooking. Ugo—Herr Messner, that is—offered to find Italian girls to cook and clean for her, but Erna has refused. "Let silly women like that Martina von Thadden have servants and grand homes!" she told Herr Messner. His eyes glowed with admiration. He sensed the strength of her will, her determination. She will not be corrupted by the warm weather and aristocratic ease Italy offers its conquerors.

Erna sees through all that seductive courtesy. Behind each fawning smile, there is trickery and insult. Mouths wish you *Buon giorno, Buona sera, Buona notte.* Eyes wish you dead.

Ugo is Italian, too, but different, of course, being Aryan by blood. She could never have established this household so quickly without his help.

Happy to be in the company of other good Germans, Ugo appeared out of nowhere, pointed out this house, and arranged the removal of all its awful modern furniture and degenerate Jew art. Most of the house was as clean as could be expected, given the dust and smoke from the bombing, but—*Scheibenkleister!* That horrible library! Enough dirt in there to plant a garden and raise potatoes.

Not even a good, strong German woman like Erna could have carried all those filthy Jew books away to be burned, so she agreed to let Ugo's men get rid of them for her. A few days later, he told her about some lovely antiques, available for a very reasonable price, and had them delivered on approval. Erna's favorite piece is a sideboard of ebonized walnut, magnificently carved. Difficult to dust, but worth the effort. An ornate mirror hangs above it. "The glass is four hundred years old," Ugo said, "and you're the most handsome woman it's ever seen."

Such a flirt! But courteous. Respectful. And so attentive, although he travels on business regularly, gone for several days at a time. He always brings her little gifts: handsome old drawings, lovely candlesticks, lace linens to grace her table. Nicer than anything she had back in München.

She enjoys Ugo's visits. Even at home, she was often lonely. After Mutti died, she kept house for Papa until he, too, passed away. When her brother, Artur, asked her to come to Italy as his housekeeper, Erna was grateful and determined to justify the expense and bother he went to, bringing her here. She had long since resigned herself to spinsterhood. She never expected to meet anyone as pleasant as Herr Messner, and in Italy, of all places!

The mantel clock chimes six. She straightens her apron and waits in the vestibule, knowing Artur will arrive at 6:05. Already, they have established their daily schedule. She'll take his hat and briefcase. He'll remove his coat and make a brief reply to her greeting while she hangs up his things. She'll serve his supper in silence; he works even while he eats. "That was good," he'll say when he finishes, then retreat to his study, a collection of files in hand. When he goes to bed, he'll find beautifully ironed pajamas, a silk robe, and Turkish slippers laid out in his room. In the morning, his suit will be sponged and pressed, his shoes blacked and shining.

Each evening Erna clears away his dishes and eats her own meal, standing, in the kitchen. "I wish Artur were more like you, Herr Messner," she confessed yesterday. "He barely speaks, and he never listens to me!"

"Artur is lucky to have you looking after him," Ugo said, "but naturally he is preoccupied by affairs of state. Noticing things like furniture and cooking would be a sort of dereliction of duty. You serve the Führer by serving Artur, Fräulein!"

"I never thought of it that way," she said.

"Men always love to talk about their professions," Ugo said thoughtfully. "Perhaps if you take an interest . . . ?"

The door opens. Her brother steps inside. "Good evening, Artur," Erna says, taking his hat and briefcase. "You look tired. How was work today?"

November 1943

EN ROUTE TO BORGO SAN MAURO
VALDOTTAVO, PIEMONTE

Osvaldo Tomitz smacks a wrench into Renzo Leoni's palm. "We're lost," he says. "Admit it!"

"We're not lost." The disembodied voice beneath the little milk van is serene, but the Alfa Romeo appears to spit the wrench out. "A *socket* wrench, Padre! Female connector, right angle to the handle. Fits around a bolt."

Osvaldo tries another tool.

"That's a socket wrench," the voice says patiently, "but not the nineteen-millimeter socket wrench. The dimensions are on the handles."

"Bless me, Father, for I have sinned: I skipped the course on engine maintenance in seminary." Osvaldo paws through the contents of a metal box. Twenty-one, seventeen . . . At least the numbers aren't divisible by five. "*Ecco!* A nineteen-millimeter female coupling, right angle to the handle."

Metallic sounds issue from beneath the engine, along with a stately procession of quiet curses. "*Porca vacca. Porca miseria. Porca bagascia . . .*"

"Where did you learn—?"

"To curse? The Royal Italian Air Force."

"—to fix engines?" Osvaldo finishes.

"Same place. Know why Italian pilots fly in squadrons of four?" There's a grunt of effort, followed by another steady stream of profanity. "So they'll have one working radio at the end of the mission. We could never get spare parts even in the thirties. Kept the planes airborne with electrical tape and scraps of tent canvas— *Porca puttana!* Is there any wire in that toolbox?"

Osvaldo digs around. "You were a mechanic, then?"

"*Belandi,* no!" Renzo exclaims, offended. "I flew a Caproni 133 triple-engine high-wing fighter-bomber," he says grandly. "Had a whole crew of fitters and riggers at my command, but those were my very own balls in the cockpit. *Mondo cane!*" Another convoy of curses rolls out from under the truck before Renzo continues: "I always did the work myself—damned if I'd trust some ignorant *cafone* with a hammer... There! Climb into that pig-bitch and crank her, Padre."

Using the hem of his cassock to protect his hand, Osvaldo opens the gasogene chamber and stokes the coal fire before swinging up into the cab. The starter fails. He pulls the choke out a bit more. The engine catches, then roars unmuffled.

"That's good! Cut the engine!" Renzo eases himself from under the truck and gets up slowly, groaning like an old man. Wipes grease from his hands with a rag, dusts off his coveralls. Reaches into the cab of the Alfa and pulls out a bottle of grappa. "Medicinal purposes," he says, toasting the priest and taking a long swallow. "Got a cigarette?"

Osvaldo offers a package of Macedonias. Renzo's face twists, and Osvaldo shrugs. Macedonias taste like burning straw, but they're better than nothing. The men light up and listen to the breeze in treetops that meet over the center of this gravelly road.

"*Porca troia!* It's going to rain," Renzo grouses. "Which reminds me: those blank identity papers you bought? You haven't distributed them yet, have you?" The priest shakes his head, and Renzo asks, "What made you choose Troia for the addresses?"

"The papers needed a municipal stamp. A group in Genoa got one from a village called Troia down in Apulia. The town's behind Allied lines, so nobody can double-check the documents."

Renzo flicks ash. "Padre, do you happen to know what *troia* means in the Ligurian dialect?" When Osvaldo shakes his head, Renzo prompts, "It's a female occupation... Not a very respectable occupation." The priest still looks blank. "*Troia* means prostitute, Padre."

"But... no!" Osvaldo moans. "So all those people would be walking around with papers that say they're—"

"Children of Troia! The sons and daughters of a southern whore!"

"Am I correct in assuming that I am the only person in north-western Italy who didn't know that?"

"I rather hope my mother would be just as surprised. The Germans wouldn't get it, but *repubblicani* would piss themselves laughing, and then arrest anyone carrying the documents."

"So I've ruined two hundred identity cards."

"In the future, you might check criminal intentions with your more disreputable colleagues." Renzo slumps onto the truck's running board and inspects his scraped knuckles. "Can I ask you something, Tomitz? Why the hell are you up here, looking for Hebes on the run, in God-Knows-Where, Piemonte?"

"You admit it! We're—"

"We are not lost!" Exasperated, Renzo closes his eyes. Folded and forested, the hills must seem impossible to navigate from the ground, but he's seen this landscape from above. He sees it at this moment as though he were flying over the countryside. The plains sweep north from the coast, breaking into long valleys rimmed by wooded mountains that crumple into higher and higher terrain until they merge with the Maritimes. "We are five kilometers by air from Borgo San Mauro, which is that way," he says, pointing. "It's twenty kilometers on this miserable dirt track, which is a pain in the *coglioni* to drive on, but better than getting picked up by a German patrol on the main road. Answer my question."

The priest straightens. "We are taught: Do not stand by while your neighbor's blood is shed."

"Sounds like Leviticus," Renzo remarks, watching the clouds.

"We must place ourselves on the side of those who suffer persecution!" Osvaldo insists, as though arguing with someone. "I am here without permission," he confesses. "You know what they say in the Curia? *Tutti preti sono falsi.*"

Renzo looks surprised. "All priests are frauds? Not all, surely! There's your friend Leto Girotti. Archbishop Boetto in Genoa, and his man Don Repetto. That nuncio in Turkey."

"Roncalli?"

"Yes, that's the one." Elbows on his knees, Renzo hunches over, cigarette shielded by his palms from the rising breeze. "You know what I think? Ten percent of any group of human beings are shitheads. Catholics, Jews. Germans, Italians. Pilots, priests. Teachers, doctors, shopkeepers. Ten percent are shitheads. Another ten percent—salt of the earth! Saints! Give you the shirts off their backs. Most people are in the middle, just trying to get by." Squinting through tendrils of smoke, he leans away to look at Tomitz. "You are a very dangerous man, Padre. You are an ordinary, decent fellow who aspires to saintliness."

"And you?" Osvaldo demands, flushing angrily. "You have false papers—Stefano Savoca could simply disappear. As Ugo Messner, you could go to Berlin if you wanted to! Where do you fit in this moral taxonomy?"

Renzo grins derisively. "Oh, I'm definitely a shithead. I'm just trying to commit a better class of sin than I used to." Renzo takes a drag, holds smoke in his lungs, blows it out slowly. "You know anything about Yom Kippur, Padre? The Day of Atonement. Jews are supposed to fast and ask God's forgiveness for sins against Him, but not even God can absolve sins against someone else. So. We're supposed to go to the people we've harmed, beg forgiveness, make things right. Which is why some sins are unforgivable." He studies the wooded hillside that borders the road. "Murder, for example."

"Because one can't ask forgiveness of the dead."

"Too true. You know what Cain's sin was, Padre?"

"Why, killing his brother, of course."

"Catholics! One answer per question, end of discussion. No, Padre, Cain's sin was depriving the world of Abel's children. My theory is, if Abel had lived, the percentage of shitheads in the world might be significantly lower." Renzo stands and shuffles bent-kneed for a few steps before he can straighten. "Can you reach that Beretta from where you're standing? Don't move, just tell me."

"The pistol? Yes, it's on the dashboard." Alert now, Osvaldo whispers, "What do you see?"

Renzo seems to study the clouds. Raindrops roll off the leaves and hit his face. "Who, not what."

Osvaldo Tomitz is carrying sixteen thousand lire in cash, its bulk concealed in the black cincture around his waist. There are, Leto Girotti estimated, over a thousand Jews hiding in his mountain parish, and he'll distribute the money to families sheltering them—assuming Osvaldo isn't robbed this afternoon. He grabs the gun and thrusts it into Renzo's hand.

Casually, Renzo drops the cigarette butt to the dampening ground before bellowing, "*Sh'ma,* Israel! *Adonai Eloheynu!*"

"*Pazzo!* Are you crazy?" Osvaldo cries.

"It's the one prayer even a half-assed Jew like me knows: Hear, O Israel! Adonai is God . . ."

The answer comes back in an adolescent quaver: "*Adonoi Echad!*"

". . . Adonai is One," Renzo concludes.

A bedraggled boy appears at the hilltop and plunges toward the road. Sledding down the steepest section on his backside, he arrives possessed of nothing but dirty clothes, a big nose, and greasy brown hair.

"*Juif? Jude?*" Renzo asks. The boy hesitates, not sure what to admit. Renzo points to himself. "*Ebreo.*" The boy considers the Beretta with an expression of profound skepticism. "Behold! A Jew with a gun," Renzo confirms, and sings a verse of Kaddish to prove it.

"*Sprechen Sie Deutsch?*" Osvaldo asks, wiping rain out of his eyes.

A sullen resolve appears. "*Solo italiano.* No more German-speaking!"

"That should spare us a great deal of superfluous juvenile commentary," Renzo mutters cheerily. Depositing the pistol in the cab, he reaches for a lunch pail and a can of milk.

"I am Don Osvaldo," the priest says. "What are you called?"

"Duno."

"Do you have family near here?"

"*No famiglia!*" the boy swears. "*Solo io.*"

"And how old are you? Nineteen?" Renzo asks, with every evidence of sincerity. The boy considers the question and nods. "A linguist, and a liar as well," Renzo remarks admiringly. "Skills much in demand these days."

Don Osvaldo points to the lunch pail in Renzo's hand. "*Siete affamato,* Duno? Are you hungry?"

"I Germans want to fight!" the boy says, shivering in the sudden chill.

"Well, you've come to the right place," Renzo assures him warmly, pouring milk into a tin cup. "Italy has a surplus of Germans at the moment. The Allies are presently being slaughtered at Anzio, so I fear you may soon constitute the totality of the opposition, but lack of manpower enhances opportunities for advancement. A bloodthirsty young savage like you should be a major general by December."

Duno takes in perhaps every fifth word, but Renzo is enjoying his own performance. "Eat first. Fight later," Don Osvaldo suggests, handing the boy a *panino.*

The boy drains the cup, then devours the sandwich in three huge gulps, Adam's apple prominent in his skinny neck. "*Partigiano, voi?*" he asks, wiping his mouth on a filthy sleeve. "*Il prete rosso?*"

"We are not partisans, and I am not the Red Priest," Osvaldo says slowly. "We'll take you to him."

"Gentlemen," Renzo says, "may I suggest that we get in out of the rain? And who the hell's the Red Priest?"

The three of them climb into the truck, Renzo settling behind the wheel, the boy taking the middle of the bench. Osvaldo slams his door twice before the latch catches, then says, "He means Leto Girotti. Leto's not a Communist. People call him that because he had a big dispute with a landlord named Malcovato years ago— the factor was keeping two sets of books. Leto got more money for the tenants."

"Oh, wonderful!" Renzo shouts over the roar of the engine. "And did Don Leto take out an ad in *La Stampa,* or just nail flyers on all the trees? Radical priest desires martyrdom! Please arrest at earliest convenience."

The racket is deafening: chuffing *gassogeno,* grinding gears, rain hammering on the roof of the cab. "It's just a nickname," Osvaldo yells, "but I think your mother would like him."

Fed and warm after weeks of stealing food and living rough, Duno Brössler bicycles to school. Hurrying and late, as usual, he pedals frantically. Then he's waiting at a train station, and no amount of pushing yields headway through the crowds that block his way. Suddenly he's on a road, in the middle of a traffic jam—

The milk van's engine stops. The priest shakes his shoulder. Duno jerks awake. "Put these on," Don Osvaldo says, handing him a pair of well-oiled work boots two sizes too big. "Give me yours."

"*Perché?*"

"Because they're looking for the Jews who crossed the Alps," the Jewish milkman says. "They arrest anyone with worn-out street shoes."

Don Osvaldo hands Duno a jacket that fits as badly as the shoes. "You're a mute, understand? Don't say anything!"

Duno squirms into the coat. "Nobody will believe this is mine."

"It's not supposed to be yours," the milkman says. "Shut up!"

The queue on the main road is a kilometer long: farmers in mule carts, young people walking beside bicycles, peasant women shuffling on foot with bundles balanced on their heads. It takes them nearly an hour to snake across a stone bridge toward a pair of carabinieri inspecting documents.

Two civilians in brown leather trench coats stand behind the policemen, looking hard at each person who passes. "Germans," Duno whispers. No one answers. Thinking they haven't understood, Duno repeats, "Those men—they're *Tedeschi!*"

The milkman cranks his window down, checks on the queue lengthening behind the van, flashes a grin at the priest. "Ready?"

The priest inclines his head. *"Prego."*

"Listen!" Duno cries. "Those are Germans—"

"Permit me to explain what *shut up* means," Osvaldo says, driving an elbow into Duno's belly.

"Bravo!" the milkman murmurs. "See you in Sant'Andrea." Sticking his head out the window, he begins to pound on the truck horn and yell. *"Vaffanculo!* I gotta d' orphans' milk here! Lemme t'rough, y' fuckin' *castrati!"*

Snarling people whirl to see not just the maniacal Sicilian in the milk van's cab waving his arm out the window, but the serene priest and the winded wide-eyed boy. Eyebrows shoot up. The priest nods ever so slightly.

The queue convulses into a crowd. Horn blaring, the milk van bulls its way forward, its driver screaming, "Milk for'a da *innocenti!* Lemme t'rough, y' *leccacazzi!"* Peasants pump their fists, yelling back just as passionately. Closer to the checkpoint, documents wave in the air, babies squall. A young woman with a bicycle picks a fight with the carabinieri, one of whom studies her papers minutely, while the other serenely assures the Germans that everything is under control.

"Perfect," Osvaldo says, flinging open the passenger door. He hops down and hauls Duno out of the truck. "Keep quiet," he orders, gripping Duno's arm and dragging him toward the policeman who's busy with the girl. Leaning toward the policeman's ear, Osvaldo says, "This boy has no papers, *figlio mio.* His family was killed by a bomb in Sant'Andrea. He's a mute, but neighbors said he has relatives around here."

"*Sì, sì, sì,*" the carabiniere says, operatically distracted. "Take him to the rectory. Padre Girotti knows everyone in the parish. *Ecco, signorina,* this address doesn't look correct to me."

Marching quick-time, Osvaldo starts uphill, the boy in tow. Duno giggles, looking over his shoulder at the chaos behind them. "That was great! Where's he going?"

"To an orphanage." Swiftly changing directions, Osvaldo leads Duno into an alley. Glancing left and right, satisfied that they are alone, Osvaldo shoves the boy against a stucco wall. "If you say one . . . more . . . word," he promises in a low soft voice, "I will hand you to the Gestapo myself."

Five silent minutes later, at the far end of the village, a church comes into view. The blank-walled exterior is as plain as pabulum, but when Duno steps over its threshold, he stifles a gasp. "Sit!" snaps the priest, pointing at a pew. "I'll be back in ten minutes."

Duno obeys, too stunned by the surroundings to argue. No Viennese is a stranger to decorative excess, but this!

Not so much as a finger's breadth of wall, floor, or ceiling has been left unadorned. Dancing angels crown a sort of chuppah over the altar. Swags of dusty red fabric trimmed in tarnished gold enclose the bima. Two smaller altars flank the main one. Duno recognizes the Virgin by her blue robe and chastely bowed head. Candles, lit after a Mass, gutter and smoke at her feet. The season's last few roses scent her air. Above the altar on the right, her unlucky husband, Joseph, stands diffidently, carpenter's tools in hand, candleless and unpetitioned.

Halfway down the nave, off to one side, a plaster man is enclosed in a smaller canopy supported by baroque carvings of what might be wiggly trout, or maybe dolphins, or possibly just vines. San Mauro, according to a hand-lettered sign. A bishop, judging from the fish-head hat and shepherd's crook. The walls of his alcove are completely covered with paintings and drawings that appear to have been done by children, or by untutored adults. One, drawn in colored pencils, shows a train station. A man in a blue conductor's uniform has fallen from the platform between two cars, saved from wheeled decapitation by the bishop, who floats on a nearby cloud, two fingers raised in blessing. In another, Alpini guard a mountain pass, but there has been an avalanche. Two soldiers tumble tragicomically in the snow, uniformed arms and legs sticking out of whiteness in all directions. The bishop hovers in the corner, blessing the third soldier, who kneels in thanksgiving, palms pressed together.

Duno snickers. "I guess San Mauro didn't like those other two."

"Perhaps they didn't ask for his help," a soft voice replies.

Don Osvaldo stands in the tall doorway at the back of the church, but it is a second priest who's spoken. Frail and bony in middle age, but with amused eyes and an unlined face, he holds out both his hands, and something about him draws Duno forward. "*Agnus Dei!* Another of God's lambs come down from the mountain!" this priest declares. "Welcome to San Mauro. I'm Leto Girotti."

"*Piacere, signore.* I am called Du—"

"No names!" Don Leto warns sharply. "If I'm arrested, I can't reveal what I don't know."

"And yet," Osvaldo points out, "everyone's heard of the Red Priest."

"The people here know me, and they protect me. I'm in no danger. Ah! Here is Signora Toselli, who makes the best polenta in Piemonte! Signora, a place at the table for this young man," Leto tells the tiny, wrinkled lady in black. "The other padre and I will come to lunch soon."

When he and Osvaldo are alone in the church, Leto stumps down the center aisle like a cinema pirate. Gripping the back of a pew, he genuflects as best he can and slides sideways, lowering himself onto the front seat. Osvaldo brings a kneeler over, and Leto lifts his peg onto it. "All this rain! The ankle that isn't there aches this time of year! Now tell me the latest, Osvaldo! I haven't seen a newspaper since All Souls'!"

"The Soviets have pushed the Germans out of the Caucasus. And they've retaken Kiev."

"And here? There are rumors of strikes at Fiat."

"Yes, but the Germans arrested fifteen hundred hostages and forced the workers back to the factories."

"The unions will find a way around that," Leto says confidently. "And in the south?"

"Stalemate. The Allies can't get past Monte Cassino. The British Eighth managed to cross the Sangro, but winter's closed in and the offensive stalled. Leto, there are terrible reports from the areas occupied by the Allies. It's chaos. People are starving."

Leto grins at Osvaldo's bulging waistline. "You seem to be eating well." Osvaldo blinks, then unwraps his cincture. "How much did you bring?" Leto asks, eager as a child on Epiphany to see what La Befana has brought him.

"Sixteen thousand." Osvaldo stacks the bundles of bills and rewraps a less impressive waistline. "That's all that was left after we took care of those hiding in the city. We lost money converting it to occupation lire."

"Like the loaves and the fishes, it will be enough."

"Leto, the Gestapo is offering a huge bounty for Jews."

"Trust in God, and in my parishioners." Leto smiles. "I knew you'd come, even if you had to disobey."

Osvaldo's face darkens. "You know what the archbishop said? 'We should do what we can for the Hebrews, but we are shepherds of our own flock.' Leto, how can he be so cold? These people are innocent!"

"You were never very clever about politics, Osvaldo. Popes make archbishops into cardinals. Tirassa wants a red hat from Pacelli. Pacelli is a pragmatic pontiff who wishes to protect the Vatican's neutrality."

"Neutrality!" Osvaldo snorts. "When in history has the Vatican ever been neutral? Leto, why hasn't His Holiness excommunicated Hitler?"

"Be serious, Osvaldo! Vatican City is surrounded. All that stands between the pope and the Gestapo is the Swiss Guard! If the pope were to speak out, he'd be arrested immediately."

"And all Christendom would rise!"

"Catholics across Europe would be persecuted. Innocent people would pay for his boldness."

"Innocent people are already paying—for his silence!"

"Precisely. Either way, lives are lost." Leto massages the place where his stump meets its peg. "What we need are deeds, not words! And that," he says, eyes shining, "is exactly why *you're* here."

EN ROUTE TO SANTA CHIARA

"Your leg, she go in *la guera?*" Duno gasps, trying to keep up.

"*La guerra,*" Don Leto corrects, rolling the *r*'s as vigorously as he climbs. "No, I did not lose my leg in the war. My family are tenant farmers. When I was small, I stepped on an old land mine." The priest stops to gesture a fountain of rocks and dirt, exploding from the ground. "My mother was a strong-minded woman, and when my brothers carried me home, she took a knife and "

He mimes a decisive slash. Duno shudders.

"It was only hanging by a little bit of skin," Leto says. "I lived through the night, and then through the day, the week, the month, and the year. Repeat the words! You must learn!"

"*Il giorno, la settimana, la mese . . . l'anno!*"

"*Il mese.* As in German, month is masculine. Do you need to rest?"

Duno tries to breathe through his nose, but his mouth drops open again. How does the man do it? he wonders. Don Leto looks like he'd blow off the mountain in a stiff breeze.

"It's hard for people born in the lowlands," the priest says. "I'm used to the altitude. Sit! There's no hurry."

The cloudless sky is aquamarine. Mountaintops sparkle, their snowcaps virginally white. The priest reaches into a battered canvas pack. He pulls out two crusty rolls and hands one to Duno. "So," he resumes, "I lived, but I was no good for farming. My family held a meeting. All the uncles, the older cousins. What can we do with this boy who can't work but still eats?"

Swallowing, Duno flinches at the phrase.

"It was good luck for me—*buona fortuna*," the priest insists, "because they sent me away to school! I learned to read, to write. I was good with numbers. I was fifteen when I left my family," he says, glancing at Duno.

"Me, too! *Anch'io*," Duno says. *"Quindici anni!"*

"Yesterday you were nineteen."

Duno's eyes drop.

"A proverb for you, my son. *Pensa oggi, parla domani:* think today, speak tomorrow. You must keep your stories straight." Leto finishes his roll and brushes the crumbs from his palms. "You have time to learn." He gestures toward the mountains that surround them. "Hannibal attacked in the winter, but the Germans are more sensible. The fighting will be in the south until spring. Drink some water," he advises, producing a canteen. "We have a long way to go."

Hours later, terraced fields and the hysterical barking of dogs announce the existence of Santa Chiara. Don Leto points to a large rock with a little shrine to the Savior's nonna nearby and makes sure Duno understands he's to wait there, all night if necessary. "Stay out of sight, *capisce?* I'll send someone to take you the rest of the way."

Leaving the boy with the last of their food and water, Don Leto stumps down one last switchback, and is immediately encircled by small children. Old men wave from the fields, but their wives and daughters come close, drawing drop spindles from apron pockets, working even while they greet him and chat. Leto speaks to each, calling them by name. Two strangers hang back, despite the reassurances of young Bettina Lovera, who chants, "Don Leto! Don Leto!" while formal introductions are made.

The Belgian gentleman is not nearly so old as Santino Cicala believed, nor is the green-eyed Claudia quite the goddess of the lovestruck Calabrian's description. Startlingly tall and slim among the stunted mountain-bred peasants, Claudia is indeed pretty but she looks sturdy as well. And she's already learned to spin yarn like a Valdottavo girl. Yes, Leto decides, she might make Santino a good wife. Perhaps she and her father will be brought to Jesus that way.

He accepts Tercilla Lovera's hospitality, content to be the beg-

gar to whom she can be generous. Bettina is preparing for confirmation, and when she recites the prayers she's memorized, Leto
rewards her with a holy card. Tercilla sends Bettina and Claudia
outside. When the adults are alone, the talk turns inevitably to the
war. No, there has been no word from Tercilla's husband or
brother. No, the Allies have not invaded Genoa. The planes passing overhead are American, but they're based in Corsica, not the
mainland.

"The Allies have a difficult job," Leto says, rising to leave.
"They are up against bad weather and bad terrain, but," he insists
cheerfully, "those very conditions favor the partisans here in the
north!" He stands and takes Alberto Blum's hand. "The mountains belong to us, signore. You and your daughter will be safe in
Santa Chiara." Dirt underfoot, Leto thumps to the door but
swivels on his peg. "*Prego,* signore, is there anything you or your
daughter need?" The gentleman looks doubtful, and Leto presses,
"Anything at all. I can't work miracles, but . . ."

Signor Blum steps outside to whisper, "We don't wish to give
offense to such kind people. But . . . a bath? To be clean, after so
many weeks!"

"*Sì, sì, sì!* I understand. The peasants up here believe that dirt
keeps fleas away, but I have a tub in the rectory, and there's wood
for the boiler. We'll find a way for you to get to San Mauro for a
few hours so you can bathe."

"Padre! Wait!" Bettina calls, and gives Signor Blum's daughter a
little push with her elbow. "Go on, Claudia! Ask him!"

"If it's no trouble," Claudia says shyly, "a book, please?"

"She was a good student," her father says.

"She's read Pierino's books already," Bettina says. "Are there
books about plants, Padre? Claudia Fiori, we call her. She's always
asking the names of flowers."

"A botany text, then! Yes, I can find something like that for
you, signorina." With that Don Leto beckons Claudia to follow
him a few steps farther, where they can speak alone. "I have a message for you," he tells her, eyes bright with fun, as though he were
passing notes in school. "From Santino Cicala!"

"Santino! Is he all right?"

"He's safe, and he didn't forget you, *figlia mia.* He was looking for you, but got lost. He's staying on another farm for now. They're snowed in, but with your father's permission, I'll arrange a meeting in the spring."

He expects excitement, but the extraordinary green eyes fill. "Signore, I don't . . . I can't remember what he looks like!"

Just as well, Leto thinks, amused. Rather than tease, he invites her to consider Santa Chiara, a hamlet so poor that a single metal spoon may be the only heirloom passed from mother to daughter. "No one here has a mirror, Claudia. Do you remember what you look like?"

She stares, and laughs, and wipes her nose on the back of her hand. "No!" she says, astonished. "I don't!"

"The soul is more important than the parcel it comes in! Your Santino has *una buona anima*—a good soul, signorina. Wear his love like a crown."

He bids her good day and stumps away, with one last errand to perform. "Pierino!" he calls, entering the barn.

Tercilla's son appears, silent as a ghost. Leto sets his backpack down and pulls out an oiled rag wrapped around something heavy. "A gift from the milkman. Unfortunately, it's air force issue from '35. I don't know what ammunition it needs."

Pierino takes the Beretta.

"How many are up there now?" Leto asks.

"T-t-twenty-one," Pierino says.

"What about food?"

"P-p-people b-bring it. Nnn-not much, b-b-b-buh—"

"But enough." Leto puts a hand on the veteran's shoulder. "Moses was halt of tongue as well, *figlio mio*. Be proud to share his burden. Does your missing arm ache in all this rain and cold?"

Pierino shrugs noncommittally.

"Think of our Lord, who suffered on the cross. He knows your pain, *figlio mio*. So do I." Struck by a thought, he says, "Pierino, did you hear? Last week, the Valdottavo postman was caught in a German labor sweep."

Pierino nods but frowns: Yes. So?

"A postman with one arm," Leto suggests, "would be of no interest to the Germans. A veteran of the war against the Soviets would be above suspicion among the *repubblicani*. Such a postman could travel anywhere in the valley."

Pierino nods again, this time with a grim smile.

"I'll speak to the district officials in Roccabarbena. It will be my honor to recommend a hero who sustained grievous injury in the service of our nation!" Leto lifts his chin toward the mountain. "There's another recruit waiting for you up at Santa Anna's rock. He's young, and foolish, but he wants to fight."

Pierino grabs a jacket with one sleeve amputated, its extra fabric undoubtedly harvested for other use. When the priest has helped him into it, he asks, "A b-b-blessing, P-padre?" Leto makes the sign of the cross and uses his own left hand to shake Pierino's.

"Spring will come, *figlio mio!*" Leto calls, lolloping away. "We're both alive, Pierino, and we've got three limbs apiece! God is not done with us yet!"

Cadenza d'Inverno
Winter 1943-44

One way and another, on every continent, a war has raged for three thousand years. Mummies, twisted by Pott's spinal variation, have been found in Egypt's looted graves. In the Dark Ages, the wolfish lupus gnawed at skin. When neck glands were attacked, the enemy was known as scrofula, or the King's Evil—defeated, French peasants believed, by the touch of King Clovis, who lived briefly and died without passing his tactics on. White death, the British call it, but unlike its cousin leprosy, tuberculosis is not white. It is the Chartres blue of Robert Koch's methylene stain, the brilliant red of arterial blood.

The field of battle is commonly the human lung, but any organ can be affected. The enemy infiltrates, takes up a defensible position, waits for weakness. Once inside the body, the bacillus is indestructible, its waxy carapace resisting the assaults of drugs and prayer. Attack and retreat, parry and riposte. Stalemate alternates with all-out offensives. Not *Blitzkrieg* then, but a war of attrition, often dismissed in the beginning as civil unrest. A persistent cough? Coal dust in the air, or asthma, or a smoker's just deserts. Weight loss, a general decline in health? Too much work, a poor diet. Gathering exhaustion and irritability: unrefreshing sleep, an overburdened mind. Chills and night fever—influenza, perhaps, or lingering grippe.

Nineteenth-century poets, capable of romanticizing anything, adopted as fashionable the high-necked collars originally worn to hide lesions caused by strumous glands. They made consumption a sign of genius, sensitivity, refinement. No popular novel was complete without a pale young person, delicate and languid, prone to fainting fits. Prima donnas expired beautifully in operas; slum dwellers and industrial workers coughed up their cheesy bleeding lungs without benefit of orchestral accompaniment.

Schiller, Keats, Shelley all lost their private battles. Chopin, Thoreau, Balzac, Paganini were among the famous casualties. Elizabeth Barrett Browning, Robert Louis Stevenson, Ralph Waldo Emerson. Anton Chekhov—physician, dramatist—died of it as well. He once coughed blood for three days and three nights, but decided the hemorrhage was "a burst artery in the throat."

How could a *doctor* have missed the diagnosis? Werner Schramm once wondered, but he understands it now. He has seen starving men chew shoes and eat rats raw when the reward for survival was just another day of ceaseless labor and pitiless beatings. He himself fights for breath after agonizing breath, hating each moment of pain but desperate for the next. The soul craves hope, as the body hungers for food.

In November, he left Sant'Andrea in a coffin, dead drunk but not quite dead, packed with a decaying pigeon whose nauseating odor discouraged inspection of the coffin's contents. "Taking him home . . . the family plot," he heard Renzo say when the truck's movement stopped. Troops at checkpoints saw a young mother who wept while an old one sat dry-eyed next to the box. Soldiers manufactured details on their own. A bereaved widow, a fatherless baby. A mother who never liked the dead son-in-law. "Sì, certo, signori. Your papers are in order. Move on."

Schramm remembers little else from the jolting ride, beyond one short conversation, overheard. "Renzo," the old woman said testily, "I will never understand why I let you talk me into this." "Mamma," her son replied, "I'm paying a debt to a surgeon who was killed in Abyssinia. He can't collect."

"And this surgeon can?" the younger woman asked. Renzo must have nodded.

All winter, that nameless surgeon's beneficiary lies bundled against the cold beneath layers of wool and fur, marking time by the light on a mountain visible through a hayloft's unglazed windows. On windless days, Schramm gazes at the peak—thoughtless, motionless, waiting for the next storm. Sometimes the snow is so fine and weightless it fills the air like fog or smoke. Twice blizzards have struck like hurricanes, lightning exploding within clouds so heavy with snow they seemed to press the air from his rattling chest.

Sweating through fever dreams, he awakens now and then to frost on his dampened blankets, and to the old woman's hard, thin face. The young mother is like the distant moon, filling his sky briefly, at long intervals. But he knows she is near, in the small house connected to this barn by a second-story passage. Schramm hears her baby cry sometimes and listens, weeping stupidly, to the lullabies its mother sings.

You'll spoil that child, he thinks. And then he sleeps again.

Northwestern Italy

1944
Anno Fascista XXIII

March 1944

"Where is the other lady?" Schramm asks when the young woman appears two days in a row.

She sets a basin filled with warm water onto the floor, pushes the hayloft shutters fully open, stands outlined by the sunshine. For the first time since they arrived here, the breeze carries no knife. "Signora Savoca took advantage of the weather. She's down in San Mauro for a few days."

"The signora is your mother?"

"Stefano's. The man who brought you here?" she prompts. "Stefano Savoca?"

"He said his name was Renzo."

She calls herself Marisa. Lovely, even if it's not her real name. He knows almost nothing about her except that she is gentle, and he is half in love. A weakened man. A pretty nurse who is not contemptuous of that weakness. The situation is banal, and she counters it by making herself sisterly: casual and matter-of-fact in caring for him. Staying windward, she pulls his blankets off and airs them over a laundry line strung between the house and barn. Returning to his bedside, she makes a move for the sheet. Well enough to be startled, he snatches it back.

Dipping a rag into the water, she wrings it out. "Herr Schramm, you are in Italy," she reminds him, washing his face, neck, chest. "No country on earth is more densely populated by male nudes. Nuns in Florence know more about reproductive anatomy than whores in Marseilles!"

He stares.

"Sometimes I forget you're German. That was a joke," she says, resoaping the rag. "Should I have applied for a permit before I told it?" He smiles, and she hands the washcloth to him. "You're well enough to do the parts that make nuns blush." She leaves the hayloft with his chamber pot. "How old is your baby?" he asks when she returns.

"Rosina?" Marisa pauses to count. "Six months! Imagine that!" She busies herself, using a clean handkerchief over her hands to collect the dirty ones she'll boil. "No blood for three weeks!" she notes. "Signora Savoca is right. You're going to live."

"Life is full of missed opportunities." It's her turn to stare. "A joke," he says.

"Next time, get a permit!" Marisa stoops to give the washrag one last swish, twists it nearly dry. "I'll bring soup later," she says, flinging washwater out the window. The clothesline pulley squeaks as she reels the line in.

"I should begin to walk a little. Tomorrow perhaps."

She pauses, a blanket over her arm. "Why not today?"

That afternoon, she brings him a paisley robe that must have been Renzo's and helps him to the edge of the bed. Spent, he sits, rests, then manages a few steps on shaking legs. After his soup he tries again, and with Marisa's encouragement, he crosses the hayloft to a chair and back before they hear the baby's waking wail.

"Mamma's coming, *cara mia!*" Marisa calls. "If the weather holds," she tells Schramm, "I'll open up the house tomorrow. You can come down for a visit."

The clouds pile up overnight, but the temperature stays warm enough for rain, and a change of scenery is a powerful incentive. With frequent stops, Marisa guides him across the sloping covered passage that connects the barn to the house, through an open door, and across a swept plank floor. Feeble as a good intention, he watches his own feet until she settles him at a table. Propped on his elbows, he wills his heart to slow, concentrating on each breath until he can spare the energy to look around.

"*Terra nova!*" she says. "Do you feel like Columbus?"

A pedal-powered sewing machine sits on a sturdy worktable under the window, where the pale winter light is best. An oil lamp hangs from a metal chain in the center of the ceiling. Suspended from a tripod in the open hearth: an iron pot. The fire's been built up, to counteract a chilly breeze through the open door. A cupboard holds a jug of olive oil, a bottle of wine, and three slumping burlap sacks—cornmeal, dried chickpeas, and chestnut flour. Rafters, posts, door, and windowframes—all retain the shape and color of the branch or trunk from which they were hewn. The house is simple, but beautiful in its way. Long ago, someone plastered its thick stone walls, and these have been adorned with trompe l'oeil windows that reveal summer landscapes or the sea—

"Mirella," his hostess says firmly.

"*Scusi?*"

"My real name is Mirella. The other lady is Lidia."

"*Grazie,*" he says, touched by her trust. He lifts a hand toward the walls. "Are you the artist?"

"More artisan than artist. My father was a *stuccatore* a specialist in fresco restoration. He started me on forced perspective when I was very young. My son's age, now that I think of it. Angelo's almost eight."

"I have a boy that age! And another, of six years. They are Klaus and Erwin. Where is your son?"

"In a boarding school. He was safer there, away from the bombing. My husband couldn't leave his work. He's still in Sant'Andrea."

"And this is Rosina," Schramm says. Her cradle is on the floor, near the fire and as far from the sick man as it can be in this tiny house. Arms flailing, legs pumping at a restraining blanket, she is practicing B's: "Bub, bub bub."

"You must miss your family, Herr Schramm."

"Yes. As you do, no doubt."

They glance at each other, and Mirella clears her throat. An unspoken agreement is reached: they will not speak of absent family. The emotions are too raw, tears too close.

"Trompe l'oeil is very common in Liguria," Schramm observes.

"Painters are cheaper than masons and sculptors."

"It's also cheaper to employ relatives than strangers, I think."

She smiles. "My father had me bagging pigments when I was four! I loved the blues: lapis lazuli, cobalt, ultramarine. All I have here are pastels, but the colors please Rosina."

"Signora Savoca has not returned?"

"No, and I expected her back by now."

"She hates me, I think."

"Bub, bub, bub. Bub!" the baby shouts, thrilled by her own volume.

"Signora Savoca lost children to influenza in 1918." Mirella
picks Rosina up and *bubs* back at her for a time. "She thinks Bayer
aspirin was poisoned. Her theory is that Germans were exacting
revenge for their defeat in the Great War."

"That's absurd!"

She smiles at the baby. "Two of her older girls took the aspirin.
They died. The youngest children didn't. They lived."

"Coincidence."

"Probably." Mirella plants noisy kisses on chubby cheeks, her
eyes on Schramm. "Distressing to be hated because of lies, isn't it."

He shifts uncomfortably in his chair. "Especially when there are
so many legitimate reasons to be hated."

"You people do keep starting wars," she says tartly. "Every family in Italy has lost men because of Germany, and this occupation
isn't helping your reputation."

"I imagine it would make a nice change if we tried tourism."

She laughs, genuinely amused. "The Allies aren't especially
popular here either. They leveled Monte Cassino a few weeks
ago."

"For God's sake, why?" Sitting on a hill between Naples and
Rome, the fourteen-hundred-year-old Benedictine monastery
was the jewel of medieval Italy.

"The Americans said the Wehrmacht was calling in artillery
strikes from the abbey. The Germans deny it. Either way, it's
gone." She jounces Rosina on her knee. "The Allies are still south
of Rome. On the other hand," she reports cheerfully, "the Russians have pushed your panzers all the way back to Poland! And
there've been huge bombing raids on Berlin and Cologne— *Dio
mio,* I'm so sorry! Do you have family there?"

"They are in Freiburg."

"Then they're all right," she says, awkwardly.

"Probably." Schramm turns his attention to a hand-carved
crutch hanging from a hook by the front door.

"The last tenant was a hunchback," Mirella tells him. "Tuberculosis of the spine, I think you'd call it. People around here are still frightened of the house. It's been empty for years."

"I am probably not contagious anymore, but are you not concerned?"

"My uncle died of tuberculosis when I was fifteen. He lived with us when I was a child." She sets the baby back into the cradle. Astonished, Rosina produces a scowl of imperial displeasure, large brown eyes following her mother's move toward the iron pot hanging in the open hearth. "X-rays show spots on my lungs, but they're encapsulated." Mirella tucks her apron between her legs, to keep the fabric away from the fire, and ladles thin soup into a thick pottery bowl. "Renzo explained about keeping the windows open and so on. And Rosina is upwind." She brings the bowl and a wooden spoon to him. "The soup's very bland, I'm afraid. Salt is like gold these days. Your Italian is quite good. Did you study Latin?"

"Yes, in school."

"And your accent is Florentine."

"I spent a year in Florence when I was young. Words come back to me. I worked hard last fall to remember the grammar." She steps to the window. Light from the setting sun makes a nimbus of her hair. "It must be close to the equinox," he remarks, waiting for the broth to cool.

"Yes—it's March already! Friday, the seventeenth, I think. Easy to lose track up here."

An experimental howl issues from the cradle. Mirella takes an oil lamp from the top of the cupboard and puts it next to the one already on the table. She doesn't light either, though it's getting dark. Rosina begins to wail. Mirella stoops to lift her.

"Don't pick her up!" Schramm says sharply.

"Why on earth not? She's probably hungry."

"She should wait. It's good for her."

"I can't imagine how. She's not a prioress fasting her way into heaven."

"You should put her on a feeding schedule," he insists, eyes averted as Mirella tosses a cloth over her shoulder and unbuttons her blouse behind it. "If you pick her up, she'll cry for what she wants."

"German babies submit their requests in writing, I suppose."

Rosina snorts and gulps and snuffles before settling in to nurse steadily. Schramm, too, concentrates on feeding himself. By the time he pushes the empty bowl aside, the spoon feels as heavy as a shovel. Leaning on the tabletop, he gazes at Mirella. "You look so familiar . . ."

Wryly, she strikes a pose with Rosina. "Have you been to the Staatliche Museum in Berlin?"

"That's it! The Botticelli—"

"*Madonna and Child with Angels,* 1477. Also the first angel on the left in *Primavera,* at the Uffizi. According to family legend, my many-times-great-grandmother was one of Botticelli's models."

Looking at her, Schramm realizes the full genius of the painter, who captured the ordinary tiredness of a pretty mother who's breast-fed for six months, and whose Son still wakes up most nights. "The resemblance is strong," he says.

"It's a lovely story, but . . ." She shakes her head.

"Inheritance halves each generation," Schramm agrees. "There would be little continuity over four centuries." He had forgotten the pleasures of conversation. "So! You don't like Germans. You don't approve of the Allies. What are your politics?"

In a singsong voice, she tells Rosina, "Mamma thinks politicians are frauds at best, and tyrants, given half a chance, *cara mia,* but kings can be decorative *and* useful!" She smiles at Schramm. "Renzo calls me an anarcho-monarchist."

"Are you the one who wouldn't marry him?"

"He told you that?" She seems surprised. "It was a long time ago." The sated, sleepy baby quiets, and Mirella lays her in the cradle, humming softly. Standing at the window, her back to Schramm, she buttons her blouse. "Sun's almost down!" she says, shivering.

"I should get back to the barn so you can close these windows."

"*Prego.* Stay awhile more." She brings a loaf of chestnut bread from the cupboard to the table, and then a bottle of local wine and two small glasses. "The bread's overdone. I haven't quite grasped the nuances of baking on a hearth." Snapping a straw from a broom by the fireplace, she presses the end on a coal, then uses it as a match to light the two oil lamps. A tendril of smoke rises when she blows the straw's flame out. Without a word of explanation, she closes her eyes and holds her hands before them. *"Baruch ata Adonai, Eloheynu melech ha-olam . . ."*

Friday. Sunset. The unfamiliar language. "You're Jewish!"

Her eyes open. *"Sì, certo!* Didn't you know?"

"I thought you must be Catholic. Renzo said you didn't marry because of religious differences."

Mirella shakes her head as though to clear it. "I married a rabbi. That could be construed as a religious difference," she says, pouring the wine. "Ordinarily, the husband says the next blessing, but these are not ordinary times." Another chanted prayer and she hands Schramm a glass. "Loosely translated," she informs him, "that one means, Thank God grapes ferment."

"I'll drink to that," he says.

"A moment longer." She places her hand on the bread and sings a third prayer before breaking the loaf into pieces and giving Schramm a share. *"L'chaim!"* she says, raising her glass. "To life!"

Schramm reaches gingerly across the table to clink glasses. "If you're Jewish, then why didn't you marry him?"

She chews and swallows before answering. "Have you ever read Svevo? Like Balli, Renzo loves women very much, but all of them equally, and only when he's in the mood." She sips the wine. "I wanted a more settled life than he was likely to provide. Now look at me! On a mountaintop, in a hunchback's cabin, with a German officer. Not the bourgeois domesticity I envisioned." She breaks off a smaller piece of bread thoughtfully. "And when Renzo came back from Abyssinia, he was . . . different. Herr Schramm, do you understand why he drinks so much?"

Schramm puts his glass down. Looks away. "Yes," he says. "I believe I do."

The storm that night is silent but relentless. By morning the entire valley is enveloped in the peculiar hush of deep spring snow. With Rosina and Schramm still asleep, Mirella is happy to lose herself in small tasks. She swings the pot of soup back over the coals, and nudges a kettle of water closer to the heat. She did as many chores as possible before sundown last night, but she has to tend the fire or they'll freeze. The Polish Hasidim would be scandalized, but Mirella suspects that in ancient times women never had a genuine day of rest.

Thanks to Renzo's contacts, she has real coffee beans and a grinder. She pours boiling water over the grounds and steeps them like a Turk. While they settle, she hurries out to the privy, shuffling through the snow to clear a path. When she returns, the full fragrance greets her, and she pours carefully, savoring the quiet. Thank God for simple gifts, she thinks. I am alive and well rested, with a cup of coffee to warm my hands and raise my spirits.

For nearly a week after Renzo brought the four of them to Decimo, Mirella was all but unconscious. She slept, woke to nurse Rosina, and slept again. A husband, three pregnancies, small children: there was a time when Mirella Soncini could count on one hand the nights of sound sleep she'd had since 1935. When the war began, things got worse.

Screamed awake by sirens, she and Iacopo would leap from bed, grab the children, and run to a shelter. When the all-clear sounded, her relief at seeing her own home intact was always blighted by others' losses. Iacopo would hurry off to comfort the bereaved, leaving Mirella to face the tedium of clearing away the dust and grit and ash blown in from the harbor, again and again and again.

Even if there was no attack, she had to be up early to do the marketing before everything was gone. Her youth has been squandered in queues, shuffling forward step by step to claim a kilo of greenish potatoes at one store, the children's milk ration at another, the family's bread ration at a third. The only thing she could predict was the shortage of something basic: oil, sugar, eggs, salt, pasta, rice. Three meals a day to get on the table, and every one a struggle.

Slowly devotion to family and community condensed to stubborn determination. She would stay at Iacopo's side, even if that meant huddling in bomb shelters. She would give Angelo the courage to enjoy the excitement of a raid, even if her own heart pounded with fear. She would teach herself to appreciate moments of fleeting peace. The feel of her son's cheek against her own. The taste of a fresh tomato. The weight of her sleeping husband's hand on her breast.

Since leaving home, Mirella's longing for Iacopo and Angelo has been keen and constant, but there are compensations here. Without the demands of congregational life, she's been free to spend hours with Rosina, gazing at her daughter's perfect little body, playing with her, singing to her, watching her grow. In this small, safe place, Mirella can keep order and count on a routine. For her, the solitude and silence of the mountain are daily pleasures.

Lidia, by contrast, has been as restless as a dog on a chain, and craves politics more than fresh fruit. Once or twice a month, Renzo hauls supplies up the mountain, including a stack of newspapers: *La Stampa, L'Italia Libera, Gazzetta del Popolo, Avanti!* As welcome as he is, Mirella dreads his visits. She herself prefers any sort of book to current events and hates the political wrangles Renzo and his mother get into.

She shivers, notices the fire, adds a bit more wood. Pulls the blanket over Rosina's cradle and opens the shutters to reel in a few diapers, dried crinkly-stiff on the line. Back in Sant'Andrea, Mirella never thought about the peasant laundresses who came into towns and carried off huge baskets of linen. A knock on the door, a shy smile, a few lire pressed gratefully into a rough, chapped palm. A week later, jumbled sheets and shirts and underthings, soiled and smelly, were transformed into neatly folded, beautifully pressed stacks of cleanliness.

Since coming here, her cracked, red hands and aching back have taught Mirella to respect the work behind so many things city people take for granted. "Now you understand!" Don Leto said happily. "You know the people, and you know their labor! When I was young, I kept accounts for our landlord and found out how little his tenants got. The *contadini* raise rabbits and pigs for his table. They live on polenta. Polenta with beans, polenta with potatoes, polenta with cheese or milk, but always polenta."

Renzo made her look at things with a shrewder eye. "Peasants aren't stupid, Mirella. They've got rabbits and chickens in pens hidden in the woods. Almost everyone keeps a piglet aside— where do you think they get their sausage? Most of these houses have false walls for wine and olive oil left off the inventory."

"The *padrone* steals big, the *contadini* steal small," Don Leto said when she asked him about that. "When larceny and lying are a way of life, the sin is the landlord's. You can see for yourself the effects of poverty. Children grow up stunted in mind and body. When everyone in a family must work so hard, no one can stop to think of a better way."

Lidia is convinced that the Communists have a better way. From each according to his abilities, to each according to his need. No landlords living off the misery of sharecroppers. Workers sharing equitably in the fruits of their labor. Lidia is thrilled by the courage of factory workers in Milan and Turin. Daring the *fascisti* to break their strikes, they mean to starve the Nazi war machine. This much Renzo was willing to commend, but when his mother praised the Soviets' stupendous military production, he snorted. "Do you know how Stalin taught Russian peasants to show up at factory jobs on time? He had the ones who were late shot. So much for the people's paradise, Mamma."

What are your politics? Schramm asked last night.

Mirella answered with a joke, but the truth is that she doesn't trust her own opinions. As a child, she reveled in the pageantry surrounding Benito Mussolini. He was as handsome as a storybook prince, and he rode a beautiful white horse. Her father believed in *il Duce*'s greatness and in the Fascist drive to make unified Italy a world power. She loved her father, so she believed what he believed, flattered when he talked to her like a grown-up. When someone questioned why Italian sons and taxes should be squandered on an African adventure, her father supported the Abyssinian war. "Italy's destiny is to rule lesser nations! And let no one question our loyalty! Jews have always been and will always be a part of the national glory."

For all her father's political passion, when Mirella turned seventeen, it was not empire that enthralled her but Iacopo Soncini. And it was not war that frightened her but Renzo Leoni. "Mirella, there's a sky above the sky! Let me show it to you," he pleaded. There were currents in the ocean of air above the world, he told her. Rivers of wind carving valleys into a countryside of cloud, a geography of blue and gold and white. "One quick flight, Mirella. No barrel rolls, I swear! And I'll land her like a kiss."

Why did she refuse?

Above her, the roof slates have warmed. A chunk of snow slides off noisily, hitting the ground with a slushy thud. Rosina wakes up with a wail. Mirella sets her thoughts and coffee cup aside. The day begins in earnest, with all its necessary tasks, Shabbat or not. She has no more time to think while the sun is up.

Hours later, her day ends as usual. She checks on Werner, banks the fire, kisses Rosina's forehead one last time, and crawls onto her own lumpy mattress, pulling three woolen blankets up to cover her shoulders. Ordinarily she falls asleep with grateful ease, but tonight, she watches firelight on the shallow vaulted ceiling and thinks again of the men she chose between.

Soft-bodied, soft-spoken, the scholar she married now lives like a spy in his native land. Braving checkpoints with false papers, open to denunciation at any moment, Iacopo risks his life to bring comfort and wisdom to frightened foreigners who expect from moment to moment to be found out, sold out, bombed out, burned out of their hiding places. The once-dashing pilot came home from Africa with a hero's medal, and a thirst for grappa that seems unquenchable. Why had she heard Iacopo's hesitant proposal of marriage more clearly than Renzo's call to courage? Was it a failure of nerve or a triumph of common sense? If she had married Renzo, would his life be better, or her own life worse?

God knows, she thinks turning over, but God be blessed: at seventeen, I made the right decision.

Borgo San Mauro

"Will you look at that! And her, named for the Virgin!" Adele Toselli whispers, scandalized in gray morning light. "How could her parents let her out of the house in that skirt!"

"She probably rolls the waistband after she leaves." Lidia moves the curtain slightly. "Watch the soldiers."

Adele sighs. "Can you remember the last time a man looked at you like that?"

"December 13, 1898." Lidia lets the curtain fall. "Nobody ever watches old women, and that's what we can use against them." When Adele hesitates, Lidia asks, "Do you know what the Germans call us? *Alte schwarze Krähen*—old black crows."

Widowed before God gave her children, Adele Toselli has worn mourning and served the priests of San Mauro for over fifty years. There was gossip in the beginning, but the first Father was very old. The second was very holy and cared nothing for women. And Don Leto? "I knew Leto Girotti when he had two legs!" Adele informs anyone who asks, and most of those who don't.

"You're sure you know what to do?" she asks Lidia.

"*Cara mia,* I heard more about engines at my dinner table than I care to remember. That's all my husband and son talked about!"

Adele drums arthritic fingers on a table she has scrubbed for half a century. "Why not? Why not!"

Lidia turns her back, wraps something in a handkerchief, then slips the little packet into her handbag. Bending at the waist, she smiles hollowly at Adele, who giggles like a schoolgirl and deposits her own dentures on a cupboard shelf. They leave the rectory in lumpy layers of black wool, taking the long way to San Mauro's central market. Turning down a deserted side street, they age step by step. By the time they reach the crowded piazza, they're tottering in pitiable anonymity, pinched and wrinkled faces aimed at the cobbles.

Adele tenses, rehearsing what she'll say if someone recognizes her, but Lidia was right. It's cold. German soldiers in greatcoats loiter with casual menace in front of what used to be the municipal hall. Wrapped to the eyes in scarves, townspeople want to finish their shopping unmolested and get back inside.

Lidia increases pressure on Adele's arm, glancing at the *latteria.* Their unwitting accomplice emerges from the shop with her can of rationed milk. Dimpled knees flashing under the roll-topped skirt, legs pinked by wind and chill, coat unbuttoned despite the cold. The younger Germans grin and nudge one another. The boldest calls out a crude remark, but a blond and haughty corporal stares hard with hooded blue eyes. Favoring him with a side-long glance, the luscious Maria Avoni slowly raises a hand to brush back heavy mahogany-colored hair, its glory undiminished by anything so sensible as a hat. The movement is intended to press her nipples more firmly against a too tight sweater, and it achieves its purpose. Head high, she feigns indifference to cheers and whistles.

With all that to enjoy, what soldier would waste a glance at two *alte schwarze Krähen* with their cheeks falling in, clutching each other's arms with blue-veined and spotted hands? The old crows pass between a pair of BMW motorcycles that lean on kickstands outside the garrison office. One huddles solicitously over her toothless companion, who crouches next to the engines just long enough to . . . oh, tighten the laces of a high-topped shoe, perhaps? Two quick moves, and the ladies hobble on.

March is as shameless a tease as Maria Avoni, with hints of spring and reminders of winter by turns. Overnight the wind shifts, the air warms. Tuesday's sun heats up the gravel track that leads to Decimo. Lidia Leoni is tired, her feet chilled and sore, but she does not go inside, not yet. She picks her way across the yard to the edge of a high cliff near the hunchback's house.

"You're back!" Mirella calls, standing in the doorway. "I was starting to worry. Is everything all right?"

"Yes, of course! Splendid sunset," Lidia comments, without turning. Casually, she reaches into her handbag, withdraws a pair of ignition wires, and flicks them into the void with a slight movement of her wrist. She faces Mirella and smiles brightly. "Adele sends her regards."

TABACCHERIA MARRAPODI
VALDOTTAVO

"Where's the cash coming from?" It's cold again today, but Tino Marrapodi's face is pasty with sweat. "Eight years, I run this store, and I never saw so much cash!"

There's enough of the new postman's arm below the elbow to serve as a sort of hook, and Pierino Lovera uses it to keep the leather mail pouch open while he paws through its contents with his left hand. "*Nnn-n-niente, sssignore,*" Pierino announces regretfully.

"Look again. Maybe a postcard, down at the bottom?" The storekeeper's older boy was sent to North Africa in 1941. Three

months ago, his younger was drafted into a Republican army unit
that's been sent to Germany for training. Neither's been heard
from since. "Nobody paid cash before," Marrapodi says worriedly.
"A man would come in for kerosene, tobacco. Some corduroy.
He'd pay with lard, cheese. Maybe a basket of eggs. We eat the
eggs. Couple days later, I get a stack of wood for the lard. I whole-
sale the cheese in San Mauro. One time, I ended up with a wagonful of broom straw! What good is a wagonful of broom straw?
my wife wanted to know. More good than a ledgerful of scrib-
bling, that's what I told her!"

The large black sign behind the counter bears the king's crest
and the Fascist sheaf of wheat. "Bertino Marrapodi is the official
licensee of a state store," the sign proclaims, "authorized to sell
the monopoly goods of the Italian government: tobacco, salt,
matches, stamps, and quinine." Sale of any other goods is forbidden. To prosper in the midst of poverty, the storekeeper must
make two and two equal five in accounts receivable, but only three
in accounts payable. Like Jesus, he turns water into wine, making
ten liters of *nebbiolo* into eleven, fiddling the arithmetic accord-
ingly. Tino's days are spent negotiating complicated deals, his
nights rehearsing his defense if someone rats on him. "I have the
only store on this side of the valley, Your Grace. The *contadini*
would have to walk all day to get to San Mauro, so I make a few
other items for sale. Pots, pans. Safety pins. Pasta, cloth."

Tino is confident such infractions of his license will be overlooked, but it's strictly forbidden to sell liquor to the old men who
meet here every day to play cards. The law forbids playing cards
on the premises, so Tino makes them sit outside in the cold, and
they're resentful. It's only a matter of time before somebody puts
the bite on him: "Pay me off, or I'll make trouble for you!"

Pierino finishes his rummage through the mailbag. "*Nnn-n-
niente,*" he says again.

Marrapodi presses his fingers into his belly. "Heartburn," he
says. "Keeps me awake all night! How can I sleep with so many
worries?" His boys are missing. His strongbox is filled with
German-printed occupation lire. There are shortages in the Roccabarbena warehouse. Without a kickback to the wholesaler, his
store's tobacco supply would dry up completely. There've been

ugly scenes—people shouting, accusing him of profiteering—but he only raised his prices to cover the bribes. "The cash worries me," he says again, pressing harder into his stomach. "What if someone denounces me?"

Pierino offers his left hand to Marrapodi. "Www-wa-watch mmmy b-b-bi—?"

"Your bicycle? *Sì, certo.*"

They step outside together. It's chilly, but the sun is shining through a break in the clouds. The hamlet centered on Tino's store is just a few small stone houses next to even fewer big stone barns. Tino lifts his chin toward a footpath that leads upward toward ever tinier and poorer places, where the most isolated sharecroppers scratch at thin soil and raise small, skinny children. "The last postman used to leave mail here for them," Tino says. "You don't have to take it all the way."

Pierino shrugs and mugs: I know, but I can't help myself. I'm a conscientious man.

Taking Pierino's good arm, Marrapodi draws close. "Be careful," he warns the postman quietly. "They're Communists up there."

In the beginning, war seemed like a good idea. The army was a big new market for produce and grain. Piemonte sent four divisions of draftees to Russia, and the boys got nice uniforms with leather boots. With so many young men drafted, there were plenty of jobs in the towns and cities.

Soon, though, old taxes got higher, new ones more imaginative. The dog tax was infuriating. First a small tax on watchdogs, then a larger one on truffle dogs, and finally an impossible levy on hunting dogs. What's next? people asked. A chicken tax? A tax on piss, like Vespasian's?

The war is bleeding everyone dry. The *contadini* already split their harvest with landlords and their crooked factors. When the Blackshirts started showing up, you couldn't slaughter a hog without a gang of enforcers demanding a quarter. Resist, and they'd open your scalp. Now it's Germans sweeping through the valley, dragging anyone in trousers from the fields, taking anything they want. In a good year, the *contadini* make a bare living, and now they're squeezed from all directions. The Germans are offering huge bounties for Jews and partisans, and they're burning out anyone who hides them. Would you blame the *contadini* for informing?

"*Ei!* Pierino!" Attilio Goletta yells from his hayloft when the postman comes into sight. "Did you hear? Ocelli's truffle dog has learned to sniff out *fascisti!* You know how you can tell when he finds one?"

Pierino grins up at him, waiting for the punch line.

"He shits!" Attilio laughs hugely and tosses his pitchfork aside. Brown, bald, and barrel-chested, the farmer clumps down the exterior staircase in wooden clogs. "How can you tell if a new bridge is good?" he asks, wiping both hands on his pants and offering his left. "Drive over it with a truckload of Germans. If it falls down, it's a good bridge!"

A tiny six-year-old runs over from the garden to tug on Pierino's empty sleeve. "*Ei!* Pierino!" he pipes. "What's the difference between a dog and a Nazi?"

Smiling expectantly, Pierino shakes his head: I don't know.

"The Nazi lifts his arm!"

Pierino smiles, and Attilio roars, but gives the kid a shove toward the garden. "Get those rows ready! I don't want to see any weeds!"

The ground the Golettas work is so bad they need every child, every daylight hour, six and a half days a week, year in and year out, to feed themselves without going further into debt. Attilio's oldest boy, Tullio, is with the partisans, which makes everything harder. The Golettas aren't just supporting themselves and their younger kids, either. There's Florina's mother, plus Attilio's widowed sister and her two daughters, and three *ebrei* besides.

Pierino holds out an envelope, and Attilio grins. "Holy cards from Don Leto?"

Dollars from Hebrews in America become francs in Switzerland. A priest at the border smuggles them to a bishop in Genoa, who turns them into lire. The milkman brings that money to Don Leto, who distributes it to those who come to Mass. Pierino delivers the rest to isolated families like the Golettas and Canobbios and the Ocelli, who've taken in foreign Jews the way his own family has.

With his youngest son out of earshot, Attilio leans toward
Pierino and whispers, "You hear about Pinocchio? He goes to
Gepetto and says, Every time I make love, my girl complains she
gets splinters! Gepetto gives him some sandpaper, *ne?* Couple of
weeks later, he runs into Pinocchio again and says, *Ei,* Pinocchio,
you getting along with the girls now? Pinocchio says, Who needs
girls?"

Laughing, Pierino hefts his bag. He knows where Attilio's getting cash, but God knows where he gets his jokes. "Mmm-marrap-
podi's ssssusp-picious. B-b-battista, too."

"Marrapodi's a moron. And my cousin's a sack of shit, just like
his father. Battista's always saying, 'I'm a Knight of Labor! I
worked for everything I got!' *Merda!* Battista bought that farm with
money that should have been my father's, and I hope the bastard
gets a cancer. Florina!" Attilio yells, fuming. "The postman's here!"

Florina hustles out of the house with three loaves of bread and
a sweater knit from lumpy yarn. People say she was once the prettiest girl in Valdottavo, but ten pregnancies on, Florina is bowlegged and bent, with more fingers than teeth. She wraps the
bread in the sweater and slips the bundle into Pierino's mailbag.
"Bring thith to my thon," she lisps. "Tell Tullio: I pray for him and
the otherth."

Pierino resumes his climb toward the Cave of San Mauro, but he
stops when he sees the red thread tied around a certain branch.
Removing it, he veers onto a goat track, climbs alone and unob-
served for half an hour. He arrives at the appointed place, lets the
mailbag thump to the ground, and sits beside it. Still awkward
with his left hand, but getting better, he unbuckles the leather flap
and pulls out the chunk of cheese and apple Signora Toselli
packed for him this morning.

Across the valley, half-buried in snow, the hamlet of Santa
Chiara looks like part of the mountainside, its sloping slate roofs
as dull as the sky. He hasn't been home in nearly a month, but Don
Leto's housekeeper looks after him. The rectory has lots of books,
and Don Leto likes to talk about them. "I, too, am the first of my
family to be literate," the priest said. "We who love to study are
like pigs with wings, *ne?*"

Or warriors with one arm, Pierino thought.

He has steeped himself in the classics, reading late into each night, until he dreams of battles fought in stately, sonorous words. Like Scipio Africanus, Pierino has set himself to learn from the enemies of Rome.

He is only twenty-one—his education aborted by war, his arm truncated by war, his tongue tied up like a dog by war. Pierino Lovera's name will never be in a book, but he understands war, and he knows how to win this one. He's studied the tactics used against Giulius Caesar by Cassivellaunus; understands the trap laid by the German chieftain Arminius, who destroyed the Legions of Publius Quintilius Varus in the Teutoburger Wald. Supplied from the countryside, aided by relatives and neighbors, highly mobile indigenous irregulars have always been able to tie up conventional troops, disrupting and delaying their movement, confusing and defeating much stronger regular forces. History will show that Adolf Hitler is not Caesar but Pyrrhus, who won battle after battle but lost so much each time that he lost his war in the end.

Now, at last, Pierino has found a man who can make others hear what Pierino can only think. The man who has watched him all this time. "Ready?" Jakub Landau asks, stepping into view.

Pierino hoists his mailbag, and leads the way.

CAVE OF SAN MAURO

Duno Brössler hunches on a lump of rock, a dirty blanket around his shoulders, an oily rag draped over his knees. His fingers are blue and he shivers convulsively, but he's learned to ignore the cold.

Methodically, he takes a 7.65mm RIAF Beretta '35 to pieces. Removes the magazine, turns the safety on. Locks the slide, pushes the barrel back, lifts it from the rear. He is not worried about being disarmed on duty. He can field-strip and reassemble the pistol in sixty seconds, and he can do it one-handed. Like Pierino.

Duno takes the afternoon watch, because that's when Pierino's likely to arrive. Most of the boys loathe sentry duty. It's lonely, boring, and cold, but Duno doesn't mind. Pierino was colder in Russia.

Duno detests the Republic of Salò because Pierino detests it. He despises the *repubblicani* because Pierino despises them. He loathes the Germans on his own account, and Pierino hates them, too, but that puzzled Duno in the beginning. "Why do you hate the Germans so much, and the Russians so little?" Duno asked. "Russians took your arm!"

Duno remembers Pierino's answer as if the maimed man had spoken with the fluency of an orator. "The Russians were defending their homeland," he said. "We, too, will defend our homes against the Germans, and against the Allies if they try to rule us. We'll fight the landlords and the *repubblicani*. We will defeat anyone who comes to take land we've watered with our sweat."

Pierino was patient with Duno's struggle to learn Italian; Duno appreciated the time Pierino required to finish a sentence. After Don Leto introduced them, it took the whole of their climb up here for Pierino to explain where they were going. The Cave of San Mauro, high in the mountainside, has hidden fugitives for centuries. When Napoleon invaded Italy, the valley's women were hidden from the French here. In this war, it's the young men who are at risk during *rastellamenti*.

Una rastella is a hay rake, Pierino explained. The Germans descend on groups of potential laborers and rake them up for work gangs: "*Un r-r-rastellammmmento.*" By the time Pierino got the word out, Duno had memorized it.

Apart from Duno himself, the San Mauro Brigade consists of local kids born in the unlucky years of 1924 and 1925. Draftees could either serve in the Republican army under German command or risk being raked up. Many of the eighteen-year-olds who reported for duty have deserted, bringing home their guns, and stories of German insult and abuse.

Four notes: whistled. Duno stands and returns the notes, higher. *Nessun dorma! Nessun dorma!* The signal was Duno's idea. He has loved the aria since he was small, when his father booked an opera company touring *Turandot*. Duno knows now what the lyrics mean. *Nessun dorma!* No one sleeps! Appropriate, he thought, for those who keep watch.

When Pierino rounds the last switchback, Duno hurries to meet him, Beretta in hand. "Pierino, watch me strip this—!" He skids on the gravelly slope.

Pierino's not alone. Tall, blond, and powerfully built, the man with him looks like a recruiting poster for the SS. Swallowing his surprise, Duno says, "I know you! I was at Sainte-Gisèle. You're Jakub Landau!"

Everyone in Sainte-Gisèle knew Jakub Landau's story. He was a Polish Jew, but one who spoke perfect German and looked so Aryan that a gauleiter actually believed Landau's claim to be a *Volksdeutscher* named Hans Obermüller, whose papers had been lost in the bombing of Warsaw.

Landau looks hard at Duno. "Yes. I remember. You're bigger." He gestures at the Beretta. "Show us."

Duno kneels and closes his eyes. His whole body shakes with cold, but he does the job with cool competence, and his chest swells when Landau is impressed. "I can do the Breda, too," Duno brags, "*ma due minuti*—two minutes for the machine gun."

Pierino points to Duno's right hand: if you lost your left, could you manage with your right?

"Not as fast yet," Duno admits, "but I will be. I'm learning to shoot, too. We need bullets, Pierino. Some of us need more practice."

Duno doesn't mention what the other boys say about him: that he couldn't hit dirt if he fell out of a wagon. He suspects they're just teasing him—nobody could see the kind of targets they pick out for him. This leaf, that stone . . .

Pierino unslings the mailbag and pulls out a sweater wrapped around several loaves of bread. He gestures for Duno to put the sweater on. Shuddering with cold, Duno considers it, then refuses. "There are others who have less," he says stoutly.

"*Il postino* told me you would be a good comrade," Landau says, his Italian heavily accented. "Wear it on sentry duty," he suggests. "Then share."

"That's fair," Duno agrees.

He's started to put the sweater on when a cautious voice calls from somewhere to his left. "Duno! Who's that with you? He looks German."

"That's my relief," Duno tells Landau. "*Va bene,* Nello! Pierino brought him."

Circling a bald boulder, Nello Toselli reveals himself: short and baby-faced, the sort who'd be a fat kid, given a decent meal even once a day. "I was just making sure," he says. The rifle he clutches is unloaded, but a stranger wouldn't know that.

"Good discipline," the blond man notes, "for boys."

Nello shoots him a look and is about to say something rude when he notices what Duno is wearing. "*Ei!* Duno! Nice sweater! Did your girlfriend bring it up here?" It's only a joke, but Duno flushes. Giggling, Toselli smacks him on the shoulder. "So that's why you volunteer for sentry duty! You've got *una bella fica* coming up in the afternoons, *ne?*" He gestures obscenely. "*Fare la chiavata?*"

"*Bastardo lurido!*" Duno sneers. "Go to hell with your dirty mind! Pierino brought the sweater, and bread, too." He waves a loaf in Toselli's face. "I was going to give you some," he taunts, snatching it back when Toselli makes a grab for it, "but after that remark—"

"*Ei!* Duno! I was only giving you a hard time," Nello whines, making another try for the bread Duno holds just out of reach.

The blond man grabs the loaf and tears off a small piece for Nello. "Sometimes we must impose a tax, *ei,* comrade?"

"The rest goes into *la nonna's* basket," Duno says, peeling the sweater off. "Whoever's freezing his *coglioni* off on sentry duty gets to wear this, understand? Share and share alike!"

The San Mauro Brigade of the First Alpine Division of the Armed Anti-Fascist Resistance, that's what the boys here call themselves. Their "brigade" is seventy-one short of a hundred-man company and they're armed with a haphazard collection of shotguns and hunting rifles that belonged to someone's *nonno,* but bombast comes naturally when you've heard Fascist propaganda all your life. Gangly adolescents slouch against the cave walls or huddle around three campfires, filling the air with talk and body heat. Several wear uniforms, insignia removed. Most wear the clothes they ran away in last fall, when the weather was still warm.

"Comrades!" Jakub Landau calls out, his voice cutting through their murmur. "I ask hospitality of the brigade!"

They leap to their feet at the sight of this blond stranger. A Republican deserter holds a Carcano '91 at the ready. Landau recognizes Attilio Goletta's son Tullio from descriptions: he is hairy as a boar, and just as attractive. A tall old woman, slender and severe in black, comes forward to place a hand on Tullio's gun barrel. "Pierino and I have met with *il polacco* before, boys. We can vouch for him," Lidia says, as Landau bows over her hand.

"I am called *il polacco* because I am from Warsaw in Polonia," Landau tells the boys.

"Pierino brought this from your mamma, Tullio!" Duno holds the bread high, then adds it to the basket of food *la nonna* arrived with this morning. Most nights the brigade's suppers consist of Signora Goletta's cornbread, and boiled chickpeas washed down with rough red wine. For this occasion, *la nonna* has supplied a feast: two big tins of tuna and half a wheel of *parmigiano-reggiano* that her son brought up the mountain last month.

Even here, in a cave, they mind their manners in front of Lidia, making small talk, exchanging pleasantries and news with the stranger until he is ready to explain his presence among them. Wiping his mouth, Landau begins his standard recruiting speech, picking bits of cornbread from his palms, so as not to waste a crumb. He represents a fighting force called the Volunteer Corps of Liberation—led by Italian army officers, manned by demobilized Alpini and regular army, as well as by patriots like themselves. The corps is aided by good men working inside the Republican government, who pass information to the partisans about Fascist military plans. Landau himself is an organizer for a growing coalition of Resistance groups brought together by the Committee for National Liberation. He is trusted precisely because he is a foreigner without local loyalties, untainted by vendettas or jealousies.

His voice is ordinary, factual; his Italian ungrammatical, but adequate. "I have no family," he says quietly. "The Germans, they kill all my family. My wife, my children, my parents, my brother, my sisters. Why?" He looks up. The boys are listening, wide-eyed. Softly, caressingly, he says, "Because they are *ebrei*."

Standing, he speaks now with the tone of a man who expects no reply. "Four years, I was alone. Four years, I was afraid. Four years, I ran. No more." He points toward the Soviet Union. "Like the sun, an army of patriots rise in the east. In Russia, in Polonia, in Yugoslavia, in Greece—the people rise against *fascisti* everywhere. I have joined my fate to theirs."

If the San Mauro joins this corps of liberation, he promises, they'll become part of a genuine brigade: three companies, each divided into platoon-sized units officered by a lieutenant in command of three squads: thirteen men each with a sergeant and corporal. Company commanders, subcommanders, logistics and intelligence officers will support the fighters.

Tullio Goletta scratches with a furry hand at the lice in his hair. "I had enough of officers when I was in the army."

"I have heard of Attilio Goletta's son," Landau says, looking at Tullio. "People say you and your babbo are two loaves from same dough. Both fearless, both strong. But Babbo's jokes are better." The boys all laugh. "In the Corps of Liberation," Landau resumes, "officers do not order any personal slavery. Italy don't shine Germany's boots, and men of the corps don't shine officer shoes. We tell them, You officers: you clean your own dishes! Wash your own stinky shirts!" When the laughter dies down again, Landau adds soberly, "And you fighters: respect the peasants! They are mother and father, grandparents and sisters of the armed anti-Fascist partisan movement. You do not steal from them! You leave the women pure!"

There are cheers this time, but Tullio points to their flea-market armory. "What we need are weapons, ammunition. Warm clothes, and shoes! What are you offering—besides officers?"

"Lugers. Mausers. Schmeissers. Uniforms. Greatcoats. Boots— good ones. All," Landau says, "from bodies of enemy." Tullio snorts, but the Pole knows his audience. These kids are young enough, and bored enough, to believe that they can do anything. Quickly, he outlines a plan.

The effect is galvanic. Arms wave, eyes glow, voices rise in volume, echoing against the glistening stone walls. "I think it could work," *la nonna* says judiciously. "I'm willing to do my part, and so is Nello's *zia* Adele."

Nello looks doubtful. "I'm not so sure. Borgo San Mauro could end up like Boves. The Germans burned a priest and an important businessman to death. Twenty-five people were shot. The whole town was leveled."

"We've got to do something," Duno says. "We can't just sit up here forever!"

That, Landau suspects, is exactly what Nello would like to do. *Attesimo,* Italians call the policy. Wait and see. "Comrades," he says, "this is war, with casualties, with reprisals. Our enemy knows only force. He listens only if we use his language."

"Pierino, what do you think?" Duno asks.

All eyes turn to the only combat veteran among them: a one-armed reminder of the risks that soldiers run. The postman stands. He makes a humming sound, shrugs, grimaces: apologetic, annoyed, resigned. "M-m-m— Mmmm-mo—" His Adam's apple spasms, his lips convulse. He jerks his head to break the jam. "Mmmoses!" finally bursts through. Then, as sometimes happens when he is alone, or unself-conscious, the next word slips out with a breath. "Aaaaron," he says, pointing at Jakub Landau.

At first the boys don't understand. "He speaks for you?" Duno asks. When Pierino nods, Duno turns to his comrades and says, "That's enough for me."

Forgotten in all the talk, the fires have burned down. Duno Brössler reaches for a chunk of chestnut wood. "We fight? The Germans kill." He holds the wood above one of the hearths. "We don't fight? The Germans kill." The firewood drops. Sparks explode into the damp air. "I say: we fight!"

One by one, boys stand. One by one, they toss fuel onto the embers, until the fires blaze. Somewhere in the cave, a sweet-voiced tenor begins to sing, "Nessun dorma." One by one, the boys of San Mauro join in. "My secret lies locked up within me. No one shall ever know my name . . ."

Closing his eyes, Landau listens silently. He is moved by the melody and the lyrics. Moved by the gallantry of old women and skinny kids who propose to take on the Republican army, the Wehrmacht, the Waffen-SS. Moved almost to tears by the final stirring declaration of a victory that must come from beyond the grave.

The Germans have Tiger tanks, he thinks, but these boys have *Turandot,* and courage, and history on their side.

A week later, the equinox is past, and the days noticeably longer. Even so, when Lidia returns to the hunchback's house this time, it's an hour after sundown. She is surrounded by violet mountains floating like islands in a sea of clouds illuminated by a gibbous moon, but she is blind to their beauty.

Lidia Leoni knows now why men love war. To plan together, to be audacious. To fear, and risk, and win! To triumph over contemptuous conquerors! What could be more thrilling?

The wind shifts. Mirella has a fire burning, and the fragrance brings Lidia to her senses. Shod in awful peasant clogs, her feet are freezing, and she hobbles inside at last. The baby must be sleeping. Mirella sits alone in the firelight.

"*Cara mia,* wait until you hear what we just did!" Lidia says, unwinding her muffler. "Four ambushes, no casualties! Hardly any of the Germans were hurt either—Nello didn't want to give them an excuse for reprisals. We got twenty-four uniforms, all good wool, enough for all the boys. Pistols, rifles, even a machine gun! Ammunition." Stamping her feet, Lidia makes sure she's knocked the caked March mud off her clogs. "I swear, I feel like a girl again! What's wrong?"

Mirella, mute and frightened, looks past her to a figure sitting in shadow by the door.

"Signora Savoca. Home at last!" a suave male voice says. "Or perhaps I should call you Gramma? All good partisans should have *nome di battaglia,* signora, in addition to those on their false papers. I understand your battle name is *la nonna.*"

Reluctantly, Lidia Leoni turns to face him.

"I'm afraid it really doesn't do to walk into a house and blurt out your troop strength, signora. People ordinarily have to be tortured to give up the kind of information you just tossed into my lap."

Standing as straight as she can, Lidia unbuttons her coat and hangs it on a peg next to the hunchback's crutch. "Renzo, I—"

"*Prego,* Mamma! Call me Stefano, one last time." He reaches into his breast pocket for a set of identity papers and tosses them into the fire casually. Mirella flinches. Lidia stares. The pasteboard curls and blackens. "They're compromised," he says. "As far as I can tell, everyone in this valley knows Stefano Savoca's mother is supplying partisans with the food he brings up the mountain."

"I—I'm sorry," Lidia stammers. "I didn't . . ."

"You didn't what, Mamma? You didn't think? You didn't look? You didn't listen? You didn't investigate fresh wheel ruts leading directly to your barn? You didn't notice the trampled ground around your own doorway?"

Lidia feels behind her for the chair and sits, a little harder than she intended.

"Renzo, please!" Mirella whispers, stepping between them. "She's your mother! Don't do this—"

"Don't do what?" Renzo asks with chilling mildness. "Don't speak harshly to her?"

A knot in the wood pops. The fire flares. Mirella backs away.

"If you are going to play this game, Mamma," he continues softly, "it's important to learn the rules. The rules are: partisans are shot. People who aid partisans are shot. People whose houses are used by partisans are shot. People who live near those houses, and didn't turn the partisans in, are shot. The relatives of those who have been executed are immediately under suspicion. They are arrested, and ungently questioned. If they don't know anything, they make something up, so the beatings will stop. Anyone they mention under torture will be arrested—"

"And shot! Thank you, *caro*. You have made your point." Tears well and spill, but Lidia's eyes remain level. "Tell me," she asks with flinty curiosity, "what exactly are the rules for those whose sons ask them to shelter Nazi deserters?"

The door slams behind him. Mirella opens it in time to see him stride unevenly across the yard. Hurrying, she follows him into the ramshackle barn that serves as Schramm's private sanatorium.

"Go back inside," Renzo orders, voice low.

She tugs a cardigan more tightly around her but stands her ground.

"Mirella, I am not a quartermaster for the San Mauro Brigade!" Gripping the rear of a wooden mule cart, he lowers himself onto his knees and drags a case of tinned army rations from within a false bottom. "The food I steal is for you!"

He lurches to his feet, but something happens. He cries out in pain, loses his grip on the flimsy crate. Cans and curses roll in every direction. The mule snorts and shies, but Mirella is not intimidated by male anger anymore. Boys, she thinks. Renzo, Angelo, Iacopo. They're all just *boys.* "They're hungry, Renzo, so we share what we have. Everyone around here is taking them food—"

"All the more reason why you should eat what I bring you!" White-faced and furious, Renzo hops toward a bale of stale hay and lowers himself onto it with an involuntary whine.

Schramm's uncertain voice comes from above. "Renzo, do you need a doctor?"

Renzo shouts, "*Verdammte Scheisse, nein!* Go back to sleep!" Lowering his voice again, he tells Mirella, "Pick up the cans!"

It's a plea, not an order. She turns her back and makes a cradle of her apron to gather the tins. Wincing, she listens to the agonized grunt he makes as he does whatever he must to his kneecap. When the cans are stacked, she tries again. "Renzo, your mother just wants to make things better," she whispers, coming close. "If everyone brings one brick, we can build a new world!"

"Or a new prison." He glances upward. "Has Schramm ever told you why he became a Nazi?"

She brushes hay from her apron and shakes her head.

"Ask him sometime. The answer's instructive. God save us from idealists!" Renzo cries softly. "They dream of a world without injustice, and what crime won't they commit to get it?" Rubbing at his knee with both hands, he mutters, "I swear to God, Mirella, I'd settle for a world with good manners."

She feels the familiar prickle: her foolish breasts let down milk whenever anything arouses pity or protectiveness. She reaches toward him, but Renzo rises suddenly and takes three lopsided steps toward the mule's stall. Clucking and murmuring, he coaxes the dissenting animal back into its traces. "It's dark," Mirella says. "Stay the night." He yanks a leather strap, snugs up a coupling. "When did you learn to harness a mule?" she asks, to fill the silence.

"When the milk van was stolen at gunpoint. Or should I say, when it was requisitioned to serve the people? Evidently, children who need milk do not qualify as the people." He rounds the cart and stands in front of her, moonlight on his face. Her hand moves toward the large bruise yellowing on the side of his forehead. He jerks his head away. "If the partisans don't like being called Communist bandits, I suggest they stop pistol-whipping people they rob."

There's liquor on his breath. "Renzo, why do you drink so much?"

"My legs hurt. Cold weather and high altitude make them worse. Grappa," he says precisely, "is easier to obtain than aspirin."

Mirella crosses her arms over her dampened blouse and settles onto a hay bale. "It's warm in Sant'Andrea."

He stares, then laughs, then slumps beside her: forearms on his thighs, hands loose between his treacherous knees. "Not a single morning passes without my thanking God that you married Iacopo."

"Liar."

He smiles a little. "You were the only one I could never fool." She puts her arms around him, resting her chin against his back. "Rosina's beautiful," he says.

"She's already trying to walk! She talks, too! No words yet—it's still nonsense, but she knows what questions and answers sound like."

"You must be relieved."

"Yes, except . . . This time the surprises don't seem so miraculous."

He draws a little pouch of tobacco from a pocket, rolls a cigarette in a square of newsprint. "December thirtieth, 1935," he says, as though answering a question. "And they gave me the Silver Medal for it."

"I'm sorry?"

The match trembles slightly in Renzo's fingers. "You asked why I drink. I'm telling you." He shakes the flame out and releases a jet of smoke. "The Dolo raid. That was my squadron."

"Dolo? But . . . my father said that was British propaganda. He said the British wanted the League of Nations to put sanctions on

Italy so they could take our colonies." She looks into the middle distance, trying to take it in. "The British weren't lying?"

"No, and neither were we. That's the hell of it," Renzo says, his face in shadow. "The Abyssinians were a pack of brutal, thieving warlords who used the Ethiopians as beasts of burden. Haile Selassie's signature on the Geneva Convention was an obscenity, Mirella. He had prisoners of war crucified! I knew those two pilots—Minniti and Zannoni were friends of mine. They were castrated alive and crucified. So we hit Dolo."

"But why? Didn't you see the Red Cross?"

"Mirella," he says wearily, "the Red Cross was painted on the roof of every brothel and bar in Addis. At Quoram, our planes were hit by AA from gun emplacements marked by the Red Cross. At Harar, the ammunition dumps were in warehouses with hospital signs."

Hands over her mouth, she looses a shuddering breath. "But Dolo—that really was a hospital? Forty patients," she whispers. "That doctor."

"Forty-two patients." The tip of the cigarette brightens, and he lifts his head to exhale. "The doctor's name was Lundstrom."

"The Swedes said a nurse tried to wave you away. Is that true? You dropped the bombs anyway?" There's no denial. She searches for something to say. "Renzo, it was war. If you hadn't dropped those bombs, somebody else would have."

"Yeah, sure. But maybe—just maybe—they wouldn't have done such a damn fine job of it."

For a time, he sits silently, remembering: hilltops and hollows veiled in mist, like a woman in bed: asleep, peaceful, erotic. The targeting trance, the long tense descent. The release, the red and orange chaos blossoming below.

"You tell yourself it doesn't matter, until nothing else does." Without looking Mirella in the face, he pinches off the end of the cigarette, works his way onto his feet, flexes experimentally at the knees. "As good as they get, up here." He reaches up to grasp the boards of the mule cart's frame. Hesitates, then hauls himself up in one quick motion. When the pain's grip loosens, he says, "Osvaldo Tomitz has a friend in the Vatican. He got a list of the Yom Kippur deportees."

The change of subject takes her by surprise. "But—no! Your sister?"

"Ester. Her husband. The kids. Nobody will tell Tomitz where they were sent. He's not . . . optimistic. I can't find either of my other sisters. Susa's family was with Catholic friends, but the house is gone. There's been a lot of bombing in Turin."

"But Debora lives in Florence! Surely they won't bomb there!"

"Monte Cassino is a ruin. Who knows where Allied command will draw the line?"

"Renzo, did you find my father and sister?"

"*Belan*—I'm sorry." He passes a hand over his eyes. "I meant to tell you right away, but then Mamma— Your father sends his love. Etta says he's driving everyone crazy, and the neighbors hiding them should be canonized when this is over. But, yes—they're fine."

"Susanna probably is, too. And Debora. They're smart, Renzo. They have Catholic family and friends."

He clears his throat, then digs into his pocket, and hands Mirella a paper packet, heavy for its size. "Like salt," he remarks when he can speak again, "my female relatives once seemed an inexhaustible commodity. Trade some of this for eggs and produce."

She doesn't ask him how he got the salt. She doesn't want to know the risks he takes. Suddenly, the constant ache of longing for her family is as gut-twisting as hunger. "Renzo, I need to see Angelo! His teacher wrote—he thinks we sent him to the orphanage because we didn't love him after Rosina was born. Suora Corniglia explained, and I've written, but— I have to see him! And I have to see Iacopo, even if it's just for a day—an hour!"

She expects an argument: It's too dangerous, too difficult, too impractical. The checkpoints, the bombing, the arrests. She must be patient, sensible, mature. She knows all that, but she's desperate for Angelo to be solid flesh in her arms. She yearns to hear Iacopo make an aria of her name. Renzo, she is prepared to plead, Renzo, if you ever loved me—

"I'll work something out." He leans over to unwind the reins, then shoves the cart brake loose. "Take care of my mother," he asks in return. "Tell her about Ester when the time is right."

He looks over his shoulder to judge the turn he'll need to maneuver out of the barn. "Mule!" he says sharply, slapping the reins. Ears twisting, the animal complains but squares in the harness and pulls.

Above, forgotten in his hayloft, the late Dr. Lundstrom's unlikely heir listens to the rumble and squeak of iron-clad wheels and squeaking wooden joints. Listens to Mirella's footsteps as she returns to the hunchback's house. Listens until there is nothing to hear but the skittering of barn mice, and wind in the pines nearby.

I knew you understood, Schramm thinks in the darkness. The most appalling things can become . . . just part of the job, and afterward . . . Christ, there are days when you're ashamed to be sane. Ah, Renzo, God help us both. *Scheisse,* we're a pair.

DIVISIONAL HEADQUARTERS,
12TH WAFFEN-SS WALTHER REINHARDT
PALAZZO USODIMARE, PORTO SANT'ANDREA

Minutes before midnight, Helmut Reinecke lays the last report on Erhardt von Thadden's desk. "Essentially the same as the first three, Gruppenführer."

In the past nine hours, four company commanders in widely spaced towns were approached by groups of old women declaring themselves loyal to *il Duce,* and offering to lead the Germans to partisan hideouts. The Reds were stealing food, the women said. They were interfering with girls. Enough is enough! It's time for *i Tedeschi* to impose some order!

The commanders dispatched patrols with these elderly guides into the forested hills flanking Valdottavo's mountains. Each group was led through a particularly narrow ravine, where they had to string out single file. With gestures and pissing noises, the old crows indicated the need to relieve themselves, then disappeared into the woods. Armed partisans stood up along the ridges. The soldiers were ordered to lay down their arms and strip off their boots and uniforms. Officers resisted in three of four cases. One was killed. Two were injured. The humiliated survivors eventually found their way back to base in their underwear.

Reinecke says, "I wouldn't have believed it, sir."

Von Thadden tosses the report aside. "At least Franck's patrol had the sense to wait until dark to slink back. New orders: every company commander clears his decisions with us." He rises to study the wall map of Valdottavo, where each partisan action has been marked with a red pin. Harassment, mainly. Petty thievery, mostly from the farmers in the region. Without turning, von Thadden asks his adjutant, "What's their gambit, Helmut?"

With a single exception, the red dots are just east or west of the San Mauro River. Reinecke leans past von Thadden and taps a finger on the north end of the Valdottavo funnel, where the valley ends in a broad band of low mountains. "That's their stronghold. They're trying not to draw attention to it."

"Where would you move to respond?"

Reinecke's finger falls on the railhead. "Borgo San Mauro."

"No. Choose six villages, three on each side of the river. Hang five men in each. Burn the buildings, confiscate crops and animals." The Schoolmaster turns on his heel and smiles brightly, though his eyes are red-rimmed with fatigue. "Explain my strategy."

Reinecke thinks for a moment. "Let the peasants see what happens when they tolerate Communist bandits in their midst. They'll do our job for us."

"The partisans may be driven into Valle Stura or Valle San Leandro, and thus . . . ?"

"They'll become someone else's problem."

"Or they'll concentrate near Borgo San Mauro in the northern end of the valley, where they'll believe themselves safe. Much easier to deal with when we're ready."

Reinecke collects the stack of reports for filing, but he pauses before leaving. "Sir? Anneliese asked me to thank you for the flowers and all the baby gifts. Very thoughtful of you and Frau von Thadden."

"Go home, Reinecke! And give that baby a kiss from her papa's boss."

April 1944

CASA DI GOLETTA
VALDOTTAVO

The work begins with stripping out: an old wall taken down, its stones reserved for later use. Santino Cicala holds each stone in his hand, memorizing its weight and form. Thoughtful, deliberate, he twists left for large ones, right for smaller ones, laying them in a crescent that forms behind him.

Most wallers strip out like bulls pawing the ground, but when Santino apprenticed, his master taught him patience. "Building a wall is like making love to a woman," he said. "Take your time. Find her rhythm. Hurry, and you'll botch the job. Dawdle, and you'll lose it."

The toolshed was rebuilt before Christmas. Bad weather delayed work on the barn for two months, but the repairs were finished last week. All that's left is this sheep pen, and Santino will have it done by Easter. Two faces of stone, hearting between, a one-to-twelve taper. Halfway up, a layer of throughs—large stones that bridge the faces and tie the wall together.

Battista Goletta pauses in his own labors to watch Santino study the wall, then bend to select a stone. Hefting it, the Calabrian twists the rock, considering it from all sides, and turns it over again. Bracing the stone against a leather-aproned thigh, he brings the hammer down sharply.

Wiping her gnarled red hands on a faded flowered apron, Rosa crosses the yard to her husband. On Santino's third rap, the stone fractures along some hidden fault. Remade, it clicks into place between its neighbors on the wall, neat as you please.

"Magic," Rosa says.

"Hard work," Battista counters.

When the snow melted and the path to Goletta's place was clear, Don Leto hiked up the mountainside to see Santino's work. "You are an artist!" he cried as Santino swept up stone chips and packed them firmly into the hearting of the wall. "Is that to neaten the job site," the priest asked, "or do you do it for a reason?"

"Both," Santino said. "Strength comes from the inside—from the inside, not from what you see."

"And the same is true of people, as I told your *ebrea*. It's what's inside that counts. Of course, it doesn't hurt for the outside to be beautiful, *ne?*"

"You found her?" Santino had almost given up hope. The winter, the Germans . . .

Don Leto pointed across the valley at a hamlet just below the treeline, visible only because the chestnut branches were still bare. "She's in Santa Chiara. The *contadini* call her Claudia Fiori. Come to the rectory after Mass on Palm Sunday. I'll arrange a meeting, but we must be careful."

"Because of the *rastrellamenti?*"

"No, the roundups aren't so bad as they were last autumn, but we have Waffen-SS in the municipal building. Don't worry. We can manage them."

Today, sweating in spring sunshine, Santino lays his hammer down and mops his face with a rag. At this pace, he'll lift four tons of rock by sunset, for two and a half meters of chest-high mortarless wall, topped with a ridge-cap of triangular copestones.

All around him, mountains cleave the air like mauls. Hazelnuts are dropping. Bees hum. Across the valley in Santa Chiara, chestnut trees are in bud.

Battista says you can still get snowstorms this late in the season, but mare's tail clouds promise good weather for a day or more to come. Santino brushes stone dust from his hands, sucks sweat and blood and powdery lime from a fresh gash in his palm. Three more days, he thinks. And then I'll see her again.

RECTORY
CHURCH OF SAN MAURO

Adele Toselli has hoarded ingredients for a month. Two turnips, an onion, a potato, a quarter of cabbage. "Three carrots as wrinkled as I am," she mutters, but it doesn't matter. Simmer the vegetables with a handful of chickpeas: *minestrone*. Don Leto has contributed four fresh eggs from three parishioners, and given his own weekly ration of bread. There's a tin of anchovies in the pantry. Two days ago, the Sant'Andrese priest Osvaldo Tomitz brought early peas from the coast along with money for the Jews. And there's still a chunk of Parmesan from Stefano Savoca's last bad-tempered visit.

With the *zuppa* simmering, she shells the peas, tears most of the bread into small chunks, beats the eggs, mixes it all in a clay pot. With Parmesan grated over the top, and the oven hot, she shoves the casserole in to bake. Sliced onions, spring dandelion leaves, add a little vinegar to the oil from the anchovies. *Ecco! Insalata con acciughe.*

She stands back from the worktable to consider the young couple outside, gauging appetites. A big strong boy, a slender girl. There's enough, Adele decides, and enough is as good as a feast.

Don Leto stumps into the kitchen. "The table is beautiful, Signora Toselli!" He lifts the pot's lid and breathes in the soup's aroma. "Do you want some help in here? Hand me a knife—I'll chop that onion."

"Get off your foot," Adele orders, reducing the onion to paperthin disks. "Men don't cook."

"In France, the cooks are all men. Chefs, they're called."

"France. Put perfume on Germans. That's your French."

Don Leto pulls the window's curtain aside. Santino's carbine leans against the cemetery wall. Nearby, the two young people walk decorously. Santino's hands are clasped chastely behind his back. Claudia's are filled with flowers. "She looks like an angel, Signora Toselli. And Santino? Well, Santino is—"

"A good boy," Adele says firmly. "Aren't you glad I talked Tercilla Lovera into this?" she asks, making sure to get credit. "Baths, clean clothes, a civilized table! A nice young couple should have something special when they're courting."

She wipes her hands on her apron and joins Don Leto. For the boy, Adele borrowed a nephew's suit. The coat won't close across Santino's chest and the trousers puddle over his shoes, but the corduroy's so finely waled it feels like velvet, even though it wears like iron. The Cavaglion company has sold kilometers of that cloth to peasants in the districts around Cuneo. The family is Jewish, underground now, but after the war, they've promised there'll be wedding dresses for the girls of any family that hides a refugee.

Someday Lidia and I will make a wedding dress for Claudia, Adele thinks. But for today, there's a frock the color of sunflowers, from a bag of donated clothing. When Claudia stoops at the edge of the grave, the skirt fans over freshly turned earth, gold over gray.

"Thin as a broom straw, poor child, but still lovely," Don Leto says. "If only her papa could see her."

The inscription carved on the wooden cross reads simply ALBERTO FIORI 1894–1944. "But look," Claudia says, pressing the dirt away. Low on the base, where the gravelly soil covered it, Santino sees a tiny six-pointed star. "Don Leto put it there, after the funeral." She pushes the dirt back, to conceal the telltale sign.

Typhus, the padre told Santino. A bite from a flea or louse. City people were more vulnerable. Signor Blum had a weak heart, and the fever carried him off within two days. Santino rubs a palm against his trousers and offers it, to help Claudia stand. The shock of contact makes his breath catch, but she quickly pulls away.

"I'm sorry," she says, embarrassed. She brushes the dirt from her callused hands and the hem of her dress. "The farmwork . . ."

Emboldened, he reaches for her hand and turns up the palm. "You should be proud," he tells her earnestly, holding it next to his own. "Hands like these mean you're honest, you work hard. No gangster or landlord has hands like mine. No prost— Good women have hands like yours."

She touches his borrowed tie and jacket lightly, smiling at his scrubbed face and carefully combed hair. He has not changed, but she has. Claudette Blum was a silly, sulky girl who could still believe that hard times were a temporary annoyance. In her place stands a solemn young woman named Claudia Fiori, her prettiness chiseled by loss and illness to marble beauty.

"Would you like to sit down?" he asks.

There's a stone bench surrounded by small-leafed lilacs and roses pregnant with buds, and embraced by a stone Virgin's outstretched arms. Santino whisks dust and pollen from the cool, pitted surface and takes off the too tight jacket, laying it on the seat so Claudia won't get her dress dirty.

He sits beside her. "Don Leto says you like the people you're staying with."

She looks toward the mountain across the river. "After Papa died, Zia Tercilla wanted to adopt me. Don Leto knows a lawyer who would do the papers for free. But I still have a mother. I'm not really an orphan."

"Don Leto found me a job in Sant'Andrea."

"Is that far from here?"

"It's on the coast, near Genoa. There's a train. So I could—" he swallows. "I could visit. You. Sometimes."

"I'd like that," she says, but she is looking at her father's resting place. "When you visit a grave, you're supposed to put a little stone on it. In a Jewish cemetery, if there are lots of little stones on a grave, it means this was a good person whose memory brings many visitors. I can't do that while the Germans are around." Tears well, but do not fall. "So I bring flowers, instead."

Ready to cry himself, Santino wishes he could make it better somehow. But dead is dead. What can anyone do?

Just like that, the solution comes to him. He selects two pebbles from the garden walk and returns to the grave, squatting beside it. With a short, thick finger, he gouges a hole in the crumbly dirt and holds out one of the pebbles. "Yours first."

Green eyes swimming, Claudia looks at him as though he is a miracle, a genius. She wipes her eyes, comes to his side, drops her pebble into the hole. He sends his own after it and covers them both, patting the dirt flat.

"That's good," he says, holding her as she weeps at last. "He was a good man. He deserves tears, and stones on his grave."

Reaching into an unfamiliar pocket, he pulls out the clean handkerchief that Signora Toselli provided in anticipation of this very moment. Claudia wipes her eyes with it and blows her nose.

"After the war," he tells her, "there'll be work for masons in cities, because of all the bombing. Everyone says a man with my skills could make a good living here. I might stay. Up here. In the north. If you would— We—I mean, I'd still like to visit my family back in Calabria, but—" He scowls at the grave, sorry for his presumption. "I meant to ask your father."

She's fifteen. She should be studying geometry and grammar and French literature. Memories of Belgium, paved streets, electric lights, and school have faded as dream fragments do, forgotten when the day begins. From her first week in Santa Chiara, she has worked side by side with the other women, harvesting grapes in September, chestnuts in October, olives in November. She knows how to choose unflawed ears of corn and tie them into bunches to hang in the *soffitta*. Her hands feel empty without a spindle to work while she sits. She has begun to think in dialect.

On the hillsides across the river, mountain orchards are dressed like brides, pink and white with blossom. Water slaps at the mill wheel's plank blades, softening the eerie moan and creak of wooden gears. In a garden just beyond the cemetery wall, an old man sings as he works.

"Papa taught me a song when I was small," she says. "*Wo man singt, da setze ruhig nieder:* Where one sings, take your place without fear." Claudia lays her callused hand on Santino's cheek, turning his face toward her. "We'll live here," she says simply, "but after the war, we'll visit your family."

"Really?" he says, amazed. "Really?" he asks again.

She nods, and his glorious gap-toothed grin appears, utterly transforming the homely face. To make a man so happy! she thinks. To make this man so beautiful . . . "Yes," she says. "Really."

Hand in hand, they sit like an old married couple with everything in their lives already decided, and all life's sorrows but one behind them. Her hand tightens around his fingers. "Promise me something?"

"Anything," he says, stunned and stupid with love.

"After the war, we'll find my mother. We'll bring her and my brothers here, and you'll build a house for them."

He squeezes her hand, then lets it go and approaches her father's grave as though it is a judge's table. Kneeling, he puts a hand over the secret place where the pebbles are buried. "I will find your wife and sons, signore," he swears. "I'll build them a house with stone floors, and thick walls, and a slate roof. The rafters will be chestnut, and the windows will have real glass. Four rooms. Two up, two down. I'll teach your sons my trade, and when they marry, we'll build houses for their wives to be proud of." He looks across the river, seeing these structures in his mind: measuring out the foundations, estimating the loads. "Your sons and I will build houses so strong no bomb or war can touch the ones inside. Every stone we lay will be in your memory, signore. But the house I build for your daughter will be stronger and larger and more beautiful than any of them."

Santino Cicala stands and faces the woman who will be his wife. When he speaks, his voice is firm with an authority he has never felt before. "We will name our first son Alberto."

She smiles, and holds out both her hands.

"Young love!" the German says with supercilious scorn, eyes on the tearful couple in the garden. "*Lieber Gott!* Isn't life awful enough?"

Head cocked back on her scrawny neck, Adele Toselli is ready to shut the door in his face. "What do you want?" she asks ungraciously.

He whirls and grasps her spotted hand, kissing its prominent blue veins fervently. "Vat do I vant?" he cries, his accent comical. "I vant your undying devotion, Italian goddess!"

Horrified, Adele snatches her hand away.

"Run avay vit me to ze Black Forest! Ve'll eat cherries, und ski!" he wheedles. The accent disappears. "Not at the same time, of course."

"You!" she cries, pointing. "You're—"

"Ugo Messner, at your service, Frau Toselli." He clicks his heels and inclines his head sharply. "I am here to pay a call on your employer."

Grabbing his arm, Adele pulls him inside, amazed by the transformation. Freshly barbered, closely shaved, the former Stefano Savoca is almost unrecognizable. The milkman's ill-fitting coveralls have been replaced by a well-cut tweed suit. A frayed shirt collar has been expertly turned, and no longer betrays its age where it folds over his beautifully knotted tie. Adele is getting used to men whose names change from month to month, and she has always known that Lidia's son was only pretending to be a Sicilian, but he even seems . . . taller, somehow.

"You're sober!" she says.

"And bearing up bravely," he says breezily as she leads him down the hall toward Don Leto's office.

The new heels on his gleaming shoes ring smartly, if arrhythmically, on the stone-tiled floor. "What's wrong with your legs?" Adele asks over her shoulder. Lidia would never tell her.

"When small airplanes make unscheduled landings, knees and ankles rarely meet aviation standards for shock absorption. My legs, however, have many other fine qualities," the astounding Herr Messner declares as Adele knocks on the padre's door. "They are reasonably functional during the summer, and at sea level. They are also complete from hip to toe, which is more than some can say. Ah! Don Leto! The famous Red Priest, about whom one hears so much! We are, of course, alone—I've been watching the rectory since dawn. I must inform you that our Sicilian friend Stefano Savoca has died again—this time permanently. I am the late Ugo Messner of Bolzano, freshly resurrected, and ready to assist in the building of a new world! Perhaps you will permit me a few words before I convey your package to Sant'Andrea?"

The office door closes, muffling the cannonade of words. Adele lingers in the hallway. Her ears aren't what they used to be, but the voices quickly rise. "And I told *you* before," she hears Lidia's son shout. "Keep the women out of it!"

Lips compressed, Adele frowns at his tone, but before she can work up a good bout of indignation, the door opens so suddenly she almost falls into the visitor's arms.

"If it isn't Giulietta's nurse!" he says caustically. "Go tell Romeo it's time to say good-bye, signora. His train leaves in half an hour."

Renzo Leoni watches, face hard, until the old lady harrumphs and leaves. "That is exactly what I'm talking about," he says, slamming the door. "You are all amateurs!"

Leto Girotti neatens his desktop, papers here, pens there. Folds his hands. Looks up. "Amateur," he says. "From the Latin *amator—*

lover. Thus: one who engages in an enterprise for love, not money. In the case at hand, for love of Italy. For love of liberty. For love of those who flee tyranny, and who resist it."

"Explain what love had to do with this."

Leoni snaps open a leather document case and drops the March 24 issue of *La Stampa* on Leto's desk. The front page is dense with tiny print. Centered at the top in a fine ascetic font is the headline: THIRTY-TWO GERMAN SOLDIERS, VICTIMS OF BOMB ATTACK IN ROME. In smaller letters beneath, it says, "The Reaction: 10 Communist-Badogliani Shot for Each German Injured."

Leto whispers, "Three hundred and twenty . . ."

"Three hundred and thirty-five. The Germans evidently miscounted. Civilians, machine-gunned in groups of five. It took hours."

Ashen, Leto Girotti pushes away from his desk and stumps to the open window. Out in the garden, Signora Toselli is telling Claudia it's time for Santino to leave. "The Resistance didn't kill those poor wretches," Leto says. "The Nazis did."

"A comfort to the corpses, no doubt. My sources say Hitler wants reprisals set at fifty to one from now on. Are you keeping track of the numbers in Valdottavo? The SS is."

Claudia looks as slender as a willow wand, Santino as solid as one of his own stone walls. Leto Girotti closes his eyes, but it does no good. He can see in his mind the Calabrian's muscles burst by bullets, Claudia torn to pieces behind the false shelter of that sturdy body. "The Republic of Salò is a puppet government," he says without facing Renzo. "If we can't strike at the Nazis, we'll cut the strings of their marionettes."

Behind him, there is a bark of stunned laughter. "That's your solution? Civil war? Italians shooting Italians, for the love of Italy! What kind of priest are you?"

Leto turns. "The kind who's visited Fascist prisons. The kind who has given the last rites to prisoners with no eyes, no ears, no fingernails! What kind of *man* are you?"

"We've been over this, and over it! I'm doing what I can!"

"It's not enough! Old women are risking their lives to get weapons for the Resistance!" Leto points out the window toward the Cave of San Mauro. "There are boys up there—kids who should be in school. The only veteran among them stutters so badly, a battle would be over before he could get an order out! They are hungry for a leader. Renzo, the Communists have already made contact."

"I should think the Red Priest would be delighted."

"Don't be a fool," Leto snaps. "There are sins of omission, my son. If you refuse to oppose those who do harm, you are complicit! You were a military officer, a professional. And I believe you are a patriot. Fewer will die if those boys are well armed and well led."

A long minute passes. Leoni stands motionless, his expression somewhere between pity and loathing. "Your day is coming," he warns softly. "God help you when you learn what I know." He stares until Leto's eyes drop, and when he speaks again, his voice is tight. "I can get them weapons—but that's as far as I'll go. And I have two conditions. One: the brigade goes to ground until I get back from Sant'Andrea next month. No action at all, understand? If I'm setting something up, I don't need a crackdown before it happens."

"And the second condition?"

"The women stay out of this."

"Not even the love of God can keep the ones we love safe. Nevertheless," Don Leto agrees, "I will do what I can to keep your mother and the rabbi's wife out of harm's way."

More tears, more embraces. With nothing else to seal their promises, Santino hands Claudette his carbine. "Keep this for me," he says. "I can't carry it in the city."

The man who calls himself Ugo Messner grips Santino's small suitcase in one hand and Santino's large arm in the other. "I'm sorry, Giulietta. Time, tides, and Mussolini's trains wait for no man, not even your Romeo."

Pulled downhill toward the station, Santino looks over his shoulder for a last glimpse of Claudia, and stumbles. "Watch where you're going, Cicala!" Messner's German accent has disappeared, a no-nonsense Ligurian one taking its place. "We don't have much time, so listen carefully. The Germans are worried about an amphibious assault near Genoa. God knows why, considering what a mess the Allies have made of their campaign so far." Messner waits until they clear a corner and he can speak again without fear of being overheard. "The Wehrmacht is building a seawall with bunkers for heavy machine guns and seventy-five-millimeter cannon, from Savona to Varazze. You'll be working for a German engineering firm, Lorentz and Company—"

Santino stops a few steps uphill. "I won't collaborate!"

Messner turns. "Don Leto told you about this job, *vero*? Would he ask you to collaborate?" Messner waits for Santino to consider this. "A man who knows how to make a good wall also knows how to build a bad one, true?"

Santino squints. "Are they using concrete?"

"Of course."

Santino catches up. "Enough sand in the mix? It'll crumble by November."

"Precisely. Turn here." The station in sight, Messner speaks quickly. "I'm taking you to meet a man named Fichtner. He thinks I'm a *Volksdeutscher*—an ethnic German from Bolzano who's perfectly delighted that the *Vaterland* has retaken Südtirol. Fichtner's desperate for skilled workers." He glances at Santino and adds sourly, "I'll see if I can get you a better salary. You'll need the money if you're going to get married."

"You're not so nasty as you pretend," Santino tells him. "Don Leto said you were a war hero—"

"Don Leto is completely full of shit."

The locomotive looses a piercing blast. Porters wheel pushcarts stacked with luggage past crates of produce, cages of chickens, sacks of dried corn. Passengers mill nervously, waiting to display their documents to men in long leather coats.

Messner leans against a low granite wall engraved with the names of men from San Mauro who died in the last war. Rubbing his knee with one hand, he reaches into his suit coat with the other. "Here's your ticket. That's the queue for third class. Get off at Sant'Andrea."

"Aren't you coming with me?"

Messner's voice drops. "Ugo Messner, I'll have you know, is a member of the fucking master race. The fucking master race travels first-class!" He stands and assesses the crowd casually. "Sometimes it's safest to hide in plain sight," he says even more quietly.

"If anything happens to me, get off in Sant'Andrea and go to Fichtner anyway, but in that case, don't mention my name. Tell him you heard he was looking for masons."

Messner starts to leave, but Santino grabs his arm. "Signore, I—I never traveled alone. There was always an officer."

The hard eyes soften. "Your papers are authentic. You're doing nothing wrong. Show the man your ticket. Find a seat. And *buon vi-aggio*—enjoy the trip."

En Route to Porto Sant'Andrea

The train stops repeatedly, taking on passengers until they fill every seat, every corridor, even the linkage platforms between cars. Small children nap on overhead luggage racks, pillowed on bundles. Everyone stinks: unwashed bodies, unwashed clothing. "Soap is cheap," Santino's nonna used to say. "There's no excuse for dirt." But nothing's cheap in wartime.

There's a long stop in Roccabarbena. A lot of people get off, but Santino isn't sure he's allowed, so he sits by the window watching the people at the station. A young woman gets on just before the train pulls out again, and sits next to him with a quick smile. The train rolls out, crosses an iron trestle, rounds a wide bend that skirts the last of the mountains.

Abruptly, Piemonte's high country flattens into a vast plain. *Contadini* stagger behind oxen. Black ribbons of fertile soil curl away from gleaming plow blades. Santino wishes he'd paid more attention when they'd studied Piemonte's characteristics in school, but he'd never thought he'd see it himself.

"*Tanta bella!* The land is so beautiful!" he remarks to the young woman at his side. "In Calabria, it's all rocks. What do they grow in those fields?"

"Mostly corn, but—" The train slows, and she sighs with exasperation. "This trip used to take four hours! We'll be lucky to do it in twenty..."

She's friendly, and her skirt is so short it rides up above her knees. She's wearing short socks, too; the skin of her legs is bare. They chat awhile, and Santino tries to make up his mind about her. At home he'd be certain she was a prostitute, but the north is different, and he decides to give this young woman the benefit of the doubt.

Moving toward an arc of mountains, the train picks up speed, then slows to a crawl, then stops inside a tunnel. The girl waves a hand at the dense darkness around them. "What's worse? Getting bombed outside or buried alive in here?"

"Arches are very strong," he says. "The tunnel won't collapse, and the bombs can't reach us in here. So tunnels are safer. Stuffy, but safer."

She rears back, to get a better look at him in the gloom. "It was a rhetorical question, but I like your answer."

Prostitutes wouldn't know a word like that "torical" one. "Are you a student?" he asks.

"I was, until they closed the universities."

"*La mia fidanzata?*" He stops to savor the moment: he's never called Claudia his fiancée before. "She was a good student. Reads any book she can get. Me, I only had the mandatory. Soon as I finished my four years, I was glad to get outside and do something useful."

"Then your children will be smart like their mamma and practical like you, *ne?* A good combination."

The train quivers and begins to roll. Santino closes his eyes. Smart, and practical, he thinks. And maybe good-looking, like their mamma.

Content to let the prophecy linger in his mind, he dozes off, head against the glass. When he awakens, it's night. The train is stopped, but this time out in the middle of nowhere. He stretches as compactly as he can and rubs at crusty eyelids. Several seats away, a badly dressed boy of about twelve clutches a knapsack, his frightened eyes on the girl at Santino's side.

The young woman taps her fingers on the armrest, and grips it when two German soldiers board. "Madonna," she says quietly. No one else speaks.

Beams of light sweep through the car from the soldiers' flashlight. "*Dokumente!*" one of them shouts. Many of the passengers moan and reach for their papers, but the girl next to Santino hardly breathes as the Germans work their way down the aisle. Suddenly, she stands and addresses the other passengers. "*Dio santo!* Why don't we just paint a target on the roof?"

Startled, the soldiers pause in their task.

"Can't you people hurry?" she demands, motioning with her hand like a wheel turning faster and faster.

"Yes!" someone else yells. "We're sitting ducks for Allied bombers!"

In the next instant, half the passengers crowd into the aisle, thrusting papers at the Germans, complaining loudly about the delay. The soldiers shout back, and bash somebody with a club. A woman screams. Men shout. Santino untwists in his seat in time to see the pale boy drop from view. Moments later, there's a tap on Santino's boot. He crosses his legs, and does not look down when the fugitive wriggles past him on the floor, moving toward the section of the car the soldiers have already checked.

Eventually the Germans leave. The passengers settle down. The train pulls forward again. "Brava!" Santino whispers when the young woman sits beside him. "Who is that boy?"

"I have no idea." She takes a shuddery breath to settle her nerves. "Since last September, half of Italy is hiding the other half. If someone looks scared, you do what you can."

It's past dawn when the train slows yet again. Outside, forests, hills, villages, and fields have been replaced by bombed factories and wrecked apartment buildings, some still smoldering.

The young woman slides forward on her seat. "This is my stop," she says, yanking her skirt down. "Sant'Andrea is next." Santino helps her pick up her bundles. "You shouldn't talk to strangers," she warns. She meets his eyes, and adds, "Neither should I."

PENSIONE USODIMARE
PORTO SANT'ANDREA

"She was probably a *staffetta*," Messner says quietly when Santino tells him what happened. "A messenger for the Resistance. Turn here. That's the house. Naturally, I stay elsewhere. Members of the master race do not share accommodations with treacherous Italian scum," he whispers as they enter the lobby. "Ah! Signora Usodimare, I have another boarder for you."

Suspicious, the old woman looks Santino up and down. "Sicilian?"

Santino hands her his papers. "Calabrian, Signora."

"No better!" she snaps.

"He's a nice boy," Messner assures her, "with a job, and a housing voucher from Fichtner at Lorentz."

Trying to look harmless, Santino waits politely while Messner takes the lady aside for a murmured conversation. Something Messner says makes Signora Usodimare laugh girlishly as she trades a key for a pack of cigarettes.

Messner jerks his head, and Santino follows him down a hall that changes elevations three times for no apparent reason, and then up three flights of stairs. At the end of a corridor Messner unlocks a tiny room, taller than it is wide and stiflingly hot. He pushes the window shutters open to let in some air and sends his hat twirling onto a peg by the door. "Give me ten minutes. I need to thaw out," he says, sitting in the room's only chair and massaging his knees after the climb. "*Belandi,* how I hate the mountains!"

Santino sits on the edge of the bed. "You were going to tell me about *staffette.*"

Messner pulls a silver cigarette case from the inside pocket of his suit coat and offers it. "You don't smoke?" he asks when Santino refuses. "Good! Filthy habit." Messner shakes the flame from a match and coughs on the first puff. "*Staffette* . . . Where to begin?" he asks. Rhetorically. "Apart from ordinary gangsters, there are about a hundred bands of anti-Fascist partisans in northwestern Italy. Gruppi di Azione Patriottica in the cities, Squadri di Azione Patriottica in the countryside. Liberals, Christian Democrats, Socialists, Communists. Garibaldi Brigades, Catholic Action Brigades. Bread and Justice Brigades. Liberty and Justice Brigades. Most of them couldn't organize a bun fight in a bakery." Messner shifts in the chair and gazes absently out the window. "They all use girls like the one you met on the train as messengers because women travel more freely."

Thinking of Claudia, Santino says, "Dangerous."

"You have no idea. When *staffete* are caught . . ." Messner lifts his chin, sending a plume of smoke upward. "The Great War killed courage with machine guns, Cicala. This one's murdering chivalry."

Santino joins Messner at the window. The boardinghouse sits on high ground, and Sant'Andrea is laid out like a map. At least a third of the buildings are damaged, the streets holed with craters bridged by planks for foot traffic, or boarded over with salvaged doors. Piles of rubble block the ground-floor windows of the buildings still standing. Broken glass glitters in the sunlight. A barber cuts hair in the midst of the wreckage. A skinny housewife has strung a clothesline between two chimneys; clothes flutter above what was her kitchen floor a few days ago. Smoke and dust drift in the soft spring air. The white shirts will be dingy before they are dry.

"Are you from Sant'Andrea?" Santino asks.

"Ugo Messner is from Bolzano."

"Even for a stranger, it's a pity to see it like this," Santino says, playing along.

"The city was never picturesque," Messner admits quietly. "It's been an industrial port for five hundred years. Tanneries and weaving in the beginning. Shipbuilding before the forests ran out. Chemicals, iron, steel mills later on— *Porca miseria!* Look at that!"

"What was it?"

"The Ospedale Incurabili."

The smoking ruins of the hospital are nearly lost in the haze over the Mediterranean. "Maybe the pilots thought it was a factory."

Silent, Messner takes a drag, filling his lungs with as much smoke as they can hold before flicking the butt out the window. Taking his hat off the peg, he stands still, as though weighing some decision. "There's a company of *bersaglieri* guarding the construction site for the seawall," he says. "The *bersaglieri* are—"

"*Repubblicani.*" Santino nods knowingly. "Old *fascisti,* with a new name. And corrupt, like mafiosi."

"Is that what Don Leto says?" Messner asks, his voice light with sudden anger. "Allow me to explain something about city life, my son. We've got two armies confiscating trainloads of food from us. Civilian rations are down to one hundred grams of bread a day, two hundred grams of cheese a month! People are starving, and unlike the Red Priest, *bersaglieri* have families to feed. I know one of them is selling supplies from the seawall project. Cigarettes, food, medicines. And he's got access to explosives, small arms, and ammunition. So he may be corrupt, but Don Leto's friends can use what I can buy from him. Do I make myself clear?"

Santino's eyes remain level.

"You don't have to approach the man, Cicala. Just find out who he is."

The wind shifts south, bringing with it the musical tinkling of bricks being tossed into piles.

"You don't trust me," Messner replies to Santino's silence. "I consort with Germans. I could be an informer. Maybe I'm using you to find the black marketeer, so I can denounce him for money. Fair enough. Would you like a hostage?" Messner spreads his hands and presents himself. "Like the inestimable Claudia, I am a Jew. I can drop my pants to prove it, but if you insist."

Santino crosses his arms. "What's in the little boxes? The black ones that look like little houses?"

A slow smile of appreciation spreads across Messner's face. Closing his eyes, he speaks as though reading from a book in his mind. "You shall love the Lord your God with all your heart, with all your soul, and with all your might. Teach these words to your children. Speak them when you sit in your home, when you walk, when you lie down and rise up . . ." One eye opens. "*Belandi.* What comes next? Bind them for a sign upon your hand . . . and for frontlets between your eyes, whatever the hell frontlets are." The other eye opens. "Et cetera. Close enough?"

"I'll watch for the man who's selling things."

"Bravo." Messner takes a last look out the window. "The Allies are bombing us, the Axis is starving us, and the Communists will grab whatever's left at the end. *Mondo boia!* Executioners rule!" he swears softly, shaking his head at the destruction. "I need a bottle, and a whore whose politics can be trusted. Care to join me?"

Santino shifts uneasily. "There are bad diseases. I don't want to bring anything home. When I'm married."

Caught between amusement and envy, Messner smiles. "I'll check back at the end of the week. If you need help before then, go to the basilica. Find a priest named Osvaldo Tomitz. Tell him you heard from a shithead that Don Osvaldo was a decent man. He'll know what that means."

"Don Osvaldo," Santino repeats. "A decent man."

"Don't forget the part about the shithead!" Messner calls, disappearing into the hallway.

Santino sits on the bed and bounces a bit. The mattress is better than any he's slept on. He's never had a room to himself before. Suddenly lonely, he returns to the window. I'll save every lira, he thinks. No drinking, no cards. I'll get work on the side. The moment there's enough money, we can get married.

Something white catches his eye: snapshots fluttering through the piazza in front of the boardinghouse. A lady wearing mismatched shoes scurries to collect them. German soldiers stand on the corner. Civilians hurry past, impatient, nervous. One photograph keeps tumbling just beyond the lady's reach. The soldiers laugh. Santino tenses to run outside and help, but before he can put motion to the thought, a gust of wind blows the photograph decisively away.

WAREHOUSE DISTRICT
PORTO SANT'ANDREA

Glissando, a harbor siren hits high A before its brief solo is lost in a chorus of inland Valkyries. German anti-aircraft fire provides percussion. Ears straining to pick out the sound of the approaching aircraft, Iacopo Soncini watches the warehouse rats. They are smart, and their hearing is more acute than his own.

"What do you think?" he asks them. "Yanks or Tommies?"

All winter, B-17s have flown over northwestern Italy, winging toward the Reich. Like wharf rats, many Sant'Andrese have learned to distinguish the engine note of the American bombers from that of the British planes. In mild weather, neighbors come outside to watch squadrons in the starlight. People chat in low voices, sitting together in dark courtyards or leaning out of windows. Then they go back to bed, hoping for a few hours of rest before sirens announce the Americans' return to Corsica.

When the rats dash for cover, Iacopo does, too. "RAF," their skittering tells him. "Our turn tonight."

One of the rats creeps back into sight. A pregnant female, teats prominent, she balances on sturdy little haunches and begins to groom her soft brown fur. "False alarm?" Iacopo asks. He blinks, and she's vanished.

A thudding explosion a few hundred meters away. Dust sifts from the rafters. Iacopo's eyes shift from floor to walls to roof, searching for signs of collapse. Ground-floor corners are the safest, left standing when the rest of a building goes down. The next detonation is so close, he feels the concussion in his chest.

There is a mathematical pattern to a raid. No matter how tight the pilots' formation, bombardiers vary slightly in the release of their cargo. The earliest of the explosions can be heard separately. Soon individual sounds merge into a toneless crescendo.

He could give a lecture on the natural history of terror. Survive your first air raid, and you thank God, laughing and giddy. Survive your tenth, and the element of luck cannot be ignored. If we'd been there, not here; if the breeze had carried that fire a few meters closer . . . Funerals become a commonplace annoyance as you make your way through the city. The notion of luck begins to turn on you. What worked before may not save you this time. Dash through the street, and you could be crushed by falling masonry. Race to a shelter, and you could suffocate as the fires' carbon monoxide sinks into the cellar.

Survive your thirty-first raid, and you'll sit tight for number thirty-two. You'll waste no energy. You're too tired, too familiar with the outhouse stench of your own fear to run from it. An abandoned, rat-infested warehouse next to a shipyard is as good a place as any, if your luck runs out.

Hunched on the floor, the cool stone cobbles hard against his hips, Iacopo feels his shoulders rise and his head duck in a pointless involuntary effort to protect himself. He tries to think about his family. The exercise is fruitless. Mirella is no longer pregnant, but he cannot picture her any other way. Angelo exists as the memory of a little boy marching off, stiff-backed, hand in hand with a short, round nun. Rosina will be crawling by now, perhaps saying a few words as well. Changed beyond recognition.

The only face he can picture clearly is a stranger's. A girl, perhaps sixteen: fast asleep, eyes open, wandering along Via Massini. Sleepwalkers are common in cities under bombardment—no one understands why. Dreaming perhaps of a journey to some safe place, dressed only in a nightgown too short for her, the sleeping girl drifted through shreds of morning fog. She was so young that he could see in her face the infant she once was, the toddler, the schoolgirl. He ached to take her in his arms and kiss her with all the tenderness he still had in him. A delayed detonation shook the ground. In an instant she was transformed from lovely girl to terrified animal. She circled frantically, unable to decide which way to run. When he came toward her, she screamed and screamed, as though he were the embodiment of all that had blighted her childhood.

The air raid's thunder beats against him like a club. Puddles shiver and gleam in the pale light that pours through holes in the warehouse roof. Pesach's full moon illuminates tonight's coastal targets, and his own shaking hands. Coal dust draws black crescents beneath his nails, and makes intaglios of his knuckles. His forearms are muscled like a sailor's. The back that bent over books now curves around the willow basket he uses to lug his stock-in-trade. The RAF is his business partner, he supposes, and the thought is vaguely funny. If he's alive and reasonably whole in the morning, he'll leave this leaky den, assess the pattern of bomb damage, choose a direction. The first hours of the day will be given not to prayer and study but to scavenging charcoal in wrecked buildings. When he's filled the basket with chunks of fuel, he'll deliver it to housewives who still have stoves to cook on, and who are sharing the little they have with fugitive Jews.

At last, the explosions slow, become sporadic. Above him, tons lighter, British bombers wheel and begin their flight back to base unburdened by ordnance. One by one, the rats reappear.

He listens to the shouts and secondary explosions outside. The rats make themselves tidy, combing dusty whiskers with delicate, pale paws. The sirens wail the all clear. Once again the angel of death has passed over him. He tries to thank God, but can't help feeling like a thug's wife who believes she is loved if a punch goes wide.

Twenty minutes, he thinks. The trembling will stop in twenty minutes.

Running feet pound along the alley beyond the warehouse walls. Iacopo remains where he is. He's picked up too many clumps of flesh and bone, found too many families cooked in the water from burst boilers, heard too many screams, smelled too much charred meat, seen too many corpses lying doubled up in pools of their own melted fat. Tonight he will sleep. In the morning, he will make his rounds, delivering courage with the charcoal.

"*Lo amut, ki echyeh, v'asaper ma'asei Yah,*" he whispers with threadbare resolution. "I shall not die but live, and I will declare the works of God."

IMMACOLATA CONVENT
PORTO SANT'ANDREA

Suora Marta pulls out the handkerchief she keeps tucked into her tight black inner sleeve and hands it to Frieda Brössler. The woman must have been handsome once, but her pale skin has been spoiled by weather, and worry, and grief.

"I told Steffi—don't talk to anyone! Wait here, and we'll come back for you. Then—"

A white-veiled novice enters, eyes downcast, carrying a tray. Noiselessly, she sets out two glasses of water, two bowls of diluted milk flavored with roasted *cicoria,* some rolls that aren't too moldy. "We can't offer anything better," Suora Marta apologizes as the novice backs away. "Dip the bread into the milk," she suggests. "You won't notice the mold."

Frau Brössler shakes her head: I can't. Sighing, Suora Marta nods permission to the daughter Liesl, who stares at the bread but reaches only for the milk. "Frau Brössler," Marta says, "if we are to find your other daughter, you must try to tell me as clearly as you can what happened."

"There was an ultimatum," Frieda says, gripping the handkerchief. "Anyone caught after the deadline would be shot, and so would the owner of the property they were caught on. How could we put that farmer in danger, after he had been so kind? Duno—my son—he said we shouldn't do it, but Herrmann was so sure! I don't know where Duno is. He wanted to join the partisans. He left us the day before we went to San Mauro—"

"One thing at a time," Suora Marta says. "Please—take a little water. What happened when you reached Borgo San Mauro?"

"At first, Italian soldiers put us in an armory. They were good to us—there was food, and they even let us go into town to shop. Then the SS came. They started beating people. Old people, women, children. They were shouting and pushing people onto freight cars. They had guns and dogs—savage dogs. A little boy started to cry, and a soldier hit him! That child couldn't have been four! Steffi started screaming. I was afraid the soldiers would hit her, too. I took her to a side street. I told her, 'Stay right there until we come back.' My husband thought he might be able to trade his wristwatch for better seats on the train. He went to the Germans to inquire, and—and—"

"The tall one shot him," Liesl says, dry-eyed.

Frau Brössler seems dazed. "One moment Herrmann was asking a perfectly sensible question, and the next, he was— He was on the ground. He was gone. Just like that. Gone! I couldn't move. I just stood there. His blood . . . poured—just *poured* out over the cobblestones."

Suora Marta is the only nun whose German is good enough to speak to many of the Hebrews. The weight of these stories, the endless repetition . . . How does the rabbi stand it? She glances at the wall clock. Half past two, and he is long overdue.

"A lady saw Papa on the ground," Liesl says. "She pulled us inside."

"Signora Giovanetti, her name was." Frieda accepts the glass of water the nun presses on her. "She hid us." The wonderment almost dries her tears. "She was so kind, so kind! I asked, *Perché?* Why? She said, '*Anch'io vedova.*' Something like that. What does that mean, Sister?"

"Dear lady," Suora Marta says gently, "it means: 'I, too, am a widow.' "

"Mutti looked for Steffi later, with Signora Giovanetti," Liesl says while her mother sobs. "They couldn't find the doorway."

"We were afraid to ask too many questions," Frau Brössler continues, tears streaming. "The lady hid us for a month in San Mauro. Then she took us to her cousin's house farther away. He kept us all winter, but in March there were German sweeps. It was too dangerous, so a priest brought us here."

"*Bitte,* Frau Brössler," Suora Marta presses, "what did the doorway look like? Do you remember anything at all about the place you left your daughter?"

The woman's reddened eyes lose focus. "The door was very short. Even Liesl would have to duck to go through it."

"Nothing else?"

The daughter speaks. "There was a statue of a little man. He was wearing that kind of hat with the two points."

"A miter." San Mauro, most likely, the town's patron saint. "A short door, near a statue of San Mauro." It's not much to go on, but it's a start. Suora Marta once again pushes the plate of bread toward the Brösslers. "Please—you must eat!"

"We can't eat that," the girl says firmly.

"Don't be fussy, child! I know there's some mold, but have—"

"It's almost Easter. So it must be Passover now. We don't eat bread during Passover."

"Of course!" Marta says. "The Feast of Unleavened Bread!"

"We're supposed to eat matzoh," the girl says.

"They won't have matzoh, Liesl." Her mother glances toward the door, then at the bread. "Someone said a rabbi visits? He could tell us what to do."

Suora Marta looks again at the clock. "He must have been delayed, but I've heard him help others when they must make a decision. He always says, 'Choose life.' In my village there was a saying, Frau Brössler: 'Bread is life.' "

When the two have eaten, Suora Marta leads them to the novitiate dormitory. There are no rugs on the floors or pictures on the walls, but the room is large and airy, divided into cells by posts and clotheslines, from which hang a series of canvas sheets. The novices themselves have mostly moved to Roccabarbena, their places taken by Jews. Mother and daughter will sleep side by side, in the last bed left. Safe from the Nazis if not from Allied bombs.

Marta climbs the back stairs to the professed sisters' quarters and opens the first door on the right. Sitting at a small desk, she takes out a piece of white stationery, now half its original size, makes a sharp crease along the top, and carefully strips away another bit of paper. Uncapping a fountain pen, she writes a few words, blows gently to dry the ink, and folds the note twice. Reaching through a slit in the side of her outer gown, she buries the note deep in the black cotton pouch that serves as a pocket.

Suora Marta stops by the linens room for a handkerchief to replace the one she gave Frau Brössler. The refectory next. The kitchen is deserted: dinner long over, supper not begun. A packet of food waits on the scrubbed wooden table, and it joins the note in her pocket. Hands under her scapular, Marta proceeds to the mother superior's office. The door is open, and Suora Marta sticks her head inside. "Reverend Mother, may I take Suora Ilaria for a walk to the basilica?"

Mother Agata smiles coolly. "Give my best to our friend in the cleaning closet, Suora."

Suora Ilaria has no idea why she serves as Marta's companion on such errands, but she asks no questions as they cross the piazza. When Marta tugs the side door open, the elderly nun peeks into the basilica. "I'm going to die soon!" she confides with a girlish grin.

"How wonderful!" Suora Marta replies, propping the door open with her foot. "Watch your step, Suora."

Ilaria points her head toward the ground and takes a big step over the threshold, as though it were a sleeping dog that might jump up and knock her down. "Soon I'll be with our Lord, and his Blessed Mother!" she says cheerily. She grips Suora Marta's arm. "I don't mean to brag."

Marta pats the spotted hand. "Pray for me when you see them, Suora."

In middle age, Suora Ilaria was the convent's Living Rule—the very embodiment of the order's customs and laws in all their myriad minutiae. Her meticulous observance was a silent reproach to her less scrupulous sisters in Christ, and earned her the nickname Suora Malaria. For years, the principal result of Suora Marta's weekly examination of conscience was a tabulation of uncharitable thoughts about the woman at her side. Thirty-four years later, Marta's a little sad at the thought of losing the old girl.

Not that I'd begrudge her a moment with You, Lord, she thinks with a pious glance toward the crucifix.

The basilica is dressed in Lenten purple, nearly deserted this time of day. Two poorly dressed, thin-faced laywomen kneel in the vaulted silence, lips moving as each prays a solitary rosary. A skinny laborer rests his bony rump against the pew behind him and stares vacantly: too tired to pray but comforted to be in church. Sitting in the back of the basilica, apparently lost in thought, a heavily mustachioed gentleman in an expensive suit strokes a long jaw, blue with the kind of beard that needs shaving twice a day.

Marta supports Suora Ilaria's creaky genuflection and leads her to the left. When the old nun settles in to pray near the Virgin's altar, Suora Marta slips away.

Until a few weeks ago, Rina Dolcino brought meals to Giacomo Tura. Sometimes Suora Marta was in the basilica when this happened, and it did not escape her notice that Rina seemed more vivid, somehow, when she emerged from the scribe's small room. If either of the pair had been under seventy, Suora Marta would have put a stop to the visits at once. Perhaps she should've been more suspicious. Giacomo Tura has mourned like a widower since Rina was killed.

Naturally, the old gentleman is lonely. Suora Marta passes some time with him, discussing war news. South of Rome, the front is quiet. The Red Army has taken Odessa. The Allies control the air over western Europe and Germany. By the time Marta returns to the nave, Suora Ilaria has fallen asleep kneeling, forehead on gnarled hands still folded in prayer.

Palming the note concealed in her habit, Marta removes the handkerchief from her sleeve and steps forward as if to dust the base of the Madonna's statue. She gives the plaster feet a bit of a rub to remove some smudge and slips the piece of paper under a vase of flowers. Turning, she sees the gentleman with the mustache note her attention to the altar's cleanliness. Suora Marta nods slightly, acknowledging his approval.

Tasks accomplished, she returns to the pew and slides in next to Suora Ilaria, who is snoring peacefully. There, until the basilica bell tolls the hour, Suora Marta prays for the soul of her friend and co-conspirator Rina Dolcino, who may not have been in a state of unblemished grace when she was pulled out of a market crowd last month and shot by Artur Huppenkothen's Gestapo.

PALAZZO USODIMARE
PORTO SANT'ANDREA

"Reprisals are an effective tactic for encouraging good citizenship,"
Erhardt von Thadden admits, knifing into a huge slab of Florentine beefsteak on his plate, "but they can be overused, Artur."

While the Gruppenführer chews, his toady Helmut Reinecke
takes up the theme. "In the Soviet Union, many Russians and
Ukrainians were eager to join the Waffen-SS in opposing communism. The same will be true here, Herr Huppenkothen, but
reprisals against civilians easily undermine willingness to work
with us."

"The Geneva Convention is clear," Artur insists. "When civilians take up arms under the banner of a government that has capitulated, they lose their protected status."

Von Thadden tips the last of the wine down his throat. Crystal
flashes as he raises his glass toward the maid. "Artur, you haven't
touched your meal!"

"I neither eat meat nor drink alcohol."

Reinecke's mouth twitches, but von Thadden looks stricken.
"Like our Führer! Of course! How could I have forgotten? Shall I
have the chef prepare something else for you?"

"I didn't come here to eat, Gruppenführer. I came to discuss a
coordinated campaign against terrorists and their supporters.
When Italian deserters bring guns home and use them to assassi-
nate German officials, they've made their homes subject to attack.
When an old man gives vegetables to partisans, he and his garden
become military targets. The rosy-cheeked woman who sews
dresses for her daughters and mends clothing for bandits puts her
own children at risk."

"Certainly, Herr Huppenkothen," Reinecke agrees, "but the
Führer also instructs us to make our rule more tolerable by dulling
the senses of the local population. They must fear us, but they
must also believe that they will not be harmed so long as they do
as they're told. One can make use of Alakhine's defense as well as
Steinetz's offense."

"The lure, not the cudgel," von Thadden explains. "Do you play
chess, Artur?"

"Games are for children."

"Chess teaches strategy and tactics for any conflict." Von Thadden turns his benign gaze on Reinecke. "So: Alakhine's defense, Helmut . . . What do you propose?"

"Put German construction crews to work rebuilding damaged churches, sir, as von Treschow did in the Soviet Union. He encouraged Russian Christians to come out of hiding and worship in public again. This tactic gained such goodwill among the clergy that many priests joined anti-Communist fighting units. They make excellent spies—"

"And excellent collaborators!" Artur points out. "They're conspiring to hide Jews all over this country."

"Then we must open their eyes," Reinecke insists. "Jews put their parishioners at risk. Jews are bandits and thieves. Jews are to blame when reprisals fall on Italian Aryans."

"Italian Aryans." Artur snorts. "Have you ever looked at Italy's coastline? These people have been seafarers for millennia. What do you think sailors do when they get into port?"

"Good point, Artur," von Thadden concedes. "The appeal to race rarely stirs Italians, Helmut. They define blood by direct kinship only."

"Then remind them that their own gallant sons died fighting Jewish Bolshevism in the Soviet Union. Remind them that if the Communists take over here, they will seize private property, just as they did in Russia."

"While promising the peasants that we'll break up large holdings and redistribute the land after the Bolsheviks are defeated," von Thadden says comfortably. "The Italian is not logical. He won't even notice the contradiction!"

The room is decorated with exquisite frescoes, beautiful furniture, heavy silver serving pieces. Everything surrounding von Thadden speaks of loot and unearned status. Artur rises to inspect a chess set on a side table. "Sixteenth century," von Thadden tells him. "Rose quartz, onyx, and white marble. The pieces are sterling, of course. I have a board in every room. I like to keep games going with various opponents."

Artur's hand hovers over the board, as though he is considering a move. Putting a finger under one corner, he tips it over, sending stone and silver crashing to the floor. Reinecke is on his feet, but von Thadden raises his hand and shakes his head.

"You, sir, are a venal, self-satisfied thief," Artur Huppenkothen says with quiet conviction. "You are unworthy of the Reich, and unworthy of our Führer. I will do whatever is necessary to restore order in this city, with or without your cooperation, Gruppen-führer."

The bedroom door is open. Martina von Thadden turns from her dressing table, all pearl-colored satin and pale pink skin. "A new negligee!" Erhardt notes on his way in.

"Do you like it?" she asks, twirling. "It was very expensive, but Ugo told the shop owner, 'This lady is the Gruppenführer's wife, you fool!' You should have seen that man's face, *Lieber*. He said he'd send it right over as his gift to the Gruppenführer's lovely lady. And look at these shoes, and this handbag! Have you ever seen such fine leather?"

Erhardt pretends to admire the latest acquisitions, letting her happy musical voice bubble around him while he undresses. Childless, surrounded by servants, Martina has nothing to do but shop for clothes and prepare for the moment when her man returns.

He holds out his arms. "Come to me, little chatterbox," he says, and she does, giggling like a girl. His hands float down a satin river, then grip the heavy hips. Martina has put on weight since coming to Italy, and Erhardt is glad of it. He likes the heft of her, the depth of the shapes, the luxurious distance of bone from his touch. She seemed made for babies when they married, but their first died shortly after birth, and she has miscarried ever since. A blood incompatibility the doctors said.

She breaks away and moves backward, pulling him by the hand toward their bed. "You'll never guess who I saw today!" she says the moment he's through.

He tries not to sigh. This is her only flaw. She likes to talk, after. "Who?" he asks, eyes closed.

"Erna Huppenkothen! She's still not married. With a name like that, I'd have run off with the first man named Müller I could find. She told me she has a gentleman friend—guess who!"

"I can't imagine."

"Ugo Messner! She says he's *ever* so nice to her. She made sure I knew that he's never touched her even once, except to kiss her hand. She thinks that means he's respectful, not repulsed. Dry and skinny as a stick, Erna is."

"Messner's just polite because of her brother. The rest is her imagination."

Martina goes still. "*Lieber,* you don't think Ugo is . . . ?"

"Paragraph 175?" Erhardt says, using the customary legalism. "No, my sweet, but have you noticed that his gait is somewhat impaired? There's a rumor of a terrible war wound." He clears his throat, and adds, "Not unlike Göring's."

Her lips form an astonished O. "How awful!" she cries. "I knew there was something about him. I feel so safe with him."

Erhardt knows what she means. There *is* something about Messner: a sort of brave melancholy that makes his attention to bored and lonely women seem more a service to their men than a reason for jealousy. "I suppose it's possible he really is courting her. Of course, Gestapo connections never hurt."

"Erna told me that she embroiders AH on all of Artur's personal linen. Poor little man! He tries so hard to be like the Führer—and he fails so gloriously!"

When her husband chuckles, Martina rises on an elbow to kiss him, and makes her eyes warm as she straddles him. "I love to make you laugh," she murmurs. She leans over, letting her heavy breasts brush the hair of his chest and belly lightly, lightly. He stretches like a cat, almost purring as her lips go to work.

For the good of the race, the doctors told the couple, the Gruppenführer should take another woman, but Martina is damned if she'll give all this up to some cow who'll drop one calf a year.

Morale is on the rise, she thinks when he finally stiffens, and hides her relief in renewed determination while his eyes wander the ceiling. There, painted satyrs chase nymphs, who smile over milky shoulders. Diaphanous scarves fall gracefully from legs parted half in flight, half in invitation. Arbors encircle a garden full of pink roses, and plump grapes hang from twisted vines. Foliage does not quite conceal a variety of couplings. Standing, bending, above, behind . . .

Erhardt raises a languid hand and points. "Let's do that one now."

Like many maritime estates, the Palazzo Usodimare is absurdly large. Four great wings surround a central piazza larger than San Giobatta's. There are stables, storerooms, kitchens, baths, residential quarters, two ballrooms, a dining room for fifty guests, and a seaward gallery of offices, where the prince's staff once scanned the harbor for incoming ships. The whole is ringed by massive stonework. Four hundred years on, and the Usodimare family is nearly extinct, their palace appropriated by the latest of Italy's invaders, but the purpose of the palace walls hasn't changed: to demonstrate raw power while shielding the splendors within from the eyes of the vulgar.

Dry-mouthed, Osvaldo Tomitz hands his papers to a sentry. "I have an appointment with the Gruppenführer."

The guard studies the priest's photo minutely and logs a notation while a second sentry frisks him, grinning when he gets to Osvaldo's crotch.

"You're expected," the first man says, handing the identity papers back. "Follow that walkway."

The garden behind the wall is stunning in its prewar beauty. Almond and lemon trees in enormous terra-cotta pots line paths perfumed by roses and mimosa, clematis and jasmine. Roman and Egyptian statues preside over a view of the water far below, softened by a living frame of cypresses, holm oaks, umbrella pines and palms. Luxuriant foliage breaks the noise of the city into small, distant fragments. All other sound is quiet and close. The rasp of brooms grooming paths. The scraping of rakes. The clank of a wrench as a plumber works on the dry fountain's pump. The casual chat of SS troopers with submachine guns, overseeing the work.

In a far corner of the garden, filthy and tattered, Iacopo Soncini stacks half-burnt scrap wood and bits of broken furniture around a pile of uprooted plants. Appalled, Osvaldo stops abruptly.

"*Wunderbar, ja?*" a cultured voice behind him remarks. "In such a garden, one may forget the ugliness of war."

Osvaldo turns. An officer smiles in greeting, fair skin crinkling around clear blue eyes. "Erhardt von Thadden, at your service," he says. "Thank you so much for coming! I appreciate your making time for me, Hochwürden." The traditional form of address for a German priest is "Highly Honored," but in von Thadden's mouth the title is mockery, and his smile broadens when Tomitz bristles. "My apologies. I was merely extending a courtesy," he says smoothly. "What does it say in the Gospels? 'Call no man Father.' Sant'Andrea is most assuredly not Rome, but I shall do as the Romans do, if you prefer, Padre."

"Tomitz will do."

"Excellent! And you may call me von Thadden, of course. My office is in this wing," he says, leading the way. "I ordinarily prefer to meet with people in their native habitat, so to speak, but lately it has seemed the better part of valor to invite visitors here. I don't mind dying for the *Vaterland,* but there's no glory in being assassinated by a bandit on a bicycle."

Von Thadden leads the way past glass cases displaying detailed models of ships, vellum charts of the Mediterranean, brass navigational equipment. Somewhere, typewriters clatter like small-arms fire. Von Thadden stands aside, allowing Osvaldo to precede him into the office. Its walls are dominated by frescoes immortalizing the naval battle of Lepanto, and by a map of the Gruppenführer's fiefdom.

Von Thadden invites Osvaldo to sit in a chair upholstered in coral damask, but he himself lingers by a small gilt table that supports a simple wooden chess set. "My grandfather carved the pieces," he says. "He taught me to play when I was eight— Ah! There's a mate in two." Chuckling with satisfaction, von Thadden plays the white rook from C1 to C8. "Leisure is so important. You leave the game, and come back to it refreshed. May I offer you something to drink? Coffee perhaps? Tea? It's a bit early, but I do have some very good French Cognac."

Osvaldo remains standing. "Nothing, thank you, Gruppenführer."

"Are you sure?" Von Thadden takes a seat behind a neoclassical table. "Please, Tomitz! Relax!" he urges pleasantly, and waits until Osvaldo perches on a chair. Well-tended hands come to rest upon a thick, unopened file. In red letters, the word *Geheim* is stamped:

Secret. "This isn't an interrogation," von Thadden assures him. "I simply like to get to know important people in my district."

"Then you should make an appointment to visit the archbishop, Gruppenführer. I am merely his secretary."

Von Thadden chuckles. "Admirable modesty, Tomitz, but I am an academic by training, and any professor will admit that his office and all his affairs are run by his secretary!" Von Thadden opens the file, lifts the top sheet, scans it briefly. The blue eyes rise, and von Thadden smiles happily. "You see? I am correct! His Excellency does indeed speak very highly of you." He sets the précis of that interview aside, then picks up another report, and another. And another. "Tell me about yourself, Tomitz. Where did you grow up?"

"Trieste."

"Yes, of course! When it was still part of the Habsburg empire, explaining your flawless German!" von Thadden says brightly. "Interesting city, Trieste. Mittel-europa at its mongrel worst! Austrians, Italians, Slovenes, Greeks! And Jews, of course," von Thadden says genially. "Your parents were . . . ?"

"My father was in shipping. My mother is a widow."

"I meant, what is your parents' race?"

"Italian."

The expectant smile fades. "Father of Austrian ancestry. Mother, Venetian. A German head, an Italian heart, *ja?* Mann's Tonio Kröger, come to life." Von Thadden smiles encouragingly this time. "Brothers? Sisters?"

"Two of each."

"My family was the same. Three boys, two girls." Von Thadden consults the file. "I am the fourth of five, but you were the middle child, I see. Sisters older, brothers younger. One in the army. Karl?"

"Carlino. Yes."

"*Ach!* It says here that Karl has been missing for some time. How terrible for your poor mother!" Von Thadden looks up, eyes rich with sympathy. "Would you like me to see if I can ascertain his whereabouts?"

Osvaldo hesitates. "I'm sure my mother would appreciate that."

"Naturally! She worries about her Karl! It would be my privi-

lege to alleviate such suffering. Unfortunately, my wife and I have
no children, but my Martina would be frantic in your mother's
place. Karl's unit was . . . ?"

"Ninth Army, Third Corps, Venezia Division. He was stationed in Greece." Osvaldo glances at the file. "Surely you know
that already."

Von Thadden looks hurt. "Your dear mother's anxiety would
only be prolonged were I to waste time making inquiries on the
wrong front." He returns to the file. "You went to the Tortona
seminary."

"Yes."

"And taught there later . . . Tell me about your education. I'm
not a Catholic. I've always been curious about the training of
priests."

"Latin liturgy, theology, philosophy. Are you a Lutheran, Gruppenführer?"

"I'm afraid I am a bit too knowledgable to cling to my natal religion, Hochwürden. My academic field was Near Eastern philology. I know a creation myth when I hear one, even if it's the myth
I grew up with. What do you think of Genesis?" von Thadden
asks curiously. "Do you honestly believe your god made mud-pie
people, and then became so angry with them for eating a piece of
fruit—"

Osvaldo rises. "If you'd like to discuss the Church's position on
natural selection, there's a Jesuit at the Gregorian who—"

"*Sit down.*"

Slowly Osvaldo drops back onto the chair.

"Genesis is merely a Jew variation on the Babylonian creation
story *Enuma elish*," Von Thadden says, scholarly once more. " 'Blood
I will mass, and cause bones to be! I will establish a savage: man
shall be his name.' Thus spoke Marduk—the first divine sculptor
of people. Flood stories were commonplace in Babylon, Sumeria,
the Hittite kingdoms. Genesis is simply a degenerate version of
earlier myths." Utterly at ease, he leans back in his chair, crossing
one knee over the other. "Christianity, of course, has no validity at
all severed from its Jew roots—a persistent logical problem. Having declared Jesus divine, you must mistranslate and misrepresent
Hebrew prophecy. The Jew messiah is to be an earthly leader

who'll bring political peace to Jerusalem and, by extension, to the world. The past nineteen hundred years have been very bloody." Von Thadden smiles cheerfully. "No peace, no messiah."

"Jesus will come again—"

"Ah, but as a Jew peddler might say: Cash, not credit, *mein Herr!* Jesus had his chance." Von Thadden rises to pour coffee from a silver service on a side table. Adding a generous measure of sugar, he stirs thoughtfully with a sterling spoon. "Christians backed the wrong horse, messianically speaking. So you changed the rules to make Jesus the winner of the race. And if a Jew messiah ever does materialize, you've taken the precaution of declaring him the Antichrist, and enemy of Christendom! Goebbels could hardly have done better!" He lifts the exquisite porcelain cup toward his nose, breathing in with evident pleasure. "You're sure you wouldn't like a coffee?"

The aroma is intoxicating. "No," Osvaldo says. "Thank you."

"Let me guess! You've given it up for Lent?" Insouciant on damask, von Thadden lets his gaze travel around the office. "Christian mythology, I'm afraid, is also lacking in originality. Zeus visits virgins who give birth to demigods. Mithras was born of a virgin—on December 25, no less! His cult had a communal meal and prayer that went, 'He who shall not eat of my body and drink of my blood shall not be saved.' Let me see . . . A kingdom to come? Zoroaster. Blood sacrifice followed three days later by a resurrection? Attis, who returned from the dead on the spring equinox."

Osvaldo checks his watch. "I do have other obligations this morning, Gruppenführer."

"Of course! You are a very busy man." It seems, almost, a compliment. "My men call me the Schoolmaster—I do tend to fall into old habits! One last thing, with your indulgence." Von Thadden unfolds a small strip of paper and reads six words. " 'The convent is short on charcoal.' " He doesn't bother mentioning where the note was found, or how he knows Osvaldo is connected to it. "You're certain you wouldn't like a brandy?" he asks.

Mouth cottony, Osvaldo says, "No. Thank you."

"Is it normal practice," von Thadden asks with catlike curiosity, "for an archbishop's secretary to be concerned with a convent's charcoal supply?"

"These are not normal times, Gruppenführer. Italy has no coal. German authorities prevent us from importing fuel. So we use charcoal. Church institutions work together on such matters as heating and provisioning."

"Well, heating shouldn't be a problem anymore. Lovely weather!"

"Charcoal is also needed for cooking and washing, Gruppen-führer."

"Obviously! Why didn't I think of that?" Von Thadden all but smacks himself in the forehead. "Charcoal makers figure promi-nently in Italian history, I understand. The Carbonari of 1849 were rebels who gathered in forests pretending to be charcoal makers while planning attacks on foreign rulers. Karl Marx ad-mired them. He believed guerrilla warfare was the best way for a weak force to confront a stronger and better-organized army." Seraphic eyes glowing, von Thadden inquires, "Do you admire the Carbonari, Tomitz?"

"I am notoriously obtuse about politics, Gruppenführer."

"A humble servant of the Prince of Peace!" He taps Osvaldo's folder with a blunt finger. "And a very . . . busy . . . man."

Von Thadden stands, stepping out onto the small balcony overlooking the garden. "I'm told the botanical collection had five thousand exotic species," von Thadden says, his voice raised for Tomitz's benefit. "Plants from Asia, Africa, and the Americas. They have no place in Europe. Rip them out, and burn them! That was my order." He faces Osvaldo. "The laborers are con-scripts living in a guarded barracks. I'm inclined to let them go when the work is complete, but if something unfortunate were to happen? I'm afraid I'd have to wash my hands of them."

Dropping all pretenses, he returns to his desk. "Communist criminals have had their way in Rome, Milan, Turin, Genoa. Not here. Tell your Bolshevik friends, Tomitz: if Germans in this dis-trict are harmed, reprisals will be set at twenty to one."

"Tell Renzo: explain to Angelo," the rabbi whispers urgently as the priest passes.

Giving no outward sign that he has heard, Osvaldo strides away from the Palazzo Usodimare. Bogus mythology, he thinks, nauseated by anger. What about those magical Nordic runes on his collar? Nazi hymns to Wotan? Numerology, telepathy. Divining rods, phrenology, magnetic cures. Neo-pagan looniness, all of it! The German people have forsaken Jesus for a maniac who believes in cosmic ice and Atlantis, and a Grail filled with Aryan blood.

Arrest is inevitable. Osvaldo knows that now. He feels momentarily safer merging into a market crowd on his way back to San Giobatta, but a broken-nosed stranger falls into step with him. When his arm is seized, Osvaldo is surprised only by how soon his time has come. He opens his mouth to shout.

"I won't hurt you, Padre," the thug whispers, "but you have to come with me."

Oblivious pedestrians stream past, like water around a rock. Everyone has a great deal to do, very little to do it with, and always: the checkpoints, the document inspections, the petty tyrannies to circumvent.

Warily Osvaldo follows the man through unfamiliar alleys. At the entry to a small, ruined apartment building, the thug whistles a few notes of Puccini and is answered by a bit of Donizetti. Stepping over wreckage, he leads Osvaldo to the remains of a corner flat that still has most of its walls and some of its ceiling.

On a smoke-damaged easy chair, an elephantine figure rubs the inside of a fleshy thigh where a shrapnel wound has ached for a quarter of a century. "Signor Brizzolari!" Osvaldo cries, "*Grazie a Dío!* I should have come directly to you—"

Serafino Brizzolari holds up a clean pink hand in warning. From the inside pocket of his tentlike suit he withdraws a small medicine bottle. "This should help your sister's little boy, Beppino. Give her my best wishes."

The thug slips the bottle into a pocket. "*Grazie, signore.* Padre, I'm sorry I scared you. A blessing, please?"

"Go in peace, *fíglio mio.*" Osvaldo waits until he is alone with the fat man. "Signor Brizzolari, von Thadden has—"

"That's why you're here. And no—never come directly to me about anything." Brizzolari lifts a manicured finger to indicate a pile of not very clean clothing. "Put those on."

"But why?"

"Huppenkothen has an arrest warrant out for you. The

Gestapo knows you and Suora Marta are doing something suspicious, and that others are involved."

Osvaldo curls his lip at a pair of filthy trousers. "Then why didn't von Thadden—?" He freezes, one foot in the air. "He told me to warn the partisans that he'd kill his hostages if they took any action in Sant'Andrea."

"He also had you followed out of the palazzo." Brizzolari shifts his bulk in the chair. "Beppo's brother-in-law will have taken care of your tail. And von Thadden won't move against the partisans yet."

Osvaldo pulls on a patched shirt that stinks of another man's sweat. "How can you possibly know that?"

"Renzo Leoni's made friends with von Thadden's wife and Huppenkothen's sister. Lonely women talk." Brizzolari glares over his belly at a massive gold pocket watch. "Damn the man! He was supposed to be here fifteen minutes ago. His drinking is—"

"The principal arrow in my quiver!" Renzo stumbles through a gaping hole in the apartment wall and looks back at the rubble behind him, to see what he tripped over. After a puzzled shrug, he makes a sweeping bow. "A man among men," he declares himself, "and graceful as well!"

"Is this the end of a long night," Osvaldo asks, "or the beginning of a bad day?"

"Does it matter?" Renzo collapses onto a broken-backed sofa and scrubs at his face. "My apologies, gentlemen. Something came up last night, or this morning . . . or whenever it was." The trembling hands fall into his lap. "Don Serafino, what would you take in trade for a cigarette? Would my firstborn son do, or will I have to promise you a daughter?"

Brizzolari growls but tosses him a pack of Macedonias. "You are out of control."

"Those who are without sin are also without information. I've endured an unimaginably tedious evening with Erna Huppenkothen, and God knows, that required a great deal of drinking."

Aghast, Osvaldo sits on a wobbly, water-stained chair, a dirty sock in one hand. "You didn't—"

"O Dío! If you could see your face!" Renzo laughs loosely. "No, fornicating for Italy exceeds my patriotic limit, Padre. Even the perpetually virginal Erna might recognize a clipped dick if she saw one. Nevertheless! At the cost of hours of excruciating boredom, I have learned that her brother, Artur, is frustrated as hell. Italian Jews have Catholic friends, Catholic in-laws, Catholic business partners. Nobody's ratting them out. Local police are tipping neighbors off before every sweep. So poor, dear Artur has decided to concentrate on foreign Jews. There will be a Gestapo raid on Immacolata after midnight tonight."

"The convent!" Osvaldo says. "But the Concordat! They wouldn't dare—"

"International borders didn't stop them," Brizzolari rumbles. "Did you think a cloister would?"

Shoving his feet into battered work boots, Osvaldo stands. "I should warn the sisters."

Renzo says, "It's been taken care of. When Huppenkothen shows up, Immacolata will appear *judenfrei,* but the convent will be watched from now on." He shakes a cigarette from the pack and offers it to the priest. "You're compromised as well, Padre."

Osvaldo nods, accepting the cigarette as well as the logic. "With me out of the network and the rabbi in custody, who'll take care of the refugees?"

Renzo's bloodshot eyes focus sharply. "Wait—Iacopo?"

Brizzolari sighs. "I knew there was a warrant out for him, but I didn't—"

"That's what I was trying to tell you!" Osvaldo says. "Von Thadden has him pulling weeds in the garden at Palazzo Usodi-mare. I don't think they know who he is. He got raked up for a labor gang, but von Thadden threatened to kill the entire group if the partisans make trouble."

Swearing steadily, Renzo walks in tight circles. Slows, then stops and looks up. "Don Serafino, can you get custody of von Thadden's hostages?"

"It depends," Brizzolari says cautiously.

"Doctors are still allowed to go from house to house, right? Anytime, day or night—same as priests?"

"Priests, midwives, and doctors, yes. Curfews don't apply."

"With a doctor's bag and the right papers . . . What do you think, Tomitz? We could cut your hair differently, get you some glasses perhaps. You could wear my suit—"

"And pick up Iacopo's rounds . . . Yes! Nobody ever remembers me anyway."

Brizzolari considers Osvaldo's forgettable face above the ordinary clothing. "It could work, assuming you don't have to set any bones. You could keep the refugees' money in a false bottom. Roll bills up and put them into medicine bottles."

Squinting through smoke, Renzo holds the discarded cassock up to his shoulders. "A little tight across the chest. . . How does this work? Do you wear it like a dress?"

"It goes over a shirt and trousers. You can use mine."

"Don Osvaldo, if he's caught wearing that, every priest in Italy will be suspect!" Brizzolari looks from one man to the other. "Leoni, you can't be serious!"

"Not often," Renzo admits, "but I'm sobering up, and the idea still makes sense to me. Don Serafino, if you get the hostages transferred into the municipal jail, I think I can solve a number of problems simultaneously." He tosses the cassock onto the sofa and slumps beside it. "It's up to you, Tomitz, but there are places I can't go as Ugo Messner."

Osvaldo shrugs assent. "Giacomo Tura can alter my papers for you."

Brizzolari wipes his sweating crown with a pristine handkerchief. "Tura takes too long. There's a man in my office who can be trusted." He motions irritably for his briefcase. "Who'll take care of these while you two play dress-up?" Opening the case to reveal hundreds of ration cards, Brizzolari recites, "Bless me, Fathers, for I have sinned: I have lied and I have stolen."

"I was selling them to raise cash for Iacopo to distribute," Renzo explains.

"I can fence them," Osvaldo says. Renzo and Brizzolari stare. "Priests, and doctors," he informs them delicately, "are acquainted with all manner of persons."

Squaring a straw Borsalino on his large, round head, Brizzolari heaves himself onto his surprisingly dainty feet. "I'll send Beppino back with the paperwork in a few hours. And I'll do what I can for Rabbino Soncini and the others. Padre, Dottore," he says, tipping his hat. "Good day to you both. And God save Italy, if He can."

Side by side, the younger men watch him pick his way through the wreckage. Slumping onto the sofa again, Renzo says, "When this is over, remember what that fat Fascist bastard has done. He'll need you to vouch for him, Padre. We're in for a civil war, the moment the Germans leave."

"And if the Germans don't leave?" Osvaldo asks. "Kesselring's making the Allies look like fools!"

"He's as good a tactician as Germany's got," Renzo agrees. "And the military record of the Allies in Italy remains unsullied by a single well-run battle, but they've got time and brute force on their side. Germany's running out of both." He levers onto his shoulders and heels to pull a hip flask out of his back pocket. Osvaldo's eyes narrow. Renzo rolls his. "Don't tell me you've never seen a drunken priest."

Osvaldo snatches the flask away and pours its contents onto a waterlogged Turkish carpet that was once some housewife's pride. "I've seen you," he says. "In the streets. During air raids." Standing in the darkness. Waiting for a bomb with open arms, a bottle in his hand. Osvaldo waits until Renzo's eyes shift to change the subject. "There's a rumor that the Allies are withdrawing troops from Italy."

Renzo flicks ash off his cigarette. "They're being redeployed. The Germans're expecting an attack on Calais. Von Thadden thinks the Allies'll settle for holding southern Italy, because of the airfields and ports. The rest of the peninsula's of no strategic value to them."

"And what will become of us, here, in the north?"

Hands dangling between his knees, Renzo stares at an upstairs toilet leaning crazily on a pile of rubble. Laths and broken joists stick out of its bowl, like dead flowers in a cracked vase. Gathering himself for one last bout of coherent thought, he takes a long drag, and flicks the butt away. "The Reds will hold eastern Europe. The Americans and British could take the west. The Wehrmacht's best bet is to shoot Hitler and negotiate terms: Germany keeps Mittel-europa from the Baltic to the Arno. The war's over. Everybody celebrates, and I'll get hanged instead of Brizzolari. Although, with my luck," Renzo mutters, stretching out on the sofa, "the damned rope will break."

The sun has found the gaping hole in the roof. Renzo throws

an arm over his eyes. Within moments, he's asleep, and Osvaldo sits quietly, studying the man. Raids, fires, smoke: the air is often sickly yellow, but it's not just sour light discoloring Renzo's skin. Suicidal bravery, or cirrhosis of the liver—he's killing himself. And he knows it. Osvaldo has been tempted to ask about Renzo's past, but what might seem normal curiosity in other times could raise suspicion now. His only real clue lies in what Renzo himself said of Schramm, the day they met in San Giobatta. "I'm inclined to respect a soldier who has to get that drunk before confession. He must have an admirable conscience to be so ashamed."

Twice, Osvaldo has tried to speak to Renzo of the prodigal son, of God's loving welcome for the penitent. Both times, the words stuck in his throat. Hypocrite, he snarled at himself. Offering absolution to one sinner but not the other. You want to pick and choose who is worthy. And yet— Nothing Renzo did in Abyssinia could possibly rival Werner Schramm's tally. Not a tenth of 91,867 were killed in the whole of the Abyssinian war!

Lord, how often shall my brother sin, and I forgive him? And Jesus said, I do not say to thee seven times, but seventy times seven . . . That's 490, Osvaldo thinks. Is it a matter of scale, then? Is the murder of one human being less heinous than the murder of 91,867?

Yes, he thinks stubbornly. Yes! It is 91,866 times less heinous!

Osvaldo Tomitz has tried and tried, but he cannot make words like guilt and forgiveness, atonement and absolution fit around what Schramm confessed, or around what others like him are doing today, at this very instant. Yes, of course! Forgive as you are forgiven! But Jesus spoke directly: forgive those who sin against you yourself. Surely that can't mean forgive those who murder by the trainload. Forgive those who willfully commit atrocities. Forgive everything, anything!

Osvaldo knows himself quick to anger. Outrage comes over him like an eagle sinking talons into his chest, tearing at his heart. Is it satanic pride, tempting him to believe that God feels that same outrage? To believe that some sins are so vast, not even Jesus could be willing to forgive them?

Nearby, shockingly loud, the air-raid sirens begin to howl. Osvaldo jumps to his feet. Renzo groans and rolls onto his side, his back to the priest. "Sit down, Tomitz," he mumbles. "Nothing we can do yet."

Except pray, Osvaldo thinks.

But pray for what? He used to pray that Sant'Andrea be spared a raid. That seems tantamount now to wishing death on other cities. For survival? Of whom? Who dies, and when and how, is long divorced from any moral dimension Osvaldo can detect. Even so, he prays: for the souls of those who'll be vaporized by the blast of a direct hit; for those whose bodies will be crushed by falling masonry; for those who'll suffer; for those who'll grieve.

Squadrons release their whistling cargo. Each bomb has a task. Two-kilo incendiaries ignite rooftop fires. Fifteen-kilo bombs penetrate deep into structures, setting them ablaze from the inside out. Blockbusters—as massive as small trucks—destroy entire buildings, cratering streets, filling them with rubble to hinder firefighting equipment.

The detonations come closer. Osvaldo begins to wish he hadn't dumped Renzo's liquor on the floor. He wonders if it is easy to push a button or pull a lever and cause a hundred deaths you do not see. He asks himself if he could do it.

When he gets his answer, he prays for the pilots and their navigators, for the gunners and the bombardiers. Forgive them, Father, for they cannot see the burns, the crushed heads, the splintered limbs, the shattered lives. And bless them, for they are fighting those who've made a charnel house of Europe.

When at last the all clear sounds, Renzo sits up and scrubs at his hangdog face. "On your feet, Padre," he calls, trudging toward the street. "Work to do."

Osvaldo hesitates only long enough to pull his rosary from his pocket, to look at the crucifix and bring it to his lips. "The sick require a physician's help, not the healthy"—that's what Jesus taught. But gazing at the emaciated figure on the cross, what Osvaldo sees are the cool, clean hands of a doctor touching the warm flesh of a starving Jew. The hands of a physician who touches not to heal or comfort but to push a syringe full of poison into his 91,867th victim's heart.

If that can be forgiven, Osvaldo thinks, hell is empty.

MOTHER OF MERCY ORPHANAGE
ROCCABARBENA

Everybody thinks Isma is a half-wit, but Angelo Soncini is pretty
sure she's Jewish.

At first, Angelo thought he was the only Jew in the orphanage.
Then one time he was doing chores, and scrubbing circles on the
floor made him hum. Riccardo came over and whispered, "Quit
that!" Angelo thought he wasn't supposed to scrub anymore, but
when he started to get up, Riccardo said, "No, stupid! Just shut up!
You were humming 'Hatikva'!"

After he knew about Riccardo, Angelo looked for other kids
pretending to be Catholic. He watched at meals to see who kept
kosher, but that didn't work. There's never any meat, so there's
nothing you can't mix with milk, so everything's pareve. Mostly
there's zucchini, or potatoes, or polenta, or rice in watery soup,
and a little bread after school. You might get an egg if you're real
sick, but you have to have spots or something. The sisters can tell
when you're faking it. Sometimes there's soup with real old pasta,
and little worms floating in it. Worms are definitely not kosher,
but everybody picks them out, except the biggest boys, who eat
them to make the girls scream and get in trouble.

You have to be quiet all the time, except at recess and on Sunday after Mass. You have to act real serious like the sisters. You
have to walk in lines, two by two, and you wear dark blue uniforms
with white shirts if you're a boy, and white blouses if you're a girl.
You have to be obedient, and you can't have anything that belongs
to you alone, so you have to be careful with everything. Because
it's not yours, it's just "for your use." When you outgrow your

pants or something, you turn them in and get bigger ones. For your use. If you talk or get out of line, you'll get a smack from Suora Paola. Suora Paura, everyone calls her: Sister Scary.

Sister Scary always yells, and she calls you by your last name, and sometimes Angelo forgets that his name is supposed to be Santoro, and he gets in trouble because he doesn't answer right away. After he figured out about Isma, Angelo snuck up and told her, "Watch out for Suora Paura—she'll smack you one if you do something wrong!" Isma just stared at her feet and said, "*Isma glai,*" or something like that. That's all she ever says, so that's what everybody calls her: Isma.

"Suora Paola has to be strict," Suora Corniglia told Angelo. "If soldiers are coming, you have to do exactly as we say without asking why, or somebody might get hurt." Suora Corniglia always explains stuff, and she never ever yells. Not even soft. Suora Corniglia calls everybody by their first names, like a mother, and she's pretty, and nice, and she has dimples. Angelo is going to marry her when he grows up, because she's always kind. She'll wear pretty dresses then.

But she can still go to Mass.

Sometimes Suora Corniglia hides half an apple in her big sleeves, and she secretly gives a quarter to Angelo and a quarter to Isma. Suora Corniglia is real careful that nobody else sees. That's another reason Angelo thinks Isma's Jewish.

Plus, another reason is, Sister Scary let Isma keep that stupid doll. It's just a china head and a rubber body with the arms gone. The hair is all scrabbly. It's ugly, and nobody's allowed to have private stuff, but when Sister Scary tried to take it away, Isma screamed so much you could hear it all over the school, and everybody thought their ears were going to fall off. "It's all the poor little thing has," Suora Corniglia told Sister Scary. And then they looked at each other real serious. That's how Angelo figured out for almost sure that Isma is Jewish. If she was a Catholic kid, she could've screamed until she turned blue. Sister Scary still wouldn't have let her keep that doll.

A lot of girls cheat, though. They make little, tiny dolls out of a stick and a scrap of cloth or a leaf or something. They hide the dolls in their uniform pockets. At recess the girls take the dolls out and make them talk to each other in real high squeaky voices. It makes Angelo sick.

Most of the time the boys and girls are apart, so Angelo doesn't see Isma much, except at recess. And Mass. Everybody goes to Mass together at 6:30 every morning, which surprised Angelo a lot the first time. In synagogue, ladies and girls had to sit up in the gallery, but in church, they sit right in with men and boys! Angelo understands that now. In the synagogue, the women always came late, and then they talked too much, and the men would always be looking up and glaring at them, and when the women got noisy, Signor Tura would hiss like a snake. But Catholic girls know how to shut up. The sisters teach them that in school.

Angelo likes Mass, except for the crucifix, which is scarier than Suora Paura. One time, when Angelo went to visit Don Osvaldo at San Giobatta, Babbo told him, "In the old days, the Romans did that to anyone who made trouble. There was a slave called Spartacus who fought for freedom, and the Romans crucified six thousand of his followers, all along the Via Appia." When Angelo asked Suora Corniglia what kind of trouble Jesus made, she said, "He died for our sins." Which still doesn't seem fair, even though Suora has tried real hard to explain it.

Mass is mostly very nice. The candles are like when Mamma lit the candles for Shabbat. Near the end, the priest chants, "*Sanctus! Sanctus! Sanctus!*" just like when Babbo chants, "*Kadosh! Kadosh! Kadosh!*" And the priest wears fancy stuff that looks like what Aaron wore in the Tent of Meeting in the desert—Angelo had a picture book about that when he was little. Plus, the singing is good.

Angelo likes school, too. There aren't many books, so they memorize a lot. Multiplication tables, case endings, trees, stars, how to use punctuation. Angelo has a good memory, but sometimes he pretends he doesn't know an answer because there's this big kid named Bruno Ceretto. Bruno's older, because he got held back. He'll twist your arm real hard if you show off. Bruno hates show-offs, but he's more show-offy than anybody.

The whole school has recess after lunch. Angelo doesn't play with Isma, but he watches out so nobody picks on her. Once Bruno took Isma's stupid doll away from her, and Angelo slugged him in the stomach so hard Bruno couldn't even talk, and then recess was over. Bruno leaves Isma alone now, but then he started kicking Angelo whenever he got the chance, so Angelo would punch him. Sister Scary caught them fighting, and made them both kneel for an hour on pieces of real hard, dry corn, which hurt worse than getting kicked, and made marks in his knees that are still there! So now Angelo just says, "Girls kick. Are you a girl, Bruno?" Bruno gets mad, but he can't do anything because Sister Scary is watching them all the time with real fierce eyes.

Someday his parents will visit, and Angelo is definitely going to tell them how mean Sister Scary is. Angelo got a secret message that he was going to see Babbo at Passover, but he didn't come. When Angelo cried, Suora Corniglia said it was too dangerous at Passover because the Germans might suspect. But still.

His parents will visit pretty soon. Angelo is almost practically sure of that. He's going to tell them they should adopt Isma. They can change her name to Altira because Isma's not a real name. It's a pretend name, like Angelo Santoro. Or Sister Scary.

"You can come and live with my family after the war," he promises Isma at recess every day.

Isma just hugs her stupid doll and looks at her feet. *"Isma glai."* That's all she ever says.

Long white fingers grip a wooden-handled brass bell at 5:15 A.M., and Suora Ursula calls, "May Mary's immaculate heart . . ." From every cell, the responsum comes: ". . . be forever praised."

Suora Corniglia pulls off a plain cotton nightgown and dresses as she has each morning since she became a postulant: in a fog of half-remembered dreams. Hands clumsy, she ties the laces of stout black shoes, then pulls a blue-violet gown over white cotton undergarments. She tightens the belt around her waist, adjusting the soft pleats of the gown. There are more pleats now than ever. She's never been a large person, but since the occupation began weight has fallen off her and the other nuns like leaves from a tree. They are bone-tired and always hungry, but this is no more than anyone else suffers, and much less than many endure. Together, she and her sisters in Christ remember Jesus in the desert, and join their hunger to His.

A plain woolen scapular goes over her head, falling almost to the floor in front and behind. Beginning to wake up, she kisses the silver crucifix and slips its long chain around her neck. In the corner of the cell, propped overnight on a mop pole: the white coif and cape with its new black veil. She settles it onto a forehead grooved by the stiffly starched headband that sits just above her brows, and fastens its laces at the back of her neck. Muffling sound, the fabric embraces her face, and she adjusts the drape of the cloth that covers her shoulders.

Her clothing, like the cell she sleeps in, is merely "for her use." The practice of poverty is meant to free the mind and heart from concern for worldly goods, but before she came to the convent, she never thought so much about material things as she does now. She conserves the tiniest slivers of soap. She is aware of each millimeter of candlewick burned. In spare moments she repairs hems, patches holes, mends stockings for the children. The fabric is old. Careful stitches come apart. Sometimes it's all she can do to keep from weeping.

Turning back loose outer sleeves the prescribed twelve centimeters, she stands and waits. The bell rings a second time, and she joins her sisters in procession to chapel. She used to pray for the end of the war, but she suspects God doesn't need a nun to nag Him about that. These days she prays for patience with the children and the mending, with her superiors and herself.

Ite, Missa est: Go, the Mass is ended. Older orphans shepherd littler ones to a refectory where peasant women dish out polenta. The nuns return to the convent to share a breakfast hardly more substantial than the communion wafers they have just received. When the bell rings again, Suora Corniglia stands for the two-by-two procession with the other teachers to the school.

The classroom for her use is large and high-ceilinged, floored with gleaming chestnut. Whitewashed walls reflect the light pouring through enormous windows that look out over an old Roman bridge. On the eve of its third millennium, Ponte Ligure seems determined to carry people and goods across the river forever, but British *bombardieri* cannot let this insult to their manhood stand. They return for round after round in a lunatic boxing match: twentieth-century explosives versus first-century stonework. At least once a week she has a nightmare about the classroom windows. In her dreams, they're shattered by concussions, and the children are cut to pieces.

At 8:00 the students file in, two by two, their lives as regulated by brass bells as her own. They take their places next to scarred wooden desks bolted to sleighlike iron runners, shortest to tallest, so the ones in the back can see over those in front. When Bruno Ceretto arrives at the last desk in the far corner, they chorus, "*Buon giorno,* Suora Corniglia."

They are unsmiling except for Angelo, who sneaks a grin at her like a secret lover. Embarrassed by the thought, Suora Corniglia frowns when she replies, "*Buon giorno,* children. Bruno, will you lead us in the *Credo?*"

Prayers are recited in singsong Latin. Permission is granted to be seated. Floor bolts creak as small bottoms hit wood. The boys know the schedule as well as she does, but they wait for her cues.

Religion. History. Grammar. The morning passes. Desktops bang open, slam closed. The boys wait. She nods approval and faces the blackboard in a swirl of dark blue wool. Raising her arm, she places a centimeter-long stub of chalk against the blackboard. "When subtracting a—"

Two planes flash by, level with the hillside school. For an instant, she sees a pilot clearly. Machine-gun fire spits in both directions. Bombs bounce off stonework into the river. Water erupts into the air. Boys surge toward the windows.

"Get away from the glass!" she shrills, seizing Angelo and Bruno by their shirts. She can hear the planes' engines as they climb and bank to reapproach German gun emplacements. Fabric gives way as she flings the boys toward the door. "Into the corridor! All of you! Now! Now! Now!"

"Did you see him?" Angelo asks Bruno excitedly. "The pilot looked right at us! Did you see him?"

Trembling uncontrollably, she wants to slap the child for not being terrified, but by the time she has the whole class crouched along the edges of the hallway floor the attack is over, and someone is tugging on her sleeve, announcing, "Suora! Mario peed hisself!"

Mario stares at his lap, fat tears slipping down thin cheeks. "*O poveretto!*" she sighs with exasperated sympathy. "Don't make fun!"

she orders sharply, glaring until nervous laughter lapses into suppressed giggles. "Bruno! You and Angelo take Mario to the dormitory. Ask Suora Idigna to help him clean up and change. Get clean shirts for your use and bring the ripped ones to me for mending. Be back here in ten minutes! The rest of you: into your seats!"

The three boys march off: Mario bowlegged around the shamefully stained trousers, Angelo and Bruno tattered and torn from her own assault. Next time, she tells herself, grab arms, not collars.

The balance of the day is uneventful, until the school portress knocks. With a stern look toward the boys, Suora Corniglia lays down her chalk and goes to the classroom door.

"Sorry for the interruption, Suora," the portress whispers. "There's a Padre Righetti here to see you. He's waiting at the convent."

She glances at the wall clock. "Grazie, suora. Ask him to forgive me, but I can't leave until recess."

There are, in the event, two additional minor crises to manage. Sweeping into the convent receiving room, she says, "I'm sorry to have kept you waiting, Padre. One of the boys—"

The priest turns from the window. Suora Corniglia's mouth drops open. So does the visitor's.

"*You're* Angelo's teacher?" He snaps his fingers twice, trying to recall where they met. "You—you were scrubbing the floor at San Giobatta!" he says. "September eighth, right?"

"Yes!" she says with quiet excitement, placing him now. "You helped with the broken glass! You're the—" She stops herself.

"The Jew who went off with the German. I see you got a promotion." His eyes flick toward her black veil. "You're an officer now! How have you been, Sister Dimples?"

"It's Suora Corniglia," she says primly, hands under her scapular. "And if that's a costume for Carnevale, you're a little late in the season. What are you doing in a cassock?"

"Trying earnestly not to get arrested." He holds up the biretta's square crown, with its three shark fins and pompon, and puts it on his head, vamping like a Parisian model before sitting at the table.

"I borrowed the ensemble from Osvaldo Tomitz, who was carrying a doctor's bag last time I saw him."

"Not getting arrested seems to be Italy's national sport," she remarks, feeling a great deal less tired now. "I need to get back to the students in fifteen minutes. What was it you wanted, Padre?"

She expects him to laugh at the title, but he sobers instead. "I'd like to meet with Angelo, if that can be arranged."

There's something about his tone. "But—no! His parents?"

"His mother and baby sister are safe. His father's been jailed as a hostage." He holds up a hand when the nun gasps. "For the moment, everything is fine, but I'd like to speak to Angelo. I led him to believe I could arrange a visit, and I want to explain. Is there any way I can talk to him without arousing suspicion?"

"If he were older, you could pretend to hear his confession, but his class hasn't had First Communion yet." She thinks for a moment. "On Sunday afternoons, the children are allowed to hike up toward the monastery. Within reason, we let them do as they please for a few hours. They can play or read. Most of them hunt for mushrooms or berries—there's so little food. If you were to wait by the monastery gate, I could steer him toward you."

"Do you think I could stay with the brothers until then?"

"Ask for Fra Edoardo. You won't have to explain anything to him." She hesitates. "When Angelo comes to you, he'll bring a little girl along. She's only three, or maybe four. We think she might be one of the refugees who came over the Alps last year."

"What's her name?"

"We don't know. She's almost mute, poor thing. The children call her Isma. The only thing she ever says is, 'Isma glai.'"

"Isma glai . . . ? Ist mir gleich? Is that what she says?"

"I suppose . . . Yes! That could be it—nursery German for 'I don't care'?"

"Don't say anything to her yet. Let me talk to her first." Fussing with unfamiliar fabric tangled around his legs, Renzo stands. "Until Sunday, then, Suora Fossette."

"Until Sunday. And don't you dare call me Sister Dimples in front of the children!"

A slow grin forms above the Roman collar. "The thought," he lies, "never entered my mind."

Wrung out by five minutes' effort fueled by a diet of poor-quality starch, spring chard, and not much else, Suora Corniglia leans against a terrace wall to muster strength and catch her breath. Beside her, tiny brown lizards dart into crevices between stones. Fig trees bake in the basil-scented warmth above meticulously tended vineyards that crisscross the hillside. The Mediterranean is a stripe of silver between gray-green foothills, and when the wind shifts, the astringency of pine from nearby mountains is replaced by the barest hint of salt and seaweed.

The breeze carries Angelo's heartbroken angry wail as well, and Corniglia aches for him. In her first year of teaching she's learned that the emotions of eight-year-olds are as outsized as their new front teeth, big as barn doors in their little faces. Frowning curiosity, stunned surprise, and joyous vindication appeared in rapid succession on Angelo's face when she said quietly, "Take Isma to the monastery gate. A man is waiting to see you there." Before she could tell him the visitor was not his father, Angelo took off up the hillside, Isma running after him, china-faced doll flopping in her hand. "I knew it!" Angelo yelled. "I told you, Isma! I told you Babbo would come!"

Leaning forward to take better advantage of rubbery muscles, Corniglia climbs again until she reaches two small children and the ersatz priest, sitting on a bench shaded by the brothers' grape arbor. Gravely, Renzo Leoni shifts Isma from one black-gowned knee to the other. "Suora Corniglia! Permit me to introduce Signorina Stefania. Stefania is this many," he says, holding up four fingers, "and lived in Austria when she was little. Angelo was just telling me about a squadron of British pilots who strafed the school yard on Friday. Blow," he says, holding a large white handkerchief over the little boy's nose.

Face blotched by the purple stigmata of childish rage and anguish, Angelo swallows. "What I meant was, they didn't really strafe us."

"Well, they might have," Renzo allows, his sincerity less specious. Switching to German, he asks Stefania quiet questions. She starts to cry, and he pulls her close. "Of course, you were scared! Planes are scary!" He winks at Angelo. "Just like Suora Paura! Angelo, Suora Corniglia has a nickname, too! It's—"

"—very likely to get Angelo in a lot of trouble if he uses it," Sister Dimples warns.

Stefania holds up her doll and whispers. Renzo brings his ear closer to her mouth. Stefania repeats something almost inaudibly. "I am requested to tell Suora that Antoinette is also from Austria."

Word by word, with frequent asides to Angelo and the nun, Renzo draws the little girl out. As the conversation progresses, infant allegiance to her mother tongue begins to loosen and it becomes clear that she understands more Italian than she's been willing to admit. Gradually, Renzo brings the questioning around to the painful topic of parents. All he can get from Stefania is "They went away."

Angelo, by contrast, is voluble on the topic, hurt and angry that his parents haven't visited either. "Angelo," Renzo reminds him, "I told you—your babbo can't come yet. He's locked up, but he's in a safe place—"

"Well, you should just go and get him out!"

Above the starched white collar, Renzo's eyes rise to meet Suora Corniglia's. "It's not that simple, Angelo."

Abruptly, Renzo lifts Stefania off his lap, plunks her onto the bench, and limps toward a bicycle leaning against the monastery wall. Between grief and grievance, Angelo stares open-mouthed at his neighbor's back. Just as stunned, Suora Corniglia's lips part. You can't just leave! she thinks, appalled. You can't just walk away.

As if in answer, Renzo stops and takes a deep breath, willing the fun back into his face. "But wait! I almost forgot!"

Drawing something from a rucksack draped over the handlebars, he returns, hands concealed behind his back. "Which?" he asks. Angelo points to his right. Crestfallen, Renzo moans his dismay. "Too bad! I thought you'd like to have this."

He reveals a left-handed miracle: an orange. Horror-stricken at having guessed wrong, Angelo's face falls. Renzo lets him suffer for an instant before tossing it. The fruit, heavy with juice, drops into Angelo's palm with a thwack, and he tears the peel like a ravening wolf. "Share it with Stefania!" Renzo orders.

Angelo rips the fruit in half and hands Stefania her portion. With the bliss of a soul ascending directly to heaven, the little boy bites into a segment and staggers with pleasure as the juice slides over his chin. Stefania may never have seen an orange before, but the item is demonstrably edible, and she too stuffs orange segments into her mouth, one after the other.

"Suora Corniglia," Renzo says sternly, "you've neglected the subject of table manners."

Suddenly dizzy, the nun closes her eyes, but summons enough presence of mind to say, "In my defense, there is very little for us to practice on."

"Sit," he says quietly. "Put your head down." She leans over, and hears his footsteps as he walks to the bicycle and back. "Drink this," he says, handing her a silver flask. She shakes her head. "Don't argue," he says, "unless you fancy me carrying you back to the convent."

Hesitantly, she takes a swallow, coughs, eyes tearing, and hands the flask back. He takes a healthy swallow himself and sits next to her. "There is a special place in hell for the man who invented bicycles," he says, massaging his knees. Tucking the flask away, he rummages in his pack, produces a second orange, and digs his nails into the peel. The world contracts to the size of the fruit in his hand. She stares, motionless, struggling to keep her head clear. "Eat this," he says. "Now."

She does as she's told. The juice is acid and sweet. When it hits her stomach, she retches. He hands her a canteen of water from his rucksack. This time, she drinks deep. Then she finishes the orange.

He makes the children drink as well, and when they're done, he folds his handkerchief to a fairly clean spot, wetting white linen with the last of the water. Feinting left, he anticipates Angelo's dodge to the right. Doing the same for Stefania, Renzo says, "Let's see if the sisters have done a better job with your religious lessons than with your table manners. Angelo, who were the first man and the first woman?"

Angelo rolls his eyes at how easy this is. "Adamo and Eva!"

"And when were Adamo and Eva created?" Renzo asks, busily cleaning juice from Stefania's fingers.

Angelo cries, "On the sixth day!"

"Right. And what happened next?" Renzo asks cagily.

Staggered by this evident contempt for his biblical acumen, Angelo yells, "God rested!" with a great show of exasperation.

"Wrong!" Renzo yells back triumphantly. Suora Corniglia blinks, and Angelo scowls. "God rested on the seventh day," Renzo admits, handing Corniglia the damp handkerchief, "but what happened before that?" Silence reigns. "Before the evening of the sixth day," he informs them patiently, "there was the sixth afternoon! And what happened on the sixth afternoon?"

Wiping her fingers and refolding his handkerchief neatly, Suora Corniglia bats her eyelashes in a parody of flirtation. "Do tell, Padre! We are breathless with anticipation!"

"I should think you would be," he says huffily. "On the sixth afternoon, Adamo and Eva and the animals were all sitting around in Eden enjoying the lovely weather when something strange happened." He pauses dramatically. "The big round yellow light up in the blue place—"

"The sun!" Angelo hollers. "In the sky!"

"Well, *you* know that, but Adamo and Eva had just been created, remember, and hardly anything had a name, and they didn't know how anything worked! So when the big yellow thing started slipping down the blue place toward all that green stuff, Adamo wondered, 'Why is the big yellow thing doing that?' Eva said, 'You're asking me? I just got here myself.' So Adamo asked the animals, 'Why isn't the big round yellow thing sticking up there in the blue place?' And the animals said, 'We were hoping you'd tell us!' "

"Except," Suora Corniglia breaks in, "there was one little mouse who just looked at her feet and said, '*Isma glai!*' "

Stefania giggles, a tiny silvery sound, and lies back against the black worsted cassock, relaxing into the story. "The big round yellow thing disappeared," Renzo continues, pulling Angelo onto the bench. "Eden got dark and chilly. Adamo and Eva and the animals were all cuddled up to keep warm, just like this. *Santo cielo!*" he cries wickedly. "No one is cuddling with Suora Corniglia!"

"*Grazie,* Padre," she says smoothly. "I am quite warm enough!"

"Are you sure?" he asks. "Because I'd be happy to—" Stefania tugs the crucifix hanging around his neck and whispers something. "You're right. I'll finish the story. So there they were, all cuddled up. Adamo said, 'I wish God had let us keep that big round yellow thing.' But Eva said, 'Well, those new little twinkly things are pretty, too.' "

"*Stelle,*" Stefania whispers.

"Stars! Exactly! But nobody knew that then. One by one, the animals went to sleep. Adamo whispered, 'What a lot of trouble for God, making that big yellow thing for such a short time.' But Eva said, 'He's the Boss.' " Renzo's tone changes. "What do you think happened next?"

"The sun came back!" Angelo yells.

"The sun came up! The animals stretched and started walking around, mooing, and roaring, and so on. Adamo said, 'Look, Eva! God made another big round yellow thing, but this time He put it over on the other side of the garden!' " Renzo lifts Stefania from his knee, his fingertips meeting across her little back. "What do you think, Stefania? Does God make a new sun every morning?"

She looks at her feet. "I don't know," she says. Not, Suora Corniglia notes, "I don't care."

"It just goes around to the other side!" Angelo tells her. "You can't see it, but it's still there!"

"Yes," Renzo says softly. "The sun is still there, even when you can't see it. And your parents love you, even when you can't see them." Out of the corner of his mouth, he mutters to Suora Corniglia, "Even when you can't stand them."

Corniglia smiles. Renzo stands, groaning when he gets up. "I can't promise to bring your parents to you," he says, "but I can promise I will try. Before I go . . . Angelo, take Stefania over to the bicycle and look in the other bag."

The children race off. "That was beautiful," Corniglia says.

"It's midrash: a story behind a story in the Torah. My oldest sister told me that one when she left home to get married. She was killed last October, trying to get to Switzerland."

"I'm sorry."

"Chocolate!" Angelo shouts, dancing with a candy bar. "Chocolate, Suora!"

Renzo looks over his shoulder. "Angelo, you little savage! Offer Suora some!"

"Just share it with Stefania!" she calls.

"Thank you," Renzo says quietly, "for taking care of them."

They are not my children, she thinks, but they are a son and daughter for my use. Renzo looks at her so searchingly that she turns away, her veil shielding her eyes. "You're not a bad fellow," she hears him say, "for a nun."

She glances at him. "And you're not a bad fellow, either. For a fake priest."

Once again, a slow grin transforms the mournful Renaissance face. Pleased, but aware that she is skirting sin, Suora Corniglia regains custody of her eyes, and keeps them on the path as she strolls with him toward the bicycle.

"Angelo," Renzo asks, "do you have a message for your mammina?"

Angelo scrunches up his face. Teeth brown with chocolate, he looks at the monastery wall, at the ground, at the arbor. At Stefania. He squints up at his neighbor. "It's a secret."

Renzo leans over. Angelo rises on tiptoe, putting grubby little hands around the man's ear. "That's a good message," Renzo says, when the whispering ends. "I'll tell her that."

Below them, at the school-yard gate, Suora Ursula rings the brass bell. Well trained, the children race down the hill, knowing the day's outing is over. Suora Corniglia returns to the bench and retrieves Stefania's doll, forgotten in the excitement. "You, too," she tells Renzo, coming nearer. "Get going!"

Not caring if anyone can see them, the black-gowned Jew takes her hand and kisses it, watching her reaction. Challenged, she refuses to pull away and meets his eyes, unflustered. Vanquished, he clutches at his heart and staggers backward, as though struck by an arrow.

"*Pagliaccio!* Clown!" she says with affectionate reproof, as though he were one of her eight-year-olds. Hiking up the cassock, he throws a leg over the bicycle seat. While he's busy fitting a clip around his pants leg, she impulsively removes her rosary. "To complete your disguise," she says.

He holds out his hand, and she drops the plain black beads with their simple silver links into his palm. After a long moment, he says, "Take care, Suora Fossette."

"I'll pray for you, Padre Pagliaccio." She watches him push off, her rosary in his pocket, bicycle tires grating on gravel. "Don't get arrested!" she calls. He raises a hand without looking back, and disappears over the crest.

THE HUNCHBACK'S HOUSE
FRAZIONE DECIMO

Drying laundry snaps in the breeze. Ravens squabble in the tree-tops. The garden is green with seedlings. Content in his high-backed chair, Werner Schramm turns his face toward the late-spring sun. The women wear faded cotton frocks, and though he himself is wrapped in woolens to guard against a chill, he feels remarkably well. As long as he doesn't raise his arms, there's no chest pain at all.

He's begun to take short walks, an ambition little Rosina now shares. Plump hands in her mother's firm grasp, she lumbers with baby industry between Mirella's legs. "You shouldn't make her walk too early," Schramm advises. "Her legs won't grow properly."

"Nonsense! She loves it!" Mirella bends to kiss her daughter's silky curls, and returns undaunted to her topic. "Anyway, you don't have to be Freud to work it out. All those stiff, raised arms. All that talk about how hard he is. He's covering something up!"

"You'll have to excuse Signora Soncini, Herr Schramm." Lidia pops peas into a bowl and drops the pod into the apron stretched across her lap. "Like everyone who takes Doktor Freud seriously, she seems to have only one thing on her mind. Thank God, her husband will be visiting soon."

"Babbo's coming, cara mia!" Skirt ballooning, Mirella swings Rosina up and around. "He'll see how you go flying!" she cries, de-lighted when the beaming baby repeats, "F'ying!"

Halfway down the mountain, a church bell tolls. Sunday Mass is over, but the parish choir is rehearsing for some saint's festa. A polyphonic hymn floats up through air so clear and light so true,

Schramm dreams again of painting. Lidia's dark eyes in their spiderweb of parchment-colored skin. The crescent curls of Rosina's red-gold hair. Mirella's cheeks, like ripe peaches beneath freckles she earned planting their kitchen garden. Focus on the near, forget about the distant. War becomes a memory, a rumor, a myth . . .

"Admit it, Werner," Mirella says. "Doesn't the Führer seem sort of—I don't know . . . prissy?"

Werner blinks and straightens. "He isn't married, but there is a woman. She is never spoken of in public—"

"So every girl in Germany can dream that the Führer would choose her," Lidia says cannily. "My grandmother was in love with Bonaparte." She reaches into the willow basket for more peas. "She saw him once when she was twelve. He was young then, and dashing. He smiled down at her from his white charger, and she very nearly swooned. Later, he gained weight and lost charm, but for several years, she was enthralled, and kept a scrapbook of his battles."

Schramm knows these two women better than his own mother or his wife. After months in this isolated house, no topic is off-limits. Female combativeness no longer shocks him, but he still hasn't decided if it is an Italian trait, or Jewish, or simply Lidia and Mirella. His own wife, Elsa, is a bland, blond memory, but he wonders now if he ever really listened to her.

Looking up, the baby buzzes her lips like an airplane. "Airp'ane, Mamma!"

"Say *prego!*" both women correct reflexively, and when she does, Mirella rewards her with another swoop through the air.

Rosina is tiny but seems startlingly precocious. She can already tell birds from planes. "My boys didn't speak so well until they were two," Schramm says.

"Girls talk early." Lidia hands the baby a pea pod to gum, to give Mirella a rest. "Renzo had almost nothing to say until he was almost two and a half. He's made up for it since."

Refusing to be sidetracked, Mirella asks, "Has Hitler's secret woman had any secret children? Are there any little *Überkinder* fathered by the Führer?"

"No," Schramm admits, "there are no children."

"Heavens!" she says archly. "He denies his own superior germ plasm to the nation, when it's every good Aryan's duty to breed?"

"I think what you suggest of him is not quite correct," Werner says delicately. "But all his energy is—" He makes a gesture suggesting a funnel. "He puts everything into his speeches. To hear him is almost—*scusi,* ladies, but it is almost pornographic. He begins very gently. He takes the crowd into his confidence. He speaks, and you think, He speaks to me alone. The others disappear. I have felt this," Schramm confesses. "Thirty thousand around me, but I felt alone with him. He is like a strong friend who knows your secret thoughts, who is more experienced, more wise. Everyone moves toward him. Your heart is faster, your eyes see only him. His voice rises. He—"

He swells, Schramm thinks. He grows tumescent—larger, more powerful—before your eyes. Your heart and soul open to him, like a girl's legs. He fills you. Nothing in the world exists but this man, his words, his voice, his power to make you believe, to adore him, to let him do as he pleases with you.

Schramm comes to himself, and clears his throat. "When the speech ends," he says quietly, "it is a climax. For him. For us. A seduction, and a climax."

For some reason, Mirella will not meet his eyes, but Lidia is judicial. " 'The serpent deceived me,' " she quotes aridly, " 'and I did eat.' "

"I met him once," Schramm says. "I was invited to the Berghof—his villa in the mountains. He is less impressive in private, except for his eyes. They are not beautiful, precisely, but extraordinary. Hypnotic! But he can be so boring! The same stories, over and over. 'When I was a soldier . . . When I was in prison . . .' He talks and talks. All night, every night, when others want only to sleep. He knows a great deal about medicine and biology, but much of what he said was not correct."

Or was simply absurd. A Turkish porter can lift a piano by himself. Humanity depends on the whale for nourishment. Fifty thousand Irishmen went to America in 1641. No one in the Middle Ages had high blood pressure. When their blood rose, they'd fight with knives; now, thanks to the modern safety razor, the world's blood pressure is too high. Anyone who paints a sky green and pastures blue should be sterilized. Roosevelt's a Jew. Jesus wasn't. The Czechs are really Mongolians. Look at the way their mustaches droop. Roman legionnaires were vegetarians and had magnificent teeth.

Rosina starts toward the garden on little hands and knees. "And no one argues with him?" Mirella asks, retrieving her daughter before she can crawl over the zucchini.

"Not twice." Schramm shudders at the memory. "He said to me—it was very late, about three in the morning—he said, 'Uncooked potatoes will cure beriberi in a week.' I said beriberi is unknown among those who eat sufficient meat. He was—" Dumbfounded, Schramm thinks, but he doesn't know the word in Italian, so he mimes Hitler's astonishment. "I thought, *Wunderbar!* He is impressed with my knowledge! So I said also that potatoes do contain some thiamine, but that vitamin is unaffected by heat. Ergo: potatoes need not be raw."

Brows up, Schramm invites comment. The women shrug: So?

"He began to scream at me!" Schramm says. "There were ten of us that night. No one could move! I was—" He mimes his shock, eyes bulging with astonishment and fear. "For two hours, three hours, he screamed and screamed about the evil of meat, and the absolute necessity of not cooking the potatoes to cure beriberi! I thought he would have me shot!"

"It wasn't the potato. It was the contradiction," Lidia says. "Men like that want everyone to marvel at their power and superiority, but they're terrified of competition. When such a man proposes a footrace, he intends to begin by battering his opponent unconscious with a rock." Lidia sets the bowl of peas aside. "Tell me, Herr Schramm, what did you do to merit an invitation to the Führer's exalted presence?"

"I wrote a public health pamphlet on the importance of mother's nutrition during pregnancy for the fitness of the infant. That was my medical speciality before the war. I made a study of the causes of incorrect infants. He heard of my work."

Gripping Mirella's skirt, pulling herself upright, Rosina thumps her mother's legs. "Mamma! Up!"

Mirella ignores her. "What do you mean by incorrect infants, Herr Schramm?"

"*Osteogenesis imperfecta, pes equinus. Meningocele, spina bifida.* Pardon— I know these terms only in Latin. *Hydrocephaly, microcephaly, anencephaly:* heads very large from water on the brain, or very small heads, or without a brain. Also—very small people. Blind, deaf. Such conditions might be an error of heredity, but if good seed falls on poor soil, the results are disappointing. Hitler was interested in this idea."

"Tell me, Herr Doktor," says Lidia. "Is idiocy among the defects caused by poor nutrition?"

Mirella flinches, but Lidia's brows are raised in calm curiosity. "Some forms, yes," Schramm tells them. "Cretinism and goiter are often together. Both result from deficiency of iodine."

"*Pègo!* Up!" Rosina demands.

Mirella pulls her skirt from Rosina's fingers. "Wait," she says, first walking, then running toward the hunchback's house.

Bewildered, Rosina watches her go. "*Pègo* up! *Pègo* up, Mamma!"

Schramm asks, "Did I say something wrong?"

Lidia takes her apronful of pea pods to the compost heap and tosses them on top. She says nothing, waiting for the younger woman to return.

When Mirella reappears with a photo that trembles slightly in her hand, Schramm needs only a glance. The anatomical atavisms are unmistakable: almond eyes with medial epicanthic folds. Midface insufficiency with pronounced saddling of the nose. Fat pads like an orangutan's around the face and neck. If he could examine the child, its palms would surely present the diagnostic undivided crease. "A younger sister, perhaps?"

"My second child."

"*Ach.* Unusual for such a young mother. The condition occurs once in, perhaps, fifteen hundred births among women under thirty."

"Is there something I could have done? Something I should have eaten, or not eaten?"

What can he say? When Langdon Down described the syndrome, the Englishman believed it represented reversion to prehuman stock. Others say such children are evidence of Mongol ancestors, who raped their way across Europe. Modern authorities blame mothers too feeble or exhausted to bear healthy offspring. Wishing to be kind, Schramm says, "The condition is not associated with malnutrition. I know of nothing you could have done to prevent this tragedy. Where is the child?"

Ignored, Rosina begins to cry in earnest.

"There was an accident," Lidia tells Schramm when it's obvious Mirella can't. "Altira died when she was three."

He draws himself up in the chair, familiar with the sensation of being across the desk from a devastated parent. "Mirella, you must not grieve: I assure you that a mongoloid idiot is better off dead—"

The slap is so sudden, so unexpected, Schramm can only stare.

Mirella snatches back the photograph. She tries and fails to say something. Scooping Rosina up, she stalks away, slamming the hunchback's door behind her.

Lidia sighs. "Go in there and apologize, Herr Schramm."

Schramm stands, astonished. "Apologize! For what?"

Lidia leans over to retrieve the wrap that's fallen from his lap. Shakes its dust out. Folds it loosely in her lap. "You insulted her child."

"I spoke as a physician, signora! There were many worse things I could have said!" Swept by an ancient anger, he jabs a finger in Mirella's direction. "Mothers like her—they think only of themselves! They are the ones—they don't see! They refuse to see!"

"To see what, Herr Schramm?"

The wrecked families. The broken dreams. The teeming institutions, like satanic zoos filled with every sort of biological failure.

Approach the children's yard: mongoloids and cretins would rush the fence, faces contorted in caricatures of human emotion. Grunting, tongues protruding, their mouths issuing wordless shrieks or meaningless, mindless babble. When they saw you had nothing for them, they'd wander away, sit cross-legged on the ground, clustered together. Drooling, laughing horribly at nothing. Picking up pebbles, eating bits of debris, tugging at the few remaining tufts of grass in the barren courtyard.

There was an entire ward for the hydrocephalics. White plaster walls, white iron cribs, white cotton sheets, and on each white pillow an enormous head. Immense egg-shaped domes tapering to tiny wizened faces connected by birdlike necks to emaciated bodies. His sister Irmgard's withered little hand would reach through the guardrail to touch his fingers. "I hope it's sunny tomorrow," she'd whisper, her voice like a breeze passing through dead leaves. "We go for a walk when it's sunny." A walk? Schramm wanted to cry. Hospital attendants pushing high-wheeled baby carriages like peddlers' carts, laden with grotesque vegetables.

And the nurseries—Christ! The nurseries were filled with the worst that could happen to human zygotes. Babies with gaping holes where their mouths and noses should be. Fragile little skeletons wrapped in a thin layer of blue-white skin the color of watered milk. Spastic, or rigidly immobile. Children so crippled they'd never leave their cribs. So impaired they'd never learn anything. Their only communication was the ceaseless, tearless, wordless moan of those trapped for years in a life of unspeakable, inescapable pain. Free me. Free me. Free me—

"Herr Schramm? Herr Schramm!" Lidia says sharply. "Are you all right?"

"Those children are like a bomb!" he says raggedly. "A bomb that kills the whole family, that breaks everything in a home! All the mother's time and attention go to the weakest. She deprives her other children of her care. She neglects also her husband. It is natural that he should leave! And for what? A child who will never contribute anything to society!"

When Lidia speaks, her voice is emotionless, factual. "Yes. I knew a mongoloid when I was young. A neighbor's child. His nose ran constantly. He never used a handkerchief. Disgusting. His tongue was always out. He couldn't learn to control his bowels."

"They never do!" Schramm declares. "A proven fact!"

Lidia raises her hands, adjusts a hairpin, tightening the iron-gray chignon. "When Altira was born, everyone told Mirella the condition was hopeless. Some of us also believed—" She hesitates. "I believed the child would reflect badly on the Jewish community. It would give comfort to those who believed us an inferior race."

Schramm looks away from the level eyes, dry beneath lined and looping eyelids.

"Mirella stood up to us," Lidia recalls. "You've seen how she can be. I told her she was being unreasonable. She said, 'The world is filled with unreasonable hate. What's wrong with unreasonable love?' Sentimental nonsense, I thought, but she kept Altira. Mirella treated that hopeless child like any other beloved baby. The results were . . ." Lidia pauses to choose her word. "Stunning."

The wind carries the scent of rock and warming soil. A few meters from where they sit, a hawk rides heat from sunlit crags. Feathers rippling in the wind, the bird lifts one wing and wheels.

"I was surprised by Altira's sweetness," Lidia continues, voice light, controlled. "She was often rather boring. All small children are boring, frankly. They love to do the same thing over and over. Altira had a capacity for repetition far beyond the limits of my patience. Even so, there was a light in her eyes."

The breeze shifts. The hawk rocks slightly, working to maintain his position, yellow eyes sweeping the tangle of spring-green vegetation at the edge of the hunchback's terraces.

"When I was thirty-four, I had a child—not like Altira, but not . . . *right*. When she was born, I swore she'd never be ridiculed as that neighbor boy was. We told everyone the baby died. My husband took her to the Cottolengo Institute near Genoa. She lived there for seven years." Her chair creaks as she eases sparely fleshed bones on the unforgiving surface. "I never went to see her."

The hawk stalls for a breathless moment, folds his wings, plummets. In the silence, they hear the brief, small cry of his hapless prey.

"Regret changes nothing." Lidia waits until Schramm's eyes meet hers. "Go to Mirella," she says. "Beg pardon, Herr Doktor."

Inside, dripping rag in hand, Mirella scrubs furiously at the trompe l'oeil drawings on the wall. When Schramm appears in the doorway, she plunges the rag into the bucket of washwater and wrings it like a chicken's neck.

"Doctors! Doctors like you— She won't live, that's what they told me. But she did. She'll never talk, but she did, Schramm. Not clearly, I admit that, but lots of three-year-olds are hard to understand! And she understood what we said to her. She was not an idiot!"

A chalk ocean disappears. Rosina sobs. Schramm sinks onto the stone platform near the fireplace.

"They said she'd never walk, but she did. Yes, she was clumsy. So what? Not everyone is a ballerina. She was sick a lot, but everybody gets colds. And yes! I probably did neglect Angelo, but he didn't need me as much as she did."

"Mirella, please—"

The washrag, filthy with land and sea, smacks against his shoes. "It's Signora Soncini to you!"

"Signora, no parent would wish for the kind of children I have—I have seen. If such conditions could be prevented—"

"The race would be improved?" Mirella wipes her nose on the back of her hand. "Homer was blind. Beethoven went deaf—"

"Signora, you don't seriously believe that a mong—that your daughter could have been a composer?"

"We don't know what she could have been! She died before we found out!"

Frightened by her mother's anger, Rosina crawls to Schramm. He bends stiffly and takes the baby onto his lap. Mirella snatches Rosina away.

"Doctors," she says contemptuously, oblivious to the child wailing on her hip. "You look at people for ten minutes, and you think you know everything about them!"

Less, Schramm thinks. Ten seconds, perhaps? Five?

"Airp'ane!" Rosina sobs, pointing.

"She wasn't a tragedy, Werner! She was a little girl. She was my daughter. And she loved to dance."

Rosina squirms out of her mother's heedless embrace. "Airp'ane!" she cries, patting at the door.

The noise outside grows. A shift in tone: acceleration. "*Mein Gott,*" Schramm whispers.

"You're not even listening!" Mirella cries, aghast. "You doctors never—"

They have, perhaps, half a minute. He grabs Rosina, thrusts her at Mirella, flings the door open. "Get out!" he shouts. "Get away from the buildings! Run!" he yells to Lidia, pushing Mirella out the door. "Run for the trees!"

The first Stuka shrieks by. Mirella makes for the woods, the baby clutched to her chest. Head between his shoulders, Schramm runs toward Lidia, grips her arm. A second gull-wing shadow sweeps over the ground. They both stumble when the engine backblast hits them.

Mirella crouches, shielding Rosina with her body. Rosina's terrified screams join the high-pitched wail of the Stukas, and the rattle of their machine guns. The first concussion nearly knocks Lidia off her feet. Schramm staggers but keeps his grip. The second bomb explodes farther up the mountain.

Fifty meters into the forest, they scrabble sideways, skirting the mountain's incline, scrambling over vines and rocks. Keep track, he tells himself. Center-mount 500s, away. Four SD70 fragmentation bombs on the wing racks. How many left?

Schramm spots an ancient chestnut. Thin mountain soil has eroded away from a snaking tangle of tree roots, creating a little cave. Pointing, he gasps, "In there!" He takes Rosina. The women crawl through an opening like a Gothic arch made of roots as thick as Rosina's body. One of the planes lets its rack of 70s go. Stones and dirt shower down through treetops. He hands the shrieking baby in to Mirella.

"Get in!" Mirella shouts. Schramm shakes his head. She and Lidia move to the edges of the little space. "Get in!" Mirella yells again. "There's room!"

A second rack of bombs falls. The detonations merge into a single titanic blast. He squirms under the tree and wedges himself between the women. "Luftwaffe! They want the partisans, not us!" They nod, trembling. He puts his arms around them.

Another pass: explosions are replaced by the rattle of machine guns and answering small-arms fire. Engine noises doppler away. Six, perhaps eight minutes after the raid began, it's over.

For a time, only the baby's hiccuping sobs break the forest's stunned silence. The adults stare straight ahead, gathering their wits.

When cramped muscles demand movement, Schramm delivers himself like a breech birth, feet first. Mirella hands Rosina through, crawls out on her own, takes the baby back. "Wasn't that exciting, Rosina?" she cries, voice high with forced cheer. "*Santo cielo!* What a racket!"

Lidia accepts Schramm's help, and doesn't release his hand as they pick their way back through the forest. "They know about San Mauro," she whispers.

"It was a message," Schramm says. "We know where you are."

Mirella, a few steps ahead, holds Rosina close. "Yes, *cara mia,* those were bad airplanes, but they're all gone!" she soothes. "You're such a brave girl! Everything is fine now."

The hunchback's house is still standing, and the ramshackle barn no worse. Schramm collapses onto his chair. Lidia sits next to him, equally drained. They watch, slack-jawed, as Mirella swoops the baby through the air.

"What noisy airplanes!" Mirella cries. "Wasn't that fun?" she asks a doubtful Rosina, whirling until the baby's short, sharp terror begins to yield to her mother's insistent merriment and her own sunny nature.

"Extraordinary," Schramm says, shaking his head when Rosina repeats her mother's "Flying!" with increasing conviction.

Lidia extracts a handkerchief from her apron pocket, presses it against a flushed and dirty face. Eyes sidelong, she considers the winded German beside her while dabbing at the trickle of sweat slipping down her crepey throat.

Schramm looks down the gravel path that leads toward San Mauro. "Someone's coming," he says.

"It's Don Leto!" Mirella shouts joyously, swinging Rosina around and around. "That means Babbino's in San Mauro, *cara mia!* We're going to see your babbo again, and your big brother!"

A black-clad figure is hobbling hurriedly up the gravel path, and there's something familiar about the man, but— "That's not Don Leto," Schramm says. "The limp is wrong."

Lidia shades her eyes with both hands. "Old as I am," she notes drily, "there are occasions when I am forcibly reminded that I have not yet seen everything. That's my son. In a cassock."

Renzo waves to them briefly before Mirella reaches him. Hands on her shoulders, he speaks quietly and at some length. Mirella puts the baby down, and sits heavily on a tree stump. Rosina babbles. Mirella sketches a smile, her face crumpling as Rosina crawls off to play.

"Her husband," Schramm supposes.

"*Poveretta*," Lidia whispers.

Leaving Mirella, Renzo approaches, limping heavily. "Schramm! You're looking less cadaverous! And Mamma." He kisses the thin-skinned downy cheek Lidia offers. "Pale, but otherwise undamaged?"

She reaches out to grip his hand. The long, uneven breath he exhales is the only sign of the dread that drove him to sprint the last half kilometer up this mountain. "Iacopo?" she asks.

"Arrested. Just bad luck: he was raked up with forty other hostages." Still trying to get his breath back, Renzo unbuttons the cassock and tosses the sweaty woolen garment over the laundry line. "Mamma, exactly how bored are you—?"

"Don't move," she says.

Schramm and Renzo follow her stare. Half-buried in the soft soil of the garden, the bomb's stablizing propeller rotates slowly in the breeze. Straddling it, arms wide, Rosina makes buzzing noises with her lips. "Airp'ane!" she announces happily.

Lidia fastens a clawlike hand on Renzo's arm. "She doesn't know you. I'll go. Keep Mirella away."

Mirella hears her name, sees Rosina, rushes toward her. Renzo blocks her path. "No!" she screams, struggling as Renzo lifts her off her feet. "Rosina, no!"

Lidia moves steadily through the garden. When she is close enough to hear ticking, she glances over her shoulder. Schramm and Renzo have manhandled Mirella behind the hunchback's house. Bending at the knees amid feathery carrot seedlings, Lidia points toward the sky. "Rosina!" she says. "See the airplane?"

The baby looks up. Lidia seizes the child under the arms, steps over the bomb, and starts for the stone barn. The ticking pauses. The baby is heavy but Lidia hurries, thin old legs stumping along decisively.

They're just inside the door when the blast lifts her off her feet for a weird, short sail through the air. There is no sensation of impact, only the need to keep Rosina in her arms. Her shoulder goes numb when she hits a bale of hay, but she hangs on, curling around the baby while they're pelted by stones and dirt.

Straw is still falling when the others reach her. Schramm stoops to feel along Rosina's limbs. The baby is crying, but there's no blood, and she's safe now in her sobbing mother's arms. Ears ringing, Lidia reads Schramm's bleached, anxious face, his moving lips: She's fine. She's fine! Are you all right? "Yes, I think so," Lidia says, faintly amazed by the whole experience. She will be badly bruised, no doubt, but she's too keyed up to feel pain.

Renzo helps her stand, holds her briefly. Schramm looks more shaken than she feels, and says something. Lidia taps her ears and shakes her head. "I can't hear you!"

They make her sit on a hay bale. She paws bits of straw from her hair while Schramm examines her. Renzo spots her spectacles, straightens the frames, and puts them on her face. Still laughing, she catches sight of the view beyond the barn, and her face loses its shape.

The garden is a crater. The chairs she and Schramm sat in a minute ago: vaporized. The laundry posts have remained upright, the rope bizarrely in place. Renzo's cassock lies twenty meters away, unscorched, in the weeds. Diapers smolder nearby. Smoking-hot chunks of metal are everywhere: jammed between the stones of the house and barn, embedded in trees, littering the ground. "A miracle!" she says, stupefied. "A miracle."

Werner Schramm has witnessed the phenomenon in others many times: the buckling knees, the helpless weeping. Under fire, your training takes over. When the danger's past, the shaking and crying begin. Renzo stands behind Lidia, his hands on her shoulders, both of them taking in the devastation. Mirella's forearm makes a seat for Rosina's bottom. Her other hand cups the back of her baby's head, fingers lost in red-gold curls. So ordinary. So normal. But they might have died half a minute ago . . .

Schramm wipes his eyes, ashamed of going to pieces. "Cataplexy," Schramm tells the others, tears spilling. "It's nothing. Reaction. Truly. Just reaction." But the recoil intensifies as he looks from face to face. Lidia. Renzo. Mirella. Concerned. Understanding. Sympathetic. The faces blur. He knows who they are, but he cannot see them. They become, with terrifying ease: items, categories. Jew, too old to work. Jew, able-bodied. Jew, with child. Left. Right. Left.

Sinking in a heap on the packed dirt of the barn floor, he gives himself up to the weeping, until he hasn't strength for more. Finally, exhausted and empty, he pulls himself together and sees two adolescent boys. Out of breath from their long run, they stare at what's left of Mirella's garden. Lidia goes to them. A hurried conversation, and she points to Schramm. They come toward him, their anxious faces pinched by shock. They take his arms, lift him to his feet, pull him toward a path that leads to the Cave of San Mauro.

"You have to come!" they are saying. "We need a doctor!"

The sun has dropped behind the mountains on the other side of the valley when Renzo emerges from the hut with the household's sole remaining chair. He settles it onto a patch of level ground, making a courtier's sweeping gesture, and Lidia accepts the seat. They are alone. Rosina is napping, Mirella beside her. Schramm, depleted by the events of the day, has sent word from the cave that he'll stay tonight with the San Mauro Brigade, which has sustained its first casualty.

Renzo shakes a cigarette from a package of Nazionales and offers it to Lidia. "What happened to that silver cigarette case?" she asks.

"Sold it." He leans over with a match. "I sold Zia Elena's credenza, too."

She dismisses the news with a queenly wave. "All that carving! Made me think of skin diseases."

Cigarette dangling in the corner of his mouth, he lowers himself to the weedy ground, using his hands to ease his knees as he stretches out. She holds her own breath until he leans back on his elbows and his face relaxes. Smoking in companionable silence, they watch a flock of swallows dive murderously through clouds of insects.

"I saw Angelo a few days ago," Renzo says, tapping ash. "He has a little girlfriend. Austrian, probably Jewish. About four. I asked Angelo if he had a message for his mammina. He wants his parents to adopt Stefania. He said he was 'practicing up on being a big brother.'"

"Eight-year-olds can be rather sweet little people. Does he miss his parents?"

"Yes, and—" Renzo shakes his head at his own foolishness. "I may have a way to get his father out of jail, if you—"

"Very." Lidia sends smoke upward.

"I'm sorry?"

"Just before Rosina and I took our first flight," she reminds him drily, "you asked how bored I am. Very," she repeats. "I am very bored, and I want to go home!" They are both surprised that her voice is shaking. "Well, look around!" she cries, waving at the bomb crater. "How much more dangerous could a city be? I can help you, Renzo. Old women are practically invisible, and that gives us a kind of power."

Who else is there? He is a member of no group, working alone, making things up as he goes. He pulls out a flask. "To the death of chivalry!" he says before offering it to his mother.

She sips delicately, returns the flask. Steadier, she asks, "So what do you have in mind?"

He watches the sky turn from gold to pink, and waits for the liquor to do its work. When benign indifference has claimed him, Renzo gestures carelessly at the twilight. "What color would you call that? Would you say that's ultramarine or—"

"Renzo, darling," Lidia says wearily, "don't be an ass."

"Mamma," he says grandly, "we have two tasks before us, and you may have your choice of them. One of us will go to jail, while the other blows up a building."

Lidia Segre Leoni was the first woman in Sant'Andrea to ride a bicycle in public. She started smoking in 1916 and kept it secret for a decade, even from her son. She has faced down German officers and led their soldiers into ambush. She reaches for Renzo's flask and tips the last of its contents into her own mouth. Eyes watering, she hands it back. "Going to jail, as I recall, is your speciality."

5 June 1944

PORTO SANT'ANDREA
10:15 A.M.

Relaxed, tanned, and looking a good deal the better for his month at some mountain spa, Ugo Messner waves a languid hand toward the Mediterranean a thousand meters below. "Bombing has improved this place!" he decides. "The vista is enlarged. There is a breeze."

A rabbit-toothed waiter delivers Artur Huppenkothen's breakfast: Cognac and coffee. To his sister Erna's dismay, Artur routinely ignores the heavy meal she prepares each morning and comes instead to the Café Vittorio, where white-coated waiters serve patrons in dove-gray uniforms or smartly cut suits. Artur never used to drink, and he himself blames Messner for encouraging the vice, but Ugo can do no wrong in Erna's eyes. Her reproaches are for her brother alone.

"What could be better, Artur?" Messner asks, brushing bread crumbs from his fingers. "French brandy, Ethiopian coffee, Italian sun, and German power!"

"What's left of it," Artur mutters sourly.

Messner's voice drops. "Is it true then? Rome has fallen? Kesselring's retreating toward Florence?"

All last month, the war in Europe went quiet. Italy was especially calm, until a witch's cauldron of nations suddenly attacked the Gustav Line. Americans, British, Canadians. Australians, New Zealanders, South Africans. Bolsheviks from France, Poland, Russia, Yugoslavia. Indians, Senegalese, Moroccans—Negroes, given guns by Aryans! Now Rome is lost, and the Führer has allowed a retreat from the USSR as well. Rubbing a hand over his forehead, Artur says, "Greater Germany is shrinking by the hour."

"More reason to take advantage of present circumstances," Messner advises quietly, brandy in hand. He pauses to appreciate a young woman strolling by in a tight tan skirt. Fabric cups her buttocks, and she is wearing high heels. Her flesh rises and rests, rises and rests as she walks. "No place to hide a bomb in that ensemble," he remarks, "but I imagine sentries enjoy making sure."

The slut brushes past a pair of patrolling soldiers. Both heads turn. A brief conversation, and they change direction. She stops when they call, smiling at the taller soldier, casually reaching into her blouse to adjust the strap of her brassiere. A canvas-draped army truck rumbles through the piazza. Artur loses sight of the three just as a bicyclist approaches from the opposite direction, bearing down on the café.

In an instant, Artur is on his feet, his pistol at arm's length.

The bicyclist brakes frantically, going down in a tangle of limbs and spokes. "Don't shoot!" he begs, both hands in the air. "*Per favore! Bitte!* Please, don't shoot!"

The child's eyes are huge with terror. He is nine, perhaps. Or ten. From a distance, Artur hears Messner say, "Relax! It's just a boy!" Artur fires anyway, to kill his own emotions. The gunshot makes everyone jump, but the bullet goes wide and the weeping boy runs away, abandoning his bicycle in the street.

"That'll teach the little bastard to look suspicious!" Gently, Messner extracts the gun from Artur's fingers, placing it next to a china plate flecked with the shards of a crusty roll. "Lugers—the latest thing in wartime flatware!" he announces, smiling amiably at the military men around them.

One by one, the patrons of the café return their attention to their own tables. Messner catches the eye of the rabbity white-faced waiter, points to his empty Cognac glass, raises two fingers. "Too much espresso, Artur!" he chides. "It can make a man jittery."

"So can living in a city filled with assassins! I could clear this region of Reds in a week if von Thadden would get out of my way. He's stalled for half a year, when anybody could see they've been operating out of the north end of Valdottavo. I arranged for a Luftwaffe raid myself when he wouldn't take action. He went whining to Kesselring." Artur lifts his upper lip in distaste. "No clear lines of responsibility! No coordination," he says, mimicking von Thadden's cultured tones. "Now everyone reports to Kesselring. Gestapo, army intelligence, Waffen-SS, the security police, Kripo. We're the generalfeldmarschall's Anti-Partisan Warfare Staff, and precisely nothing gets done!"

"Surely a handful of partisans can't make enough mischief to be a military threat!"

"They're better armed every day. Every gun they carry is taken from the hand of a dead German soldier."

"My dear Artur, the weapons are stolen. Italians are thieves, not warriors! They sing Puccini and eat pasta. They make love, Artur. They don't fight."

"They disrupt supply lines and communications. They're holding down troops that could have been on the Gustav Line." When the waiter sets their brandies on the table, Artur downs his own in a single gulp. "They've attacked German and Italian military headquarters," he whispers, "and blown up Gestapo offices."

"They're a rabble," Messner insists. "Incompetents. Degenerates! The explosions must have been Allied bombs on a time delay—"

"Quiet!" Artur orders sharply. His eyes are unfocused, but it's not the liquor. "Quiet!" he shouts.

Waiters freeze, trays tucked under their arms, coffee cups poised. Patrons scowl, but they follow the Gestapo chief's eyes upward.

They hear what sounds at first like a column of trucks, but there is no grinding shift of gears. Just a low, steady groan, high and far away. Wehrmacht officers and SS men come slowly to their feet, linen serviettes falling unnoticed from their laps to the cobblestone pavement. Waiters stare, amazed, as the cloudless Ligurian sky begins to fill with tiny silver sparks, winking like stars in blue daylight. Ten, twenty, fifty, a hundred: squadron after squadron of American aircraft. Two hundred, three hundred. Bicyclists slow, put down their feet, gaze upward. Five hundred. Six! Heavy bombers, fighter escorts. Pedestrians stagger slightly and lean against stone walls, heads thrown back, mouths gaping. "Madonna," a waiter says, voice loud in the dense silence that envelops the piazza. Seven hundred! Eight hundred, nine hundred . . . All on their way to Germany.

"I make it just under a thousand planes—for a single raid," Messner breathes, awestruck. "More than the entire Italian air force had at the beginning of the war. God help whoever's under that . . ."

Around the corner, just out of sight, an Italian baritone begins an ironic rendition of "*Deutschland über Alles.*" There is an angry Teutonic shout, a defiant retort in Italian. A gunshot. A high-pitched scream, cut short by a second bullet. A Sturmbannführer nearby raps his knuckles on a café tabletop by way of applause. "Well done!" he growls as a new-made widow's wailing joins the drone of Allied engines. "That ought to shut those opera singers up."

Always the first to recover from such shocks, Messner snaps his fingers at the rabbity waiter, who still hasn't moved a muscle. "You there! A round of brandy for everyone!"

Cognacs are quickly distributed. Messner stands, glass raised. "Our faith in the Führer remains unchanged!" he declares with stout *volksdeutscher* sincerity. Officers and officials greet the toast with a murmured, "*Sieg heil.*" Glasses are drained.

Loyalty demonstrated, Messner moves his chair to sit at Artur's side. "Have you come to a decision regarding the arrangement I spoke of last month?" he asks quietly. "The corduroy is first-rate, Artur. Fine wale, with a hand like velvet. Bolts of it locked in a warehouse. Getting that Jew fabric to Germany would be a service to the *Vaterland,* Artur. Another winter is coming."

Messner's voice is low and smooth in Artur's ear. "Think of Erna!" he urges. "She never complains when others prosper, but I know she loves beautiful things. She is a good woman—I'd ask for her hand, but she deserves better! Where's the harm?" Messner presses softly. "Corduroy to keep German children snug this winter. A postwar nest egg for Erna, and for the man who might have been my brother-in-law, were I more worthy."

Artur watches the planes disappearing into the distance. Why are the pilots willing to bomb fellow Aryans? he wonders, at a loss. They should be standing with us against Bolshevism! Stalin and his Jews'll turn on them—wait and see. They'll regret what they've done to us when Ivan kicks in their doors!

"The war will end eventually, Artur. You must think of your future, and Erna's."

Beneath the shimmering white tablecloth, Messner's thigh is warm. The touch is casual, probably inadvertent. Artur shivers slightly. "Trucks are hard to come by," he says, his lips hardly moving. "The best I can do is a '38 Opel Blitz."

With the barest motion of his hand, Messner taps Huppenkothen's glass with his own. "Fifty-fifty?"

Artur's glance flicks toward the other patrons. "Sixty-forty." He presses a heavy linen serviette against skin misted with sweat, then stands. "Drop by my home at noon. Erna will have an envelope for you."

SANT'ANDREA MUNICIPAL JAIL
II:45 A.M.

When Jakub Landau stopped at a routine roadblock on the way into Sant'Andrea, he still had an out-of-date work permit identifying him as Hans Obermüller. He'd nearly bluffed his way into the city when the Republican soldiers discovered anti-fascist pamphlets sewn into the lining of his jacket, and turned him over to the carabinieri. Tomorrow *il polacco* will be shot.

Iacopo Soncini is the only one who knows that the condemned man is a Jew. Landau himself considers the fact of no interest. "I am a Communist," he replied when the imprisoned rabbi identified himself as a clergyman. "Religion is a drug." Drawn by Landau's eerie equanimity, Iacopo asked the source of his calm. "The individual does not matter," he was told.

In the shadow of death, Landau has talked—to pass the time and, perhaps, to be remembered. His mother was German, his father a Pole working in Germany when they met. "When Mama died, Papa took me and my brother back to Kossow, but we spent our summers in Offenbach, visiting my mother's parents." Landau served two years in the Polish army and obtained an engineering degree from Warsaw Polytechnic, but his childhood German did not fade. Like his father before him, he found work in Berlin.

The Depression hit; foreigners were the first to lose their jobs. Landau went home, married a Warsaw girl, had a daughter. "Her birthday was the first of September," Landau told Iacopo. "She turned three the day Germany invaded in '39. The news spoiled her party." Guests huddled around Landau's shortwave as Radio

Berlin announced that the Wehrmacht had crossed the border "in retaliation for an attack on Germany by Poland." They laughed—actually laughed—at the absurdity!

Absurdity or not, Polish corpses soon rotted on the streets, and hospitals overflowed with wounded. Air attacks went on around the clock, and when the Wehrmacht was close enough to shell the city, the Soviet army invaded along Poland's eastern border. Occupation was certain; by whom was unclear. Bodies bloated in the late-summer heat, and exploded hideously. There was no food, no electricity, no water, no sewer service. The bombardment ended, and the tanks rolled in.

"The Nazis made a big show of handing out bread. There were journalists, cameras," Landau recalled. "I heard one reporter say that the German people were compelled to feed the hungry population of Poland due to the criminal neglect of the Polish government!" The cameras didn't show that the bread was a centimeter deep in mold. Nor did the reporters mention that the food depots near synagogues were called rat traps. "Poles were given moldy bread, but Jews were given beatings."

Everything of value was confiscated—a fancy word for stolen. Everyone had to register, so the population could be sorted into racial categories. "Poles of German ancestry were given Jewish farms and factories," Landau said. "They could ride in trains, they ate well. Overnight, the *Volksdeutsche* were kings! Most couldn't speak a word of German, but I could." White-blond, with glacier-blue eyes, he told the authorities he was a civil engineer, a Pole of German ancestry whose identity papers had been destroyed in the shelling. A week later, he was working for the Reich, answering to the name Hans Obermüller. Nerves stretched tighter every day, he supervised the repair of bridges in Warsaw, in German-occupied Estonia and Finland, and finally in Berlin. At the end of 1942, he made a dash for southern France. When the Italian Fourth Army retreated across the Alps last September, Landau was with them, and arrived in Italy the day its own occupation began.

"And what of your family?" Iacopo asks now.

"I sent my wife and daughter to live with my father in Kossow. I could visit them because trains ran nearby. I thought they would be safe."

The heat in the jail is oppressive, but Iacopo shivers at the echo of his own decisions. "Tell me their names," he whispers. "If I live, I will look for your family and tell them of your fate."

"They're dead," Landau says without emotion. "The Germans sent everyone in Kossow to a place called Treblinka."

All the rabbi can summon is the most exalted of banalities. "Surely, they are with God."

Around the room, conversations and card games stop. Two hundred prisoners packed into the jail stare while Landau laughs, loud and long. Amused and indulgent, the Pole shakes his head, wipes his eyes, and waves their interest off. Smiling tenderly, he pats Iacopo on the arm, like a father soothing a child. "Rebbe," he says, "what I have seen would make an atheist of Abraham."

TAVERNA IL DUCE
12:40 P.M.

The Fascist tavern near the seawall is crowded and noisy, filled with men who pay cash for what they want. At a corner table, Santino Cicala waits with a *bersagliere* in civilian clothing. His name is Giuseppe Farini. Santino pretends he doesn't know that. It makes Farini feel better. The black marketeer is so nervous, he's smoking his own stock. Every pack of Milites can buy a thick stack of occupation lire, but this will be the biggest risk he's taken so far. He glares at the door. "Where the hell is that drunk?"

"He'll be here. He's got a lot of things to arrange—"

Everyone smiles when the couple comes into view. A handsome Italian whose suit coat is tossed over his shoulders and sways with every jaunty step. A homely Fräulein, weak with laughter, made vivacious by his interest. Gallantly, the man who calls himself Ugo Messner pulls out a chair for Erna Huppenkothen, greets a couple of *fascisti,* mimes friendly recognition to other patrons. When his companion is settled, he leans over to whisper in her ear. Something he says provokes a scandalized shriek, and he weaves through the tight-packed tables, disappearing into the *gabinetto* at the back of the bar.

Santino follows, but waits outside. The Jew always locks the door while he takes a piss. When the latch slides back, Santino slips inside. *"Va bene?"*

The whispered response is ebullient. *"Benissimo! Ottimo! Perfetto!"* Messner hands Santino a packet of transport papers. "There's an Opel Blitz waiting at the Gestapo motor pool. They're expecting you. When you've finished loading the cargo, bring it to the alley just this side of the Cuneo bridge. We'll meet you there— What's wrong?"

Santino stares at the key in his palm. "I can't drive."

"What?"

"I didn't know you wanted me to drive the truck! I thought you just wanted me to load it!"

Messner's liquorish urbanity explodes into half-vocalized profanity so appalling, Santino bumps into the wall, trying to move away in the tight space.

"I'm sorry, signore! I didn't—"

The eyes close, and a hand goes up. "Forget it," Messner says tightly. "It's my fault. I should have— It doesn't matter." He cracks the door open. "Where's Farini?"

"In the far corner, near the kitchen. Out of uniform, and shitting-his-pants scared."

"Good. Heroism requires fear, Cicala, which is why I am incapable of it. Stay here for a few minutes, so we don't look like we're together. I'll work on Farini."

When Santino emerges from the W.C., Messner is back in the middle of the *fascisti,* the Fräulein hanging on his arm, enchanted. "But do you know *why* so many people hate the Jews?" Messner asks the others. "Because Jews think they *matter!* What they say, what they do, what they believe. Even when they don't believe in God, Jews think their disbelief is significant. It's positively comic, and intensely annoying to the rest of us."

At the table by the kitchen, Giuseppe Farini is standing like a figure on a pedestal: shoulders back, head high. Glancing at Santino, he throws a few bills down on the table and lifts his chin toward the door. "Let's go."

"Where?" Santino asks.

"To the Gestapo motor pool, and then to the mountains,"

Farini says in a low firm voice, gazing at Messner with a look just like the Fräulein's. "I'm through eating German shit," he swears. "And if the Allies come? By God, I'll fight them, too."

Santino catches Messner's eye. Grinning, Messner lifts a glass toward Farini. "Who will join me in a toast to heroes?" he shouts. "Bartender! A round for everyone!"

Songs and jokes and funny stories follow. He entertains the clientele, well aware of the impression he and Erna make. An aging girl with good connections. A shameless gigolo. Loose, happy, careless. No one seems to notice his sweating palms.

Ugo Messner may drink as much as any sot can swallow, while Padre Righetti wears a mask of fearless honesty and must never stagger or slur his words. Suspended between them, Renzo measures the capacity of each. Half sober, he can just keep up with the swift cunning and momentary ingenuities his restless mind provides. Half drunk, his nerves are steady, and all the chances seem worth taking.

He doesn't always get the balance right. He awakens, now and then, fully dressed in a hooker's bed, with no memory of what he said or did the night before. Head splitting, mouth foul, he fingers his clothing, deciding who and what he should be. Smooth serge? Don Gino Righetti will be ashamed, the *troia* tolerant and amused. If the rougher fabric of Ugo Messner's linen suit comes to hand, she'll be polite. Either way, she'll be happy, paid handsomely, for a quiet night's sleep. Thus far, neither of his alter egos has exposed the *mohel*'s work to the professional scrutiny of an unknown whore. Unmanned by liquor, he is also unbetrayed.

Back in Abyssinia, after the Dolo hospital raid, he could drink for hours, and still have a woman or two. On leave in Addis, he favored the girls pimped by a displaced Russian prince who kept women in a row of doorless mud-brick cabins. He drank before. He drank after. He hardly ever ate. He couldn't stomach sooty Ethiopian flatbread rolled around raw beef and red pepper, but he learned to love the *tedj*. Cheered on by other pilots, he drank that stuff without swallowing, his throat open as a drainpipe. Tanked to the top, he'd take on another of the Russian's harem. Then, sufficiently disgusted, he'd locate a bar frequented by the lower ranks and pick a fight with an infantryman of promising bulk and evident ferocity, hoping to end the evening dead.

Pilots fly now by the hundreds, kill by the thousands. It would be easy to lose his grip on guilt, but he clings to this one truth: greater crimes do not excuse his own. When the murder of forty-three people no longer matters, civilization is extinct. His shame is the last vestige of honor in a vicious, barbaric world. He drank in Addis to kill his conscience. He drinks now sacrificially: to keep remorse alive.

And because his legs hurt. And because getting drunk is the only pleasure left to him. And because his hands shake less.

He'll quit soon.

But not today. Today he'll once more seek that golden land where reckless genius lives! Timing's critical. The schedule's tight. He's made one mistake already, and can't allow another. He checks his watch, makes his farewells. May I walk you home, Fräulein Huppenkothen? Of course—the dressmaker. Compliment her for me. You always look wonderful. Take care, my dear. I'll be away on business a few days. *Ja, klar, mein Schätzchen!* As soon as I get back.

A splash of cold water in the *gabinetto.* An espresso on the way out. A surreptitious change of clothes in Giacomo Tura's cleaning closet. And Padre Righetti emerges from the basilica ready for responsibility. One blackbird in the city's flock, he walks across San Giobatta's piazza. Lifts his shark-finned hat to a pair of nuns who incline their heads as one. Raises his hand in bogus blessing over a pair of Jewish children selling holy cards to trusted Catholics on the steps of the convent. Hiding in plain sight, as Padre Righetti suggested.

He passes unremarked through checkpoints and roadblocks, progress unimpeded until he approaches the municipal jail. There the carabinieri take pains to examine papers with ceremonial attention. The queue files forward a few steps each minute, stalling completely when an old woman insists on explaining her business to them.

"My son outgrew these!" she says with a vague, worried look, clutching a bundle of rags. "I have to find a mother with an older boy and a younger one," she confides. "She can have my son's clothes for her little boy—I'll trade them for her older son's things."

"Signora," the policeman protests kindly, "your son must be a man by now. It's been a long time since he outgrew anything!"

Bent and bony, the old lady hugs the bundle to her sunken

chest. "My son outgrew these!" she says, quavering voice more in-sistent. "I have to find a mother with an older boy and a younger one! She can have my son's clothes for her little boy, and my son can wear her older boy's clothes!"

People begin to mutter. Smiling benignly, Gino Righetti steps out of the queue and comes to the carabiniere's side. "Let her pass," he says, sotto voce. "She's just a crazy old lady, *figlio mio. Completamente pazza.*"

"I heard that!" the old woman snaps. The carabiniere nods them through, and Renzo takes her by the arm. "A priest should know better! You're very badly brought up!" she scolds. "Let go of me! I have to find a lady with an older boy and a younger one!"

"Don't upset yourself, signora." He steers her toward a crude wooden bench placed beneath a high, barred window of the jail, where he tips his biretta to wives and mothers and sisters waiting their turn to stand on the bench and speak to their menfolk in-side. "I'm sure these ladies will let you sit here and rest, signora," he suggests soothingly. "When I've finished my work among these poor prisoners, I'll come back for you, all right?"

Suddenly cooperative, she allows him to take her bundle. He jams it between the heavy wooden bench support and the wall be-fore addressing the other women. "If this lady wanders away, go with her, my daughters."

They glance at one another, at the bundle, at the old lady, whose eyes are clear now, and focused.

The earliest part of the jail was solidly built of sturdy sandstone blocks. This new wing was slapped up in a hurry to deal with a glut of wartime prisoners. The women are separated from their men by a poorly mortared wall, post-and-beam construction filled with brick and stone rubble, lightly frosted with stucco.

"*Sì,* Padre!" the women murmur. "*Sì, certo!* Whatever you say."

SANT'ANDREA MUNICIPAL JAIL
4:05 P.M.

Once a week, a priest comes to hear confessions and say Mass. Ia-copo Soncini pays little attention when a new one enters the large, open room and moves through the crowd from prisoner to prisoner, speaking quietly. Whenever a priest approaches, the tattered charcoal man is humble. "Nothing to confess," he always says. "No chance to sin in here, Padre."

"Now, there's a shocking failure of imagination!" this one replies. "I found any number of illicit activities to pursue in jail! Bribery, lying, theft, gambling . . ."

"Renzo!"

"Shut up and listen carefully: the outer wall is going down in about five minutes. There's a truck waiting at the Cuneo bridge. Mirella and the children are at Mother of Mercy. If we get separated, go there and ask for Suora Corniglia—"

"We have to take him with us," Iacopo says, pointing. "He'll be executed tomorrow morning. He's a Polish Jew, but he speaks German."

"That's a Hebe?" Renzo stares. "*Belandi!* I never would have guessed! All right, he can come, too. Get behind that partition." He jerks his head at the sandstone, once the exterior of the old prison. "Stay there, and don't look back!"

Quietly directing prisoners toward safety, Renzo works through the crowd. When he reaches the Pole, the man barely glances at him before saying, "*Non sono cattolico. Sono ebreo.*"

"How nice! So am I," Renzo answers in quiet German. "Even with the rabbi over there, we're seven short of a minyan, but as God told Moses, Don't just stand there praying, cross the sea! The wall you're leaning against has three minutes to live."

A slow, hard smile forms on the Pole's lips. "I knew the CNL would send someone."

"There's an Opel Blitz waiting at the Cuneo bridge— Wait! The Committee for National Liberation? *Verdammmte Scheisse! Porca Madonna*—" There's no time to think, let alone sort out which language to swear in. "I'm freelance, understand? Not CNL! I just came for the rabbi. We'll get you out of Sant'Andrea, but then you're on your own."

Beginning to wish Padre Righetti had bought some sacramental wine, Renzo leads the last few men behind the wall. There he pulls out the small black book Don Osvaldo provided, lifts the missal in his left hand, crosses himself with his right.

Inside, a hush falls. Outside, a furor rises.

310 MARY DORIA RUSSELL

"I have to find a lady with an older boy and a younger one!" a familiar voice insists. "Don't push her, you *cafone!*" a younger woman shouts. "She's an old lady!" another yells. "How dare you treat women like this?" a third demands.

Renzo begins the chant. *"Introibo ad altare Dei."*

"Ad Deum qui laetificat juventutem meum," comes the responsum.

"You should be ashamed!" a woman yells. "Would you treat your mother like that?" someone asks. "She can have my son's clothes for her little boy!"

"Do me justice, O God, and fight my fight against a faithless people. From the deceitful and impious men, rescue me!"

Serafino Brizzolari's rumbling bass voice joins the soprano chorus, as planned. "Ladies! Ladies, please! I'm sure we can resolve this difficulty—"

"Signor Brizzolari! Tell these men they can't treat us so rudely!"

"Ladies, please! I must insist that you all follow me—"

"... *lucem tuam et veritatem tuam:* Your light and Your fidelity shall lead me on and bring me to your holy mountain." How apt, Renzo has time to think.

The high, barred window is replaced by brilliance. The bottom of the wall erupts. The sensation of motion ends almost before he can register it. Slammed backward, blinded by the flash, he lies immobile, his lungs stunned and airless.

Someone lifts him to his feet. Blinking stone powder and stucco, he puts out a hand to feel his way forward, trips over something soft, stops to wipe blood and dust from his face, and winces at a metallic stinging sensation, like needles thrust into his skin. His left eye clears long enough to see a thin man on the floor, screaming from within a skull, its face flayed by the blast. All the sounds seem far away, as though heard underwater. His right eardrum is probably broken.

"—ome on!" It's Iacopo, hair singed and pale with dust. Lost again in a red haze, Renzo lets the rabbi guide him toward the breach. His lips and nostrils and eyes burn. Lime in the mortar, he supposes. His left eye clears long enough to see women converging on the mob of men who tumble out of the jail. Everyone is shouting and running, creating as much confusion as possible.

"Belandi!" Renzo shouts, hilarious with relief that he's not blind

and probably won't be completely deaf. "We did it!" And everyone seems to have lived through it—apart from that poor faceless bastard who looked back at the wrong moment. There but for the grace of God, and an extra five meters' distance from the blast—

A brick hits his shoulder. The upper portion of the wall is beginning to collapse.

Iacopo yells something and grips Renzo's arm. The ground levels beneath them. The stink of explosives and burned hair recedes.

Renzo pulls the cassock skirt up and dabs tentatively at the mess above the Roman collar. He isn't frightened by the amount of blood soaking into the black serge. No worse than the Libyan crash, he supposes. Head cuts bleed like hosepipes.

Another swipe at his eyes, and he catches a glimpse of his mother standing at the edge of the crowd, waving. He raises a hand to let her know he's seen her. "My mother's over there!" he yells, but the rabbi doesn't seem—

Two more explosions penetrate his muffled ears. Gunfire crackles. Women scream and scatter. Someone clubs his leg out from under him. Dumbfounded, he tries to get up. Hands seize him, the fingers like iron grapples in his armpits, dragging him over the cobbles. Booted feet pound past. He lifts his head, sees his mother coming: a force of nature, determined to reach him.

"Mamma! No!" he screams. "Get down!" Above and behind him, he hears Santino shout something at Iacopo. Iacopo grabs his legs. "Wait!" Renzo screams, bucking and kicking. "Mamma, get down!"

All around them, bullets sing and smack into masonry. Santino scuttles backward, stumbling when the body in his hands goes suddenly slack. The face above the dog collar is white. "Madonna! Did he just die?"

"I don't think so," the rabbi gasps, trying to keep a grip on a leg slick with blood. Landau catches up with them. "What happened?" Iacopo yells. "Why did—?"

"We had attacks planned all over the city. They must have thought the jailbreak was a signal." A young man in laborer's clothing tosses a pistol to Landau, who begins firing to give them cover. "Go, Rebbe!" he shouts. "Get to the truck!"

Around the corner, Giuseppe Farini waits with the Opel ready and running. He jumps out to release the tailgate when he spots Santino with a bleeding priest. "Gesù! What the fuck happened?"

Santino pushes the body up into the truck, heedless of the cargo its blood will spoil, and gives the rabbi a boost as well. "Drive!" he yells.

Farini starts for the cab.

"Wait!" Iacopo shouts, pointing.

Jakub Landau sprints down the alley and dives headfirst into the truck. Slamming the tailgate into position, Santino dashes for the cab.

The Opel lurches forward, and they're on their way: a fake priest, a genuine rabbi, and the regional political officer of the Italian Committee for National Liberation, along with cargo officially bound for Germany, all transportation papers stamped "Highest Priority" and signed by Artur Huppenkothen.

Improbably jabbed and prodded by the bolts of cloth beneath him, Jakub Landau feels through the layers and pulls out a 9mm Beretta. Unfurling a roll of fabric, he finds seven more pistols. Concealed in the center: two carbines nestled like lovers, stock to barrel. Counting quickly, he makes an estimate. Fifty bolts of cloth. Four hundred Berettas, a hundred rifles. He snakes an arm downward. Crates of ammunition, beneath it all. A bonanza.

The rebbe is on his knees putting pressure on the gunshot wound in the bogus priest's thigh. "We have a good medic in the mountains," Landau yells.

Up in the cab, the driver downshifts to handle a steeper grade as they drive out of town. The engine noise adds to the ringing in his ears, but Landau can read the wounded man's lips.

Italians, he thinks, smiling to himself. It's always *Mamma* with them.

SAN MAURO BRIGADE FIELD HOSPITAL
VALDOTTAVO, PIEMONTE

The dream usually begins the same way. Duno is alert, but never scared. The planes will make a wide turn, he expects, then double back for a second run at the Roman bridge in Roccabarbena.

He hears the rattle and ping of gunfire hitting stone, sees Nello Toselli, still tubby despite a winter of hunger, racing bullets to the cave. Two planes flash overhead, German crosses, black on white, under the wings. Nello's screams are lost in a series of deafening explosions.

Duno kneels at Nello's side. The air reeks like a barnyard. The ground is brown and rust and red. Nello is facedown, his pants sticky with blood. Holes in his back and buttocks gape through the torn fabric like lipsticked mouths. Duno rolls him over. Loops of glistening bowel tumble out. The colors are astonishing. Maroon. Crimson. A bright spring green. Yellow, like chicken schmaltz.

This is where the dream can change. Most nights, the others gather to stare at the crater in Nello's belly and groin. Someone vomits. "Go get *la nonna*'s doctor!" Duno yells.

Nello whimpers, "Mamma, it hurts." Something in his gut breaks. Bright red arcs out of the body in pulses. Duno flinches when his face is splashed with hot blood, and wakes up.

Sometimes, though, the dream is different. He shouts for boiled salt water, washes dirt from the intestines, stuffs them back inside. Nello sighs. His face loses its clenched look and relaxes into a blank repose. On those nights, Duno sleeps better.

No one could have saved Nello. Duno knows that now. A swill

of blood and bile and shit obscuring the field means ruptured viscera and ripped vessels. "Reassurance is your last gift," the German doctor told him. "Speak calmly and quietly to the wounded
man, and go on to someone else."

Nearsighted, without spectacles, Duno Brössler is no good
with a gun, but he isn't squeamish, and he's not afraid of blood.
He can look at great ragged cavities left in pulpy flesh and simply . . . go to work. He has, quite likely, saved six lives under terrible conditions, and made it possible for them to return to battle.
To do that, Jakub Landau told him, is as though Duno himself
were six soldiers.

Since Nello's death, Duno has spent countless hours studying
the anatomical drawings Doktor Schramm improvised on the
plaster walls of *la nonna*'s house. The chalk sketches were almost
beautiful. "In combat, you won't see this," Schramm warned.
"Bullets make a mess." Welling blood is venous; pulsing blood, arterial. "Get the bleeding under control first," Schramm told him.
"Find what leaks." Put direct pressure on the wound—pad your
hand with clean cloth if you have it. "Don't cut a tubular struc-
ture," Schramm said. "Never close the jaws of your scissors if you
can't see their tips." A rapid pulse and pale blue gums? Shock: raise
the feet, keep the trunk warm. Use iodine for disinfectant, liquor
for anesthetic. When neck wounds bubble and chest wounds
suck, stitching the blue-rimmed hole won't help. Convulsions signal cardiac arrest. Fixed, dilated pupils confirm death.

I ragazzi: the boys. That's what the Valdottavese still call the San
Mauro Brigade, but there are no boys left, not since Nello Toselli
died. They're men now, even those too young to shave. Since the
air raid on the cave, they've moved every few nights, on the run,
but not afraid. They coalesce for planning, split up to carry out
raids. There were awful casualties at first, but they've developed a
strategy that's been consistently successful. They choose a road,
blow up the next small bridge over a stream, and take the high
ground nearby. Then they simply wait for a German column sent
to investigate. It's always preceded by two soldiers on motorcycles. Just as they realize the bridge is out, you shoot them to
pieces, collect their weapons, and take the bikes. A couple of
hours later, two German trucks carrying twenty men and small

cannons will appear. Hold the high ground, shoot them to pieces, collect their weapons, their ammunition, and the trucks. Four hours later, two Tiger tanks arrive. By that time, you're long gone: better armed, and scattered into a dozen ravines. The *Übermenschen* never change their tactics, and it's costing them the war.

"We've got the Nazis on the run," Duno tells the man he's working on. "Rome is free, and yesterday the Allies invaded France. Radio London said it's the largest invasion in history."

The wounded man is conscious, but hasn't said a word. The right side of his face is swollen to twice its normal size. Duno rinses the cloth in hot water, presses it against the half-formed scabs. When they're softened and looser, he can pry them off and get at the bits of stone embedded in the skin.

Blood starts to flow again. The rabbi looks ready to pass out. "Head lacerations bleed a lot," Duno tells him. "Don't worry. These are superficial."

"He'll be all right?" the rabbi asks.

"*Sì, certo!*" Duno says, audibly confident for the patient's sake.

In fact, the leg looks angry. Streaky, reddened. Sepsis could be setting in. "You can't be sure," Schramm told him. "Sometimes the body defeats an infection."

Today Duno has the luxury of shelter for the operation, even if it's only a barn. There's a fire, boiling water to sterilize the knife, brandy for anesthesia, the rabbi to assist. Duno motions, and the rabbi hands him the grappa. "Drink up," Duno says, putting the bottle into the wounded man's hand. "I'm going after that bullet."

The fingers refuse to grip. The man works to speak clearly through fattened lips. "Do wha' y'have to."

Duno looks at the rabbi. "Help me roll him onto his side, then hold him steady." They cut the blood-crusted trouser leg neatly, so it'll be easier for *la nonna* or Nello's aunt to repair. The entry wound is small, above and behind the knee. There's no exit, just a huge bruised lump halfway up the thigh, in front. "The bullet is lodged here," Duno says, palpating the front of the thigh. "I'm going to cut across the skin and take it out from the front," he warns the patient. "I'll be quick."

Concentrating, Duno hardly hears the shout of pain when he slices through the bruise. Two more passes through granulated blood, and the blade strikes lead. "Hold as still as you can," Duno says, using the knifepoint to midwife a slug through his incision. The man gasps, shudders convulsively, goes limp.

"Just as well," Duno remarks, popping the bullet out. "Easier to sew when they're unconscious." He cleans the entry and exit wounds again, painting them with iodine, suturing. "This isn't so bad, really. I've seen bullets pulverize the bone, rip the arteries, blow big chunks out of the meat." Duno glances up. "Sorry, Rabbino. Put your head between your knees."

With the leg bandaged, Duno starts digging grit out of the face, hoping to be done before the man comes to. It's tedious work. "Somebody told me this is *la nonna*'s son," he says to pass the time and distract the rabbi.

"He is," the rabbi says. "Was. She's dead."

Duno's hands freeze. He looks down, and realizes that the wounded man is awake beneath his fingers. "How?"

"Cross fire," Renzo Leoni says. "Finish wha' you're doing."

They move him twice, maybe three times. Always at night. The moon is quartered once, gibbous the next time. For a while, he's hidden in a wine cellar, where cool, moist air does battle with a fever that threatens to burn him to the ground. Iacopo seems never to leave his side.

"Where's Mirella?" Renzo asks.

"Suora Corniglia found a place for her and the children. She sends her love. Drink this. Then rest."

"Go home. Go . . . wherever they are. Leave me alone."

An outdoor bivouac, next. Shards of sunlight shattered by twisting leaves, falling like glass into eyes emerging from bruised lids. The Austrian boy comes and goes. Once Jakub Landau visits with a delegation from the CNL, hoping to recruit *la nonna*'s son; it is a mistake *il polacco* will not repeat.

Days become weeks. She sends her love. Mirella? Or Sister Dimples . . .

He hears conversations. Actions taken, casualties sustained and inflicted. Now and then, an adolescent comes near, pats his shoulder, and says, "I got one for her, comrade."

By August, he can walk with a crutch. They move to Castello Ritanna, a long-abandoned hilltop fortress. "Some of the smaller rooms are intact," the Austrian kid tells him. "We're using them as a more permanent hospital."

One day Schramm appears in a stone doorway, comes close, kneels at Renzo's side. The German is professional at first. "Straighten the leg. Good. Flex it, so . . . Yes. Excellent." Fingers probe the wounds. Renzo's face is turned from side to side, its pitted, livid surface inspected. "The boy did a good job." Schramm rocks onto bony haunches. "I am sorry about your mother, my friend. She was a remarkable woman."

What is there to say?

September 1944

The first time she saw the blood, she thought that she was dying. Her father was still alive then, and Claudia ran to him, weeping, but he turned away from her distress. Tercilla Lovera rushed from the henhouse to see what the trouble was. Albert Blum elbowed his daughter. "Tell her," he mumbled, and hurried off, embarrassed.

Tercilla listened, wiped her rough hands on a worn apron, and put horny palms on either side of Claudia's wet cheeks. "*Cara mia,*" she said, "nobody ever dies of a nuisance." That was the good news. The bad news was, it would happen every month, over and over. For years. "If it stops," Tercilla warned, "you're going to have a baby."

Wonderful, Claudia thought while Tercilla taught her how to fold the rags. War isn't enough? I have this to worry about, too?

A day or two later, Pierino brought home a set of safety pins he bought at Tino Marrapodi's store. The pins made things easier, but Claudia couldn't look Pierino in the eye for a week.

From then on, when she and Bettina walked down to barter cheese for pasta at Marrapodi's, old men looked up from their cards or touched their caps when Claudia passed. Sometimes if she looked over her shoulder, she saw them measuring her hips with their eyes. "You're a woman now," Zia Tercilla told her. "Like Caesar's wife, you must be above reproach, or men take advantage."

The month her father died, Claudia herself was so sick with typhus that the bleeding didn't come. Bereft, feeble, wretched, she sobbed, "I don't...want to have...a baby. Papa's gone! And

I'm . . . too young!" So Zia Tercilla explained the rest. "Is that all?" Claudia demanded with soggy resentment. "Are there any other little surprises?"

"Wipe your nose," Tercilla said. "The surprise is, it can be nice, if you have a good man like my Domenico."

By late spring, things were back to normal, and while Claudia wasn't exactly glad, she welcomed evidence that she had her health back. Kneeling now on a broad, flat rock at creekside, she weights her rags with stones and lets the water start her work. Washing them is a distasteful chore, but she's gotten used to it. Like squatting on a pair of planks to relieve herself above a public cesspool, the nuisance and mess are simply part of life in Valdottavo.

It's a life she's made peace with, a life she feels ready for. She's worked beside Tercilla and Bettina for nearly a year, kneading bread dough, sorting dried beans, beating flax, spinning wool. Since Claudia's engagement, Tercilla's constant instruction has become more emphatic. A housewife must know how and when to plant each kind of vegetable in the kitchen garden, what pests to watch out for. How to fertilize with chicken droppings without burning the crops. And how to preserve and store produce, and make cheese, and—

There's time, Claudia tells herself firmly. I'll learn what I need to know.

She and Santino will always be different—a Jew, a Calabrian. They will be without blood ties in the valley, but they won't have a legacy of grudges and suspicion to overcome either. After the war, Santino will be a sought-after mason. Claudia is already a member of the community: Tercilla's honorary niece, cousin to Bettina and Pierino. People on Pierino's postal route say, "Ei!, postino! Send your cugina Claudia to write for us!" Pierino can read, haltingly, the rare letters he delivers—you don't need a right hand for that—but Claudia does the writing.

The letters are nearly all the same. "Dear Son, we have no word of you since 1942. It's summer, so we don't worry now that you have no blanket. We pray to the Madonna you'll come home from Russia before winter."

Parents nod gravely when Claudia reads their words back to

them and watch solemnly as she folds the letter into its flimsy envelope, inscribing it with the last known address of their missing boy. In return for the paper, the ink, and her trouble, they give Claudia an egg or a bit of cheese, and offer prayers for her *fidanzato* Santino. Claudia, too, has a man at risk.

She worries about Santino, naturally, but in a way that feels pleasingly adult and serious, and anyway, the war will be over by Christmas; that's what everyone says. Sitting back on her heels, she lays a sliver of soap next to twists of cloth, stacked like cordwood on a dry rock. "*Ecco!*" she says to no one. "That's done for another month."

The skin beneath her breasts is greasy with sweat. She looks around, listening, but hears only the raucous rattle of cicadas. Satisfied that she's alone, she quickly strips off her blouse and leans out over the creek, still slightly amazed by her own body. She scoops cool water over her breasts, onto her face, down her neck, into her armpits. Hiking up her skirt, she squats to soap between her legs. This is why Mama went to the *mikveh* every month! she realizes. To feel clean. To start time ticking again.

In no hurry to get back to the village, she sits on a boulder and watches leaves flutter and twirl on their stems as her fingers work at the buttons of her blouse. Once anonymous, the plants around her are familiar now; she knows Don Leto's book from front to back. *Laburnum alpinum,* typical of subalpine mountains, she thinks. *Rosa pendulina. Geranium sylvaticum. Saxifraga rotundifolia.* The Latin binomials are like poetry. All the creekside plants are native, but nearly everything in the gardens is from America: tomatoes, potatoes, corn, squash, peppers. What on earth did Italians eat before Columbus?

Closing her eyes, she listens to the creek. Its hushed noise reminds her of applause for a symphony heard on the shortwave. The mountain is her orchestra now. She knows its music well—

Her eyes snap open. The first cry sounds almost like a birdcall, but so many songbirds have been trapped for food . . . She stands, straightens her skirt, moves away from the water's babble, listens harder. A squeal this time. Or a bleat, like a lost goat might make.

Curious, cautious, she steps from rock to rock, crossing the creek to the other side of the ravine. She hears rough laughter, and she knows—already, she knows—but she makes her way to the top. Heart pounding, she raises her head just high enough to see, just long enough to be sure. Then she runs for home.

"The Germans were kicked like dogs south of Rome, but they pulled back in good order to the Trasimeno Line," Santino says, drawing a finger across his shin. "They held the Allies there two weeks, but pulled back again to Arezzo."

"We hhheard they're d-d-dug in along the Aaarno," Pierino says.

"The Gothic Line, they're calling that one. A lot of men from Liguria and Piemonte were sent there to build walls, gun emplacements, watchtowers. That's probably where your husband is, signora. I hope he's all right."

Tercilla nods, flattered by the attention. She's heard that southerners are almost Arabs and keep their wives locked up, but Santino is respectful, full of news yet calm and steady. He always brings something from the city for Tercilla and Bettina. Little cubes of sugar this time, each wrapped in tiny pieces of paper with German words on them.

As much as she loves her son, Tercilla can see why Claudia prefers the stocky stonemason. Pierino is better looking and has a good job, but you have to balance that against the stutter and the missing arm. And the nightmares. With four girls to marry off, Tercilla never expected to have trouble settling her son. "Be patient, woman," Domenico used to say. "When the widows and orphans know who they are, any man with a dick and a job will be a prince." Now Tercilla is the one who waits to know if she's a widow, and she's lucky to have Pierino's salary, even if it's paid by the Fascist government. "That's money the *repubblicani* won't have for bullets," Don Leto told her.

She cuts wedges of tomatoes, thick slabs of chestnut bread and thin slices of cheese, and sets them on the table between the men. "Would you like some wine?" she asks them. Stretching, she takes down a bottle, and her new wineglasses.

Tercilla wouldn't like to think of herself as a war profiteer, but a lot of city people snuck into the hills this summer, hoping to swap small treasures for food. She took a silver spoon for a half liter of olive oil. That's been a disappointment, darkening day by day until the only nice thing about it is the fancy design on the handle. But the crystal glasses she got for a small wheel of goat cheese! Those sparkle like new snow when the morning light hits them.

"The Germans pulled four divisions out of Italy to fight in France," Santino is saying. "That should make things go faster here. But the British generals are . . ." He shrugs and shakes his head. "The Canadians broke through the Gothic Line in August. They lost four thousand men, but the British Eighth didn't back them up, and when the weather got bad, the Canadians had to withdraw. The *fascisti* I work with thought it was a gift from God!"

"Th-the G-germans're d-drrrilling hhhh—" Pierino holds up his hand, to ask for time. "Hhhholes! Under th-the P-p-ponte Antica."

"The Roman bridge at Roccabarbena," Tercilla clarifies, pouring the wine.

Santino takes a sip and nods his compliments. "Whenever they pull back, they blow up bridges behind them, to slow the Allies down." He brightens. "That means they don't think they can hold the Gothic: they're getting ready to retreat north." He addresses Pierino, one soldier to another. "Germans are dangerous, even after they're gone. They leave booby traps everywhere. Mines hidden under cans of food, or pieces of chocolate, or soap. Even under dead bodies! Pick something up, there's an explosion. You should watch them up here, so you know where the traps are."

"Wwwwhy exp-p-plosssives?" Pierino makes an arc through the air, and then points underneath it.

"Under the bridge?" Santino recites from memory. " 'An arch is two weaknesses that, leaning together, become a strength.' That's what Leonardo said. Bridges are built for a load from the roadbed, so they're hard to damage from above, like when planes drop bombs. But if you weaken the span from below—" He stops, his homely face almost breaking in half around his gappy grin. "That's her!" he says happily. "I just heard Claudia outside!"

She bursts into the house, rushing past them for the rifle Santino gave her to seal their engagement. "Pierino! There are soldiers—"

Both men are on their feet when she turns, the carbine heavy in her hands. "Santino!" she says, astonished. "Thank God! There are soldiers doing something terrible to a girl!"

Santino reaches for the '91 to check the chamber. "Where? How many are there?"

"Six of them. I'll show you where."

Pierino grabs a second strip clip of ammo from a shelf. Bettina appears in the doorway, eyes like eggs. Tercilla grips her daughter's shoulders roughly and spins her back outside. "Go tell Cesare Brondello," she says. "Then hide, Bettina! And stay hidden!"

They are working in pairs. One kneels on the girl's shoulders while the second pumps away. Two are done. A blond corporal smokes. A private buttons his pants. Both call encouragement while the next, slack-mouthed and rapt, waits his turn. The youngest hangs back, and the blond corporal punches him in the shoulder. "What's the matter?" the blond asks. "You some kind of queer?"

Twenty meters above, Claudia urges in a tiny, frantic voice, "Shoot them, Santino! Make them stop!"

Tercilla shakes her head. "He'll hit the girl."

"The b-b-blond first," Pierino whispers.

"Second," Santino says. The carbine's well oiled: the bolt slides back noiselessly. Motionless as the rocks that hide him, Santino braces against a tree trunk. Listens to the blubbery little noises the girl makes each time the boy rams into her. Watches, unblinking, until the soldier sags.

Santino breathes out, finger tightening on the trigger. The other Germans give a ragged cheer when their comrade grins for the last time, rolling away from the girl. The side of his head sheers off.

Before anyone can react, the blond's jaw disappears. Bone and blood fly from his neck. He tumbles backward, hair like ripe hay in a patch of sunlight.

The girl on the ground convulses, scrabbling away on her elbows and heels like a crab. The third bullet goes high. The fourth smashes into a knee and travels straight up the leg. The wounded soldier shrieks. Panicking, the others return fire, but can't work out where the rifleman is.

One grabs the girl, jerks her onto her knees, crouches behind her. Two others race for cover. Tracking ahead of the slowest, Santino brings him down with a lucky shot. The youngest disappears into the woods, and keeps on going.

Pierino lifts a rock the size of a loaf of bread and scuttles along the ridge. Santino loads the second clip, and nods. Pierino pops up, flinging the rock like a discus. It smashes down through leaves and brush. The German with his arm around the girl's neck wheels to face the noise.

It's a poor angle. Santino goes for a body shot. The round goes sideways through the boy's back. His grip on the girl flies open. His screams join hers, and those of the *castrato*.

"How many more?" Santino asks. "Where are the others?"

"Two dead, three wounded," Tercilla says grimly.

"One ran," Claudia tells him as Pierino returns.

"Fffinish them," Pierino advises.

The girl is rigid with fear, her half-nude body gaudy with brilliant red and sickly yellow. It can't get worse for her. Santino takes a deep breath. Lets it out slowly. Sights. Squeezes. Once. Twice. Three times.

Claudia and Pierino bolt down the slope. Pierino kicks bodies and collects sidearms while Claudia leads the girl up the slope. It's Maria Avoni, Tercilla realizes, disgusted. Blouse ripped, legs bare, Maria's face is all open mouth and dirt and tears. Everybody knew something like this would happen, and the little tramp has put the whole of Santa Chiara at risk, coming up here to do her dirty business.

Neighbors arrive in groups of two and three. Some carry knives. Old Cesare Brondello has a shotgun. When he sees the bodies, Cesare sends his granddaughter back for picks and shovels, and goes to Claudia's *fidanzato,* digging a rag out of his own back pocket.

"Wipe your mouth," he says, when the Calabrian's done emptying his stomach. "You never killed before?"

Pasty-faced, Santino shakes his head. "Only animals."

"Then nothing has changed," the old man says. "We'll bury the bastards, but you'd better say good-bye to Claudia. You can't stay here."

Five minutes, Claudia thinks. We had five minutes, and now he's gone off somewhere with Pierino, and who knows when we'll see each other?

She and the girl are ankle-deep in the creek. The other women stand at the edge of the water, talking behind their hands while Claudia sluices soapy water over a young body frighteningly like her own. "Sit down," she says. "I'll wash your hair."

"I'm dirty," the girl says angrily, nails scraping at her thighs. "There's still dirt."

"Those are bruises." Claudia dips the rag into the water over and over, searching for blood and brains in crevices, behind ears.

"I want to confess!"

"You didn't do anything wrong," Claudia tells her, glaring at the village women, whose eyes shift away. "My name is Claudia. What's your name? Tell me your name."

"Maria," the girl says, breaking down again. "Like Our Lady. Like the Virgin!"

Tercilla waits with a dry cloth. "Get dressed. You're clean."

"No! I'm still dirty. I want Don Leto! I have to confess!"

"Maria, listen to me!" Claudia cries. "You didn't do anything wrong! It was the soldiers—"

"But I agreed!" Maria wails. "He promised— We were hungry, and I *agreed!*" She looks at the others, her eyes pleading. "But just to one—not to six! Not to six!"

Old and young, the women of Santa Chiara look at one another, and then at Claudia, who is still pure. You see? their faces ask. You see what happens? Guard your virtue, or you'll end up like that little slut Maria Avoni! Maria can see it in their eyes. "You think I don't know what you're thinking?" She wipes her nose on the back of her hand, defiant now. "*Puttana tedesca!* Go on, say it! *German whore!*"

Suddenly furious, Tercilla Lovera splashes into the creek and hits Maria hard, twice, across the face. "God help you!" she snarls. "God help us all, when the Germans find out what you have caused!"

HEADQUARTERS, SS-PANZERGRENADIER
2ND REGIMENT
12TH WAFFEN-SS WALTHER REINHARDT DIVISION
ROCCABARBENA

The sun sets. Europe's airwaves fill with coded transmissions. Snow on flowers; grass on high hills; bright birds sing. The images of poetry, drafted for war service. Opera, too, has been dragooned. On Radio Berlin, Siegfried sings of reforging his father's broken sword: a German counteroffensive is cleared to begin twelve hours later. Tonio declares his love for the Daughter of the Regiment on Radio London: some partisan band can expect a British airdrop, this time tomorrow night. The telephone exchange between Erhardt von Thadden and Helmut Reinecke seems an ordinary conversation about Reinecke's baby daughter, by contrast.

"*Ach!* I almost forgot," von Thadden says. "My Martina sends greetings to your dear wife, and apologizes for a missing line in that recipe she sent on Wednesday. It should begin, 'Boil the macaroni.' "

"Thank you, Gruppenführer," says the recently promoted Standartenführer Reinecke. "Will you be joining us for dinner on Sunday?"

"Nothing would please me more."

Kinder und Kuchen conscripted for war work now.

Allied commanders have finally learned *Blitzkrieg.* Fluid lines, fluid operations. Commanders encouraged to be bold, to let armored columns break through wherever possible without worrying about flank protection or supply. Vast numbers of Wehrmacht troops have been encircled. The Red Army is on the Prussian border, the American fifty kilometers from Köln and the Ruhr. Soviet factories churn out three thousand planes a month, and nearly as many tanks. American armament plants run around the clock. "They can add rooks and knights and bishops to the board on every play," von Thadden said, "and Germany has no pawns left."

The two men have been close from the day Reinecke became von Thadden's adjutant. Not quite father and son but kindred spirits, they've disagreed on one issue alone: conduct of the antipartisan war. Reinecke argued for the lure, hoping to win anti-Communists to their side. Von Thadden gave it a fair trial, but every kilometer lost to the Allies has given comfort to the insurgents. Bolder by the day, they've accounted for thirty thousand German casualties since May, nearly matching the numbers lost to the British Eighth and American Fifth Armies. "It's time for the cudgel," Reinecke conceded. "Allow me to wield it, Gruppenführer."

For the first time since he left Russia for Italy, Helmut Reinecke is back in the field, no mere lieutenant but a Standartenführer at the head of a panzergrenadier regiment. With five thousand of von Thadden's men under his command, Reinecke has used the early weeks of his new rank well: deploying troops, positioning artillery. "We are to hold northern Italy, at all costs," he told his company commanders, and he read to them Kesselring's latest orders, with particular emphasis on their final lines. "The situation in the Italian theater has deteriorated to such an extent that it constitutes a serious danger to fighting troops and their supply lines, as well as to the war industry and economic potential. The partisans are a motley collection of Allied, Italian, and Balkan soldiers, and even German deserters who lead native civilians of both sexes, of different callings and ages. The fight against them must be carried out with the utmost severity. *I will protect any commander* who exceeds our usual restraint in the methods he adopts against the partisans. A. Kesselring, Field Marshal."

Gruppenführer von Thadden will arrive on Sunday evening. The action is scheduled for the following Wednesday. Everything is settled, but the plan receives added impetus when Reinecke's own adjutant—a laconic man named Scheel—appears at the office door with a dispatch. On a routine patrol this afternoon, German soldiers from the San Mauro garrison were ambushed by local farmers. A savage firefight ended with five Germans dead. A sixth escaped to report the squad's massacre.

The Geneva Convention could ask no more. Quickly Reinecke dictates the wording of the notice to Scheel. "Print five hundred," he orders. "I want them posted by dawn."

CHURCH OF SAN MAURO
17 SEPTEMBER

Leto Girotti lifts his eyes, extending, raising, and joining his hands together. Bowing his head, he turns to face the congregation once more and makes the sign of the cross over them. *"Benedicat vos omnipotens Deus: Pater, et Fílius, et Spíritus Sanctus."* Some six hundred of the faithful sing their "Amen" with the choir.

"Et verbum caro factum est," Leto chants. The congregation genuflects as a body, except for one man at the back of the church. Sixtyish, nearly bald, shoulders heavy with ax-muscle, his face the color of roasted chestnuts, the leathery skin gullied by sun. Battista Goletta is not here to worship.

Leto finishes the service by rote and returns to the sacristy to devest. He is in no hurry to deal with Battista, but when the time comes, Leto musters warmth and welcome. "Battista! How wonderful to see you at Mass. I have prayed for this day, *figlio mio.*"

"Don't give me that crap, Girotti." Battista thrusts a printed notice into Leto's face. "This is your doing, priest!"

By the time he's finished reading, Leto's voice is steady. "These are lies. Those soldiers were violating a girl. A good man caught them in the act—I won't say who, but it's someone you know yourself, Battista."

"Whoever he was, it's him or the whole valley." A short, thick finger jabs hard into Leto's chest. "Give the Germans what they want," Battista says softly, "or I'll tell what I know about you and that Commie cousin of mine."

"I don't believe you," Leto says as firmly as he can. "Attilio Goletta is your own flesh. His son Tullio is your godchild! You wouldn't betray them!"

Battista's eyes bore into Leto's. "When *il Duce* made me a Knight of Labor, I took an oath to support him. I don't go back on my word just because the Allies are winning." He glances up the mountainside. "And tell those Communist bastards this: I've already made a statement to someone reliable. If anything happens to me, he'll make sure they pay."

Six months ago, Leto knew every partisan by name. No longer. Volunteers have poured into Valdottavo. Some are from other valleys, or Milan, or Turin. Some are deserters from Mussolini's Black Brigades. Others wear squares of red cloth tied around their necks. Few know the priest by sight, and a cassock guarantees nothing. Ragged and underfed, each eats time with suspicion, but Leto dares not hurry them. Fail to convince a sentry of your honesty, and from where he sits, he can detonate an explosive around the next bend.

The cutoff to the crumbling little castle is hidden by trees and vines, netting and brush. By the time Leto reaches it, his leg and a half ache enough to distract him from both worry and prayer. Another sentry challenges him, and with patience born of exhaustion Leto explains his business once more, and then again, to a boy guarding the heavily camouflaged gate. This time, at least, it's a local kid—one of the younger Brondellos. "*Sì, certo,* Padre," he says. "See that doorway? He works in the hospital."

Inside half-ruined walls, Castello Ritanna bustles with more activity than it's seen since the fifteenth century. Leto stumps across the courtyard, determined to beg forgiveness humbly and accept whatever help or advice the other man is willing to give.

He enters a cool and shadowy stone chamber where men rest on pallets, recovering or dying. A frightened boy begins to cry, believing a priest's been called to administer the last rites. From the back of the room comes a low, familiar voice. "Relax, kid, he's not here for you."

Sitting on a milking stool, Renzo is feeding soup to a man whose hands are bandaged. Spoon poised, he waits for the priest's eyes to adjust. "Don Leto," he says with soft mockery, "you've been avoiding me."

Swallowing, Leto asks, "May I speak to you in private?"

Renzo hands the spoon to one of the walking wounded and slowly pulls himself to standing. Together, they limp across the courtyard, Renzo asking clipped questions, Leto providing brief answers. The Soncinis? The rabbi and his family are reasonably safe; Leto won't say where. Tomitz? Leto hasn't heard from him recently, but Osvaldo surfaces only when he has to. The refugees? More German pressure—three sweeps last month, but no one caught. Italian bus drivers have refused to transport Jews from a concentration camp north of Florence; with attacks on the Gothic Line, the Germans have let that situation go for now. Money? Still coming across the Swiss border.

The tension between them does not ease until they each use the same maneuvers to sit on a crude log bench without putting pressure on a bad leg. Renzo shakes his head and waves a hand at the tumble-down castle. "An appropriate setting for a couple of wrecks like us."

Leto tugs a sheet of tightly folded paper from beneath his cincture. Printed in German and Italian, the ultimatum is blunt. "Five German soldiers were murdered by assassins near the village of Santa Chiara, district of Borgo San Mauro, on 16 September 1944. The killers must be handed over to German authorities, along with the bodies of the fallen German soldiers, by noon 19 September 1944. Failing that, the harshest of reprisals will fall upon Valdottavo. Order issued and signed, Standartenführer Helmut Reinecke."

"Reinecke! He used to be von Thadden's adjutant. *Porca bagascia!* I don't suppose I have to say it."

"You warned me this would happen. No one is more aware of that than I! Renzo, it was Santino Cicala. Claudia discovered six Germans raping a local girl. Santino killed five. One man got away."

"Belandi." Renzo sighs. "I'd have done the same, but I'd have missed more than one. Cicala must be a hell of a shot."

"What should I do now?"

"Where's Santino?"

"I don't know. These notices are posted everywhere—he's bound to see one."

"You're assuming he can read well enough to understand them." Renzo uses both hands to shift his leg. "Go back to the rectory. Telephone Antonia Usodimare. Santino may have gone back to her boardinghouse in Sant'Andrea. The partisans will get the word out, too."

Leto's heart sinks. "Then you believe he must turn himself in."

"*Belandi,* no! That's exactly what I don't want." Renzo gets to his feet. "I know Reinecke, and his C.O. Let me see if I can work something out." Renzo whistles sharply and waves to a young man loitering nearby. "Find Tullio Goletta for me!" He turns to Leto. "If Santino shows up, send him to the hunchback's house, understand? He's to stay there until I tell him different."

"If Renzo says he can work something out, he probably can," Osvaldo Tomitz told Leto last year. "Give that man a handful of snarled fishing line, he'll knit you a trawler, and there'll be fish for supper."

Leto has begun to agree. Who but Leoni would have imagined getting a truckload of arms and escaped prisoners out of Sant'Andrea? And with the Gestapo's help, no less! The death of his mother was a terrible thing, of course, but it seems to have sobered him, and Leto feels sure Lidia would have chosen such a death over a useless one, or slow decline.

A slow decline is just what Leto would like—geologically, if not physically. Downhill is harder on a wooden leg. He makes poor time on gravel tracks, falling when his peg gets wedged between rocks. The sun has set when he finally steps onto the paved road that winds past Tino Marrapodi's store and downward toward San Mauro.

There's only one way back to the rectory from here, and he needs an excuse for being out after dark. He could tell the Germans he was summoned to give Extreme Unction to a dying parishioner, but they might ask the name, check his story. Someone else will be put at risk.

He's half-decided to ask Tino for a night's shelter when an unseen man whispers harshly, "Stop! Don't move!"

Leto holds his breath, raises his hands, turns slowly in the direction of the voice. Two figures rush toward him in the lavender dusk: one slender as a willow wand, the other as broad and strong as his own stone walls.

Lowering his hands, Leto Girotti holds out his arms. The three of them embrace. No one needs to say it: they've seen the notices. They all know what's at stake.

"Hear my confession," Santino says.

Claudia is trembling, but her back is straight. "Then marry us," she says.

WAFFEN-SS REGIMENTAL HEADQUARTERS
ROCCABARBENA
18 SEPTEMBER

"Sir?" Skinny, fidgety, and hardly out of diapers, the motor-pool driver paces next to a dun-colored staff car. "How much longer, do you think?"

Lounging on a pile of sandbags, Ernst Kunkel rolls his eyes. "Who knows? The Schoolmaster can talk the ears off a rabbit. He and Reinecke are probably playing chess, or some damned thing like that."

"He'd better hurry. It's a seven-hour drive. We'll lose the light!"

"What's your name, kid?"

"Meisinger, sir. Hans-Dieter."

"What are you, seventeen?"

"Almost, sir."

Christ, Kunkel thinks. Sixteen. He's still got spots. "You open to some advice, Hans-Dieter Meisinger?" Kunkel shakes a cigarette out of a pack and offers one. "You don't call sergeants sir, and you don't tell a Gruppenführer to hurry."

The boy lights up awkwardly, coughing on the first drag. He wants to look like he's smoked before, but mostly he just holds the fag in his hand, trying not to burn his fingers. "My mother didn't want me to enlist," he says, as if he's been waiting to tell somebody since he joined up. "I lied about my age. The Reich needs men, I told her, but really I—I wanted to learn to drive, you know?" The kid's hands twitch. "I didn't think it would be like this."

"Rough?"

The boy takes a trembly pull on the cigarette, coughs, and looks away.

Ernst Kunkel has spent the war cleaning Erhardt von Thadden's uniforms, pouring coffee, kissing up to the old man's wife. Sure, you can get killed—air raids, pipe bombs, hit-and-run attacks, but what the hell? Sant'Andrea is soft duty in a nice climate. In Kunkel's opinion, that's worth a certain amount of diligent boot-licking, especially compared to fighting partisans.

It's like chasing ghosts in a graveyard: they know the territory, and you see them only when they decide to show themselves. Over a hundred successful raids, and nearly a thousand Germans killed around here since April. Seven hundred wounded. Almost five hundred Fascist casualties. At least young Meisinger has the brains to worry. Von Thadden's read the reports, but he seems to think this little jaunt will be an amusing mountain holiday.

Finally, they hear voices just inside Reinecke's office. Von Thadden's new adjutant, Karl Schmidt, leans over to open the door for the Gruppenführer, careful not to step in front of von Thadden as he does so. A cipher, Schmidt is. Dull as his name. *Jawohl,* Gruppenführer. As you wish, Gruppenführer. Right away, Gruppenführer. You're a fucking genius, Gruppenführer. Reinecke recommended Schmidt as his own replacement for the job. "He has what it takes, Gruppenführer." An agile tongue and a taste for shit, Kunkel thought.

When von Thadden appears, everyone in the vicinity braces to salute. At attention, Kunkel takes a sidelong look at him. Uniform perfectly pressed, already wrinkled. Boots polished, and scuffed. A small coffee stain just beneath his ribbons. Von Thadden thinks being sloppy is endearing. "—a pleasure to see your planning come to fruition, Helmut," he's saying. All jovial and generous, like Father Christmas with a riding crop. "The master always likes to see his apprentice do well!"

Reinecke snaps his fingers at the driver. Young Meisinger salutes and rushes to open a door for von Thadden, then scurries around to the other side of the car. When both officers have settled into the backseat, Kunkel climbs in next to Meisinger, who starts the engine.

Reinecke comes to von Thadden's side. "You won't reconsider, Gruppenführer? Let me assign an escort."

"Your concern is noted, Standartenführer, but I will rely on the isolated queen's pawn."

The officers exchange Heil Hitlers. Reinecke raps the fender with his knuckles. Meisinger looks to Kunkel before pulling away. "No escort?"

Kunkel shrugs and whispers, "That's the way he likes it, kid. Drive."

Roccabarbena is the closest thing to a city up here, but only barely big enough to qualify. Petrol for civilian use is long gone. There's hardly any traffic. In less than fifteen minutes, they're out of town and into the neck of the Valdottavo funnel. Mountains rise almost vertically on either side of the river, paralleled by train tracks and the road they're on.

Kunkel jerks his head toward riverbed stones barely covered with water, and pitches his voice so only Meisinger can hear. "Trout must be bumping their balls on the bottom."

The kid manages a twitch, but the smile never really develops. His knuckles are bloodless on the steering wheel, his eyes darting left, center, right, and back again. "It's crazy not to have an escort," he mutters.

Kunkel agrees, but he also knows when to keep his mouth shut: all the time. Von Thadden's probably convinced it's more valorous to go alone, or some old-time crap like that.

The valley widens. Whenever there's a good stretch of road, the kid speeds up, working the clutch and gearshift, the wheel and the brakes. Tanks and trucks have beaten the shit out of the pavement. Potholes. Ruts. Lick your lips, and the next jounce could take off half your tongue.

Kunkel watches the passing countryside, but there's nothing much to see. Tree stumps and burnt farm buildings for two hundred meters on either side of the riverbed. It's good bottomland, crops growing further out. Corn, tasseled off. Women bent over, harvesting something. Beans, maybe. Raggedy skirts riding up, scrawny legs showing. Nobody worth getting excited about, although the kid keeps gawping. Maybe he likes 'em skinny—

Meisinger makes a small whining noise and hauls hard on the wheel. The car careens left and jumps the road, nearly tipping over. For thirty meters, they smash along the shoulder, flattening low weeds and whippy saplings before lurching back onto the pavement.

Swearing nonstop, Kunkel climbs back into his seat. "*Scheisskerl!*" Schmidt shouts, helping von Thadden off the floor in the back. "What is the meaning of this?"

The kid doesn't even slow down. "Land mine in the road. Sorry, sirs! Did you see that lady stand up and block her ears? She was expecting a bang. If you look back, you can see where the ground was disturbed, and then smoothed over."

Still fuming, Schmidt twists in his seat to look behind them. "Yes," he admits. "Yes, I see it, Gruppenführer. Good work, ah—?"

"Meisinger, sir," Kunkel supplies, glancing at the kid with new respect.

"Meisinger!" von Thadden repeats heartily. "Very alert. There'll be a commendation for your file!"

Made bold by praise, Meisinger raises his voice over the noise of a tortured suspension and the diesel engine. "Pardon me, sirs, but we really should turn back and get an escort. Motorcycles. A couple of armored cars. Partisans have attacked two convoys in the past twenty-four hours, and—"

"Do you play chess, Meisinger?"

"No, Gruppenführer, I never learned."

"If you had," Schmidt chimes in, "you'd see the potential of the isolated queen's pawn, which prevails by not attracting attention to an attack."

"Make a note, Schmidt," von Thadden says. "Have those women questioned."

An hour passes, and then another, with no additional excitement. The officers in the back spend the time going over some big report, but every time the car approaches a curve where you can't see the road ahead, Meisinger tenses up.

It's hard not to do the same, but hell, Kunkel thinks, you can't stay scared forever. With the top down, the afternoon sunshine pours onto them like balm, and Kunkel starts to relax . . . His head jerks up when Meisinger pulls onto a gravel track.

"I need to refill the petrol tank, sirs. And sirs? Up this high, with night coming on, it'll get cold soon. I can put the top up while you—if you'd like to—"

Von Thadden saves him. "Yes, thank you, Meisinger. Very thoughtful."

Bladders emptied, trousers buttoned, officers and men climb back into the car. The gravel road rises, skirting a hilltop. Kunkel shifts in his seat and looks back the way they've come, catching glimpses of the valley through rare gaps in the everlasting god-damned chestnut trees. The view isn't bad. East-facing slopes in shadow. Sun setting behind them, throwing pretty light on the other side. The river breaking into creeks, like a girl's braid coming undone.

Kunkel would feel better if he could see some gun emplacements. Valdottavo's a lot bigger than he expected. Which means Reinecke's regiment is stretched thinner than von Thadden thought it would be, sitting behind that fancy desk in Sant'Andrea, talking about fucking chess. Jesus.

Meisinger downshifts, guns the engine. The emptied jerrican rattles in the back as the car jolts over ruts and rocks, grinding over a crest in an alpine meadow. It's a giant fruit bowl of a place, tipped west, orchards catching the last bit of daylight. Pear trees, apples. Goats grazing on windfalls. Von Thadden looks up from the reports. "Excellent cheese up here. Not as tasty as German cheese, of course, but good for the type." He lifts a chin toward the goats. "Fruit for fodder. Sweetens the milk."

Knows everything, von Thadden does. "How much longer?" Kunkel asks Meisinger softly.

"An hour. Maybe more," Meisinger whispers. "We should've left earlier."

"—and the local *prosciutto crudo* is good as well," von Thadden is telling Schmidt. "Rather like a *Schinken,* although a different breed of swine."

A few hundred meters ahead, a peasant has finished pruning suckers off his apple trees; his big hooked knife leans against a pile of brush. When he spots the car, he pulls a cloth cap off his stubbly head and dodders arthritically into the center of the road, waving his hat at the camouflaged staff car and yelling.

"*Gott,*" Meisinger murmurs. "Partisans."

"This could be trouble, sir," Kunkel warns.

"Not necessarily," von Thadden replies. "Schmidt, take care of the report. Just as a precaution."

A few meters ahead, the peasant mimes with conspicuously empty hands: You can't go any further. Meisinger hits the gas.

"Don't hit him," von Thadden calls from the backseat. "He'll damage the radiator. Slow down, Meisinger, that's an order."

Kunkel glances over his shoulder. "Shall I shoot him, Gruppenführer?"

"In a moment, perhaps."

Meisinger gears down to a crawl, swings off road slightly, coming to rest at the side of the road. His eyes are closed, and his lips are moving. Kunkel checks the backseat again. Crumpling the papers von Thadden has been reading, Schmidt stuffs them back into the attaché case. In his patient schoolmaster voice, von Thadden says, "Get out and speak to the man, Kunkel. Give Schmidt some time."

Kunkel opens his door. When nothing happens, he stalls, twisting from side to side to stretch his back, and then strolls out to meet the peasant. Bald, bandy-legged, and barrel-chested, the farmer clumps closer, wearing wooden clogs, a filthy faded shirt, and stained corduroy trousers. The old man hesitates, pulls out an ancient handkerchief, sneezes into it. *"Ponte nicht gut!"* he says in pidgin German, wiping his nose. "You gotta turn back, signore! Bridge no good!"

"Scheisse! That's a pain in the balls," Kunkel says. "Between bandits and bombing, it's getting to be more trouble than it's worth, going on a picnic these days."

The man sneezes into his rag again. *"Non capisco, signor Herr."*

"Signor Herr! Aren't you the cute one?" Kunkel looks over his shoulder at the Gruppenführer. "He says the bridge is out, sir." Indistinct in the backseat, von Thadden shakes his head.

The peasant scratches his crotch and grins uncertainly. "Bridge no good," he repeats, looking confused but earnest.

"Ja, klar, I heard you the first time," Kunkel says affably. Where the hell would a peasant learn even that much German? Again he turns toward von Thadden. "I have reason to believe this gentleman is not being entirely candid with us, sir."

Schmidt rolls down his window slightly. Smoke escapes. The peasant's grin turns wolfish. *"Zigaretten?* Got cigarettes?" he asks hungrily, inching sideways toward the car. *"Für Apfel? Gut, ja?* Cigarettes for apples?"

Unexpectedly, Von Thadden gets out of the car and comes around it quickly, blocking the peasant's view of Schmidt and the burning papers. Gratifyingly impressed by a general officer's uniform, the peasant gapes.

In the next instant, he drops from sight, rolls under the car, shouts something.

Firing into the air, a pack of screaming partisans rise from the orchard brush piles, charge the car, disarm Kunkel and von Thadden, thrust gun barrels into the faces of the two men inside. It's over in ten seconds.

Rolling from beneath the chassis, the peasant motions with a pistol for Meisinger and Schmidt to come out of the car. Meisinger gets out immediately, hands up, shaking and mumbling. When Schmidt fails to do the same, the peasant gives an order to a skinny young bandit with close-set eyes and huge nose overhanging a rudimentary mustache. "Put that fire out!" the boy shouts in Viennese German. "Do as you're told or I'll shoot, *Schlappschwanz!*"

"I don't take orders from Jews," Schmidt says.

Bad move, Kunkel thinks, and he's right. The little kike fires into the backseat and takes a startled step backward. Glowering under a chimpanzee's brow, a hairy thug pushes the Jew aside, reaches inside the car, and hauls Schmidt's body onto the road.

Foamy red blood pulses from the neck. Legs scrabble at the gravelly road. Trousers darken. Feet twitch spasmodically, flop sideways. Wooden matches spill from a cardboard box in the curled and lifeless fingers. Meisinger moans.

With apelike agility, the hairy one hops into the car, cursing as he beats the flames out with his own hands. The contents of Schmidt's bottle dribble onto the roadbed. The strong, sweet scent of petrol joins the stench of burnt gunpowder and urine.

The Ape climbs out of the staff car with a sheaf of charred and smoking papers that go to pieces in the evening breeze. Schmidt died doing his duty, Kunkel thinks. Whatever was in that report, it's unreadable now.

The old man presses a pistol barrel into von Thadden's temple, bringing the smell of cordite close while the general's arms are bound behind his back. Von Thadden asks, "Do you intend to kill the rest of us as well?"

Meisinger starts to cry. The bandits snigger. The old man issues a string of orders to his ragged young subordinates. Rat Face listens, nods, and turns to the Germans. "You are our prisoners, Gruppenführer Schlappschwanz. Make trouble, and they'll shoot your tiny dick off."

Tullio Goletta waits until the Germans have disappeared beyond the orchard. "Bonehead!" he yells, cuffing Duno. "You were told: no killing!"

"He was trying to burn those things! So they had to be important, right? Anyway, he moved!" Duno squawks. "It was supposed to be a warning shot!"

"*Gesù!*" Tullio fumes. "The first time you ever manage to hit something! We needed hostages, not more bodies!"

"*Va bene,* Tullio," his father says. "Gruppenführer Schlapp-schwanz will count extra." Attilio Goletta laughs. "General Limp-Dick! That's a good one!" he says. "Wait'll I tell that one to Pierino!"

THE HUNCHBACK'S HOUSE
FRAZIONE DECIMO

When moonlight finds Santino Cicala, he is lying on the sacking mattress filled with dry and crackly leaves, gazing at his wife of thirty hours. The night chill has raised gooseflesh, and he curls around her, belly to back, to warm her, not to wake her.

Their first time, it was the stripping out: walls of awkwardness and modesty taken down. Thoughtful, deliberate, he stood behind her, kissing her neck, smelling her clean hair, reaching around her for the buttons. He pulled the blouse from her shoulders. Felt her bare back against his chest. Cupped her breasts, memorizing their weight and form. Most men go at it like bulls pawing the ground, but stones have taught Santino patience.

When the time came, he did what he had to, as gently as he

could: he hurt her. And when he was done, he kissed and kissed her. "The first time's bad for girls," he said, and promised, "It'll be better from now on."

They talked, after, about the life they'd lead. The houses Santino would build. The garden Claudia would grow. The children they would have. They know life will be hard: one bad year can sink a mountain family for a decade. But there will be chestnuts to roast or boil whole, and to grind for sweet brown flour. Wood for tools and furniture, and to burn for warmth. Cornmeal for polenta. Eggs, and the occasional chicken to stew. "Stonemasons get paid in cash sometimes," Santino said. "I'll buy you some goats with money, or I can take them in trade. You can make cheese for us, too."

She giggled then and told Tercilla's story about making cheese when she was a bride. There were a dozen ways for cheese to fail, and Tercilla found them all. When at last she proudly unmolded her first successful wheel of fontina, Domenico found a long black hair sticking up right in the middle. Solemnly he pulled it out and held it up for her consideration. Tercilla said, "I guess that's why Mamma told me to wear a kerchief," and for some reason it struck them both as madly funny. "Domenico and I—we laughed and laughed and laughed," Tercilla said, "and from that time on, we were truly one."

Smiling, Santino rose on an elbow and kissed his wife again. He took his time. He found her rhythm. He kept his promise: this time it was better.

Sleep overcame them, and they woke next to full light. They ate, and played house, pretending the hunchback's place was their own. Santino walked around the ruined barn and told her how it could be repaired. There must have been a garden here last spring, Claudia decided. A few tomato vines survived bombing and neglect, their fruit sweeter than apples. A lone corn stalk stood in one corner. "Why aren't there any ears?" Santino asked, lifting its leaves and finding nothing. Claudia told him, "They have to be in a big group of plants, or the ears don't get fertilized—"

She stopped, blushed, but did not turn away. Instead she held out her hand, and led him back into the house.

Once, when he was fifteen and apprenticed, Santino worked in the garden of a rich man. There was an old statue of a naked girl, lean and strong, and unafraid. "Diana, the huntress," the master told him. The marble girl watched over them as Santino swept stone chips, and packed the hearting, and learned how strength could fracture but be rebuilt.

Now that girl is his. Living skin like cool marble. Lean and strong. No longer afraid. "*Moglia mia,*" he whispers, his fingers grazing her breast, her hip, her thigh. "My wife. My wife."

Claudia awakens, turns over. She meets his need with a woman's certainty, her hands on his arms, his shoulders, his broad back. Measuring the shape and feel and weight of him. Learning him by heart. "My Santino," she whispers when he shudders. "Always my Santino. No matter what."

She does not cry when her husband leaves. Save your tears, she thinks. You may need them later.

BORGO SAN MAURO
19 SEPTEMBER

Sunlight glints off a river that looks chrome-plated. A sudden, sharp heat headache begins, just behind Eduard Knyphausen's eyes. He sweats in full battle dress under the Italian sun's assault. Summer's last stand, he thinks. Not even noon, but hot already.

San Mauro's been sealed off for three days, surrounded by a reinforced company of an armored grenadier division, part of three Waffen-SS battalions in position all over Valdottavo. "Sturmbannführer, there are no combatants in San Mauro," the peg-leg priest claimed. "Only women and children. Old people, sick people!"

"And where are the men who have left all these poor people behind?" Knyphausen asked icily. "In the mountains, among the partisans and bandits, that's where! Listen carefully: I want the bodies of my men back. I want the guilty to surrender. If they choose not to turn themselves in, they will be responsible for what happens here, not I."

Finally the church bell strikes ten. Knyphausen nods. Noise erupts. Officers shout through bullhorns. Troops standing ready at the edges of the town yell, "*Raus! Raus! Raus!*" smashing open every door, pounding through every building. Houses vomit skinny-legged old men, women ugly with fear, screaming children.

With whips and dogs, squads of soldiers herd them toward the center of town. It seems like chaos, but every move is choreographed. Several hundred townspeople join scores of peasants relieved earlier of their market produce and corralled since dawn in the central piazza. There are machine gunners at the corners, riflemen on rooftops. Men with dogs patrol the perimeter. Knyphausen glances at his watch. Seventeen minutes, he notes with pleasure. All set in motion by his nod. "Get a head count," he orders.

A sergeant approaches and salutes. "Sturmbannführer, there is a man trying to get into the town. He has no papers—he says he's a *Volksdeutscher* from Bozen. He claims the bandits have taken Gruppenführer von Thadden prisoner, along with eight other Germans. They want to negotiate."

Von Thadden failed to arrive last night; that much is true. Knyphausen flicks at his boot top with a ceremonial riding crop. "What proof does he offer?"

"Oberleutnant Schmidt's papers, sir. He says Schmidt was killed, but the bandits want to arrange an exchange for the others. The man's unarmed. Shall we let him through?"

Temples throbbing, Knyphausen says, "I'm getting out of this sun. Send him to my office."

His headache worsens when he hears what the *Volksdeutscher* has to say. His name is Ugo Messner, and he has been held prisoner since June, when bandits confiscated a truck and the load of fabric he was delivering to the *Vaterland*. Perched on a wooden chair, Messner looks nervous and ill-fed. His well-made suit is dirty and ragged. He claims to know both Reinecke and von Thadden personally. Schmidt's papers are genuine and bear rust-colored evidence of a wound, although there's no telling how serious or whose.

"I'm not sure how many Germans they've taken hostage," Messner says. "At least nine. If the bandits see your troops withdrawing, all prisoners will be released. If not, they'll execute the captives. They say those five German soldiers who were killed— they were caught raping a local girl. The partisans are peasant boys, Sturmbannführer, sentimental about their sisters' purity.

The whole incident is unfortunate, but with a little finesse, no more German blood need be shed over this."

Neither of Knyphausen's choices are attractive. Negotiate with terrorists or be held responsible for a general's death. Less than two hours to deadline . . .

Messner says, "*Bitte*—if I could just speak to Standartenführer Reinecke myself?"

It's an out: pass the problem up the line. Raising his voice slightly, Knyphausen calls, "Buntenhof: get Reinecke for me."

Waiting, Knyphausen goes to his office window to check on the situation in the piazza. The crowd is nervous but cowed. Messner asks for a cigarette, coffee, and food, relieved to be among Germans, and full of questions. The bandits told him that the Führer had been wounded in an assassination attempt, that the Wehrmacht has lost ground in France, the Low Countries, in the East, in southern Italy. Reluctantly, Knyphausen confirms it all. In the past two weeks, the Soviet army has reached Yugoslavia, linking up with Tito's partisans. The Americans and British have taken Brussels, Antwerp, and Liège. Messner looks stricken, but Knyphausen is happy to provide the facts he pins his own hopes on. "We've blown up the dikes and flooded the lowlands. That will slow them down. And the Führer has a stupendous new weapon, even better than the Vengeance I missile. What we need are more tanks and a little time. We can turn this—"

Buntenhof appears in the doorway. "Sir, I have Standartenführer Reinecke for you."

On the telephone, Knyphausen briefs Reinecke on the kidnapping. Messner watches worriedly. Wincing at Reinecke's response, Knyphausen holds the handset a few centimeters from his ear. Messner motions for it. When Knyphausen refuses, Messner shouts, "Helmut, my friend! You must help! Think of Martina!"

"Buntenhof!" Knyphausen calls. "Get this man out of here!"

Messner is pulled from the office, still pleading at the top of his voice. It's difficult to follow what Reinecke is shouting. Clark's Fifth Army has launched a huge attack. A ferocious battle is under way. Kesselring wants the partisan threat behind his lines liquidated.

"But Gruppenführer von Thadden—?" Knyphausen asks.

"Damn you, Knyphausen—we have our orders!"

Reinecke cuts the connection. Knyphausen stands, straightening his jacket with a tug. Outside, a sergeant is waiting for him. "A total of 318, Sturmbannführer: 231 from the town, plus 87 peddlers here for the market, sir."

Six hundred short of the figure in their own municipal records. Lies. Deception. They had their chance. "Messner!" Knyphausen shouts. When the anxious *Volksdeutscher* presents himself, Knyphausen points to the mountains looming above this wretched little nest of vipers. "Tell those bandits they are to release the hostages unharmed by noon, or pay the price. There will be no negotiation."

Messner looks stunned. "Sturmbannführer, an hour and a half! Even on a motorcycle, I couldn't— Please! Allow me to ask Reinecke for a little more time!"

Knyphausen turns on his heel. He needs to get out of the damned sun, back into the relative cool of his office—

"*Prego,* Sturmbannführer! A moment! I beg you!"

It's that damned one-legged priest again, at the edge of the piazza crowd with a stocky little goblin of a man at his side. "Sturmbannführer, I have the man—"

"I'm the one," the ugly brute is saying. "Just me! No one else—"

Messner shouts something. The sergeant shoves him on his way.

"They were abusing a girl," the priest says. "Santino only wanted to—"

Knyphausen stomps down the steps, into the glare, his head pounding. "Are you telling me that this—this one man, this *one* man, this single piece of stinking shit killed *five* German soldiers?" Knyphausen draws his Luger, points it at the priest's head. "He is some kind of spaghetti-sucking *Übermensch?* Is that what you expect me to believe?"

The crowd surges forward, their shouts and cries drowning Knyphausen's rage. Sentries push back with rifles at present arms. Dogs lunge. Officers' arms rise and fall, whips striking at anyone in range. A soldier smashes his rifle butt into the priest's shoulders. Cawing and clawing her way to the priest's side, an old black crow screams abuse at the soldier, and then simply screams when she, too, is knocked to the ground between the goblin and the priest.

Three flat, loud reports echo against the buildings. Bodies jerk, flop, go still. In the sudden silence, Knyphausen does not need to shout. "Get the rest of these people into that church."

Hazy sunlight yields to featureless cloud cover. By late afternoon, the valley seems to steam. Claudia Cicala sits on a high rock ledge, her husband's Carcano '91 cradled in her arms. A man she does not recognize works his way up the mountain toward the hunchback's house. Trudging doggedly, he disappears around a switchback or behind the trees, reappearing whenever a terraced field interrupts the forest. His limp is obvious, but long before she can see his face, she knows this is not Don Leto. He has two arms— not Pierino then. He is too tall, too slim to be Santino.

Two hours later, close enough to speak, he shows himself unarmed, and removes his hat. "Giulietta, I have bad news."

She looks more carefully. He is changed, but she remembers the day he called her that. He is not a German, Don Leto told her. He is a Jew. An Italian Jew who was once a soldier.

"*Sono desolato,*" he says. "Your Romeo was an honorable man."

With painful effort, he lowers himself, sitting at her side. For a long time, they watch the darkness gather. A widow of sixteen. A cripple of thirty-one. In the distance, thousands of birds coalesce in the smoky dusk, wheeling, diving, soaring in unison on scythe-shaped wings.

The man lifts a hand toward them. "*Apus apus,* of the family Micropodidae," he says. "I was killing time in a library once, and looked them up. 'The common swift is the most aerial of birds,' " he recites, " 'so perfectly adapted to flight, the species' feet are nearly vestigial.' "

"Micropodidae," she whispers. "Tiny feet . . ."

"They never land on the ground or perch on branches. Swifts ride air currents all night, sleeping. They eat, and preen—even mate in the air. I wouldn't have believed it, but I saw them when I was a pilot. They collect nesting material on the wing. Straw, dry grass, flower petals. Anything light enough to be carried by the wind. Swifts nest just long enough to raise their young, and then . . . They return to their element."

"We thought if he turned himself in, no one else would be hurt," she says.

The wind rises. To the south, there are flashes of white light within and below the clouds. Lightning, and artillery. She knows the difference now, instructed by Pierino. Each evening all summer, Mussolini's San Marco brigades have blindly lobbed 155mm shells into Valdottavo; the partisans replied with captured 81mm mortars, aiming just as blindly at the sound of the San Marco guns. Any effect on the opposition was purely accidental. Today was different. Across the valley, there were battles and skirmishes. Fires, everywhere. Borgo San Mauro and a dozen other towns smolder. Santa Chiara is gone. Zia Tercilla, she thinks. Bettina. Cesare Brondello. All the people who took Claudia and her father in, and treated them like family.

The temperature begins to drop. Outrunning the coming thunderstorm, birds swarm in a blurred, shadowy shape that swirls into the next valley. Tonight's rain will be a blessing and a curse: dousing fires, chilling the dispossessed.

The man gets to his feet, graceless as a grounded swift. "We have a roof," he says. "We should get inside." The first fat drops hit her face. She lets him help her up. "*Prego*," he says, trying to take the heavy rifle from her hands. "Let me carry this for you."

She lifts the rifle, holds it closer. She studies this strange, scarred man she barely knows. "Will you use it?" she asks. He looks away, then meets her eyes. She waits until he nods, and then she hands it over.

Standing at his window, Helmut Reinecke stares at the teeming rain while his adjutant reads the draft report. " 'In response to recent partisan ambushes and attacks, three battalions of the 2nd SS-Panzerkorps Regiment, 12th Division Waffen-SS Walther Reinhardt, were ordered to engage the enemy in Valdottavo, where partisan bands have roamed freely. A show of force near their strongholds was sufficient to cause the male population to flee into the mountains, carrying firearms and grenades. The bases of these bandits were destroyed. A number of houses were burned to the ground when partisan munitions hidden within them exploded. Several Communist sympathizers were executed.' " Scheel looks up. "Should I have mentioned the civilians in that church, Standartenführer?"

Reinecke's conscience is clear. Huppenkothen said it: when soldiers take off their uniforms and conceal their weapons, they are no longer protected by the Geneva Convention. And neither are those who support them. "Items of military importance only, Scheel." Perimeter floodlights create pyramids of gilt raindrops so close together they seem solid. "What is it the French say? *Après moi, le deluge!* Something like that . . ."

"I don't speak French, sir." Scheel waits a beat. "It never seemed to be of military importance." Reinecke grunts a laugh. Scheel continues reading: " 'Following these engagements, the regiment was attacked by men in civilian clothing. We estimate their numbers to be close to twenty thousand. Despite heavy fighting and a number of casualties, we broke their resistance. We are presently regrouping. Gruppenführer Erhardt von Thadden and eight others are missing in action, presumed killed.' "

Hands behind his back, Reinecke turns from the rain to stare at a silver-framed photograph recording his daughter's first Christmas. Anneliese holds little Margot, dazzled by the gorgeously decorated *Tannenbaum.* Erhardt and Martina von Thadden look on, like proud grandparents. "Type the report up for my signature," Reinecke says. "Make arrangements for me to go to Sant'Andrea. Don't inform Frau von Thadden yet. I'll bring the news to her myself. And contact Artur Huppenkothen at Gestapo headquarters. Set up a meeting."

Two, perhaps three months before they must retreat behind the Alps. We'll make them pay, he'll tell Martina. Before we leave this place, we'll make the bastards pay.

CASTELLO RITANNA
21 SEPTEMBER

Nine men, unshaven and half-dressed, sit morosely in close quarters. Stripped of their uniforms, given dirty peasant trousers to wear, they were brought here blindfolded, shoved into this little cell. Each has a story of ambush or attack. They've had no food for twenty-four hours. The water jug is nearly empty, the slop bucket nearly full. No one expected to live through the night, so they count themselves lucky when they awaken to hunger and the stench of their own waste.

Beyond their prison cell, an argument rages. "They are prisoners of war! The Geneva Convention—"

"—is a crock of shit! They are murdering civilians. They're war criminals."

"Which is what you'll be if you shoot them!"

The shouting gets louder. A new voice ends the dispute. The language is Italian, the accent Teutonic. Kunkel boosts young Meisinger up, to peer out a small high window. "I see a German," Meisinger reports excitedly. "Standartenführer Reinecke must have sent a negotiator after all!"

Regaining some dignity and bearing, the Gruppenführer stands, and urges the others to do the same. They wait, clawing straw from hair and rubbing at teeth with their fingers.

The wooden bar scrapes back and the heavy timber door is dragged open. The clouds are low and gray, but the captives blink in the dull light pouring into the dim cell.

"*Herauskommen!*" a blond man orders.

Von Thadden addresses the Aryan, whose tone indicates that he does not realize to whom he is speaking. "*Guten Tag, mein Herr.* I am Gruppenführer Erhardt von Thadden—"

"Shut up. We know who you are."

Shoved toward the center of a small castle's piazza, their protests rewarded with blows and curses, the prisoners have no choice but to obey. A mob of men and boys with reddened eyes glare, shout and spit at the captives, but make way with deference and respect for the blond. He sits at a table crudely lashed together from fallen branches, folds his hands with an expression between contempt and satisfaction. Before him are nine small piles of documents weighted with pebbles against the breeze. Identity papers, personal items, snapshots. "My name," the blond begins, "is Jakub Landau—"

"I knew it!" a captain named Grittschneider says, thirst-swollen lips curling with distaste. "Jew dog!"

The rat-faced little Jew who shot Schmidt in cold blood snarls, "Shut your filthy mouth, *Nazischwein!*"

There are shouts, threats. Someone drives a rifle butt into Grittschneider's belly. Landau raises a hand. Order is instantly restored in silence broken only by the sound of Grittschneider coughing.

"I shall read the indictment in German for the prisoners," Landau announces. An interpreter repeats this in Italian. "During the past few weeks, three battalions of the Second SS-Panzergrenadier Regiment, Twelfth Waffen-SS have engaged anti-Fascist forces in the Valdottavo district," Landau begins. "The Third, Fifth, and Sixth Brigades of the Committee for National Liberation repulsed attacks on their positions, inflicting enemy losses of eighty-seven killed or wounded at a cost of fourteen casualties to our own forces."

Without turning, Landau pauses. The interpreter's voice is flat, unemotional and familiar, though Erhardt von Thadden has never before heard this man speak Italian. He who was always immaculately turned out when visiting the Palazzo Usodimare is shabby now, and hollow-eyed, half his face pitted by scars. "*Mein Gott,*" von Thadden says. "Ugo Messner."

"Sometimes," Messner replies. "Not recently."

"You—you sat at my table. You danced with my wife!"

"You occupied my country."

Landau's voice cuts through, continuing the indictment. "Unable to defeat combatants, German forces surrounded and yesterday destroyed the following." There are groans, roars, cries of grief as Landau reads a long list of towns and villages razed. "A thousand families have been burned out. We have received reports of over five hundred civilian casualties. Nearly three hundred were burned alive in the church of San Mauro."

"This is absurd!" von Thadden says. "We were in your custody while that was happening!"

Jeers drown Messner's emotionless translation. Again Landau gestures for silence. "In that case," he says, "explain these." He draws photographs from one of the nine stacks of documents, and spreads them out on the table so the prisoners can see them. Grittschneider looks away.

"*Scheisskerl!*" Kunkel snarls at Grittschneider. "You've killed us! Why would you carry pictures like that?"

The partisans pass the snapshots from hand to hand. On the

back of each someone has methodically recorded dates and locations from 1941 to 1944, from Russia to Italy. The backgrounds vary—forest, grassy wasteland, a stone bridge, a blank wall—but the same heavy-set man is in each. His uniforms document a rise from second lieutenant to captain. Behind him, dangling from taut ropes: as few as three, as many as twenty, people hang. Mostly men.

"They were criminals! My duty was to establish order in those towns," Grittschneider declares. "Those executed were thieves, drunkards. Murderers!"

A young woman approaches, holding out a photo. "Name two." Guileless green eyes fix Grittschneider with an unwavering gaze. "If they were guilty of crimes, there must have been a trial. Name two of the convicted."

"Claudette!" Duno cries. She does not turn. "That's Claudette Blum!" he tells Landau.

"It was a long time ago," Grittschneider says, dismissing her. "They were criminals! Justice was done."

Landau stands to face the partisans. "Justice! The very thing we seek!" he says, theatrically amazed by the coincidence. He turns to the Germans. "I will be merciful. You may all live . . . for as long as this man can recite the names of those he hanged."

"It was a long time ago!" Grittschneider repeats. "I don't remember—"

"I only wanted to drive a car!" Meisinger weeps. "I didn't do anything!"

Landau pounces, mimicking the boy. "I didn't know! I didn't do anything!" he whines. "That's what they say, comrades! But there are ten thousand places where the *fascisti* kill like this. Everywhere the Nazis go, they murder. They build factories for nothing but killing! Bigger than Fiat, bigger than Olivetti—huge factories, comrades. Thousands of people go every day into these factories—not to work, to die! Children, women, old people. Jews, Gypsies, Slavs—anyone the Nazis call *Untermenschen*. The bodies are burned. You can see smoke from twenty kilometers away! They give the ashes to German farmers—for fertilizer! I have seen these things with my eyes, and now you, too, see what they do!"

Landau points at Valdottavo blanketed by a brown haze. "Comrades! The *fascisti* have burned our houses, our villages. They have killed my family, your family! Will these men live?"

From three hundred throats, a single word.

Nine men are beaten to their knees, shoved facedown into the damp stone cobbles of the castle's courtyard.

Blood spatters, fountains, pools. A slaughterhouse stink joins the cordite. The shooting goes on and on, until the guns are emptied, the rage is sated, the silence broken only by crow calls and wind.

"That was wrong," Renzo says raggedly. "What was done here was wrong."

"Yes," Landau agrees. "It was a waste of bullets. Next time, we use rope." Focusing for the first time on the green-eyed girl, Landau frowns. "Who are you?"

"You know her," Duno Brössler reminds him. "She was in Sainte-Gisèle. She's—"

"Capable of speaking for herself," Landau says. He comes closer and asks again, "Who are you?"

She meets his eyes, then looks past him to the others. "I am the widow of Santino Cicala, and I have come to join you."

Hours later, one man sits alone on a crude wooden bench, his back against a stone wall, an empty bottle in his hand, talking to the blood, diluted now by steady rain.

"I've sworn off ethics," Renzo explains to the faint and fading pink puddles. "What's the point?" he asks.

"Too much for me," he admits, face to the rain. "You sort it out."

November 1944

VILLA MALCOVATO
NEAR ROCCABARBENA

Paradise, Mirella thought when she first saw this place. A large farm, fifteen kilometers from the nearest train station, five from the nearest village. The main house on a hillside, with a wide prospect of the broad valley, a small wooded mountain beyond. Patches of sloping cultivated land: wheat, corn, alfalfa, olives, vines.

"In the summer, it's dry as dust," Suora Corniglia warned her, "and hot! You can barely breathe! The riverbed becomes a desert—nothing but stones, with a little muddy trickle down the middle. But when it rains, the whole countryside comes to life. Everything has color again. That's when the work is hardest, but it's so beautiful..." The nun came to herself and cleared her throat. "There is a small school for the farm children. Your husband will replace a teacher who ... is needed elsewhere. You'll run the kitchen and the *ambulatorio*—a sort of clinic for the peasants. And everyone helps with harvests. You can trust the *padrone* without reservation. His name is Massimo Malcovato."

This personage arrived at the convent in a huge car. Painted in the Vatican's yellow and white, it was driven by a liveried chauffeur who looked vaguely familiar, and turned out to be Don Osvaldo Tomitz. The children were thrilled by the grandeur of riding in an automobile, but their parents were more dazzled by the ease with which the vehicle sailed through roadblocks and checkpoints. Osvaldo slowed and stopped just long enough for Malcovato to declare, "*Ich bin ein Diplomat des Vatikans!*" Carabinieri asked no further questions. Even Germans waved the car on.

Wounded three times in the Great War, Malcovato retired a major, and he is still *il maggiore* to everyone he deals with. Wearing five Silver and three Bronze Medals for valor, he became an important food distributor under Mussolini, and to this day, he strides through Fascist Italy, greeted with respect everywhere he goes. "Officially," he rumbled, "I am disabled by my war wounds. This status entitles me to first-class train compartments, and an attendant to accompany me whenever I must travel."

"*Il maggiore* has businesses in Milan, Turin, Genoa, and Sant'Andrea, all with large Jewish communities," Osvaldo said, throwing a grin over his shoulder at Iacopo. "And he has almost unlimited access to ration cards."

"To be turned into cash," Iacopo surmised, "for payoffs and bribes."

"Gifts," *il maggiore* corrected serenely. "Expressions of gratitude—as is my desire to help you, Rabbino. During the Battle of Caporetto, a soldier named Tranquillo Loeb carried me half a kilometer to a field hospital. Perhaps you knew him. He became a lawyer, and I followed his career—to its end. Shameful. Shameful! I never had any affection for the Germans, but how a civilized nation could permit such things is beyond me. I've done what I could since Loeb was killed. My daughter made me aware of your personal difficulties."

"Your daughter?" Mirella asked.

"Suora Corniglia is *il maggiore*'s youngest," Osvaldo said. "Renzo met her at San Giobatta. He kept in touch."

"It was Leoni who suggested that Don Osvaldo become my attendant."

"The *fascisti* were getting suspicious about the 'doctor' visiting so many houses in Sant'Andrea. So I've become a chauffeur. We've rebuilt the distribution network."

"The arrangement has been quite satisfactory. Ah—we are nearly at the end of our journey. I have a house in Milan," *il maggiore* told them, "but this is home. Don Osvaldo and I generally visit once a month for a few days of rest. Occasionally we may bring additional guests, but I'm sure Signora Soncini will be able to accommodate them at the table."

Villa Malcovato proved to be a self-contained kingdom straddling the border between the mountains and the plains of Piemonte. Some six hundred *contadini* on fifty-seven tenant farms are scattered across seven thousand hectares, all administered from the villa *fattoria*, with its threshing floor, an ox-powered mill, a granary, oil presses, a dairy, carpentry and ironwork shops, a laundry and stables, poultry coops, pigpens, barns. Operating on the *mezzadria* system, the estate produces wine, oil, flour, pasta, bread, cheeses, meat and eggs, fruits, vegetables, and beans.

The villa itself is unpretentious: a square sixteenth-century stone and redbrick house, its loggia overlooking a garden of cypresses and ilex. "Rosina, see how pretty?" Mirella said. "Angelo, look! There are dogs!"

"Kitties, too?" Stefania asked softly.

"Every barn has kitties!" Mirella assured her. They had to take Stefania, of course. Angelo would not be parted from her, and it felt right to add a daughter that age to the family.

When the car pulled up to the back door, the older children raced off to see the animals. Iacopo went with *il maggiore* and Don Osvaldo to meet the factor and begin learning the farm's operations. Left behind, with Rosina squirming in her arms, Mirella nearly swooned when she saw the enclosed privy. And the kitchen! Limestone floors, a marble sink under a window fitted with glass, not just oiled lambskin. An indoor pump for water. Glasses, plates, tin-lined copper pans. Beautifully crafted storage baskets hanging from the rafters. A long wooden table for her family, plentiful food to place before them! Paradise, she thought again, with a *Shehecheyanu* of thanksgiving.

Three months of relentless labor have sweated the romance out of country life. Since her first rapturous day in the kitchen, Mirella and two housegirls have rolled out highways of pasta, scrubbed mountain ranges of potatoes and carrots, ground swamps of basil, garlic, and oil for pesto. *Dio santo,* the bread alone is a full-time job! Thirty loaves a week to fill those pretty baskets—bread made by hand from standing grain to flour to kneaded loaves. Fifteen kilos of dough at a time, baked in a woodburning oven fueled by cuttings from grape vines and fruit trees.

Rosina alone is exempt from work. Like all the estate's children, Angelo and Stefania pick tomatoes, shell beans, and glean a second harvest from the wheat fields after the men have gone through with mechanical threshers. Tanned and barefoot, the two of them have shot up like the weeds they hoe out of the kitchen garden, making up growth lost to hunger.

"You came at the worst time, signora," one of the housegirls tells her as they wash dishes together. "Winter is easier. It's all handwork then. Knitting, sewing."

Before that promised respite, there will be the grape and olive and chestnut harvests, but Mirella smiles briefly, grateful for Giovanna's encouragement. Her feet are swollen, her back aches. The window above the sink reflects a woman who's begun to understand why peasants age so quickly. At least I'm not pregnant, Mirella thinks. At the end of the day, Iacopo trudges in from the barns, more worn out than Mirella. They go to their bed limp with fatigue, wanting no more than to sleep side by side, too tired to muster so much as a kiss.

You can wear out or you can toughen up, Mirella tells herself sternly, and under the circumstances—

Twin beams of light slash through the darkness. Drying her hands, she feels the rush of anxiety provoked by anything unexpected, but relaxes when she recognizes the yellow-and-white auto. The major's visit is two weeks early, but that's hardly a cause for panic. "Iacopo!" she shouts like the *contadina* she's becoming. "*Il maggiore* is here!"

Mirella sends Giovanna upstairs to put the children to bed. She herself prepares a platter of thin-sliced sausage, tomatoes, cheese, and bread. Carries the tray to the library, where the men always meet. Nudges the door open with her hip, and stops, frozen.

"I—I thought they were Africans!" Don Osvaldo's voice cracks. "I thought, There can't be Africans in San Mauro. Rabbino, they were *burned* black! Fused together by the heat—hundreds of them. Hundreds!"

At Osvaldo's side, Iacopo looks up and sees his wife. "There has been a battle in Valdottavo, Mirella. Don Leto is among the dead."

Mirella cries, "Oh, Valdo. How terrible!"

"There's more bad news," *il maggiore* says, pacing in front of the fireplace. "The Germans arrested most of the Milan network last week, and in Turin—"

Iacopo takes the tray from Mirella's hands. "Go to bed," he says in his velvety baritone. "I'll join you later, *cara mía.*"

The men talk far into the night, but when Iacopo comes to bed, Mirella is still awake. He slides under the covers, and she puts an arm over his chest, giving comfort, seeking it. Silent, he lies on his back, his hands behind his neck, staring at the ceiling. She holds the sheet to her breasts and sits up in the darkness. Waiting.

"The Waffen-SS and Gestapo have begun a coordinated campaign to root out Jews, partisans, and anyone who helps them. Mirella, they're arresting priests—someone must have talked."

Hardly breathing, Mirella closes her eyes.

"There's no choice, *cara.* We have to consider—"

"No, Iacopo!"

"Osvaldo is doing the work of six men."

"I won't listen to this. You risked your life for months. You were arrested twice. For God's sake, Iacopo—you have a family! You have children!"

"How can I hide here when other men—"

She shakes her head stubbornly, eyes brimming, chin trembling. "I have never said no to you before. Never! But I do now. No, no, no! Promise me you will not do this!"

"Mirella, I can't—"

"Promise me!"

He turns on his side, his back to her. She bites her lip, determined not to cry, and after a long time, lies down next to him.

Merely a handsbreadth of lumpy mattress between them, but they are each alone.

Christmas, Mirella tells herself, like everyone else in Europe. It will be over by Christmas. If we can just get through a few more weeks . . .

Cadenza d'Inverno
Winter 1944–45

Rome changed hands two days before the Normandy invasion, and just like that, the Italian campaign dropped off the world's front page. A sideshow, newspaper editors decided. Barely worth a mention. Four hundred thousand men, forgotten.

They'd get letters from the folks at home. "Is the fighting finished there? We never hear anything about Italy." Soldiers would try to tell them what it was like on the Gothic Line, but the words would fail, or disappear beneath a censor's thick black lines. So they wrote back about the mud.

Once the autumn rain began, it never stopped for long. Bridges washed out. Rivers flooded their banks, and fields disappeared under water. Torrents roared down mountainsides, and mud sloped by the ton onto civilian highways already hammered by heavy military equipment. Engineering battalions worked day and night, digging drainage ditches, plowing the syrupy mess to the sides of roads. They blasted rock from Apennine crags, crushed it, shoveled gravel into gouges and potholes, getting sloshed with sheets of mud for their trouble as trucks roared by carrying food and ammunition, casualties or replacements.

Wet for weeks, feet would swell something awful. Men would limp into a town hoping for shelter from the endless goddamned rain, and there'd be nothing left. Not a building untouched. Whole houses blown to hell: splinters and gravel, that's all. Nothing alive except maybe one poor damned cow, udder full to bursting, bellowing as she roamed through the muddy wreckage.

And then they'd get to the front. Christ—even the air was

muddy there, but nobody at home would read about that. The censors wouldn't let them tell how mines and shells sent geysers of the stuff into the sky, how mud-covered birds fell to earth with bits of man meat and twisted metal. Boots and socks, bearings grease, blood, crankcase oil, vomit, shattered corpses—everything churned, liquefied, sucked into the mud.

A few days of that, and everybody began to break down. Madman-hero or chickenshit draftee, they couldn't think straight, couldn't follow what the officers were saying. Men were court-martialed for disobeying orders they couldn't remember having heard.

In General Headquarters, topography and armies were repre-sented on maps by tightly packed contour lines and geometric shapes, but armies didn't fight in that campaign. It was companies at best. Platoons. Squads. Clusters of individual men struggling up narrow fingers of steep and stony mountains toward dug-in troops who could see them coming, and defended every god-damned inch.

In that murderous, soul-killing, relentless way, the American Fifth took one mountain after another, while the British Eighth fought its way through the vast watery maze of Romagna's swamps. By October, Highway 65 to Bologna was wide open and the Brenner Pass was blocked by debris from bombs. The German retreat was cut off, and behind their lines, the Italian Resistance was at work, disrupting communications, transportation, supply lines; blowing up bridges, ambushing troops, assassinating offi-cials. Action by action, partisans took possession of the country-side, the forests, the high ground, and the night. No city, no building, no household in Italy was safe for Fascists.

They could *see* the end. That was the hell of it. Whether they looked for victory or defeat, they could see the *end*. A break-through was days away, and then—

Supplies and reinforcements were diverted from Italy to other theaters. The Allies reassigned their best generals to the west-ern front and Greece. A few nights later, Kesselring's staff car col-lided with a piece of towed artillery, and he was out of action, damned near killed. The sideshow was handed over to second-tier generals: the Allies' colorless Leese, the Reich's lackluster von Vietinghoff.

Neither could win. Neither would yield. And then it began to snow.

Across Europe, dense fog and deep cold encased every branch and twig in icy armor. Generals used the bone-chilling, heart-freezing winter of '45 to consolidate broken units and hurl them against the enemy again, and again, and again. The infantry's dream of "home by Christmas" became the Great War's nightmare of stagnant lines and pointless slaughter.

And every night more fine young ghosts whispered in a knife-blade wind: Welcome to hell, brother. Damn the generals. Damn the politicians. Damn them all. Damn everyone who is warm, and dry, and *alive* tonight.

Northwestern Italy

1945

Anno Fascista XXIV

February 1945

Tracers stream by. Black puffs of AA blossom. The Dakota bucks and rocks. Simon Henley cringes, and the dispatching sergeant from Chicago laughs. "Relax! Jus' some token shit from Sant'Andrea," the Chicagoan yells over the deafening drone. "Nuttin'a worry 'bout."

The plane's crew is American, its passengers British. Three Special Ops teams of two men each: an officer who speaks Italian and a signalman to establish communications between partisan bands and Allied Command. Two teams have already parachuted into Emilia-Romagna, and now it's on to Piemonte, after cutting across the Gulf of Genoa.

As promised, the flak ends in less than the time it takes to overfly the thin crescent of Liguria, but Corporal Henley has several excellent reasons for remaining terrified. One: he is in an airplane. Two: the airplane is over enemy territory. Three: very soon, he will be required to jump out of the plane into the enemy territory.

Across the fuselage, Major Salvi grins beneath the sort of pencil mustache favored by dashing cinema stars. "Simon! How is your sphincter?" Simon registers shock, and once more provides a laugh. "Don't be ashamed!" Salvi yells. "Even Lawrence of Arabia got the shits before a battle!"

An Ancona expat who taught Dante at Cambridge, Giordano Salvi signed on with the Special Operations Executive back in '42. His English is a strange mix of academic and army, but his Italian is native. Salvi already holds the Military Cross for the work he did north of Naples before Anzio, two years ago. This will be his third drop behind German lines.

It's Simon Henley's first.

Nineteen, a baby-faced blond, Mrs. Henley's little boy spent his first winter of service freezing on coast guard duty, twelve miles from home. There he fired a Lewis gun from time to time at German aircraft passing overhead, but failed to impress either the Luftwaffe or the local girls. The latter failure, and the observable influence of a paratrooper's distinctive red beret on women, accounts for Simon's present predicament. In a fit of unrequited lust, he volunteered for paratroop training last year.

With illogic that seemed typical of the army, Simon was posted to the Signal Corps in British Guiana instead. There four Negro NCOs, each a breathtakingly fast telegrapher who'd worked for the Georgetown post office, browbeat him relentlessly until he could reliably transmit thirty words per minute without error—a skill, he learned glumly, that had no measurable effect on his sex appeal. When his group started lessons in silent killing and unarmed combat, he began to wonder if he'd been assigned to Special Ops, but then it was back to England, when he was apparently reassigned to the paratroops after all. He spent two weeks stepping out of a wingless plane propped on scaffolding twelve feet above the ground while a sergeant screamed, "Tuck and roll, you bloody little cunt! Tuck and roll!"

At last, the moment of truth: three training drops from a plane with wings and an engine. Only then did the freshly promoted Corporal Henley discover that the only thing more sickening than flying was the fear of plummeting to the ground like a rock. And the only thing more terrifying than *that* was the thought of displaying how frightened he was by hanging on to the dispatcher's knees and sobbing, "Please, sir, may I be excused?"

Tonight, like Major Salvi, Corporal Simon Henley carries a compass concealed inside a button of his tunic and a comb with a hidden saw in its shank. Less subtly, he wears a commando knife with an eight-inch blade sheathed on his left hip, a Colt .45 automatic holstered on his right, and a Marlin submachine gun slung across his back beneath the Irvine Stachute that will, he's been assured, open automatically. He's been told only that they're to get themselves to Milan and link up with a band of autonomous partisans there. Major Salvi has the rest of their orders. Everything in the SOE is need-to-know.

The pilot spots a signal fire made of hay bales, their outline blurred by wind. "Commies, pro'ly!" the sergeant blares through the noise. "You limey bastids won't sen' 'em any weapons, so dey use decoy signals to fool us inna droppin' shit onna wrong spot. Yer signal's a square shape!"

"As opposed to a square color?" Salvi asks, ribbing him.

"Smart-ass!" the Chicagoan replies, shouting a laugh when Salvi says, "Major Smart-ass to you, Sergeant!"

They continue to chat at the top of their lungs while the pilot banks for a closer look. A second signal fire comes into view, and then a third, on a different mountainside. "Shit!" the Chicagoan yells when AA opens up on them from the direction of a flaming T. "Jerries! Get ready, youse guys."

The red light comes on. The sergeant drags the door open. An icy blast of starlit air hits Simon Henley's face. At thirty-second intervals, the sergeant flings out canisters of supplies, the wireless transmitter, and the hand generator, each on separate chutes. The plane jolts and sways alarmingly. The sergeant hits Salvi's shoulder. The major disappears. Stepping up to the opening, Simon looks down, hoping to see Salvi's parachute bloom above the folded, forested wilderness. The mountains are a study in black and white. Bloody hell, Simon thinks. It's still winter here!

He's never jumped into snow.

VALDOTTAVO

"The charges are too close together," Renzo says. "Move that one about half a meter."

"Why?" the kid wants to know.

"If the second detonation isn't offset correctly, the wheels on the other side of the track will keep the train from derailing."

"All right," the boy says sullenly. He's fourteen, maybe. Full of bravado and crap. "Why don't you help?"

"Because," Renzo explains patiently, "I'm a drunken old gimp. Either I fall over, or I can't get up." They can hear the locomotive's engine now. "Move the charge."

Renzo slogs back through the snowy mud toward Schramm and the others who wait on the slope above the tracks. "You shouldn't talk like that about yourself," Schramm says. "It's bad for discipline."

Lighting a cigarette, Renzo looks up, attention drawn by anti-aircraft fire in the distance. Low on the jagged horizon, an airplane smokes into sight. "Busy night."

Schramm follows Renzo's gaze. "British?"

"American. Starboard engine throwing oil. Feather that prop, friend."

As if heeding Renzo's advice, the pilot tries to bring the propeller vertical. The windmilling goes on, creating so much drag the plane nearly stalls. "Lighten the load," Renzo murmurs. The damaged engine bursts into flame. "Cut the fuel . . ."

The train's whistle blasts as the locomotive starts through its last tunnel. Renzo beckons to the boy. "Pietro—Paolo, whatever the hell your name is—"

"It's Franco!" the boy shouts back.

"Are you going to stay there and argue with that train?"

Canisters, boxes, and a couple of paratroopers sail out of the crippled Dakota and disappear behind a nearby mountain. The crew remains on board, hurling flak jackets, a chart table and oxygen tanks into the night.

"Will they make it?" Schramm asks.

"If they bail out now."

The plane begins to climb, but not fast enough.

"*Scheisse,*" Schramm sighs when it explodes against a cliff. "Survivors?"

"The crew? Not a chance." Renzo pulls out his flask and raises it to the dead. "The jumpers? Possibly."

Franco sloshes through muddy snow, looking back through dirt-gray branches in time to see the train crew leap into trackside weeds as the locomotive blares out of the tunnel. "You warned them!"

Renzo wipes his mouth on the back of his hand. "Of course!"

"But they're Fascists! They're—"

The air is compressed by two explosions in quick succession, then ripped by the screech of metal on metal. A shatteringly loud crash seems to go on forever. Across the ravine, Tullio Goletta gives the sign and thirty men in motley leave the trees to slide down a snow-covered slope. The trainmen call greetings to Renzo, and join the partisans in emptying the freight cars of their cargo.

Mouth open, Franco turns. Renzo's eyes are mocking and mature, if slightly unfocused. "That's why I'm the boss, and you're the one who's going to shut up and carry a box back to base." Renzo waves to Tullio and pitches his voice to carry. "Anyone over there speak English?"

Tullio consults with the others. "Otello does, boss!"

"And I do, a little," Schramm says.

"We're going after that airdrop," Renzo calls. "You're with me, Tullio. Bring Otello and five or six others! You, too, Schramm. We may need a doctor."

Roman candle. That's the jump-school term for it. Occasionally chutes fail, and that's what you look like, going down.

It seemed hours before Simon felt the welcome jerk of his own straps. He lost sight of Salvi's all too rapid descent, rotating on the lines in time to see the Dakota itself crash into the mountainside. With tracers trying to find him, the long swaying float to earth seemed endless, even while the ground hurtled upward to meet him. He kept his elbows tucked and meant to roll, but thudded instead into snow, less than a minute after the Chicagoan gave Simon a shove into the frigid air.

Winded by the fall, he hears more explosions—two, three? Nearer this time. Expecting Germans at any moment, Simon tries to get out of his harness but can't move. I'm paralyzed, he thinks. I didn't roll, and I've broken my own silly neck!

In the next instant he realizes he can wiggle his toes. Crossing his eyes, he can focus on the snow just in front of him. He turns his head from side to side to clear a little airway in front of his nose. Kicks and presses and gouges with knees and elbows. Gains some space around himself, but makes no progress upward.

Not paralyzed then, but definitely immobilized.

Rest a bit, he decides.

The snow insulates him at first, but soon begins to drain his body heat away. Shivering, he tries again to dig out, swearing now, and scared. The activity makes him warmer briefly, but his muscles start to tense up. Fatigue sets in faster this time.

He rests, shuddering uncontrollably. His fingers and toes ache with cold. He tries again, digging like a demented terrier, but exhausts himself just to get his fingers up by his chest.

Astounded, he thinks, This is it then! Unless the Germans come and shoot me first, I'm going to freeze to death. Standing up. In a snowdrift. In Italy! I never even got to wear that bloody red beret.

He wishes he'd written to his mother. He wishes Major Salvi's parachute had opened. He wishes it were spring, and that the snow would melt.

In a fit of determination, he grits his teeth and puts everything he's got into last effort to free himself.

Don't cry, he tells himself afterward. Just don't cry.

"Where do you think you're going?"

Angelo stands still, one arm into a jacket that's already too small. "To the privy. Really," he says. "The explosions woke me up. I had to pee."

"Look me in the eye," Mirella orders. "Tell me you weren't going to look for bullets."

"Honest, Mamma. I have to pee."

"All right," she says, eyes narrow. "I'll just wait right here until you're done."

He jams his feet into wooden-soled boots. "You never believe me," he mutters, indignant at being caught.

Mirella sags onto a kitchen chair as her son clumps out to the privy. Oh, Angelo, she thinks, fighting nausea. What am I going to do with you?

Is it because he's a boy, or because he's nine? Is it the war, or is it just Angelo, needing a man's hand? She wishes she had Lidia to advise her. She wishes Iacopo were here to take charge. She wishes she could sleep through the night.

The door bangs shut. She looks up. "Angelo, come here," she says. He does, but he won't let her put her arm around him. "Angelo, please! Try to understand! I'm all alone here—"

"No, you're not! There's Mariano and Tomasso and—"

"That's not what I mean, and you know it! It's just you and me and the girls now. I have so much work to do, and I'm . . . I don't feel well. I worry about Babbo, and if you make me worry, too, it's just too much! I need you to be as grown up as you can be. You must look after the girls, and take care of me a little bit, too. Can you do that?"

Arms crossed against his chest, he shrugs, rolling his eyes but nodding. She tries to kiss him, but he squirms away and stomps up the stairs to the bedroom, ahead of his mother.

He and Stefania share a bed with Rosina to keep warm. Rosina's asleep, but Stefania's only pretending. She probably noticed when he got up to watch the airplane go by, and ratted him out to Mamma. Girls, he thinks, disgusted.

His mother stands in the bedroom doorway until Angelo undresses and gets back into bed. He waits, listening to the hallway floor creak under his mother's footsteps, until her door closes. Then he pinches Stefania really hard, like Bruno Ceretto taught him. Stefania squawks, and he covers her mouth with his hand. "Nobody likes a rat, Stefania. You snitch on me again, I'll cut your hair off."

"You wouldn't!"

"I'll wait till you're asleep and cut it off until you're bald."

"You'll get spanked," she warns.

"You'll be bald a lot longer than my *culo* will hurt." He pulls his pants back on, drags two sweaters over his head, opens the window, and tosses his boots out. Won't be the first time he's climbed down the vines. Throwing a leg over the sill, he fixes Stefania with a stare. "Rat on me again, and you'll be sorry, baldie."

The starlight's all blue, but when your eyes are used to it, you can see real easy because the snow sort of shines. And anyway the parachutes are easy to spot. The camouflage is all wrong—black, green, and brown against the white. Course, they didn't expect to get shot down. They probably figured they'd be past the mountains when they jumped.

Germans look for airdrops, but Angelo's not scared of them. They don't like coming into the mountains at night anymore, so they walk real slow, and won't get here for a while. Dead bodies don't scare him either. They did when he was little, but not anymore, not after that one Bruno Ceretto found. It must have been a partisan, because he wasn't wearing a real uniform. He died near the orphanage, and Bruno found the body when the sisters sent everybody out to look for mushrooms and bird eggs and *ruculo* to eat. He told Angelo, and they snuck back out that night to see it. There were flies and worms, and no eyes, and it really stank.

"Get his bullets!" Bruno said, shoving Angelo.

"I'm not touching him! You can get a disease!"

"You baby. I bet you made it up about that lady's head in a bucket!"

"Did not!" Scrunching up his face, Angelo waved at the flies, put his hand way out, and picked a bullet out of the dead guy's cartridge belt with the tips of two fingers. He jumped back and Bruno laughed, but Angelo had the bullet, heavy and cold and important, in his palm.

Bruno snatched it. "Watch! You take the lead out like this, see?" He pried the pointy part out of the brass case with a penknife he took off a littler kid. "Then you pour the gunpowder into little piles on a flat rock. Like volcanoes, see?"

When you hit the volcanoes with another rock, they explode. The kids on the farm think Angelo made that up, but it's true, so he's going to get some bullets and show them.

Angelo ignores the boxes and stuff, trudging on until he finds the paratrooper whose chute never opened and is almost for sure dead. Still, he might be faking, and taking bullets is sort of stealing, so Angelo sits down behind some trees and holds his breath as long as he can, watching to see if anything moves. When the body passes this test of deadness, Angelo looks around for a big, long stick and creeps out of the trees toward the rocks the paratrooper fell on.

He pokes at the body a little at first, then harder. The real problem is, the gun's underneath the guy. Angelo considers pushing the body over, but there's a commando knife strapped to the top leg, and that would be as good as a bullet to show the kids at the farm. Holding his breath again, Angelo puts the stick down and reaches for the knife—

A hoarse shout startles him. He falls backward, scrambles to his feet, puts his hands up, like in a cowboy movie. For a terrible moment, he thinks the men are *fascisti*, but nobody's wearing a uniform. "*Ei!* Over here!" he calls, waving his arms over his head, so they won't think he didn't know they were partisans. "I found the airdrop! Over here!"

He waits for them to arrive, dancing a little with excitement. There are nine men, clanking with guns and knives. The first ones are *contadini* for sure, short and thick: built like a brick outhouse, the factor always said. The last two must be city people, because they're taller, and look tired. Nobody talks while the tallest, skinniest one stoops down to check the body.

Angelo raises his hand, like he's in school. The second-tallest one has a scary scarred face, but he snorts a laugh and nods permission to speak. "That guy's dead," Angelo tells him. "I made sure! But there's another one up there, and I saw more boxes and stuff over there! I can show you!"

The scarred-up man looks hard at him. "What's your name, kid?"

After a moment's hesitation, he says, "Angelo," but not his last name, because you never know.

"Angelo Soncini?" the scarred-up man asks. "Schramm, this is Mirella's boy! Angelo, it's me, Renzo Leoni!" Angelo couldn't swear to it, the man seems like maybe he could be the neighbor who came to Mother of Mercy wearing a priest dress one time. "*Belandi,*" the man swears, "what the hell are you doing out here? You could get killed! Look how big you are!"

"I'm ten!" Angelo says. "Almost." He looks at the lightening eastern sky and realizes his mother is going to know he snuck out. "We should get going," he says, adding, "I saw some Germans coming, too!" to make sure everyone will hurry up.

Angelo leaps from rock to rock, like an island-hopping giant in a white ocean, having a grand time. Considerably less amused, the men struggle along in his wake, trying not to fall into the pools of deep snow between the crags as they tramp down a ravine and across a frozen kettle pond and around the hip of a hill. They find a generator, a radio, and a canister of cigarettes at fifty-meter intervals, well packed and apparently unharmed, but the last of the Dakota's cargo is higher on the mountainside in a drop zone nobody would have selected, and no footsteps lead away from the parachute.

Lifting silk away from snow, they expect another corpse. Instead a drowsy young man stares up at them and blinks slowly. "I trie' a roll," he says.

"Dig," Schramm says, and everyone does, clearing the snow with their bare hands, tugging at the Tommy's arms to pull him free. The Englishman begins to hum tunelessly, stopping now and then to make some remark and giggle. "Try not to jar him. Sometimes their hearts just stop," Schramm warns. "We've got to get him warm as soon as possible."

"I live right over there," Angelo tells Renzo. "Mamma will take care of him." The men pause and look at one another. "It's safe," Angelo says confidently. "The owner is a big shot with medals and stuff. He knows all the *fascisti,* and they don't bother us."

"Renzo," Schramm says in a low voice, "if you want this man to live . . ."

Renzo closes his eyes, weighs priorities, issues orders. "Tullio, get back to base. Send your father back here with twenty men— wait, make it thirty—as fast as they can travel. You, you, you: take the radio equipment to Monteverdi for safekeeping. You two stay here to dig. Otello, go down to the farm with Angelo, so his mother doesn't think he's making this up."

"And tell her to get a good fire going," Schramm orders. "Heat some water!"

Still half-buried, the Englishman waves to the dispersing partisans. "Bye-bye!" he calls cheerily, then begins to sing, loudly and in a variety of keys. "Weeee'll mee' tagain, don' know where, don' know wheeeen . . ."

"Hurry," Schramm says. "When they stop making sense, they don't have much time."

The paratrooper's halfway to Tipperary when they've dragged him to the surface. Breathless from the effort, they listen to the jaunty march for a few minutes, then struggle to their feet.

"Schramm," Renzo says as they make ready to carry the half-frozen paratrooper toward Villa Malcovato, "the ski instructors said if someone's hypothermic, you warm him up slowly."

Schramm concentrates on uncoupling the Englishman's harness and lines. "We did some research," he says vaguely. "Faster is better."

Hearing comes first. People whispering. Boots on wooden floors. His own existence is next. He's warm. Sitting in a chair. His legs feel heavy in an odd sort of way. He opens his eyes, blinks owlishly, takes in his surroundings a little at a time. A fireplace. A window.

"Caporale?" he hears a woman say.

She is, alarmingly, pretty as an angel, although Simon never expected heavenly beings to look so tired. Two sleeping cherubs snuggle on his lap, one under each arm, wrapped inside the same blankets tucked around him. That's when he realizes he's been stripped to his socks and army-issue Y-fronts, and that a bare-chested man is sitting right behind him.

The tired angel puts her hand against his chest, to keep him from leaping out of the chair. "*Calma ti,*" she says soothingly. "*Tu sei fra amici.*"

Amici means friends, but standing just beyond her is a group of fearsome-looking men, apparently outfitted at a jumble sale. Italian army jackets, city tweeds, hand-knit jumpers. Baggy peasant pants, trousers from woolen suits or German uniforms. Laced hunting boots, wooden clogs, street shoes, German combat boots. They're heavily armed with an equally international collection of military-issue weapons, shotguns and hunting rifles, police pistols and meat cleavers.

Their disorderly appearance contrasts with the attention and obedience they give a slender, middle-aged man with a badly scarred face and a submachine gun slung casually over his left shoulder. Noticing Simon, Scarface breaks off their conversation and comes closer. "*Parli italiano?*"

Simon spots his uniform drying on a rack in front of the fire. "There's a phrase book in my kit," he tells them, pointing with one finger. Reaching around the little girls, he mimes opening a book with his palms. "Book? An Italian-English phrase book?"

The man behind him oozes out of the chair, speaking Italian. Simon instantly feels the chill of his absence against his own bare back, and realizes why this person was there in the first place. The angel speaks sharply to a boy—her son?—and the child hurries to get the phrase book, watching wide-eyed while Simon flips through it.

"There," Simon says, and slowly sounds out transliteration. "*Sahno key eye-tar-low:* I am here to help you." He hands the book over, pointing at the phrase.

The leader's brows rise. Judging from the resulting laughter, he says something along the lines of, "Well, thank God for that! We're safe now that this bedraggled little limey is on the scene."

From the string of orders subsequently issued, Simon picks out just one word: Maria. The kitchen empties itself of partisans, leaving Scarface, the angel, and a thin man, all of whom continue discussing the situation. The bloke who sat behind him listens to them, nodding repeatedly while buttoning his shirt. "I am called Otello," he tells Simon. "I visit England for one year. We are *partigiani:* partisans. Anti-Fascists. We are all friends for you. Your comrade is misfortunately dead. This is the doctor of us." The thin man raises a hand in greeting. "He says you must rest." Otello indicates Scarface next. "The boss says it's dangerous for this lady if you stay here. So you will rest one night. Then we'll go to our camp with you. Have you undestand everything?"

"Where's the wireless? The Marconi?" Simon looks from face to face. "I have to report in. I was supposed to go to Milan, but I don't know why. Major Salvi had all the orders, and if he's dead, I don't know what—"

Otello stops him, and translates. "The boss says, 'The radio is safe. You will use it tomorrow.' " The doctor lifts the smaller of the two sleeping girls out of Simon's lap. The tired angel takes the older one into her arms and sends the boy out of the room. "Now this lady takes you to rest," Otello says.

The angel smiles encouragingly and shows Simon to a staircase.

Half an hour later, with Stefania, Angelo, and the English boy in bed, Mirella returns to the kitchen. Renzo and Schramm are alone at the table, deep in quiet discussion. "We have coffee," she tells them. "Should I put some on now? No—maybe you should get some sleep."

"Mirella," Renzo says, "stop fussing and go back to bed!"

"I'm fine. I'm fine," she says, bustling distractedly from task to task. "Are you sure about the coffee? I could put some in a sack for you. *Il maggiore* can get more. We have eggs. Should I make you some eggs? Werner, lie down upstairs awhile. I can take Rosina now."

"Ah, but it's such a pleasure to hold her." A pale dawn brightens the curtains above the sink and finds its way to Rosina's curls. Her chubby cheeks are the color of peaches, as her mother's used to be. Schramm frowns at Mirella's nervy, cheerless agitation. "You're pale," he tells her. "And thin. Are you eating enough? How far along are you?"

"Almost three months," she says, as though dismissing some minor inconvenience. "I'm fine, Werner. Some morning sickness, that's all."

She glances quickly at Renzo. "Mirella—" he says, and stops for a deep breath and long moments of tapping the tabletop. "Where is Iacopo?" he asks finally. "Why are you alone here?"

"He's in Sant'Andrea with the refugees—"

"God damn that man! Can't he *ever* put his own family first?"

She doesn't want Renzo's anger. She has her own, and the gnawing fear that goes with it. "There was no one else," she says. "Osvaldo Tomitz has been arrested."

GESTAPO INTERROGATION CENTER
PORTO SANT'ANDREA

"I never used to smoke," Artur Huppenkothen says. "My sister complains about the smell. Erna can't understand why I have taken up such a filthy habit. My nerves, I tell her. It helps my nerves."

He has smashed terrorist cells, one after another, but what good has it done? He is a blacksmith, bringing his hammer down on the anvil time after time, but there's no iron to bend to his will. The enemy is like water, like the sea. You might as well pound a rising tide.

"The Soviets have taken the Balkans," he tells the priest. "Yugoslavia, Bulgaria, Rumania. Religion is finished there. Do you want that to happen in Italy? Do you understand whom you are protecting, Father? Jews, who do not believe in Jesus. Communists, who do not believe in God at all! You are a good man, but you've been duped. You haven't seen what I've seen. Communists took over München when I was a boy, and let me tell you something—they were all Jews!"

Beneath its bruises, the face remains impassive, the eyes downcast.

"Are you praying, Father? Then pray for wisdom!" Artur pleads. "In the Gospel of John, Jesus says, 'Whoever belongs to God hears the words of God—if you do not listen, you do not belong to God.' Who do the Jews belong to then? They killed Christ in Satan's service! They poison and kill and steal from Christians. They hate us with a hate so vast, so—so violent, they want us all to die! The Jew is capable of any kind of evil. There is nothing they won't stoop to, Tomitz! Why do you protect them?"

Artur opens a thick file, shuffles through the crackly onionskin papers. "In Spain, the Communists killed thousands of priests and monks and nuns! The pope himself said Jews form the principal force of Bolshevism! Jews subsist through contraband, fraud, and usury. They have tentacles everywhere, Tomitz—in contracts and monopolies, in postal services and telephone companies, in shipping and the railroads, in town treasuries and state finance— Here!" he says, finding a clipping from *Civiltà Cattolica*. "From the Vatican newspaper! 'Jews are uniquely endowed with the qualities of parasites and destroyers. They pull the levers of capitalism and communism—a pincer assault to control the entire world! They grow fat off the arts and industry of the nations that give them refuge!' "

Silence.

Artur watches smoke give shape to light coming through the office window, trying to fathom this man. He looks so ordinary, so normal. Nothing in his physiognomy marks him as a race traitor, a

Communist dupe, a Jew lover. Sadly, once the infection takes hold, no amount of reasoning can break its grip. Artur squares the sheaf of papers, closes the file, replaces it in his briefcase. "I gave you every chance," he says. "You leave me with no choice."

He was dozing in the backseat of the car, waiting for *il maggiore* to return from a meeting in the Palazzo Municipale. By the time he was taken into custody, he'd heard so many stories, he could anticipate every detail. The Gestapo men in leather coats. The pistol pointed at his chest.

There would be prison. Interrogation. You know you'll be beaten, but you don't really *know.* You can't, until you feel that first blow, because it carries a completely unexpected message. It does not say, "Tell me what I want to know!" It says instead, "You are helpless."

Even on the battlefield, the Red Cross or the medics find their way to the wounded. The compensation for being hurt is the expectation of help, and when that expectation is destroyed, a part of you dies. You realize with numb surprise that those who hold you prisoner can do anything they like. They don't simply punch you in the face. They reach through the air and shatter the boundaries that make you an individual. They impose themselves on you as they please. It is a kind of rape.

The next surprise is heartening. Like a little boy in his first schoolyard scuffle, you discover you can take a punch. The fright and pain of the first blow fade remarkably quickly. A kind of giddiness takes hold. The pain is not, after all, unbearable. It's not as bad as a toothache, for example. Hit me all you want, you think then. It'll get you nowhere.

And so: the shuffle down an endless corridor illuminated by bare bulbs hanging from cords furred with dust. A turn, a stairwell. Another corridor three flights down. Doors on each side at two-meter intervals; men behind them weeping, moaning. "*Coraggio,*" someone shouts to the shackled newcomer. "Courage, comrade!" A man behind a different door laughs shrilly.

A large brick room. A high vaulted ceiling. His clothes are taken from him. While his hands are manacled behind his back, his eyes follow a thick-linked chain rolling over a pulley anchored in the ceiling, spooling onto an oaken uptake spindle with an iron crank.

The strappado. Machiavelli endured it, survived it. He wrote *The Prince* afterward. Or, rather, he dictated it. Nevertheless. It is possible to live through this. There can be a life after the strappado.

Huppenkothen is waiting. He is a small man, neat, with the kind of round soft features that look good-natured. "I hate this," he says, pacing. "The screaming. The shitting, the pissing. I hate it." He pauses to light another cigarette, his hands unsteady, and jerks his head toward a civilian with a flamboyant mustache and a long blue jaw that works like a pump handle as he chews the last of a sausage *panino*. "Signor Innocente does not share my distaste, Father. You'll talk sooner or later. I suggest sooner."

Innocente. It is the surname given to foundlings raised in Catholic orphanages. A euphemism for bastard.

Innocente licks his fingers, steps forward, pulls the chain down, snugs its hook into the shackles. The chain rattles. The spool creaks, taking up the slack.

"Names," Huppenkothen says. "Addresses. Meeting places."

The hook draws Osvaldo's hands upward, backward, away from his body. Sweat pops on his forehead, his upper lip. His feet leave the ground. Suspended a meter above the floor, he is able to think of Christ crucified for an instant.

And then: he is transfigured, transmogrified, all body, no soul. All that was Osvaldo Tomitz gathers into his shoulder joints. His muscles quiver, first slightly, then more violently. He stops breathing, unwilling to spend strength on anything other than holding himself at half-oblique.

"Everyone tries that," PierCarlo Innocente tells him. "It never works."

From the spindle's vantage, PierCarlo measures the naked body with a tailor's eye, deciding how much chain will be needed to keep the feet above the floor. He hoists the priest another half meter up and chocks the spindle. Drawing closer, he inspects the priest's shivering penis with detached curiosity. "Naughty worm," he whispers with an odd lilting intimacy. "Naughty little worm . . ."

He straightens and hits the priest high in the belly, under the rib cage, emptying the lungs so that no scream can mask the crackle of shattering cartilage and snapping ligaments. Torn out, lifted from behind, the balls of the shoulders spring from their sockets. The body falls abruptly, then hangs from its own muscles and skin and nerves and blood vessels. The dislocated arms are twisted high above the head.

"Torture," PierCarlo says to himself. "From the Latin *torquere,* to twist."

He watches, patient, emotionless. Soon the body's need for breath wins its battle against gravity, and the screaming can begin. When the shrieks subside to a high, thin whine like a piglet's squeal, PierCarlo begins to chant in the singsong voice of an adult wheedling cooperation from a reluctant child. "No one can hear you but me. Nobody knows where you are," he croons softly. "Give me what I want, naughty worm, or I'll never let you go."

March 1945

PENSIONE USODIMARE
PORTO SANT'ANDREA

The office is makeshift: a cheap desk pushed into an entry that was once a modest receiving room for a prosperous family. After the war, Antonia Usodimare intends to fix the place up again, but for now it's good enough. Her boarders are lonely men, too weary and dejected to care about threadbare upholstery and derelict draperies. She moves heavily on puffy, leaden legs, cooking plain meals for them, doing their washing. Between bouts of housework, she knits with red and swollen fingers, knobby knees splayed beneath the skirt of a faded black dress, bunioned feet stuffed into a pair of her dead husband's slippers.

This morning, she aches worse than usual. After all the boarders left, she added a long climb to the garret to her ordinary work, then punished her joints further by kneeling in the corner, prying up the boards, retrieving a bundle of clothing. One flight down, she wrapped the bundle in a thin towel, collected a few shirts, stuffed them into a sack with stinking underwear and socks. Layering them, like a nasty lasagna. Slowly, pausing on each stair tread, she made her way back down to the office, tucked the sack under the desk, and settled down to wait.

She's been promised that a *staffetta* called *la vedova* will give her an entire package of British cigarettes in exchange for the bundle. A princely payment, but justified by the risks Antonia takes for the resistance. The Gestapo will arrest anyone, even old women. If they search the Pensione Usodimare and find what hides under her desk, Antonia Usodimare will pay with her life.

At midmorning, a young peasant knocks politely on the open

door but stays just outside, one hand balancing the large basket she carries on her kerchiefed head. "*Prego, signora,*" she says with a slurry mountain accent, "have you any laundry for me today?"

Antonia frowns suspiciously. She was expecting someone her own age, not this pregnant green-eyed girl. "I usually do my own."

"*Prego, signora,* I'll do a good job, and I don't charge much. I need the money. I am all alone. A widow."

As she realizes that *la vedova* is not just a nickname, the landlady's lumpy old face changes. "*Poveretta,*" she murmurs, bending to retrieve the sack. The girl lowers her basket, secreting the bundle amid the sheets and shirts she's already carrying. "*Grazie tanto,*" she says. "You are very kind."

She passes the cigarettes to Antonia when the old woman embraces her. "There are too many widows," Antonia whispers. "Too many mothers alone."

"There will be more."

It is a promise, not a threat. Antonia draws back, chilled. *La vedova* pauses at the open door. "I'll have the laundry back by Tuesday," she says in a voice meant to be heard. "*Mille grazie, signora.*"

At roadblocks and checkpoints, she can play her pregnancy either way. Italians, either sentimental or in collusion with the resistance, allow the weary young Madonna to pass without a thorough search. Germans are more dangerous. Their eyes linger on her swollen breasts. They pretend to be suspicious. Italy is filled with girls who survive by doing soldiers a favor for a few lire, a couple of cigarettes, a little food. To them, Claudia is a slut stupid enough to let herself get knocked up, as bitter and embattled as they themselves. "What have you got in that basket?" such men always ask. Sometimes she flirts with them. "A bomb," she jokes. "Want to search me?"

Sant'Andrea's early spring has softened into real warmth; her blouse is half open beneath a rust-red cardigan. The waistband of a flowered skirt is shifted above her belly, and raises the hem over her knees. She shuffles forward in the queue, watching the older of two soldiers.

Stepping up to the barricade, she glances at a gang of undersized urchins loitering just beyond. Ragged, barefoot, fearless. *"Zigaretten,"* such boys beg at every German checkpoint. For sport sometimes, soldiers flick a butt to the cobbles and make bets as children fight for possession. Claudia leans over to set her basket down. The older German watches a trickle of sweat slip between her breasts. She hands over her identity card.

He may toss a cigarette toward the boys, beckon to her, demand a "toll" for her passage. He may see the signs of alteration on her papers and arrest her, or simply shoot her in the head because he's hung over and knows the war is lost. She will not know why she died, except that she is following her orders: collect the uniform, deliver it to Schramm.

"What's in there?" He means the basket, but he's looking now at her belly.

"A little bastard," she says in Schramm's Italian-accented German. "Want to search me to be sure?"

Pawing through the laundry, he gives the opportunity some thought. She's pretty, even six months along— *"Scheisse!"* he hisses, leaping back as though his hand had been bitten by a snake.

She apologizes, feigning surprise and dismay. Explains that such cleaning is part of her job. He swears again, face twisting with disgust, and tells her to move on. God knows how many people this man's killed, but rags soaked with menstrual blood have the power to horrify him.

She clears the barricade and follows a boy named Riccardo down a narrow alley, through a low plank door. The other kids filter in, delivering stolen purses, wallets, and guns. Riccardo decides what he can fence in town and what he'll sell to *la vedova.* The bargaining is swift. Two packets of British cigarettes for identity papers. He wants two more for the guns, but she shakes her head. "One pack," she says. "We've got plenty of guns."

"Bene." Riccardo lights up.

"Next Tuesday," she tells him. "The Genoa gate."

The child's cheeks hollow as he takes a drag. He coughs and nods, then raises a grubby hand in farewell. "Next Tuesday," he agrees. *"Ciao, bella."*

Near Borgo San Mauro
Valdottavo

Tonio lugs lead batteries. Maurizio totes the cumbersome generator. The twelve-pound wireless transmitter bumps against Simon Henley's own chronically bruised back. Twenty-some men form a guard around the precious radio equipment. When the sun comes up, the tracks of this mixed multitude will be plain as day through melting snow and the mud beneath it. "Won't the Germans follow us?" Simon Henley asks his guide.

"Of course not," Maria Avoni says.

"Why not?" he asks in sincere ignorance.

"Because they might *find* us." She stands still, listening. Gets her bearings, and points. "There is a spring. We will drink some water and rest."

Mirella Soncini seemed an angel of mercy who made his first day in Italy warm and safe. Maria Avoni is an altogether different example of Italian womanhood. Last month, at Renzo Leoni's order, Maria appeared at Villa Malcovato toting a machine gun, with ammunition belts criss-crossed over her lovely bosom: Boadicea as dressed by Pancho Villa. "How was your flight?" she asked Simon, as though he were a tourist on holiday, not a paratrooper behind enemy lines. "I will show you to your first camping place," she said. "We will have an enjoyable walk."

She commands a band of two dozen partisans instructed to facilitate the British signalman's work. Her English is competent, but Simon was bemused by her phrasing until she mentioned that her father was a mountain guide before the war.

She picks out a flattish rock to use as a picnic bench, and extracts *panini* from a backpack. The other partisans nudge each other, smirking, when Simon sits next to her. He wishes their vulgar assumptions were correct. He's spent hours pretending to care about Maria's nature talks, watching her hips as she climbs in the moonlight.

She is smart, and knowledgeable, and has volunteered for the thankless task of teaching him a bit of her language. Tonight's topic has been the bewildering variety of Italian politics. As near as he can make out, the Garibaldi Brigades divide their time between ambushing Fascists and preparing for a Communist revolution after the war. Matteotti Socialists are left-wing laborites, but not Communists; they support trade unions and peasant agricultural cooperatives. Christian Democrats want to restore normality, a rather cloudy concept these days. Catholic Actionists differ from Christian Democrats in some way that even Maria is hazy about. "I think they're more religious" was all she could come up with.

The Committee for National Liberation's brief is to coordinate the actions of such groups for the common good—broadly defined as making the Germans leave Italy. The British SOE's mission, in turn, is to encourage CNL cooperation with the Allies by dropping medical supplies, weapons, ammunition, money, and cigarettes, all in exchange for intelligence on enemy troop movements. Simon's own orders are to transmit said intelligence, an activity the German SS and Italian Black Brigades wish devoutly to discontinue. By day, squads of them comb the district on foot or motorbike, searching in general for partisans and in particular for an Englishman with a wireless. Maria guides him to a new transmission location every seventy-two hours.

"And what are your political views?" he asks Maria, trying to sound worldly while chewing a cheese sandwich.

She licks olive oil from her fingers. "See those two farms? There, and there." Hints of a rosy dawn flush the eastern sky. He can just make out the blackened ruins high on either side of the main valley. "The Fascists say Attilio Goletta helps the resistance. The Communists say Battista Goletta is a Fascist informer. Broken clocks are correct two times a day. The Black Brigades and the Garibaldini—they are both correct this time." She shrugs, and with an act of will, he does not watch her breasts move beneath her battle jacket. "Most of the time, they are wrong. *Fascisti* think all peasants help the partisans, so they burn houses. *Communisti* think if a farmer's house isn't burned, he must be a collaborator. So they burn houses."

"And your group?"

"We just want all these bastards to leave us alone. Germans, Fascists, Communists."

Relieved the British are not yet on her list of *bastardi,* Simon clears his throat self-consciously. "Maria, I heard that there will be a dance. A lot of the partisans are inviting *staffette* ... I was wondering if you would—"

Her face goes still. She moves her head from side to side, listening to a faint thumping on the other side of the low mountains to the south. Mortars, a valley or two away. "I'll dance when the war is over."

She stands, giving orders. Maurizio does as he's told, hefting the generator, but Tonio mutters "*Rompacoglioni*" in a tone intended to provoke. Maria replies, a whiplash in her voice.

Simon straps the wireless onto his back but looks to Maria for an explanation of what just happened. She pumps the air near her crotch with both hands and jerks her head toward Tonio. "*Ambidestro,*" she says with a sneer.

He stifles a laugh when he works it out: two-handed wanker.

"He calls me ballbuster," she tells Simon casually. "I say to him, 'Lucky I hate the Germans more than I hate pricks like you.' " She studies Simon, knowing—the way women always seem to know—that his intentions are every bit as dishonorable as those of any other man. His tactics, at least, are more gentlemanly. "When war came, there were fewer tourists, and my father's business went down. After the Germans? No tourists at all. From then on—" She meets Simon's eyes with a level gaze. "I supported my whole family. Parents. Nonna. Three brothers, a sister." She watches his reactions. Admiration. Puzzlement. The shock of understanding. He searches for something to say, but she says it for him. "I was a whore, but I am also their superior officer. So they obey."

They have begun to climb again when a small girl appears out of nowhere. She chatters and points toward a farm building about a mile down the mountainside. Simon sees a German soldier exit a barn.

Unconcerned, Maria sends the child off and leans again into the slope. Simon stumbles, looking over his shoulder. There are several Germans now, heads bowed over a map. One raises binoculars. "Maria," Simon says with all the urgency he can muster, "if they spot us, they're not likely to mistake this for a shepherds' convention."

"You worry too much," she says, her pace unaltered. "They will stay there and have a breakfast."

He has never been in combat. Maria has led ambushes, survived firefights, won skirmishes. She knows the country and the people. He trusts her judgment. With the war nearly over, many ordinary German and Italian soldiers merely go through the motions of pursuing partisans, but the SS have lost none of their zeal for hunting down unarmed Jews. In the past few weeks, Simon's seen massive operations sweep through valleys like this. Barking mad, really, given how much those troops are needed elsewhere.

Suddenly, and for no reason he can identify, he feels . . . exposed, and very frightened. He sidesteps, not knowing why, moving to Maria's left just as the machine guns open up.

Startled by the noise, he dives for cover, rolling behind a log in time to see Maria's blouse stitched in red by a neat row of bullets. Four more partisans are hit before she topples to the muddy ground.

Three rounds zip over the log, their draft riffling Simon's hair. They're shooting at me, he thinks stupidly. Those people are trying to kill me. In the next instant, all the tedious months of SOE training and discipline take over. He looses a burst from his Marlin in the general direction of the gunfire and motions for Maurizio to move uphill.

Wide-eyed, Maurizio tightens the generator's straps, scrambles through the muddy melting snow, then fires a burst of his own while Simon runs crouched and at top speed. Soon all the partisans are moving upward in pairs, alternately keeping the Germans' heads down with covering fire and scrambling like hell for cover on higher ground.

They've made fifty meters when the noise and the immediate danger begin to recede. Mouths open, they pause to reassess their line of retreat. The ground suddenly leaps to life beneath Tonio's feet. A machine gunner on their left flank quickly corrects. Tonio screams—legs, thighs, hips spattered with slugs. Another partisan grabs his arm, trying to pull the wounded man along. The gunner finishes them both.

Sprinting now like startled goats, the surviving partisans dash toward the trees on their right, struggling through the treacly surface. A third machine gun opens fire directly in front of them. Three men go down, shot or maybe only slipping in the mud. Simon scrambles into a shallow gully with Maurizio. Maurizio yells to the others. A few shout back. Simon tries to count the voices. Seven left? Eight? Scattered over a fifty-yard field of overlapping fire. In the numberless western serials Simon watched as a child, this was when the 7th Cavalry would gallop over a ridge, bugles blaring, sabers flashing.

The shooting becomes sporadic. Partisans periodically pop up to keep the Germans at bay. The Jerries return fire halfheartedly, knowing they need only remind their quarry they're still pinned down. Eventually, the Italians will run out of ammunition.

It's going to be a beautiful spring day, Simon thinks as the sun rises. He can see a small copse of chestnut trees in a rubble of boulders, about two hundred yards uphill.

He nudges Maurizio and jerks his head toward the trees, hoping that eyes and expression can convey his thoughts: Stay here, and we're fish in a barrel. Run, and we'll be cut to pieces. Understanding, Maurizio shrugs, pulling the corners of his mouth downward as if to say, Six of one, half a dozen of the other. "*Andiamo,*" he says.

They take another count of the survivors and relay the plan to make a run for it. Tensing, Simon has gathered himself for the dash when the noise suddenly triples, and military clichés explode around him. Withering fire. A hail of bullets. All hell breaking loose. A vaguely familiar voice shouts in English from somewhere uphill. "*Ei!* Simon! Get ready! We give you cover!"

Laughing crazily, Maurizio directs Simon's wild-eyed gaze toward a man waving behind a tree stump. It's the one who visited England. What was his name? Something Shakespearean . . .

Before Simon can remember more, Renzo Leoni strolls out from behind a boulder. (Cool as a cucumber. Butter wouldn't melt in his mouth.) With the Germans preoccupied by this astounding display of *joie de morte,* Simon jumps up to spray the woods with his Marlin, thinking, Run like a rabbit. Run for your life.

Vaulting a fallen tree behind a low rock outcrop, he flops onto his belly and watches for muzzle flashes. This time he aims and picks off a man feeding ammo into one of the machine guns. Rewarded with a scream, he feels for the first time the sheer unholy joy of survival at another's cost, and looks for someone else to kill.

A partisan scuttles over and hides behind the rocks with him. "*Ei!* Simon! Remember me?" he asks cheerily. "I am Otello. I visit England for one year!"

Living proof that God protects drunks and lunatics, Renzo Leoni joins them, groaning like an old man when he kneels. He speaks in a low, quick voice, his appraising eyes on Simon. "The boss is happy you still have the radio," Otello translates. "He says: you did well. He says: a corporal in the paratroops is worth a colonel in any army!"

Surprised and gratified, Simon can think of no way to reply, and in any case, Renzo seems to forget him in the next moment. "He will count to three," Otello says, watching the silent orders the boss is conveying with an Italian's manual eloquence. "The others will cover us, and you will run with me, over the hill—that way. Run very fast, understand?"

On "*Tre!*" they take off amid a thunderstorm of gunfire. Knees pumping, crouched like a crone under the weight of the wireless, Simon expects a bullet in the arse, but minutes (hours, centuries) later, he and Otello clear the crest safely and slide down behind it.

Maurizio is next, flinging himself and the generator over the hilltop and into the declivity beyond. Three more partisans follow, leaping like Olympic long jumpers. One of them has retrieved the batteries from Tonio's body. Another grins and offers a bottle of red wine. Simon stares, astounded by the idea of carrying wine into battle, but he takes a slug and passes it on.

Otello and the others confer quickly. Two partisans nod and leave. Silently, the others wait, watching their Englishman's chest heave. "Are you better now?" Otello asks solicitously. "Can you walk?"

Insulted, Simon puts his primitive Italian to use, maligning the mating habits of Otello's entire family. Laughing, they get on their way, teaching him several additional terms for such behavior as they follow the scouts.

The gunfire grows fainter as they cross hills, cut through fields, and skirt hedgerows, moving at a steady pace that seems to indicate a long journey ahead of them. The day turns warm. Birds sing. Suddenly, the scouts come running back, calling out in hoarse whispers, motioning: Down! Down! Down!

Everyone dives for cover, and Otello pulls Simon into the freezing waist-high water of a high-banked stream. A German half-track trundles over the horizon. Shivering, sweating, they wait in absolute silence while the vehicle rumbles past, close enough for them to smell its exhaust.

When it finally disappears around a hill, they scramble out of the stream. Simon shrugs out of the radio rig, determines that it hasn't gotten wet, and tries to empty his boots without taking them off. Otello holds a whispered conference with the scouts, who take positions about fifty yards ahead. "We go where the Germans came," Otello says. "Do you understand? The Germans make a radio signal to headquarters that says, 'All clear. No partisans here.' So, no more Germans will come that way."

For the balance of the day, they meander through the countryside, their only objective to avoid contact with the enemy. Three times they see German patrols in the distance, and once they duck behind a hedgerow. A platoon of Decima Mas Republicans passes: ex–motor torpedo boatmen from the defunct Italian navy, limping morosely in bad boots.

By dusk Simon is thoroughly lost, and therefore utterly unprepared when they arrive at the very spot where the ambush began. He stares at Maria's body, forgotten until this moment. Sitting beside her, the same small girl who warned them this morning, a lifetime ago.

The child is sent away with a few quick orders. The partisans draw straws. Maurizio loses. While the others draw off to a safe distance, Maurizio checks their comrades' corpses for booby traps. When nothing blows up, Otello says, "This is safe for us tonight. The Germans think no one will come back."

Alerted by the little girl, two short, thick women arrive bearing shovels on their shoulders, baskets of food on their heads. Shaped like potatoes, with faces of genial toughness, they cluck their tongues over the fallen while handing chestnut bread and skins of harsh red wine to the living. Famished, the partisans eat, talking quietly, then take turns digging in rocky mud. The women shake their heads. "*Poveretti*," they say. "*Poveretti*."

Simon slumps empty-headed beside Maria's body, listening to the shovels' crunch and slop. For the first and only time, he reaches out to touch her face; startled by her cold flesh, he draws back. When the time comes, he helps lay her and the other corpses into their shallow graves. Otello cuts branches from some sort of conifer, placing fragrant sprays of green over the slack and empty faces. Maurizio starts to fill in Maria's grave but stops when Simon asks him to. Removing the little compass hidden in one of his buttons, Simon shows it to the others. They nod with approval when he closes Maria's fingers around it.

The peasants depart with their baskets and tools. Otello posts a sentry. The others pass wine bags from hand to hand, but no one sings tonight. When the skins are empty, each man makes a pile of pine boughs to lie on, above the freezing mud. A childhood prayer runs through Simon's mind. Now I lay me down to sleep. If I should die . . .

Tomorrow, he'll be escorted to one of the many tall stone watchtowers built into the slant of Piemonte's hilltops. Seven feet on a side, the upper level ten feet above a cellar downslope, they always afford a panoramic view of Valdottavo.

Otello and Maurizio will stay with him, to help with the batteries and generator. Over the next few hours, they'll watch activity in the valley. Identify high, quiet places within a few miles of the hideout. Hike to the best spot for the first transmission. There Simon will open the radio case, fit a stone into a loop at the end of a fifty-foot copper wire, and fling it over a nearby tree branch. He'll tune to Algiers, and be amazed once again by how easily such a primitive arrangement brings in QSA5 signals.

With a onetime code pad, index finger tapping thirty errorless words per minute, he'll deliver the intelligence he's gathered in the past two weeks. "Partisan strength est 23,000 / disciplined under fire well-led / main German withdrawal hwy estimated 150 lorries destroyed / 200 KW 50 POW / partisan losses light / civilian reprisals heavy."

He'll ask to be released from the mission he and Major Salvi were supposed to have carried out in Milan. He's already with a group of autonomous partisans who deserve all the help they can get. He'll request airdrops of plastic explosives, of Stens, Brens, and automatic rifles, of ammo and spare parts for all the weapons. He'll ask for more signal flares, for salt and cigarettes, for penicillin, sulfa drugs, plasma, sterile bandages, and morphine.

Then he'll break to receive, taking down his own orders in Morse, to be decoded when he gets back to the stone tower. He'll have under an hour from start to finish—the time it would take for two German direction-finding vehicles to get a fix on him.

Today he learned he can rely on his training, rely on himself to do his duty, and do it well, under fire. In the morning, no doubt, Simon Henley will feel like a blooded veteran, ready for whatever the war can throw at him. But tonight? Lying on a bed of pine boughs near the grave of a young woman he barely knew, he thinks of the short, hard life of Maria Avoni, and he cries. Like a baby.

VILLA MALCOVATO
NEAR ROCCABARBENA

They are the bravest of the brave, these girls. The chances they take, the risks they run. The more Mirella learns of them, the more awe and sadness she feels.

When the occupation began, the Resistance printed pamphlets for wives and mothers. "Your greatest contribution to the nation is to open your door and let your men go—to fight!" But who risked arrest and rape and death to distribute those pamphlets? Girls. Women.

Staffette carried letters, documents, intelligence. Then medical supplies, then dynamite, ammunition, and grenades. They knew their fate if caught, so they learned to load and fire pistols for their own protection. Soon they joined brigades and assault groups, and now they fight beside the men. Constantly on the move, traveling on foot in the awful cold, sleeping in cellars, on concrete floors, in barns or open country. Hungry, wet, lice ridden.

No wonder, then, when a widow of sixteen becomes the mother of an infant boy born many weeks too soon.

Mirella hears a quiet knock at the door, and opens it to Werner Schramm. "The doctor is here," she tells Claudia.

Mirella moves to the fireplace, listening to Schramm's soothing murmur as he examines mother and child. In a voice as small as her baby, Claudia asks, "Will he live?"

Schramm's eyes briefly meet Mirella's. "Your son is very small, very weak," he tells Claudia gently, "but babies can surprise us."

"Why won't he suckle?"

"He is tired from being born, signora. He needs rest and warmth. As you do."

A few years ago, Werner Schramm would have whisked this doomed infant away. Out of sight, he'd have done nature's work, granting the child a quick and merciful death. He is a different man now, but it is very difficult to watch the little chest heave spasmodically, working hard for air.

Across the room Mirella refills a cooling *scaldino* with hot coals and slides it under the bedding near the girl's feet, tucking the blankets around her. Together she and Schramm step away from the bedside.

"You can try feeding him with an eyedropper," he suggests quietly. "The skin is very fragile. Perhaps some olive oil, to protect it. Keep him warm. That is most important."

Duno Brössler is in the kitchen, pacing as nervously as a young father. When Claudette went into labor, Duno sent for Schramm immediately, but the baby was born so soon... "Your young friend will live," Schramm says, "but her son won't last the night." Duno sags. "You did well to save one of them," Schramm tells him. "You should go to medical school when this is over."

Duno runs his fingers through lank and dirty hair. "Is she awake? May I go in?"

"Yes. She will like to see a familiar face, I think. Send Signora Soncini to bed. She needs rest, or she may lose her own pregnancy."

Duno steps quietly into the little room, speaks to the rabbi's wife, who kisses the infant's forehead on her way out. Duno draws a chair near, sitting close enough to stroke the dying baby's fine, dark curls. He looks more like an organ-grinder's monkey than a human child, but Duno says, "He's beautiful, Claudette."

"Thank you," she says, believing him.

"Have you chosen a name?"

"Alberto, for my father. That's what Santino wanted."

"That's a good name," Duno says. "Rest now. I'll stay with you, Claudette."

Once they knew that Osvaldo Tomitz was in a Gestapo prison on Via San Marco in Porto Sant'Andrea, the hours of discussion yielded only one good plan. "I'll say I was sent to check on his condition," Schramm argued. "My friends, you must allow me to save lives. That is a doctor's duty, is it not?" Eventually even Renzo was persuaded: Schramm could do by stealth what would otherwise require a full-scale attack on a fortified position in an occupied city.

He unwraps the bundle of dirty cotton sheets delivered at such cost by *la vedova*. Shakes the wrinkles from the uniform, holds the jacket to his shoulders with a sense of unreality. Who wore this? Werner Schramm shares a name with that man, and a biography to a point. To wear the uniform now is to put on a mask in a Greek tragedy, but Schramm is ready to assume his role.

He leaves a note of thanks and farewell for Renzo. Urges Mirella to take care of herself. She cries, and kisses him on both cheeks. A partisan escort waits outside.

They hike across pastures and through woodlands, snake along bends in the winding river, take cover in a vineyard. A church bell strikes nine. Across the road, at the top of a slight rise, Tullio Goletta waves, taps his ear, and puts his finger to his lips. Wind rattles the branches of nearby trees. Tullio raises one finger, makes a T of his hands. *Tedeschi:* Germans.

The noise grows. A camouflaged Wehrmacht command car lumbers into view, slowly dodging craters left by British bombs. Half-amused by how predictable German schedules are, Schramm brushes dirt and leaves from his uniform, squares his shoulders, and walks out onto the road. The lines come back to him. The posturing, the presumption. Herr Doktor Oberstabsarzt Werner Schramm of the Waffen-SS commandeers the car, demands to be driven to Sant'Andrea. He is obeyed by a very young, very inferior officer.

Schramm blusters and bullies his way through roadblocks and checkpoints, and arrives at his destination in early afternoon, sweating in the early warmth of the coast. Surrounded by barbed wire, sandbags, and giant iron stars, the building's windows are bricked almost to the top, leaving just a few centimeters open for ventilation.

Boot heels ringing, Schramm enters, shouts, intimidates. The jailer is a well-fed Italian toady eager to mollify bad-tempered Nazis. Grabbing his keys, he is happy to lead the way down a twisting set of stairs cut into living rock. The air is moist, damp, cooler by the step.

"A relief from the heat outdoors, *ne?*" the chatty jailor remarks. "Until your joints start to ache. Of course, these bastards have more than their joints to think about! Down this way, signore. These used to be storerooms, I don't know what for. Must have been valuable, though. Look at those doors!"

Wide, heavy planks, reinforced with iron bands. Two long rows on either side of a stone corridor. Behind one door, a man weeps and begs. Someone yells at him, voice harsh, words garbled. A third man cries, "*Coraggio, camerati!*"

"Courage, comrades!" the jailer mocks. "That one must be new." He glances over his shoulder. When the German fails to share his amusement, a scowl automatically replaces the grin. "Shut up in there!" the toady shouts, banging on doors with his truncheon. Halfway down, he sorts through keys, opens the door, steps aside. "In there," he says unnecessarily.

Illuminated by the borrowed light of the hallway, the room is narrow. Like a tomb. Like a sepulcher. The walls are tiled with porcelain-faced bricks, as a bathroom's might be, but there are no facilities beyond a galvanized bucket in one corner.

Curled on the bare basalt floor, the man inside does not rouse. Eyes swollen shut, lashes buried in purpled pulpy flesh. Broken teeth visible through torn lips. Both shoulders dislocated; vast bruises speak of ripped blood vessels. The abdomen, too— hideously bruised. Testicles blackened. Blood in a drying pool of voided urine: ruptured kidneys, a torn bladder.

A thousand years of artwork have prepared Schramm for this body. Grünewald's *Isenheim Altarpiece*. The damned of Bosch's hell. The crucifix in every church. Look without flinching at atrocity, they instruct the faithful. Imagine what the saints endured, and envy them. Behold what the Savior suffered for your sake. But not everyone learns the intended lessons; some dream of hammering the nails.

Blinking, gagging, Schramm takes a handkerchief from his pocket and holds it over his nose; not even the greatest artwork can convey the smell of ammonia and shit. "This is Tomitz? You are certain?"

"Oh, yes, sir! Absolutely!"

Voice low and controlled, Schramm asks, "Who is responsible for his condition?"

The jailer shrugs. "PierCarlo Innocente, I suppose. The Gestapo made the arrest, but Innocente specializes in priests. He says priests and Communists are the hardest to break. They believe in a better world to come. This one didn't look like much when they brought him in, but he still hasn't talked—"

"Christ! Look at his mouth! If he wanted to talk, how the hell would we make out what he's saying? Get Innocente, now!"

"I—I don't know where— He's off today."

"Find him, or I'll hold you responsible."

The jailer hesitates. "I should lock up."

Schramm points to what's left of Osvaldo Tomitz. "Do you suppose *that* is going to escape?"

The jailer hurries off. Just as quickly, Schramm kneels at the priest's side, bending to bring his lips close to the torn ear. "Father," he says, "I've come to help."

Spongy eyelids flutter. Bleeding fingers twitch. One must be ordained to give extreme unction or to hear confession, but one of the partisan priests has provided Schramm with what he needs, and given him instructions. He opens a medical bag and withdraws a small, round case that looks like a gold pocket watch.

"Receive my confession, Lord," he whispers for Tomitz. "Savior of the world, O good Jesus, who gave Yourself to death on the cross to save sinners, look upon me, most wretched of all sinners. Give me the light to know my sins, true sorrow for them, and a firm purpose of never committing them again."

He's probably getting the prayers wrong, but he doubts that God will mind. "Pray with me, Father," he urges. "O my God, I am heartily sorry for having offended Thee, and I detest all my sins because of Thy just punishment, but most of all—"

The priest's split and crusted lips begin to move, and together they finish the Act of Contrition. Opening the gold case, Schramm brings the consecrated Host close enough to touch the swollen lips. Throat clogged, he whispers, *"Corpus Christi."* The priest's tongue reaches forward to bring the dry and nearly weightless wafer within his battered mouth.

The ritual is complete, but not the task. "Osvaldo Tomitz," Schramm asks, "do you believe in Jesus Christ, who died so that others might live?"

Tomitz nods once, twice. Slowly: again, again, again.

"This day, you shall be with Him in heaven. Father, pray for me!"

Exchanging the gold case for a syringe, Schramm finds the in-tercostal space, depresses the plunger. A moment later, the suffer-ing ends. A thousand Jews, the people who harbor them, and God knows how many Resistance cells are safe.

Schramm should leave now. Just walk home, to his sons and to his wife. War changes men, but it changes women, too. He's spent the better part of two years in the company of Italian women run-ning households in the midst of war. If, by the grace of God, he lives long enough to reach home, and if Elsa is alive when he gets there, Werner Schramm is determined to make a better job of it than his own parents did after the Great War.

But somehow, he cannot bring himself to move. Slumped against the wall, next to the body of the soul he has just released, Schramm thinks, You understand now, don't you? You are with God now, Father, but after what you went through, surely you no longer believe it's a sin to prevent suffering. We were right in the beginning, but—the borders kept moving. Perversion, vagrancy, gambling, theft became diseases. Dissidents, Communists, Gyp-sies were carriers of disease. To be a Jew was to be disease itself. At the trains, I tried to choose the best, the strongest, the most likely to survive awhile. It was like a juried art show—inferior work was rejected. Yes, I know. Judge not, but . . .

We were afraid. We were all afraid. There wasn't enough of anything, and if there isn't enough, you're afraid someone will take the little you have. They'll hurt you, steal from you, and laugh at your weakness and stupidity afterward. That's what everyone believed. We were all locked away in our separate fears, and then . . . the Führer came out of his prison with a key. He would turn our selfish, despicable fear into a kind of glorious selflessness if we obeyed him, if we dedicated our lives to the Reich. If our blood was pure.

There's no point in lying, Father. With Irmgard in my family, it was judge or be judged. If I joined the Party, if I did as I was told, there was no question of sterilization. Exceptions were made. Goebbels has a clubfoot, you know. And my children—they're such fine boys. Strong and handsome. I miss them so much. . . .

Schramm's eyes fill. He tries to get a grip on his emotions, but when he sees the small cross scratched in the mortar between the stones, there's no holding back the tears. Tears for what he meant to do, tears for what he did. Tears for his broken family, his broken life, his broken nation. Sobbing, he crawls to the little cross, and places his fingers on the symbol of salvation, of love that is more than enough, love that is the antidote to all fear. Remorse claws at his lungs, his guts, his heart.

Father, I was afraid, and weak. And wrong. And I am so terribly sorry! I'll do penance, Schramm swears, choking on a laugh when he thinks, Not just rosaries, either, Father! For the rest of whatever life I am granted, I will try to make amends.

The old words come back, prayers he learned as a child. *Misere mei Deus:* Have mercy on me, O God, according to the multitude of thy tender mercies. Blot out my iniquities, and cleanse me of my sin. Lord, I am not worthy that You should come unto me, but only say the word, and my soul shall be healed—

Footsteps. Voices. At the other end of the long corridor, the jailer jabbers apologies, explanations, excuses. Another man growls ill-tempered rejoinders. Schramm clambers to his feet, drags a handkerchief from a pocket, wipes his eyes, blows his nose. He feels as though he has drained a swamp of sin, but there is no time for contemplation.

A tall man with a lantern jaw and a luxuriant mustache flings the half-closed door wide open. Schramm points to Tomitz. "You are responsible for this?"

The bastard's head tilts back. Arrogant, unashamed. It would be so easy, Schramm thinks. One in the body, one in the head. Send this hound to hell, and step over his corpse without a backward glance.

Go, said Jesus to the harlot, and sin no more. There is hope, Suora Marta said, even for a pig like you.

"Innocente, you are an incompetent swine!" Schramm snaps. "Clean up the mess," he tells the jailer. "I'll find my own way out."

Blinking in the sunlight, he gets his bearings and looks for the quickest route out of town. He's hardly walked a block when the quiet is broken by explosions, gunfire, screams. Civilians around him cry out, clutch children, race for cover. Schramm grabs a skinny woman's arm. "I am a doctor! Tell me: where is the hospital?"

She points, shouting half-coherent directions, and breaks away.

Schramm asks twice more before he finds the place. A harried nursing sister in the midst of a crowd sees his uniform and snarls. "No, you don't! Not here! Not in this hospital!"

An ambulance team pounds by, carrying a stretcher with a wide-eyed old man who holds a shaking hand over a ragged gash in his forehead. Schramm unbuttons his jacket, tossing it into a corner. "I am a doctor, Suora! I want to help!"

Maybe it's because he's speaking Italian. Maybe there is something in his face that convinces her he is not there to kill. She shows him where to scrub. Their first patient is lifted onto the table. An eight-year-old boy, breathing in short, grunting coughs. "One gunshot," another nun reports. "Hit from behind in the left shoulder. The exit's just below the right nipple."

Schramm taps the chest with the tips of his fingers. Below the left clavicle, the chest resonates like a drum. Lower down: a dull sound, like tapping a stone. The second sister hands him a scalpel and murmurs to the little boy: this will hurt, he must be brave. Quickly Schramm slices through the resistance of the exquisitely sensitive pleura, ignoring the child's shriek as he widens the knife track. The wound bubbles. Schramm holds out his hand. A drain appears in it. He pushes seven centimeters into the cavity. Blood gushes through the chest tube into a bowl held by a nun.

The child gasps and coughs in the cold sweat of agony. The basin overflows. An orderly mops it up. The nun connects the drain to a bottle on the floor. Half-filled with water, that will act as a simple one-way valve. With each wailing exhalation, air and blood burble from the submerged end of the tube. The boy's lung begins to expand. Already the next casualty is being carried in.

In the hallway, a temporary receiving station is set up to assess serious cases and assign an order of treatment. Occasionally the triage nurse has a case stretchered directly into surgery, hoping immediate intervention might save a life. Hour after hour, Schramm digs out shrapnel, opens abdomens, sews up perforated bowels, removes crushed limbs. Time stops. There is only the flesh beneath his fingers.

When the last patient has been carried off, Schramm is lightheaded from dehydration. Exhausted, but exhilarated. He pulls off his gory shirt and trudges to a sink to wash away the blood, lifting handful after handful of water to his face, head, shoulders, chest. Drying off, he asks the nurse, "Is there someplace I could stay, Suora?"

She doesn't answer. He lowers the towel from his face. The nun is as white as her coif. A Wehrmacht officer stands in the scrubroom doorway, imperious in full if filthy uniform. "There is a German doctor here." He frowns at Schramm. "You?"

Startled, Schramm stammers, "Si—*jawohl.* Yes, sir. I was cut off from my unit—"

"You're needed. We've got casualties."

There seems to be no choice. Schramm tosses the towel aside and shrugs into his uniform, a soldier again. "Are we going to the front, sir?" he asks as they climb into an open staff car and head north.

Gray in the face, the other officer looks blank. "*Going* to the front? *Scheisse,* man! Where do you think you *are?* We're pulling all the field hospitals back. The Allies have broken through."

$\mathcal{A}pril$ 1945

VILLA MALCOVATO
NEAR ROCCABARBENA

Werner was the first to come under her protection. Then Simon Henley, nearly frozen. Young Claudia was next, and Mirella hoped the girl would stay, but two days after tiny Alberto was buried, the *staffetta* left to rejoin her brigade.

A destitute old woman with five small grandchildren arrived at the villa that afternoon. Mirella took them in. On that signora's rundown heels: a Moroccan soldier, completely lost. Nobody understood a word he said. Mirella gave him a meal, and after looking at a map, he went off happily to whatever fate awaited him.

The following week brought a bewildered Sicilian draftee, terrified and begging to stay. The owner of an antiques shop in Genoa, who offered to pay for a meal with a Renaissance figurine carved from ivory. A farmer's son, desperately ill with pneumonia. A man who'd worked for an English businessman before the war: denounced by one neighbor, warned by another, on the run. Mirella kept the farmer's son in the villa's small clinic; the others moved on.

Lavinia Costa-Valsecchi was next. A ninety-year-old contessa, dotty in furs and diamonds, she was dumped at the villa by her chauffeur, who drove off to join the partisans with her auto and its petrol as his dowry. Then a little girl with an even littler baby boy on her hip knocked at the kitchen door. Their mother was dead. The girl heard that Villa Malcovato still had a milk cow. Could they stay here?

District by district, the Germans steal anything of value as they pull back. They burn whatever they can't carry away, shoot anyone

who protests and many of those who don't. Allied air raids are de-
stroying what's left. The Germans are hated and Allied bombardiers cursed, but true loathing is reserved for the Italian SS
volunteers, and for informants who buy favor with neighbors'
lives.

Civilians are of no consequence to anyone but themselves, and
tell stories of pointless destruction and casual cruelty to anyone
who pretends to listen. Kindly, naive people arrested for giving a
meal to a stranger. A little boy hit by a staff car, deliberately run
over by the tanks that followed. Bombs falling on four children
herding some geese in a field. A fifty-year-old man tortured for
three days before the *fascisti* realized their prisoner was Giuseppi
Pesce, not the Giovanni Pesce they sought.

Villa Malcovato's population doubled, and doubled again, filling the house, the stables, the barn. A dozen peasant families
burned out of their homes. Twenty-three children, overflow from
Mother of Mercy, itself inundated by orphans. Exhausted evac-
uees from Genoa, Sant'Andrea, and Savona, many in a sort of
walking coma, speechless and trembling.

Mirella shares her bedroom now with four other mothers, thirteen children among them, and shares the bed itself with Angelo,
Stefania, and Rosina. Before falling into stuporous sleep, she takes
brief comfort in the way they snuggle around her, warm and
sweet-faced, smelling of compost. Each morning she awakens to
find another little group of famished people waiting for her attention in the courtyard.

With two hundred or more to feed and shelter, she tells the
factor and his men to dig up the last stocks of cheese and flour, oil
and salt, buried for safekeeping last fall. She puts older girls in
charge of younger children, or sends them to help in the garden.
The boys work in the barns or care for livestock hidden in secret
clearings. The women cook, spin wool, knit baby jerseys. They
make diapers from old sheets, sew children's clothes from scraps
of worn-out fabric, cobble shoes from wooden soles and strips of
carpet.

The villa has reverted to its earliest form: a medieval city under
seige. The world shrinks to what can be touched, seen, heard.
Mental horizons contract to those of the most isolated peasant,

and with that narrowness comes peasant skepticism toward all plans for the future. Nothing you were, or are, or will be, is in your own hands. Society is held together by the simplest of human ties. A person in need stands in front of you; if you can help, you must help.

A war of leaflets begins. Paper flutters from low-flying planes. "Anyone who harbors rebels will be shot. Any house in which rebels have stayed will be blown up after all stores of food are confiscated and the inhabitants shot. The German army will proceed with justice, but with inflexible hardness, unless informed immediately of the rebels' whereabouts." Leaflets scattered by the Allies give precisely the opposite instructions. "Italian patriots! Continue your resistance with acts of sabotage against the German army. Cut communications, destroy bridges, roads, and electrical plants. The moment for decisive action is near!" Mirella has children collect the leaflets for toilet paper.

After sunset one evening, three Austrian soldiers knock timidly on the door. They're very young, deserters from the Wehrmacht, trying to get home. Their prospects are poor, but better than at the front, where some great battle is being fought. Mirella gives them some withered apples, shows them the map, sends them on. In the morning, four mortar rounds fall on the villa's chapel, empty at the time. Somewhere, gunners adjust their aim and the explosions shift away from the farm. Mirella sends the oldest boys to the edge of the woods to dig long trenches, line them with brush, and cover them with tarps. The women stuff sacks with straw for makeshift mattresses, ready to run with the children to the trenches on a moment's notice. The immediate menace advances and retreats, but this much is certain: the front is no longer in Africa or Russia or France, not in Messina or Rome or Florence. It is here.

"*Che sarà di noi?*" everyone asks Mirella. "What will become of us?"

No radio, no post, no newspapers, but rumors in abundance. Two villages west, Fascist troops appeared suddenly, blocked off the main street, and arrested everyone. A partisan band took a town south of here, expecting to link up with the Allied advance; the Germans arrived instead, and wiped the partisans out. London has been completely destroyed by a new German weapon. At Villa Senni, three hundred people hidden in the cellar had to flee through artillery fire into the mountains; a hundred were killed— no, two hundred! Thousands of people are dying of Spanish influenza in Bologna. The Allies have landed in strength at Genoa. A German spy has assassinated Roosevelt. The Americans have pulled out of the war.

Inured to the sound of airplane engines, the children don't even look up when bombers drop their cargo on Roccabarbena, or when small, swift groups of fighters swoop down, guns flashing, on something doomed two valleys away. A new sort of refugee turns up: fugitives from the Italian Black Brigades, begging for civilian clothes and hoping to join the partisans. "You should be more careful," one tells Mirella. "For fifty kilometers around, people told us, Go to Villa Malcovato."

A few days later, an Italian civilian appears and takes Mirella aside to tell her about an English paratrooper who needs food and money. There is something about this man . . . "No," Mirella says. "We have nothing to do with foreigners here."

"Signora," he says, moving closer, "this Englishman is a Hebrew. He needs your help."

She covers her momentary hesitation by looking for one of the children. "Rosina!" she shouts. "Stay out of that mud!" She turns back toward the man, making sure he can see how tired she is. "*Scusi,*" she says, distractedly. "What were you asking?"

"Are there any farms nearby where *ebrei* can get help?"

"None," she says heartlessly. "We have our own to care for."

Then one bright blue morning, the contessa announces it is her saint's day. "Signora, there's no Saint Lavinia," the housegirl Giovanna tells Mirella. The contessa insists there should be a party in her honor. "*Completamente pazza,*" Giovanna murmurs, but the weather has improved, and the notion of a *festa* is so bizarre, the idea takes hold. One of the older girls ties braided yarn around the children's legs and teaches them to run three-legged races. The contessa, wrapped in a fox stole, urges the children to sing Christmas songs, and caps the day by awarding a pearl necklace to the child with the sweetest voice, and a Mont Blanc fountain pen to the winner of a sack race. That night, the old lady favors Mirella with a Mona Lisa smile and says, "I think that did everyone good, don't you?"

The low booming of artillery grows nearer. Angelo runs up the rutted drive, more excited than afraid. "They're coming, Mamma! Eight hundred Germans!" An hour later, the rumor begins to change. Eight hundred become three hundred. *Fascisti,* not Germans. By evening, the three hundred are eighty, marching south toward Sant'Andrea.

At midnight, Giovanna shakes Mirella awake. "Signora, there's a partisan with a bullet in his shoulder at the door," she whispers. "What should I do?"

Mirella pulls a cardigan over her nightgown, goes to the kitchen, dresses the wound. "You can sleep in the stable," she tells the boy, "but you must leave before light."

All that night, they hear cannon fire and planes. In the morning, the ground is littered with leaflets in four languages, offering safe conduct, medical aid, food, and removal from the combat zone to any German who surrenders.

A heavily armed man appears out of the woods, begging for a meal. Around mouthfuls, he warns of two German spies. "They're wandering around east of Cuneo. They pretend to be deserters and ask for help. They were handed on from farm to farm, until they uncovered the whole network of *contadini* helping the Resistance." The man washes his polenta down with a glass of watered milk, and stands to leave. "Last Monday, Fascist troops surrounded three small villages and the outlying farms and shot everyone the spies pointed out, including four women and an old priest. So be careful of anyone asking for help."

Mirella watches him tramp away, trying to remember the Austrian boys she gave apples to. How many were there? Two of them, or three? Three, she thinks. They seemed like nice boys, but who knows? Who knows . . .

A squadron of Allied planes flashes overhead, droning toward Roccabarbena. She watches the tracer bullets from German AA emplacements in the city. Two planes are hit just as the bombs are released. The whole valley seems to explode, just beyond the hills.

At ten the next morning, a German staff car roars up the drive through a steady spring rain. Two officers get out. Without knocking, the commander shoves the front door open and shouts for whoever is in charge. Mirella lifts Rosina to her hip, willing herself to appear innocent and ignorant. Would it be better or worse if her pregnancy were more obvious at five months? Better or worse if her eyes were not sunken in half-moons of purple skin? Better or worse if she looked twenty-eight, not a haggard fifteen years older?

Without such worries, the contessa takes charge, supporting herself on two ebony canes. "How dare you come in here with muddy boots! Who are you?" the old lady demands in imperious German. "What are you doing here?"

"We require billets for a field hospital," he begins.

"What?" she asks with loud annoyance. "Speak up! I haven't all day!"

The officer tries again. "We require this property as a hospital—"

"Don't be absurd. This is a children's home, you ridiculous man! *Kinderheim,* do you understand? Children!" The contessa flicks the blue-veined back of her hand at him. "Now go away. And don't come back!"

The officer mutters something that Mirella takes to be "Loony old bat." She follows him anxiously from room to room as he inspects the property. "*Kinderheim,*" she says, taking a cue from the contessa. "This is a children's home! Do you understand?"

He leaves the house and confers with the other officer, who has evidently inspected the outbuildings. The children have been herded outside into the downpour. Many are crying. Angelo has Stefania by the hand; he glares at the Germans, who don't notice, thank God.

"*Alles,*" the commander says, gesturing. "We require the whole farm."

"But the children? *Die Kinder?*" she asks helplessly.

The officers climb into the backseat of the car. "We will return tomorrow," the commander tells her.

Mirella turns her back to the muddy gravel spun up by the staff car's wheels. Those who've hidden until now gather in the courtyard, waiting in the rain for her to tell them what to do.

Il maggiore is trapped in Milan—Allied planes swoop down and strafe any vehicle they spot. There hasn't been so much as a note from Iacopo since January, and the last time she saw any of Renzo's men was when Claudia was here. Was his band the one wiped out at Montebianco? Is it time to move everyone into the woods? How much longer will the fighting last? How many babies and old people would die of exposure? Are the woods any safer than the villa?

Mirella hardly notices the strength leaving her legs, but she lets someone take Rosina out of her arms. I'm used up, she thinks, sitting in a puddle. There's nothing left.

Behind her, the contessa stands in the doorway, watching the German car disappear down the drive. "A Prussian of the worst sort," she declares before addressing the crowd. "The Germans want this place for a hospital. They want us out by tomorrow." She waits for the cries of dismay to die down. "My late husband," she says clearly, "was an admiral when he died. I asked him once why he had chosen the navy and not the army as his career. He said, 'If you're going to be killed in battle, it's better to sleep in a dry bed the night before.'" She folds her hands over a small potbelly swathed in silk. "You may do as you please, but I intend to stay right here."

Shrugging fatalistically, the others disperse, to make whatever decisions are left to them. Mirella leans back, propping herself on her hands, unspeakably weary. "Signora, why didn't you help before?"

The contessa looks down, brows arched. "You seemed quite capable."

Too tired for courtesy, Mirella says, "I thought you were crazy."

"Possibly," the contessa allows, going back into the house, "but I am not the one who's sitting in the mud."

Sometime that night, Angelo jostles his mother's shoulder. "Mamma? Mamma!" he whispers. "Stefania wet the bed!"

Mirella hauls herself upright, cleans herself and the children, turns the mattress over. Dry bed, she thinks, and falls asleep before she can laugh or cry.

Troops arrive at dawn. Not hospital personnel but trucks, tanks, infantry, along with two donkeys laden with stolen goods, and one goat without much time to live. Germans surround the house and farm. Some fall asleep where they drop. Others tear the place apart, looking for hidden food and valuables, snarling at anyone in their way.

Mirella gets the children up and dressed in layers. "Stay here with the girls," she tells Angelo, "but be ready to go."

A young officer sits in the kitchen. Dirty, utterly worn out, he raises his head. "*Guten Tag,*" he says, and mumbles something she doesn't understand.

He seems civil and sounds reassuring. "*Kinderheim,*" she tells him. "Many *Kinder.* What should we do?"

He looks beyond her. Mirella turns. Angelo is standing on the stairs behind her. The girls clutch his hands, wide-eyed. The officer pushes himself to his feet, approaches Rosina, cups her chin in a filthy palm. He says something Mirella can't make out, but she catches the word *Keller.* She points toward the stairs.

Knees buckling from fatigue, the soldier descends partway into the cellar and looks around. "*Das ist gut.*" He beckons. "*Kinder, ja?*"

Something whizzes past the kitchen window with an eerie moan, and explodes an instant later in the garden. Shouting orders, the officer pounds back up the stairway and runs outside. A second shell explodes. "Angelo!" Mirella screams. "Take the girls downstairs, and stay there!"

"Mamma, where are you going?"

"To get the other children—they'll be safer in the cellar!"

"Mamma, don't leave us!" Stefania begs. "*Please,* Mamma! Don't leave me again!"

Mirella's heart jolts. She lifts Rosina, starts down the staircase. "Angelo, take Stefania's hand!"

There's machine-gun fire, shockingly loud, just beyond the kitchen. Another Allied shell hits, nearer. They say you never hear the one that gets you, but how could anyone alive kno

May 1945

Sant'Andrea Bluffs

Renzo is chain-smoking Gold Flakes, but his eyes are clear and he is not so lame now that they're close to the coast. He grins at Claudia's unspoken assessment. "Peak of condition, relatively speaking." A good thing, too, given that the brigade is under attack, and badly outnumbered.

They'd have been in real trouble, if not for her. Camped in yet another stone ruin crumpled atop yet another scrubby mountain, the brigade posted sentries, and everyone else went to sleep. Claudia woke up, queasy with cramps, and went to the makeshift latrine. There, she squatted, watching starlight sparkle on Porto Sant'Andrea's bay. Something nearer caught her eye. Noiselessly, she pulled up her trousers, grabbed her submachine gun, and found a vantage behind the low stone wall.

Several platoons of Republican soldiers had slipped past the guards and crept, heavily armed, toward the hilltop. She opened up on the nearest, all of whom had their hands full with climbing. A minute later, two hundred partisans were running to join her attack on what has turned out to be some thirteen hundred *fascisti,* supported by heavy and light machine guns, mortars, artillery, three armored cars, and two tanks at the bottom of the hill.

With surprise gone, the Republican assault troops have been pinned down for two dark hours by random fire. Now that dawn has exposed their positions on the hillside, they can do little more than cower and pray as they're picked off.

Behind the brigade's line, young women and younger boys break open airdrop packing, make aprons of their shirts, scuttle forward with their deliveries. In the shelter of a stone wall, partisans salute their Englishman with raised chins, grins, small waves of appreciation. Since Simon Henley jumped into the thin air over Piemonte in February, arms and ammo and crisp pound notes have dropped like confetti on this unit.

Renzo draws deeply on the butt of one cigarette and lights the next with its glowing end. "Grenades," he coughs, "on my command." Claudia runs crouched in the shadow of a stone terrace, relaying orders. At Renzo's shout, a veritable orchard of pineapple grenades fly downhill. One-sided slaughter continues until a no-man's-land is established.

Again Claudia moves along the line. "Shoot now only when you see a good target," Otello tells Simon, although the lovely green-eyed girl has said considerably more than that. Before she finishes her route, Renzo yells something even Simon understands.

"Conserve ammo?" Simon asks. "But why? We have crates of the stuff—"

"Don't worry, Simon! The boss knows what he's doing."

Renzo closes his eyes, concentrating on the topographic maps he sees in his head. Claudia summons three men to his side, and he sends their squads into the wooded ravines that rib the mountain. By Simon's count, this move leaves 120 or so to hold the high ground. Splitting your forces is rarely wise, and the odds against them are of Agincourt proportions, but none of the others seems concerned.

Now taking only light resistance, enemy troops move past the survivors of the first assault group, advancing to within sixty paces of the crumpled castle's defenses. Encouraged by the lull, a Republican officer shouts into a megaphone.

"He says we must surrender!" Otello reports gleefully. "We are surrounded. Our position is hopeless." An accurate description, as far as Simon can see, but everyone else seems amused, and the merriment is more raucous when Renzo shouts something in reply.

Roaring, the *fascisti* rise to charge. The boss's voice cracks like a rifle shot. Bullets, grenades, and body parts fly, until the Republicans can neither advance nor retreat.

Renzo calls, "Cease fire!" There are cheers along the line.

Otello giggles happily. "Their artillery is no good now! The gunners would kill their own men!"

Far below, on the road skirting the base of the bluffs, a new and larger detachment starts upward. This time the Republicans are burdened with machine guns they hope will give cover while their casualties are extricated. Their climb will take hours.

Staffette hand out wine and cheese and British battle rations. Sitting with Claudia and the brigade medic, the boss waves off food, but accepts the grog. Duno glowers disapproval. Claudia shrugs. Renzo ignores them both.

From a distance, Simon considers the three of them. Jews, he thinks. Clannish as Scots, and just as canny. The only man who enters their charmed circle is that one-armed postman who delivers directives from the Committee for National Liberation to autonomous bands like this one. Renzo is as deferential to the messenger as he is dismissive of the messages.

The British are notorious for emotional constipation, but Simon has never seen a man drink with less emotion. The boss doesn't get sentimental, or sloppy, or mean, or happy. He is businesslike and practical about drinking, as though getting blotto were a job he means to do, and do well. Renzo plays at war the way another man might play tennis: with careless grace, with thoughtless skill. Claudia works at war the way another woman might do housework: without protest, without complaint. If her own chilly quiet weren't enough to discourage suitors, Duno has made it clear to Simon that Claudia is under the boss's protection, though she is not his lover, nor is she Duno's girl.

Crows and seagulls converge to bicker over bodies. Renzo passes the time plinking at birds that come too close to the Fascist wounded, but his hands shake and he's a poor shot. The sun moves overhead. Fed and relaxed, oblivious to the moans and cries of the enemy wounded, some of the men settle down to nap. Others talk quietly. Simon's own eyes begin to drop . . .

"Simon!" Otello whispers, shaking him.

Waking in an instant, Simon shades his eyes against the afternoon light. The Republican reinforcements are just out of range, setting up machine guns. They're determined to get to their fallen comrades, but this will be the proverbial uphill battle, and they've learned to respect the commander of this brigade.

On some signal Simon does not detect, a partisan squad that's moved to the enemy rear rises to let loose volley after volley. The Republicans turn to face the threat, only to be raked from their left. Those who survive the first fusillade wheel. That platoon drops out of the line of fire from a third platoon on the enemy right.

With a perfect view of the battlefield, Simon begins to feel like a guest sitting in the Royal Box at a Wimbeldon match. Holding the whip hand, he discovers, produces warm, happy feelings of invulnerability and power. This, he realizes, is what it must have been like for the Jerries when they started all this.

Gray-and-black uniforms turn red. Helmets cartwheel downhill. Rock and weed take on the color of oxblood. Junior officers bellow conflicting commands as men crumple and fall around them. Nobody knows who's in charge, and the Republicans can expect no help. Surely, their officers won't risk more pointless casualties.

Renzo calls for another cease-fire. Before long, the wounded are begging for water, for help, for mercy in late afternoon heat.

"Look," someone yells. "They're leaving!"

On the road below, the artillery units begin to withdraw. The guns are left behind, and the remaining troops begin to melt away. Some of them throwing off their uniform jackets.

Alone, a Republican officer begins to climb in the diminishing light. His face is in shadow when he arrives at the edge of the battlefield, where his batallion lies dead or dying. With a strip of white bandage in his hand, he steps into range and calls to his partisan counterpart.

Passionate argument breaks out among the brigade officers. Paying no attention, Renzo walks into the open to meet the Republican.

Mesmerized, Simon hardly breathes while both men pick their way awkwardly through the carnage. Either side could break this truce at any moment, but their officers speak at length, shake hands, and part.

Down in Sant'Andrea, bells begin to ring, and the sound spreads from church to church across the city. No one says a thing until Renzo has made his slow and painful climb back to the brigade.

Claudia is waiting for him with a bottle. His hard, scarred face unmoving and wet, Renzo shakes his head and starts to fall. Duno provides an arm to slow the collapse. Claudia bends to listen to the barely audible voice, then straightens to address the brigade. "The Germans have surrendered," she says without emotion. "The war is over."

Simon is sure he's understood, but no one moves while she continues with something he can't follow. "The Republican commander asks us to help with the dead and wounded," Otello translates. "The boss says: they're our countrymen. Honor them."

Duno is the first to venture toward those still living. One by one, partisans put down their guns and follow.

Porto Sant'Andrea

Delirium. There's no other word for it. Half-wild and half-starved, dressed in rags with flour bags tied around their feet, partisans march into the city, singing anthems of resistance. Their pace slackens to a saunter to accommodate cheering crowds, ten deep on either side of the street. Women and girls rush forward to embrace them and plant kisses on their cheeks. Old men push bottles of wine into their hands. Accordions and guitars appear. Everyone is singing at the top of their lungs.

Palms blistered and backs aching from a long grim night as grave diggers, the boss's tattered men are very late to the party, but no one resists the joy for long.

Green, white, and red flags, stitched together from curtains and tablecloths, fly from every window. To Simon's delight, a few makeshift Union Jacks wave in recognition of Britain's real, if belated, aid to the Resistance. In every church, giddy young men clamber drunkenly into belfries, banging on the bells with mallets until their arms are rubbery and someone else appears, ready to do the same.

Soon Simon himself is crocked enough to take a turn. "*Viva l'Italia,*" he shouts over and over, until he's too hoarse to go on. When his replacement arrives, Simon fills his chest with Italy's soft coastal air and looks out over the Mediterreanean, listening to the rapturous noise around him. By God, I've justified my little life, he thinks. I did my bit to bring this day to Italy and these wonderful people.

Suddenly it seems like a hilariously good idea to slide down the church roof, and the wild applause Simon receives for the stunt makes up for the thump his tailbone takes. "You forgot to roll!" Otello wails, and the two of them howl with laughter until they're too weak to stand. "Have you seen the boss?" Otello gasps, wiping his eyes.

"Not since this morning," Simon tells him. He looks around, hoping to find Claudia, but the thought is lost when two fine young ladies present themselves for his approval. "I'll dance when the war is over," Maria Avoni said just before Simon saw her killed. In her honor, and with a paratrooper's red beret on his head at long last, he drinks and dances with every girl he can grab.

All too soon, a British officer picks him out of the crowd, and waves him to the sideline of the carnival. "Powell, S.O.E.," this captain says, shouting to be heard. "We landed by Lysander at Vesime. You were ordered to keep these men out of Sant'Andrea!"

Concentrating mightily, Simon struggles to recall such an order. Yes—there was a transmission from Field Marshal Alexander in Tunis, sometime in the past few days. "Under no circumstances are the irregulars to attack the northern cities until Allied forces arrive to lead them. They are to hold their positions and limit their actions to harrying missions."

For a year and a half, the partisans of northern Italy fought the Fascists with minimal outside help. Carpenters and lawyers, farm boys and shopkeepers, carabinieri and theology students, butchers and musicians and railway workers put aside every social and political difference among them. Together, they swarmed over roads, bridges, train tracks, airports, wiping out German columns sent to demolish Italian infrastructure, attacking every remaining Fascist garrison. They endured hunger, brutal weather, thousands of casualties, untold grief and suffering, and on the brink of victory, Alexander wanted them to stand down. Simon knew the boss well enough to anticipate his response to that. Rather than deliver the decoded message to Renzo, Simon had simply tossed the crumpled paper into a campfire.

Now, with a smart salute, he gathers all the bleary dignity he can muster and lies. "Like King Canute, sir, I tried to stem the tide. Regrettably, it did no good, sir."

"Yes, I see the difficulty," Powell says, himself distracted by a lovely brunette offering a bottle and an open-armed welcome. "*Mille grazie, signorina*. Too kind," he says formally, adding, "Carry on, Corporal," before plunging into the crowd for a dance.

PENSIONE USODIMARE
PORTO SANT'ANDREA

Above the city proper, Antonia Usodimare turns toward the footsteps behind her. Looking better for a bath, twenty hours' sleep, and a change of clothes, the man she knew as Ugo Messner joins her in the doorway and listens to the bells. "They're still having their fun," she says. "All night, they've been drinking."

"A gigantic national hangover in the making," he remarks.

"But I'll be the one with a headache." Everyone knows what happened when the Reds took over Russia. Before long, boys with guns will pronounce sentences on Republican officials, landlords, bankers, anyone faintly aristocratic, anyone with money, anyone whose death will profit a personal enemy. Antonia survived this war by taking German and Fascist boarders, and she knows she's in for trouble. "I'm an old woman," she says. "A widow with no sons. All I have is this pensione. How long before a mob comes to burn me out?"

"Duno and Claudia will be awake soon, signora. They'll vouch for you. I left British cash and a letter that should help as well. In the meantime?" He takes her hand, raises it to his lips. Kisses it respectfully, and winks. "Make a flag, *signora*. And practice looking happy."

Hands in his pockets, hat tipped back, Renzo Leoni strolls away, enjoying a peacefulness he's never felt before. "Why is it so easy now?" Claudia asked him once, when she returned to the brigade, no longer pregnant. "I can't seem to be afraid anymore."

"You have no one to live for," he told her. "It's a kind of freedom."

Ambling downhill, he finds a local barber heating water in a German helmet over a small fire, and sinks blissfully into all-but-forgotten sensations. A chair beneath him. A warm towel draped around his face. A close shave, and a decent haircut.

He tips the barber handsomely. Finds a newsstand and buys all the one-page papers available. Following the scent of finely ground coffee hoarded in anticipation of this day, he locates an outdoor café. Sits at a table in its little island of swept pavement. Lights a cigarette, orders an espresso, lays the papers out, and pieces the story together.

Sometime last month, von Vietinghoff requested permission for Army Group C to retreat back to Germany. From his bunker in Berlin, Hitler ordered Italy destroyed instead. Despairing of their Führer's sanity, Wehrmacht and SS generals burned their records, and contacted Church officials. In return for safe conduct back to Germany, their troops would not carry out the scorched-earth command from Berlin; civil authority would be handed over to the Committee for National Liberation. Bishops and archbishops relayed their messages to partisan commanders.

The CNL happily responded that Eisenhower's orders were clear: no negotiations with the enemy. The Germans were invited to surrender unconditionally. Von Vietinghoff wavered, then refused. Partisan attacks redoubled. The Reich's defeated divisions indulged in a final spasm of barbarous attacks on civilians, but by the end of the week, all German armies in Italy surrendered. The ceremony lasted seventeen minutes.

The local news is startlingly unheroic. The CNL plans to present a united front in negotiations with the Allies for control of the Sant'Andrea city government. Political parties are dividing up spheres of influence: food distribution, telephone and electric utilities, police and fire departments. He recognizes a name or two. Jakub Landau will be the head of a civil engineering group; *il polacco* will begin sewer repairs immediately.

Sewers, Renzo thinks with a snort. I'd rather be dead.

The bells have stopped ringing. A weeping girl, still plump from German food, rushes past. Her head is shaved and doused with red paint. Reprisals have begun. There's gunfire somewhere near the warehouse district. Pockets of resistance being cleaned up, most likely. Republican soldiers who held out until the end.

The wrong kind of patriots, he thinks.

He stubs out the cigarette, drops a pound note on the table. Leaving the papers for the next patron, he walks downhill, toward the center of town. The whole city seems to have had huge holes bashed in it by a colossal hammer. Walls still standing are plastered with grainy news posters: *il Duce* and his mistress hung upside down from a Milanese lamppost. Scrawled graffiti everywhere. *Down with Mussolini! Death to Fascism!* There's no intact glass any-where; shards glitter under broken masonry and rusted iron. Most of a child lies near a pile of debris.

San Giobatta's bell tower has collapsed. The gap allows a view of the docks, where Italians long past delusions of dignity hold out tin pails for food flung into the crowd by British sailors who were shelling them a week ago.

Crouched on a curb, a tiny barefoot boy holds out muddy ciga-rette butts salvaged from gutters, begging people to buy them. Like an ancient Roman tossing bread at the circus, Renzo flips the kid a pack of Gold Flakes. Stunned by this unimaginable luck, the child runs away, yelling, "Mamma! Mamma! Mamma!"

A few blocks way, the curving marble staircase of the municipal palace is exposed to smoky daylight. Scorched papers blow through the collapsed facade and flutter down the street. In the piazza itself, bodies hang from a makeshift gallows. The north wall of the palazzo still stands, decorated with dripping starbursts of red, chest-high. The executions are presided over by a sixteen-year-old boy with a Sten. The head of the tribunal is a year or two older. Renzo congratulates himself on his own exquisite timing.

Then he sees the mountainous corpse. Executed by firing squad, too heavy to risk on a noose.

With Osvaldo Tomitz dead, there was no one left to testify on Serafino Brizzolari's behalf. Despairing, Renzo tries to remember when he heard the shots. *Was I drinking coffee? Belandi. If I'd skipped that goddamned haircut . . .*

The rest of his plan is flawless—aided, even, by this final fail-ure. The piazza is filled with people eager to finger others, and now simply asking about Brizzolari is enough to arouse hostility.

"That's Ugo Messner!" cries the rabbity little waiter who served cappuccino to Nazis for eighteen months. "I heard him say, 'My faith in the Führer and the *Vaterland* is unshaken! I am a good Nazi,' he said, 'and I hate the partisans!' "

Not precisely true, but hardly worth arguing about. And in any case, the owner of a Fascist bar hurries to corroborate the waiter's accusations. Yes, that's Ugo Messner. He was very friendly with Erna Huppenkothen! Her brother ran the Gestapo!

That should have been sufficient for conviction, but in Sant'- Andrea there is, amusingly, a lawyer for the accused. The *avvocato* has two minutes to plead for each client's life, and does so with Ciceronian eloquence, despite the fact that acquittal is unlikely when there's already a rope around the defendant's neck. "I myself suffered under the *fascisti*," he reminds the mob, "but I still believe in the integrity of the law. If you won't give me time to call witnesses on his behalf, at least allow this man to speak in his own defense!"

The adolescent magistrate calls for silence. "Ugo Messner, have you anything to say?"

The crowd quiets, and the temptation of one last performance is too much. " 'I am the one who has no tale to tell,' " Renzo declaims grandly. " 'I made myself a gibbet of my own lintel—' "

He stops, mid-*verso*, amid catcalls and curses. Two nuns skirt the edge of the crowd with a line of orphans trailing them: skinny little goslings behind dark blue geese. Suora Marta hurries the children along, intent on getting them past the makeshift gallows as quickly as possible. Her wimple shields her eyes, and for a moment he believes himself safe, but— "No! Wait!" she cries when she sees him. "You mustn't— He's not a collaborator!"

Leaving the children, she pushes through the crowd, jerked backward when a man snares her arm. His face is yellow and green with fading bruises. "Look!" he snarls, pointing at jagged teeth with nailless hands. "Look at what they did to me!"

"Not him! That's Renzo Leoni!" She wrenches her arm loose, shouts to the others. "Find the rabbi! Or ask the archbishop!"

"Go back to your convent!" the nailless man yells.

"This man is not a criminal! He was using the Germans—"

The rush-bottomed chair beneath Renzo's feet wobbles. Its

legs, or perhaps the cobbles they stand on, are uneven. Below him, arguments and accusations fade away. In his mind, it's nearly sunset, and his eyes rise to a lavender sky where a thousand swifts soar and wheel. Their dark wings flash as they disappear, plunging, and reappear, sweeping upward in tight formation. He waits until the swifts dive and, in a moment of remembered ecstasy, hurls himself after them, and dangles breathlessly.

It's like flying, except you never come down.

$\mathcal{A}$utumn 1947

MOTHER OF MERCY ORPHANAGE
ROCCABARBENA

Tongue in the corner of her mouth, a little girl glowers in mighty concentration. Determined to master this skill, she sighs heavily and stops to rub at a mistake. The paper crinkles. She looks up, close to tears.

"*Va bene,* Filomena," Suora Corniglia says. "You've practiced enough for today. Go out and play."

Filomena adds her worksheet to the wrinkled and deformed stack on Suora's desk. Nearly every piece in the pile is crumpled or creased or blotted. The children do their best, but the paper undermines them. Parades of nicely ovalled O's and properly angled P's stumble over bits of wood embedded in cheap grayish pulp. The older children have fountain pens, and any hesitation in the flow of writing results in a little pool of ink soaking into the paper. The younger ones use pencils, but their worksheets are holed by erasures. "Gently," she reminds them over and over. "Don't rub so hard!" But there is something about eight-year-olds and mistakes. Errors must be obliterated. The paper suffers.

At least we have paper, she tells herself. Things are getting better . . .

Rising from her desk, she cleans the board—an eraser in each hand, arms wheeling. Stepping to the nearest open window, she claps the felt blocks at arm's length, closing her eyes and turning her head from the chalk dust. She sneezes anyway. The breeze shifts, clearing the air and carrying the shouts of workmen repairing the roof of the railroad station.

The classroom windows don't frighten her anymore. In the dormitories, orphans don't wet their beds or wake up screaming quite so often. They are better fed, growing again. No one can love them as their dead or missing parents would have, but they know that the sisters care for them.

Autumn light makes the varnished chestnut bookcases beneath the windows glow. From the time she was small, she has always loved the beginning of a new school year. Everything seems possible—

A knock at the door makes her jump. The portress pokes her head into the room. "Sorry to startle you, Suora. There's someone to see you."

"*Grazie,* Suora, I know this gentleman. Rabbino, how wonderful to see you again."

Left alone, the two of them struggle with emotions they are desperately tired of feeling. Widowed, childless, the rabbi is changed: bone and muscle, shadows and lines. They both know he did everything possible to save Suora Corniglia's father, but *il maggiore* was so closely identified with Mussolini . . . Anyone who'd had anything to do with the Germans or the Republic of Salò was likely to get strung up. Even that poor one-armed postman was hanged. He couldn't stutter fast enough to convince anyone he'd been a partisan all along.

"*Prego,*" she begins, "have a seat, Rabbino—"

The only adult-sized chair in the room is her own. They laugh, and Iacopo leans against a desktop near the window, but not for long. Filling the silence, he moves from place to place in the classroom, chatting a little too brightly about elections and political scandals, the reparations Italy must pay, the fate of territories taken by France and Yugoslavia. Rome has lost Abyssinia and Eritrea as well, but that may be a blessing. All over the world, the old powers struggle to regain control of rebellious colonies and protectorates. Nearly six years of war. Forty million dead, one way or another. Enough killing, one would have thought, to sicken everyone of the sport, but new conflicts have broken out in Palestine and India, in China and Indonesia, in Nicaragua and French Indochina.

For her part, Corniglia speaks of the school and the children. Aid money from America. The new priest assigned to Don Leto's old parish in San Mauro. Villa Malcovato.

Somehow, in the chaos after the war, the villa still passed legally to *il maggiore*'s only surviving child. Suora Corniglia arranged for the land to be broken into individual farms, and much to the bishop's dismay, gave title to the *contadini* who'd worked the land before the war. "Has his excellency forgiven you yet?" the rabbi asks, smiling when her dimples appear.

"He'll get over it," she says, unperturbed. "Do you remember the German doctor who joined the partisans? There was a letter from him, sent to Villa Malcovato, asking about your family. I wrote back to tell him what happened."

Another silence. The rabbi stands. His hat brim moves through his fingers, around and around. "I've completed my work here," he says finally. For two years, he has collected names, updated lists, sorting the missing from those gone forever. "We've established that nearly all the Italian deportees were sent to a camp in Poland called Auschwitz. A few have turned up, but we have just under six thousand confirmed dead."

She's seen photos in the newspapers. People say the newsreels are too terrible to bear. The rabbi steps to the windows, his back to her.

"There's a saying in Hebrew," he tells her. " 'No matter how dark the tapestry God weaves for us, there's always a thread of grace.' After the Yom Kippur roundup in '43, people all over Italy helped us. Almost fifty thousand Jews were hidden. Italians, foreigners. And so many of them survived the occupation. I keep asking myself, Why was it so different here? Why did Italians help when so many others turned away?" He shrugs and turns. "I've decided to immigrate to Palestine, Suora. To a kibbutz on the coast, near Tel Aviv."

From one war to another, she thinks. "You will be a great loss to us, Rabbino."

"It's kind of you to say so, but I feel—" He looks away. "I feel that life here has been amputated." He faces her a moment later, and smiles briefly. "Anyway, I wanted to thank you. And to say good-bye. And to return this. Renzo Leoni had it in his pocket when he— The mortician was an old friend of his. This was wrapped in a piece of paper with your name on it. Well, actually, it said *Sister Dimples*. The undertaker had no idea, but he kept it, and last week it occurred to him to ask me about it."

She holds out her hand. The rabbi drops a rosary into her palm. Plain black beads with simple silver links. Father Clown, she thinks. Father Clown . . .

"Thank you, Rabbino," she says when she can speak. "I will pray for him."

Coda

This is what they remember about their mother: she never cried.

Each of her children tells of some crisis that failed resoundingly to elicit maternal compassion. The cancer. The divorce. The miscarriage. In their mother's mind, nothing that happened in Canada could ever justify lament. "Safe your tears," she always said. "You may need dem later."

A hospice rabbi learns a lot about the families he serves. In the long hours old bodies require to die, gray-haired children take turns sitting at their parent's bedside. Some are genuinely devoted, distressed at the pending loss but determined to make those final hours comfortable and serene. Others go through the motions, hoping to mitigate their own postmortem guilt. Some are frustrated, almost angry at the dying parent, desperate to know what forces deformed their childhood. This is their last chance to understand, and it is slipping away.

Claudia Kaplan's three children returned from Vancouver, from Montreal, from Windsor, to sit at their stricken mother's bedside. Her face is like marble against the pillowcase. She will never speak again; cerebral hemorrhage, suffered alone, went untreated too long to remedy. Her silence feels familiar to her children. All three have gravitated toward careers that probe secrets or plumb silences. The eldest is a prosecutor, the middle child a psychologist, the youngest an interpreter for the deaf.

Their mother had many fine qualities, they were quick to tell the rabbi. Despite an endless series of part-time menial jobs, she attended every school event and checked every bit of her chil-

424 MARY DORIA RUSSELL

dren's homework. She studied English from their basal readers, and helped them with arithmetic and geography. "I didn' get no school past fourteen," she'd say. "I gotta learn what you learn."

Comically—even stereotypically—tightfisted at home, she was generous to a fault with strangers. She'd squeeze a few dollars from her own meager earnings and those of the gentle tailor she married in a DP camp. She sent contributions to the Hebrew Immigrant Aid Society every year. "And that woman could not pass a panhandler without giving him some change," her son told the rabbi. "I'd say, 'Ma, he's just going to buy booze.'"

"'If you can help, you gotta help,'" his sisters chorused. They'd heard it a million times.

Their mother was always busy—sewing, cooking, gardening, canning. She knew the Latin binomials for every plant, but never bothered with their common English names. Given how bad her English was, her children were repeatedly surprised by how many languages she knew. Occasionally, there'd be a long-distance phone call, and she would speak at length and mysteriously. "Was that Arabic?" David asked once.

"Turkish," she told him.

"When the hell did you learn Turkish?"

"After d' war," she said. "An' don' talk ugly—I don' like dat hell stuff."

"That was her modus operandi," David said. "Get too close, she'd change the subject."

Every Passover, they returned to North Toronto—the prosecutor, the psychologist, the interpreter for the deaf. Their mother provided a vast amount of food, but she seemed alone, no matter how many people were in the room. Maybe she was quiet because she couldn't get a word in edgewise, with her kids debating and arguing and making wisecracks. Asked about her life, she'd only shrug. "Nossing e'citing, sank Got! I had enough 'citement in d'war."

"C'mon, Ma, tell us about the war!" David would urge.

She wouldn't be drawn. The prosecutor could ask leading questions or say something provocative to get a rise out of her. The psychologist and interpreter watched her face and hands for clues. She knew they hoped to trick her into revealing something. She had a way of laughing questions off—a short chuckle that did not convey amusement.

History was their father's domain, and Claudia disapproved of his obsession with the war. "Abe, you gonna get bad dreams," she'd predict, and she was always right.

"What was your father like?" the rabbi asked Jacqui.

"He was never really there," she said. "A lot of camp survivors were like that. You had to learn not to be noticed."

"Was your mother in a camp as well?"

"She was hidden in northern Italy during the war. Her mother and two brothers were deported from France in 1942—we're pretty sure they died in Auschwitz, but we never found out for certain. Mom's father died of some kind of disease. Typhoid, I think. Something like that. That's all she ever told us."

Since her final illness, her children searched their childhood home, hoping for some hidden memoir: a stash of old letters or a box of remembrances that could reveal their mother's soul. An emotional Rosetta Stone to decipher. They've found only a cheap spiral-bound notebook with a few cryptic lines in their mother's small, cramped handwriting. "The bells rang day and night," she wrote. "The others danced and sang. As for me, I thought of ice."

"Ice is the right word," David said bitterly. "A coldhearted bitch, that's what she was." He blames himself for being unable to elicit her affection.

"An emotional deaf-mute," his sister Paula concluded. She prefers to believe in some disability that rendered their mother incapable of giving what her children craved.

"She never really dealt with her losses," Jacqui said, intellectualizing. "All that aggressive cheeriness was a front. She used to tap her fingers on her lips—as though she was reminding herself not to talk."

The rabbi has his own ideas. Claudia Kaplan is yet another casualty of a war that began long before it started, and has not ended yet. Immense, intractable, incomprehensible, that conflict remains the pivot point of two centuries, the event that defines before and after. Hundreds of millions killed, wounded, maimed, displaced. The last survivors are dying now. Their children and grandchildren are fulfillment of Ezekiel's prophecy that the dry bones shall live again, but the poison still seeps down, contaminating generations. So much evil. So much destruction, and at its heart—

Struck by a thought, the rabbi straightens. Years of study. Books, documentaries, interviews. It seems impossible, but he searches his memory, and nothing comes to mind . . . The Austrian corporal was a courier in the First World War, running through tunnels and trenches, delivering messages from one officer to another. There were rumors about his cousin Gelli's death, and yet, in the end, did Klara Hitler's sickly son *ever* fire a gun?

One hollow, hateful little man. One last awful thought: all the harm he ever did was done for him by others.

Author's Note

A *Thread of Grace* takes place in an imaginary landscape peopled by fictional characters, but my intent was to present an accurate portrayal of the 1943–45 German occupation of northwestern Italy. Hundreds of histories, memoirs, and published interviews contributed background, but I must single out the two books that provided impetus for this novel. The Sant'Andrea story line formed around the section called "The Priest, the Rabbi and the Aviator" in Alexander Stille's historical study *Benevolence and Betrayal: Five Italian Jewish Families Under Fascism* (Summit Books, 1991). The mountain story line took its shape from Alfred Feldman's memoir *One Step Ahead: A Jewish Fugitive in Hitler's Europe* (Southern Illinois University Press, 2001). My Web site, www.MaryDoriaRussell.info, includes an annotated bibliography of additional important sources.

I cannot overstate my debt to Alfred Feldman. Together, we retraced his steps from the Maritime Alps to the hamlets, towns, and cities of Piemonte and Liguria, where he and his father spent the final twenty months of the war. With Mr. Feldman's help, I was able to conduct personal interviews with survivors and rescuers he knew during the war. Enzo Cavaglion, Pia Cavaglion, and Miriam Kraus shared firsthand memories of resistance and rescue, while Catarina Goletto, Margharita Brondello, Anna Occelli, and Battista Cesana demonstrated to me the openhearted welcome that strangers still receive in the village of Rittana, where Alfred and his father were hidden in 1944–45.

Rochelle Losman of Traces 2000 facilitated interviews with

veterans of the armed anti-Fascist Resistance, including Carla Capponi, Rinaldo Bausi, Mario Livi, Max Boris, Gino Servi, Orazio Barbieri, Ugo Sacerdoti, Mario Treves, Giorgio Dieno, Eugenio Gentile Tedeschi, and Giovanni Pecse.

Many others in Italy and the United States told me stories of childhood and daily Italian life during the Second World War. In particular, I thank Emmanuele Pacifici, Carmello Furnari, Marietta Gettenberg, Dani Marino, Rosetta Delbiondo Marino, Renato Marino and Anna Agresta Marino, Lydia Schmalz Geiss and Anita Deibert Arndt, Father Roy Marien, Louisette Gianesini Gallegos, Ines Gianesini Zamboni, Tullio Bertini, Lucina Ronutti Cutler, Daniel B. Cutler, and Eva Angelo.

It will be eerie, I suspect, for these people to recognize elements of their own experiences mixed with the memories of others, filtered through a novelist's imagination, and assigned to a character of a different age or gender. What I have written is not real, but I hope they will find it true.

My thanks also go to Alberto, Davide, and Mirella Cavaglion, to Dr. Giovanni Varnier, Enrico Fubini, and Rabbino Giuseppi Momigliano, who aided my research in Italy, as did Dr. Susanne Bach in Germany and Rita Zitiello in the United States. A thousand e-kisses go to Massimo Weilbacher, who answered a thousand questions about Italian history and dialects with unfailing good humor.

The following provided professional insight: José Alfredo González Celdrán (Middle Eastern philology); Father Ray Bucko and Father Ross Fewing (Catholic practice); Frank Olynyk, Ferdinando D'Amico, Richard P. Doria, Charles O'Toole, and Dr. Sven Kuttner (militariana); Sister Anna Margaret Gilbride and Sister Christine Devinne, both of the Order of Saint Ursula (convent life).

To my agents, Jane Dystel and Miriam Goderich, and to the peerless Leona Nevler: thank you for your faith, judgment, and friendship. My editor Susanna Porter's enthusiasm, guidance, and support have matched publisher Gina Centrello's belief that this book would be worth the wait. Evelyn O'Hara and Dennis Ambrose have my gratitude for their patience with manuscript changes. The sales force at Random House adopted me before

The Sparrow came out and have championed me ever since. My publicist, Brian McLendon, and I are approaching our tenth anniversary; he is a joy to work with—funny, wry, and relentless in his efforts to make a literary career out of what might have been an accidental detour off the academic highway. Bonnie Thompson's meticulous copyediting keeps me coming back to her for more, and since books are indeed judged by their covers, I thank Robin Locke Monda for creating the arrestingly beautiful jackets of *The Sparrow, Children of God,* and *A Thread of Grace*. As always, I would like to express my appreciation to the wonderful people who sell books, read books, discuss books, and recommend them to others. You're the ones who keep my stuff in print.

As good as my professional team is, we all owe a great debt to my amateur editors. Jennifer Tucker, Mary Dewing, Kate Sweeney, Louise Doria, Vivian Singer, Ellie D'Addio Baehr, Maureen McHugh, Maria Rybak, Tomasz Rybak, and Susanna Bach provided insight, suggestions, and encouragement that made it possible for me to keep working on this manuscript until it was worthy of all the time they gave early, awful drafts. My son, Daniel, became a partner as I discussed the story with him chapter by chapter. (You were right, Dan: it would have been a mistake to cut Claudette.) And for over thirty-five years, my husband, Don, has been the steady heartbeat of my life: partner and soul mate. Not to mention in-house tech support.

Skeptics may believe that I have idealized the courage and generosity of ordinary Italians during the 1940s. So I will close with the inscription chiseled on the marble memorial stela erected in Borgo San Dalmazzo in 1998 by the Jews of Saint-Martin-Vesubie in honor of the people of Valle Stura and Valle Gesso.

WHEN RACIAL HATRED RAGED IN EUROPE,
JEWISH REFUGEES, UNCERTAIN OF THEIR FATE,
COMING FROM DISTANT COUNTRIES
—AUSTRIA, BELGIUM, GERMANY, POLAND—
FOUND HOSPITALITY AND SAFETY IN THESE VALLEYS.

Hidden in isolated cottages,
protected by the population,
they waited with trust and hope,
through two interminable winters,
for the return of liberty.
In homage to and in memory of those who helped them,
those refugees and their descendants
embrace the noble inhabitants of these valleys
in brotherhood.

About the Author

A paleoanthropologist known for work on cannibalism and craniofacial biomechanics, MARY DORIA RUSSELL is the author of two previous novels. *The Sparrow* and *Children of God* earned her a number of awards and have been translated into a dozen languages. She lives in Cleveland, Ohio, with her husband and their son. Her Web site is www.MaryDoriaRussell.info.

About the Type

This book was set in Requiem, a typeface designed by the Hoefler Type Foundry. It is a modern typeface inspired by inscriptional capitals in Ludovico Vicentino degli Arrighi's 1523 writing manual, *Il modo de temperare le penne*. An original lowercase, a set of figures, and an italic in the "chancery" style that Arrighi helped popularize were created to make this adaption of a classical design into a complete font family.